"In the 1960s, there were probably many women who dreamed of escaping their marriages and finding truer passions, but Beverly Diamond actually had the guts to try it. *Behind Every Good Man* is the story of one woman's journey toward the power she didn't know she had. Told in an upbeat, lighthearted, and thoroughly engaging prose, this story will hook you from page one. Confino writes with humor and insight as she shows Beverly navigating unexpected circumstances and figuring out how to outsmart one obstacle after another. *Behind Every Good Man* is just the kind of feel-good read we all need right now. Another triumph from Confino that you most assuredly will not want to miss!"

—Jacqueline Friedland, *USA Today* bestselling author of *He Gets That from Me*

"Confino has done it again! Though we take a step back in time, we step right into Bev's life and what it means to be an empowered woman . . . no matter where you're from, what your circumstances are, or how idiotic your husband is. The message? Women always prevail. With sharply written prose that makes you laugh, cry, and root for our heroine, Confino has created a charming, empowering masterpiece. A read for everyone."

—Rea Frey, #1 Amazon bestselling author of *Don't Forget Me* and *The Other Year*

"If Midge Maisel gave up comedy for politics, she'd be Beverly Diamond in *Behind Every Good Man*. Sara Goodman Confino's fourth book is another winner: smart, sharp, funny, and feminist. What a fun ride!"

—Meredith Schorr, author of *Someone Just Like You*

"Behind every good book . . . is, well, a terrific writer. Sara Goodman Confino does it again with her latest, *Behind Every Good Man*. It's got all the inside–Washington, DC, goodies: political hubby caught with his pants down and his scorned wife (our fabulous protagonist) who is not going to take the betrayal lightly. Instead, she is going to beat the cheater at his own game with some tricks of her own. Beverly Diamond goes for the gold—a woman ahead of her time, she takes on her husband *and* Capitol Hill with her own savvy political maneuvers, and in the process lands the winning punch. Confino's page-turner is full of laughs, feminine mystique, endearing characters, Jewish-isms, and lotsa heart."

—Lisa Barr, *New York Times* bestselling author of *Woman on Fire*

"The votes and been counted, and the results are in . . . when it comes to writing novels with the perfect blend of humor, romance, and strong female characters you root so hard for you get goosebumps, Sara Goodman Confino is the clear winner. *Behind Every Good Man*, her latest gem, is a lighthearted, feel-good story with a healthy serving of romance and a powerful message of female empowerment. Bev is an irresistible, Midge Maisel–like heroine who perfectly captures the hopeful spirit of America in the early 1960s, when the burgeoning civil and women's rights movements began to give a voice to the unheard. Bev's transformation from perfect housewife into deft political strategist, all while balancing motherhood, a collapsing marriage, and lots of family drama, is a master class in how to be a strong, confident, loveable, and vulnerably human woman. With a quick wit, a page-turning plot, and broad and likable cast of characters, this is one of those books that you'll read in one sitting and then wish you could pick up and start again immediately. Spend a few delightful hours with Bev, and you'll be sure to never underestimate a woman again."

—Samantha Greene Woodruff, bestselling author of *The Lobotomist's Wife*

BEHIND EVERY EVERY GOOD MAN

ALSO BY SARA GOODMAN CONFINO

Don't Forget to Write

She's Up to No Good

For the Love of Friends

BEHIND EVERY GOOD MAN

A NOVEL

SARA GOODMAN CONFINO

LAKE UNION
PUBLISHING

Published by Lake Union Publishing, Seattle

www.apub.com

Amazon, the Amazon logo, and Lake Union Publishing are trademarks of Amazon.com, Inc., or its affiliates.

ISBN-13: 9781662517723 (paperback)
ISBN-13: 9781662517716 (digital)

Cover design and illustration by Philip Pascuzzo

Printed in the United States of America

For my aunt Dolly and uncle Marvin

1

Look, I'm not saying that I was the perfect wife, but . . . Well, maybe I am saying that.

Every morning, I woke up at five. Actually, most mornings, it was 4:59. I didn't want my alarm to wake Larry after all. He needed his beauty sleep until 6:00.

No, I woke up a full hour and one minute before he did so that I could shower, put on my makeup, dress, and have breakfast on the table for him by the time he came downstairs after *his* alarm went off at six. No pounding on the bathroom door and telling me he had to shower for work in our house. No sir.

By the time he arrived in the kitchen at 6:30, breakfast was on the table. Eggs, toast, fruit, coffee, and orange juice. The newspaper folded just so at his left. I got a quick kiss on the cheek, then went to wake and dress the kids, ensuring they didn't disturb his breakfast. Honestly, the only thing I didn't do was squeeze the juice myself. A girl's got to have limits after all.

Larry left at seven on the dot every day, at which point the kids and I exhaled. It wasn't that we didn't enjoy having him around. But he spoke so highly of how well I ran the house that I preferred he keep thinking that was the day-to-day reality. Which any mother will tell you isn't how parenting actually works.

But for the ten minutes that he actually saw the children sitting down to eat their breakfast, all three of us could keep the illusion going. The second he was out the door, the real day began.

And the day that my perfect little world fell apart was a doozy.

The latch had barely clicked behind Larry before Debbie threw a fistful of soggy Cheerios at Robbie, who retaliated with a piece of toast smeared with strawberry jam. Larry complained frequently about how high our water bill was, and I blamed it on an unseen leak under the house. Which could be the case. But I wasn't admitting to how much laundry those two little troublemakers generated. They were *my* little troublemakers after all. And they were awfully sweet when they weren't throwing food and destroying the house.

"Hey!" I said, snapping my fingers at them. "Food goes in your *own* mouth. This isn't *Cinderella*. No little birds and mice are going to come help me clean up after you."

"She started it," Robbie said, pointing at his two-year-old sister. Debbie immediately burst into tears, which mixed with the strawberry jam smeared across her face.

"Well, I'm ending it," I said, wiping her face with a napkin as she squirmed to get away from me. "And even if she starts it, you know better."

Robbie crossed his arms, a scowl emerging that resembled his grown father's way too much for a five-year-old. "You always blame me!"

"She's a baby," I said.

"I big girl," Debbie said, also scowling.

"Big girls don't throw food," I countered. I checked my watch. "And if you don't behave today, you don't get to watch *Captain Kangaroo*."

"That's a baby show," Robbie said.

"Then don't watch it."

He pouted for another second, then apologized to his sister. I ruffled his hair and kissed his forehead. "Finish your breakfast—eating it, please, not throwing it. Then we'll change your clothes, and you can watch TV while Mommy makes some cookies."

"For me?" Debbie asked, rubbing her hands together gleefully. "I help!"

"For Daddy's office," I said, shaking my head. If there was sugar involved, that child would be there. Her bottom lip quivered. "Doesn't Mommy always let you lick the beaters and make sure you get a cookie?" She nodded, and I leaned to kiss her cheek. "You will today too, sweetheart." I straightened and pointed at her. "Now eat that cereal, missy." Perfect mother in addition to perfect wife. I even turned the mixer off before I let her lick the beaters.

I poured my second cup of coffee while they chewed, then nibbled on a piece of toast and flipped through Larry's newspaper, sighing at the water ring on it. I asked him not to put his coffee cup on the paper when he was done with it so I could read it too, which he never remembered, and I didn't want to nag. But you'd think he could at least do it on the sports section instead of news. I suppose he thought he was being considerate, saving the tablecloth. But there was a saucer there for a reason. And it wasn't like I didn't have to wash the tablecloth multiple times a week because of the kids. I glanced up from the paper at it. Yup. I would be washing it today as well.

Eventually, he would call my bluff and get a plumber to inspect the pipes, but that was a problem for another day.

With the kids in clean clothes—again—and planted in front of *Captain Kangaroo*, I turned to tidying up the kitchen before making my famous cookies. I usually brought them to the office on Fridays as a treat for a week well done. Sometimes Mondays if Larry said it was going to be a rough week. He was the campaign manager for Sam Gibson, Maryland's first-term senator, who was angling for his second stint.

That job was how we met, seven years ago, though he wasn't the campaign manager back then. Sam had wanted my father's support and invited the whole family to dinner. Papa had been a congressman until he retired nearly two years ago, which was a bit of a euphemism. He wasn't so sure he would win reelection after suffering a minor heart attack on the House floor, and his doctor warned him that if he stayed in politics, the next heart attack would kill him. Now, he spent his days playing a lot of armchair politics over checkers in the park, debating endlessly over how President Kennedy was doing and what those blasted Soviets were up to.

Sam's first campaign manager had gotten the flu, so Larry stepped in at dinner. He called the house the next day, and I answered the phone. I said I would get my father, but he stopped me, saying he wasn't calling for him. We went out that night, and the rest . . . Well, here we were.

I did sometimes wonder if Sam put him up to asking me out. Because Larry winning my father over definitely helped get Sam that endorsement. Larry swore Sam didn't know he asked me to dinner. But there wasn't a lot that Larry did without Sam knowing.

One more outfit change later, thanks to the chocolate from those cookies, the kids and I walked the three blocks to my parents' house. That was something I had been adamant about when Larry and I got married. I wanted Mama and Papa nearby. Larry had no objections— the Chevy Chase neighborhood was perfect. Our house wasn't so grand as theirs, but neither were we—yet. Larry swore we would get there though. He secretly had political aspirations of his own. And, as he liked to say, with me on his arm, he couldn't lose.

"Hello?" I called, opening the door, cookies balanced in my left hand. Robbie and Debbie went barreling past me into the house.

"Beverly, darling." My mother walked down the stairs, fastening a pearl earring. "Ah ah ah," she said as the children approached. "Are your hands clean?" They stopped and held them out for her to inspect, which she bent down to do. "Wonderful. You may hug me now." She opened her arms, and they threw themselves into them.

I rolled my eyes while she cooed over them. Had there been a speck of dirt under a nail, they would have been frog-marched to the bathroom to wash while I was castigated for their uncleanliness instead of them being showered with the affection they got now.

But help was help, and I appreciated that she would take them while I ran errands. As long as it didn't interfere with bridge, lunch, or her myriad of hair and nail appointments.

"I'll head out, then," I said.

"Don't you want to sit and chat?"

That was code for she was feeling neglected. But if I stayed, it meant the cookies were made in vain. "What time do you need me back today?" I asked.

"One."

"Then no, I can't."

She sighed. "Always rushing about. You need help, darling."

Do you want to pay for it? rose in my throat. Larry had been harping on about my overspending as it was. But I swallowed the words. "I do, which is why you're the best, Mama." I moved forward and kissed her cheek, then leaned down to kiss the top of each child's head as well. "You two be good for Grandma now."

My mother waved a hand in the air. "They're angels. I don't know what your mother thinks you'd ever do wrong," she said to them in a singsong voice.

"Right. I'll be back by one."

"Noon."

I felt my jaw tighten. "I thought you said one?"

"Why would I say one?"

Deep breath. "I'll be back by noon."

"Come with me, darlings," she said to the children as I left the house.

~

We only had the one car, so I took the bus downtown to Larry's office. I didn't mind, to be honest. Driving into the city was harrowing with the traffic circles and tourists. Papa said they laid out Washington, DC, to confuse the British if they invaded, but they apparently did their job too well because DC traffic was still confusing everyone 172 years later. Larry didn't work out of the Capitol though—his team was in an office just off the Hill. And on the bus, I *actually* got to read the water-stained newspaper without the distraction of my children throwing food. I had to be up on everything happening on the Hill if I was going to be the perfect wife to my politics-adjacent husband.

~

The campaign workers swarmed me when I walked in. My cookies were popular, and therefore so was I. I smiled and greeted them all by name, asking about wives and children. But Larry was noticeably absent. "Is Mr. Diamond in his office?" I asked.

In hindsight, Louis had looked alarmed when Frank said yes. But Louis was always a little bug eyed, and I didn't think anything of it. Nor of the empty desk where Larry's secretary, Linda, sat.

I also didn't knock. Which perhaps I should have. He could have been in there with Sam. Or President Kennedy. Or Khrushchev for that matter.

But he wasn't.

No. Instead, when I walked in, I saw Larry at his desk, arms behind his head, Linda's feet sticking out from the side of the desk, her blonde head bobbing up and down.

Neither of them noticed I had walked in.

For an interminable moment, I stood there, frozen to the spot. Then the moment ended. "Ahem," I said loudly. Larry jumped, and I heard the sound of Linda slamming her head into his desk.

"Beverly," Larry said, fumbling to fasten his pants. "I—uh—Linda was just—"

"Taking dictation?" I asked drily. He started muttering inanities, but I shook my head and walked out.

2

Larry chased me out of the office as I kept walking. He could have grabbed my arm, but he would never make a scene like that in front of his staff. And even in my state, I recognized that still mattered more than I did.

Instead, he waited until we were on the street. "Bev," he said, moving in front of me so I had to face him. "It's not what it looked like."

I stopped walking, arms crossed. "Oh really. What was it, then?" He started sputtering, but I held up a hand. "Let me save you the effort because all your blood is clearly still elsewhere. Linda wears glasses, so she didn't lose a contact lens. And even if she had, I doubt even you have a reason how it could have fallen into *your pants* that doesn't make this look worse. So how about you tell me how long this has been going on instead of lying and pretending I'm stupid enough to believe you?" His mouth fell open. I tapped the face of my watch—a gift from him on our first anniversary. "I don't have all day. I have to pick up *our* children—you know, the ones I take care of all day while you mess around with your secretary—at noon."

He swallowed, started to speak, then cleared his throat. "Not long," he mumbled.

"Not long like this was the first time, or not long like three years?"

"Bev—I—"

"Answer the question, please. The truth."

"Somewhere in between there."

My jaw tightened, and Louis's panicked look appeared in my mind. His whole office knew, then. And I was marching in there delivering cookies every week while they knew he was fooling around with his secretary—his secretary! Such a cliché!

"Look," Larry said, putting a hand on my arm. "I'm sorry. I just— ever since Debbie was born, you haven't exactly—"

I plucked his hand off my arm. "You're blaming *me?*"

"What are you doing here on a Thursday anyway?"

For a split second, I understood how criminals could claim temporary insanity. If I pushed him in front of traffic, as long as I had one wronged woman on that jury and told her what he had just said, I would walk away free.

But I didn't do that. "I have a hair appointment tomorrow," I said coolly. "Perhaps if you had let me know about your standing Thursday tryst, I could have rescheduled."

Neither of us spoke. "Bev," he said eventually, reaching for my arm again, but I took a step back. I was at a crossroads, staring at two alternate futures. Could I swallow my pride, pretend this never happened, and keep our lives the way they were?

Possibly. But I didn't want to spend the next fifty years wondering who he was with every time he wasn't home. Because if I let this slide, he would be doing the exact same thing for those fifty years.

"No. I've heard enough. I'm telling the kids you're working late. You can come home to pack a bag after they're in bed."

"Pack a bag?" He looked at me like I had grown a second head.

"Don't look so upset," I said, patting his arm patronizingly. "You can go stay with Linda, and there's no chance I walk in on you now."

I turned and strode purposefully down the street toward the bus stop. Larry didn't follow.

As I entered my house forty-five minutes later, I checked my watch. I had an hour before I needed to get the kids. And for a moment, I disloyally wished for a mother whom I could call and ask to keep the kids longer without having to explain what had just happened. But that wasn't my mother, and I wasn't one to dwell.

Instead I peeled the offending watch from my wrist. An anniversary present was a joke now. Anniversaries were for faithful couples. I shoved it into the drawer where we kept batteries, bills, matches, and scissors, and then sat at the kitchen table.

But I couldn't sit still either. My entire body was humming, and if I sat, the vibrations would set off an earthquake.

Instead, I went upstairs to our bedroom and looked around as if seeing it for the first time. The decor would have to go. I had selected everything, but I'd done it with an eye toward Larry's taste and comfort. I didn't want the dark wood or the beige wallpaper or the even beiger bedspread. I liked color and light and air. I went to the heavy damask curtains and pulled them open. They would have to be replaced as well.

Whether Larry came home or not.

Larry.

I picked up the photograph from our wedding, in its Tiffany frame. A gift from the Trumans. Larry had been giddy over the present from the former president, though I was certain either Bess or one of their secretaries had picked it out. Papa had invited the Eisenhowers too, though Ike was far too busy to attend. But with that exception, everyone who was anyone in DC had been at the wedding.

Larry was grinning at the camera in the picture, while I smiled up at him. Ever the dutiful wife.

I sank onto the bed, my engagement ring catching my eye, and thought back to the day he proposed. A perfect day. The cherry blossoms had been in bloom, and he suggested we go down to the Tidal Basin to see them. It was illegal to pick them, of course, but Larry plucked a sprig for me anyway. When he passed it to me, my ring was around the stem.

He told me that I was the one. That he couldn't live without me.

What changed?

A wave of grief washed over me, powerful enough to carry me away in its current. What about Robbie and Debbie? How could I do this to them? And how would I handle everything all alone?

My eyes drifted back to the silver frame, and I shook my head to clear my thoughts. Was that why he had married me? The political connections. The gifts from presidents past and current. The knowledge that Papa's name opened nearly every door on Capitol Hill.

It didn't hurt that I was pretty and could cook and knew everyone worth knowing in DC. But I looked back at the picture. Our whole wedding had been hand shaking and clapping powerful men on the back. There were no photographs where he gazed lovingly down at me. Always looking ahead, at the camera or toward the future. Never at what he had.

I ran my finger over the glass above my own upturned face, trying to remember what I had been thinking that day. But it was a blur of people and kisses and toasts.

Our honeymoon in Havana though—he had loved me then, hadn't he?

Maybe.

Or maybe just what I stood for and brought to the table.

Because once he had a ring on my finger, those tables turned. I wasn't the focus anymore. He was. His career. His needs. His wants. I looked around the room again, wrinkling my nose. His taste.

Even that watch, now ticking away in the kitchen drawer—I had been late *one* time for an event. One. And he tried to pitch that as a sweet anniversary present. Honestly, a vacuum cleaner would have been more romantic as long as he hadn't explained it as fixing a character flaw.

"Ever since Debbie was born . . . ," I said out loud, my blood boiling again. Such a load of horse manure. I bent over backward to please that man in and out of the bedroom. What, had he rolled over and wanted me there one time while I was rocking Debbie back to sleep to make sure she didn't wake him? No. *I* wasn't doing this to the kids. *He* was.

I dropped the picture frame on the bed, then went to the basement, where I grabbed the suitcases and hauled them upstairs one at a time. I set them on the bed and began filling them with Larry's things. When the first was full, I placed the wedding picture inside before zipping it. He could have his precious frame. It was a fair trade—I was going to have a life that didn't cater to his every whim in exchange.

3

"You're late," my mother said by way of greeting when I arrived to pick up the kids. They were sitting on the stairs, shoes on, as she adjusted her pillbox hat in the mirror by the front door. Hers didn't have a dent in the top as she didn't believe fashion happened by accident, no matter what Jackie Kennedy did.

I glanced at the clock on the mantel inside the living room. Three minutes past twelve. She and Larry could start a little "Bev was late one time" club.

"But if I'm going by the time you initially told me, I'm fifty-seven minutes early," I said.

"What was that, dear?"

"Nothing, Mama."

She swept by me, then stopped, turned around, and came back to cup my face in her gloved hand. "What's the matter?"

I ducked my head. "Nothing's the matter."

Her eyes narrowed. "A mother always knows."

A car horn beeped from the driveway. "That'll be Louise. Go with your mother, darlings," she said to Robbie and Debbie. "Grandma will see you tomorrow morning."

She blew them kisses as she left. Once she was out the door, both kids ran to me, embracing me with shockingly unsticky fingers. I didn't remember my mother being such a stickler for cleanliness when my brother and I were young. Then again, we'd had a nanny. Being a congressman's wife was a full-time job. Or so she said. There were a lot of bridge games, luncheons, and hair and nail appointments back then too.

"Come on. Did Grandma feed you lunch?" They both shook their heads. "Then let's do that before Debbie's nap." I held out my hands, and they each took one.

~

I half expected Larry to show up at dinner and pretend nothing was wrong. If so, I would have to wait until the kids were in bed to unceremoniously show him the door. But he didn't.

Instead, he arrived at eight. I always unlocked the door for him whenever he was expected home, but I didn't this time. I heard him try the door handle, then a few seconds later, the sound of his key in the lock.

I briefly wished I'd had the foresight to call a locksmith. I imagined his surprise at finding his suitcases on the front step, his key useless, as I peeked at him through the living room curtains, laughing at his impotent anger.

Then again, if anything about Larry had been impotent, well—he would have likely not had to use the key at all.

That thought sobered me, and as the door opened, I set my jaw.

He saw the suitcases before he even looked up at me. "Bev, please—"

"Please, what?"

He stopped for a second. "I made a mistake."

My hands went to my hips. "A mistake is wearing a brown belt with black shoes. I don't think for a moment that you were confused about what your secretary's job duties entailed."

"You know what I mean."

"Do I? Because of all the mistakes I've ever made, I was never confused about whom I was supposed to be sleeping with until this morning."

He stared at me. The perfect wife would have been willing to overlook an indiscretion or two. But I was done being perfect.

"I'm sorry," he said finally.

I waited for the "but" that always followed, but none did. And for a few seconds, I wavered. Then I remembered the wedding picture. The watch. The look on Louis's face. And his comment about the time since Debbie was born.

"I don't think that's enough."

"Bev—"

"Just go," I said. "I packed everything you'll need. Call first if you intend to stop by for anything else. I don't want you confusing the children."

"What are you going to tell them?"

"That Daddy had to go away for a while."

His shoulders sank as he realized I was serious. "You have to let me see them." The tone was somewhere in between a command and a question, but I nodded. Resigned, he grabbed the handles of the suitcases. "I'll call you tomorrow."

After he had gone, I poured a glass of sherry and filled the bathtub. I didn't have to watch *Bonanza* for once. I could pamper myself, go to bed, and wake up whenever I felt like it.

~

Which turned out to be 4:59 a.m. Apparently my internal clock hadn't gotten the memo that Larry didn't run my schedule anymore. Which wasn't surprising. It took me a moment upon waking to realize I was alone in the bed.

I tried to go back to sleep, but it was no use. So I showered and sat in the kitchen, drinking coffee and reading an unstained newspaper, until I heard the kids calling for me.

When my mother walked in, without knocking, at half past ten, the kids were helping me redecorate my bedroom. By which I mean they were jumping on the bed while I removed the curtains. The bedspread and pictures were already in a pile by the bathroom door, and I had peeled a strip of wallpaper halfway off.

"Spring cleaning?" my mother asked, an eyebrow raised.

"Just a little redecorating," I said.

"It needs it," she said coolly. "Hunting lodge chic has never been in style." She looked to the children. "Let me see your hands." They held them out for inspection, and she ordered them into the bathroom to wash before she would hug them.

When she returned, she touched the hanging piece of wallpaper. "Shouldn't you pay a professional for that part?"

I shrugged. "I thought it would come up easier than it did."

"What colors are you thinking?"

I took a few steps toward the center of the room and looked around. "Pink maybe."

She angled her head, trying to picture it. "Larry will hate that. Maybe yellow. Or teal accents if you really want to add some color."

Pink everything, then, I thought.

Then she looked me over. "Is that what you're wearing to your hair appointment?"

I was in dungarees and a blouse, my hair tied up in a kerchief. "Hair appointment," I echoed. I looked at my wrist, which was bare, then to the clock on my nightstand. I had packed Larry's in his suitcase. "I forgot."

"Whatever *is* the matter with you right now?"

"I'll just be a few minutes late," I said, dashing to the closet, pulling my shirt over my head, and then reaching for a dress that didn't require a girdle. "Can you stay a couple hours?"

"Why? Are you doing color? Are you going gray already?"

I blinked heavily and resisted the urge to check my hair in the mirror for premature aging. "No."

"It's not your fault, you know. Your grandmother was completely gray by your age."

I sincerely doubted she had a full head of gray hair by twenty-seven. And my mother claimed her dark brown hair was natural, which, at fifty, I wasn't inclined to believe was true. But heaven help the person who called my mother a liar.

"No. I wanted to go look at some new furniture and bedding."

"And wallpaper, I assume."

"And wallpaper. But they don't have that at Woodies."

"I suppose I can stay until three or so."

I turned around for her to zip me, which she did, then she brushed off my shoulders. "Thank you," I said, turning to kiss her cheek.

"And I can send Vincent over to do the wallpaper when you pick some."

"I do appreciate you," I called, already leaving the room. "Be good for Grandma," I told Robbie and Debbie.

"They're always angels," my mother said.

I shook my head as I left. A new hairdo was exactly what I needed right now.

~

I walked out of the salon feeling lighter. Larry preferred my hair long, so I had resisted the Jackie Kennedy style that most of my friends wore. But when I sat in the chair, I said it was time for a bob. And I treated myself to a ruby-red lipstick at Woodies before I went to the furniture section.

By the time I arrived home, I had done major damage on our charge card. The new bedroom set would arrive Monday; the new bedspread, sheets, and curtains were in bags on my arms. The new wallpaper would be delivered Tuesday. And my hair and lipstick turned heads in a way mousy Bev Diamond, Larry's devoted wife, never did.

And if Larry didn't like any part of it, well, he should have thought of that before assigning his secretary any marital duties.

"Hello?" I called as I walked in. No one responded. I looked at my bare wrist and shook my head. Maybe I should buy myself a new watch. One that I picked out. But that was a job for the next shopping trip. If it was later than three now, Mama might have brought the kids to her house. It wouldn't be the first time.

The faint sound of the television echoed from the den, so I put the bags down and went in to show off my new look.

The children were glued to the screen and didn't even glance up, while my mother smoked a cigarette and flipped through a magazine. When she saw me, she looked over to make sure the kids were still occupied, then stood and grabbed my arm, pulling me out into the hall.

"Nancy called," she said and took another drag of her cigarette.

"Is she okay?" Her tone had me worried. Had something happened to Arnie or one of the kids?

"Perfectly so. Although it would seem she has a houseguest."

Nancy was my best friend, and her mother-in-law was a nightmare. "I don't understand why she won't tell her she can't pop in with no notice."

My mother raised an eyebrow. "This houseguest is one you're quite familiar with. It would seem Larry spent the night there, and Nancy is under the impression that he may be with them some time." I bit the inside of my cheek but didn't reply. "Needless to say, I didn't know any more than she did—although based on the state of your bedroom, I would assume whatever he did, it wasn't good."

I leaned around her to make sure the kids were still engrossed in the television. They hadn't looked up yet.

"It wasn't," I said quietly, then took the cigarette from her hand and inhaled deeply. I had quit when I got pregnant with Robbie, and this was my first puff since then. She took the cigarette back, then gestured that she was waiting, moving her hand with the cigarette in a circle. I grabbed the ashtray from the hall table, took the cigarette from her again, and stubbed it out. "You're going to burn the whole house down the way you wave that thing around."

"The way things look, it might be better if I did. What happened?"

I sighed. The truth was going to come out eventually. And if I didn't tell her, she would march herself over to Nancy's house. "I caught him. With his secretary." She looked at me blankly. "Doing . . . things."

"Is that all?"

"All!"

"Darling, men have indiscretions. If every woman who caught her husband with his secretary kicked him out, there would be about six marriages left in the world."

I genuinely debated getting a glass of water and pouring it on her to see if she would melt like the Wicked Witch of the West.

But she was still talking. "Go tell him to come home. Honestly, this might be just what your marriage needed. He'll be so attentive after this."

"Absolutely not."

"Beverly, I love you like a daughter—"

"I *am* your daughter!"

She waved her hand. "It's an expression. But I mean this when I say it: think about what you want. Because being a merry divorcée with two young children is going to be a lot harder than you think."

"And if it was Papa? You'd be just fine staying with him and pretending nothing happened when his whole office knew, and you had just been humiliated?"

Something changed in her face, and for a moment, I wondered if she *had* done just that. If she was about to tell me that Papa had cheated on her—honestly, I think that would have been a bigger blow than Larry.

And then she surprised me. "No. You're right."

It was the first time she had ever said those words to me, and I stood there, my mouth open.

"Close your mouth," she said, tapping my chin. "You need an expression to match that haircut, and that isn't it. I'll go pack some things and be back over in an hour or so."

"Pack?"

"Of course. You need help. I'm moving in until you get situated."
She paraded into the den and flipped off the television to both children's
protests. "Wonderful news, darlings! Grandma is moving in for a little
while. Won't that be fun?"

Fun wasn't exactly the word I would use to describe living with my
mother.

"Mama, you really don't—"

"Hush," she said. "Look how excited the children are."

They actually looked angry that the television was off, but she
flounced out of the house, leaving me with no room to argue.

4

Not an hour later, the front door opened. "That was fast," I called from the kitchen. I was relieved. If she didn't pack much, she wasn't staying long.

I wiped my hands on a dish towel and went toward the hall, running smack into Nancy as I rounded the corner.

"Ow," I said, rubbing my forehead. She did the same.

"Hello to you too. Why is your husband living out of a suitcase at my house?"

I tried not to smile but couldn't fully suppress the grin. Nancy was just so perfectly Nancy. Straight to the point.

"Come on," I said. "I need your help hanging my new curtains." Nancy was handier than most handymen, let alone our husbands.

"That does *not* answer my question. When did you cut your hair? It looks wonderful. What did he do?"

"Come help me, and I'll explain."

She turned and led the way toward my bedroom. "Why'd you get new curtains?" She stopped short at the door to the bedroom, taking in the stripped bed, curtainless windows, and half-peeled wallpaper. "Did he murder someone? Are you hiding the evidence? I'll help you, of course, but I don't want to be an accomplice to Larry."

I grinned again. "I'll stand on the chair, but I need you to hand me the curtains as I put them on the rod."

"Your arms will fall off. Take the rods down and thread them through on the bed."

I tapped my temple. "This is why I need your help."

"You know who could help rehang them? Larry."

I took a deep breath and exhaled slowly through my mouth. "How much did he tell you?"

"Nothing. He showed up with suitcases, and I told him if you kicked him out, I didn't want to hear a word." She hesitated. "He told Arnie you threw him out. I think Arnie knows more, but he didn't tell me yet."

A muscle ticked in my jaw. Arnie likely already knew about Linda. Apparently everyone did except me and Nancy. But if I told Nancy that I thought Arnie knew and I turned out to be right, then two marriages would fall apart. And as appealing as the idea of moving in together and raising our children like a commune was, we weren't far enough from McCarthy to call it that.

"I went to bring him cookies at work and walked in on him with his secretary."

"Is it possible it wasn't what it looked like?"

The image flashed through my head. "No."

"Maybe it was a one-off? You know how men are."

I shook my head. "He said it's been going on a while."

"I told you when he hired her that it was a mistake. He needed someone who looked like Eleanor Roosevelt." She had said that. But it never for a moment occurred to me that Larry would be unfaithful until I saw it with my own eyes. "So now he'll fire her, you'll pick the next one, and he'll come home." She was sitting on the bed, deftly threading the rod through the new curtains. "I like these. They'll brighten up the room."

"I ordered all new furniture and wallpaper too. You can help with the new bedspread next if you want to."

"I wish Arnie would let me redecorate more. He always complains that I'm spending too much money."

"Larry doesn't know. He'll find out when he gets the Woodies bill."

Nancy looked at me a moment, then threw her head back in laughter, her blonde hair sprayed so heavily that it didn't budge. "Oh, that's smart! Maybe Arnie should have an affair so I can do the same. Larry can't say a word now. And every day when he wakes up, he'll remember how expensive it is to cheat." Nancy hopped off the bed, a curtain done, and went to stand on the chair. "Pass me the rod. I'll put it up."

I handed it to her, admiring the pastel pink with mauve paisley as she popped the curtain into the bracket with ease. "It looks good," I said.

"Fantastic. It'll be even better when the wallpaper isn't peeling off the walls." Nancy climbed down and went to work on the second curtain rod. She always made herself right at home, but in the way women did. A man's version of "at home" meant putting his feet up on the coffee table. If Nancy walked in while I was cooking, she'd set the table and make the sides. I sometimes thought she would explode if she ever sat still, and she probably talked in her sleep.

I stood a few feet from the window, studying the new curtains and thinking about what she had said. She and my mother both agreed he would be the perfect husband if I let him come home. I imagined him going on weekend adventures with me and the kids, swinging Debbie onto his shoulders at the zoo like he used to do with Robbie.

But the fantasy faded. Yes, I could likely scare Larry into fidelity with enough overspending and time sleeping on Nancy's sofa. But what kind of marriage was that?

"I don't want him to come home," I said, still looking at the curtains, not sure if I was convincing her or myself.

"Well, not yet of course. You have to make him sweat more than a night or two on my couch." She paused. "He'd better not actually sweat on my good couch."

"I'll take you shopping on his card for a new one if he does."

Nancy laughed. "He can sweat away, then."

I went to the corner where the blanket lay and pulled the new bedspread from the bag. "I mean, I don't think I want him back at all."

"You need to wash that before you put it on, or it'll just be a wrinkly mess," Nancy said. "I suppose you could just iron it, but probably best to wash it first."

I sighed and tossed it to the floor. It would have to go in soon if I wanted it to be ready for bedtime tonight. "I mean it."

Nancy put the curtain rod aside. "What does that mean? You want a divorce?"

I flinched slightly. My mother's warning about being a merry divorcée rang in my ears. I knew two divorced women, and everyone acted like it was contagious. Nancy and I were just as guilty of that. "Are you still going to be my friend if I'm divorced?"

"No. I'd ignore you on the street." She rolled her eyes. "What do you think?" She went back to the curtains. "Can I kick him out of my house too?"

"What will Arnie say?"

"When I come home and tell him how much happier you are without a husband? He'll say whatever I want goes." She reached out to touch the end of my new hair. "This does look great, by the way. Are you sure you don't want to go blonde too? Drives Arnie wild."

I did not want to picture Arnie going wild, with his comb-over and gut that he tried to hide by hiking his pants too high. "I think I'll stay brunette for now. I don't want to drive your husband wild."

Nancy stood and dragged the chair to the other window. "Pass me the curtain rod, then go start the washer—unless you got a new dryer too, it's going to take a while."

"Not a bad idea."

"Might as well go get yourself some jewelry too. If you're not going to take Marilyn Monroe's advice about gentlemen preferring blondes, you can listen to her that diamonds are a girl's best friend. Other than me, that is."

"Marrying a guy named Larry Diamond didn't exactly prove that one true."

"Wrong kind of diamond, clearly. But best do it now, before he can cut that card off."

I admired the second set of curtains. "I'll keep that in mind."

"You really need new valances too. And did you get a dust ruffle to go with the new bedspread?"

"Not yet."

"Back to the store tomorrow, then," Nancy said, climbing off the chair and dusting off her hands. "You can always drop the kids at my house if you want them to see Larry without you having to."

I wasn't a crier. Most women would have shed a lake's worth of tears over this whole situation. But at that offer, I felt an unfamiliar lump in my throat. "Thanks, Nance."

She wrapped me in a quick hug. "What are non-diamond best friends for?"

"Oh, hello, Nancy," my mother said from the doorway. "Beverly, darling, bring up my suitcases. I assume I'll sleep in here with you until you clear out the guest room."

Nancy looked at me, her eyes twinkling. "Oh, this just got much more interesting." She kissed my mother on the cheek as she went to leave. "You take good care of our girl, Millie."

My mother bristled slightly, though whether it was at the too-familiar use of her first name, the "our girl," or the uninvited kiss, I did not know.

Nancy turned back at the doorway. "I'll be back tomorrow to help you clear out that guest room," she said with a wink.

"You're going to need to wash that bedspread before we can sleep in here," Mama said as Nancy's footsteps echoed down the hall.

"Heading to do that now," I said, gathering it in my arms.

"And don't forget my suitcases!"

Larry might have gotten the better end of this deal sleeping on Nancy's sofa.

5

Life without Larry was both more peaceful and more chaotic, though he had little to do with the latter, as the burden of the chaos descended directly from my mother. She slept in my bed for the first four nights, snoring louder than Larry ever had, until the guest room was set up to her liking. Which did require three more trips to Woodies and one to Hecht's to procure the exact sheets, bedspread, and mattress that she would need to deem it acceptable.

If I had suffered any illusions of training my body to sleep later, Mama dispelled those quickly. A lifetime of waking up before Papa doesn't come undone in four days. And I hadn't learned to be a wife in a vacuum, though I didn't put my makeup on and then go back to bed as she did with him, pretending she rose each morning with perfectly flushed cheeks, lined eyes, and lipstick. She started to do that the first morning at my house, then stopped herself, remembering. But the habit of waking up at 4:59 refused to die for either of us.

Robbie questioned where Larry was, but Debbie went on her merry way. I told him it was a work trip—Larry didn't have to travel often with Sam, but he had done it a few times. But on the fourth night, as I tucked him in, kissing his forehead as I always did, he looked up at me. "When is Daddy coming home?" he asked sleepily.

I froze, then choked out, "I'm not sure, honey." He looked sad, and before I could stop myself, I asked, "Do you miss him?"

Robbie nodded, then closed his eyes.

I sat on the edge of his bed for a long time, wondering if I had made a mistake. The change in our relationship *had* followed Debbie's birth. Because when Robbie was little, there was no father as proud as Larry. Had it been the affair? Or had it been me all along?

And could I still salvage what we'd once had?

My mother called for me from the hall, breaking my reverie, and I hurried out of the room so she wouldn't wake the children. Why people forgot how to be quiet once their children were grown, I would never understand.

Neither child asked for Larry in the morning, and I didn't bring him back up. And having my mother there, who was much more hands-on with them—as long as their hands were clean—than he had ever been, felt like a treat.

To them.

To me, well, the constant critiques were a lot.

"How will you have any energy if that's all you eat?" she asked as I brought a piece of toast to my lips. Apparently her grapefruit provided more nutrition, with its two heaping spoonfuls of sugar on top.

"The children watch too much television." I avoided pointing out that she parked them in front of it far more frequently than I did.

"The house is a mess. Children should learn to put their own toys away." I didn't remember putting toys away once as a child because of the household help.

"You really should have a maid." I would love one. If she planned to pay her salary. Larry was going to lose his mind over the new furniture charges as it was.

"You're going to eat that?" she asked as I took a bite of a jettisoned cookie. "You really can't afford to let yourself go now."

"Actually, that was my entire plan. If I let myself go, I won't have to worry about cheating husbands because I just won't have one." I didn't say that. Okay, I did later to Nancy when we took the kids to the playground. But saying that to my mother would have started a third world war.

But by Thursday, as she ordered me around the living room, making sure everything was just so for her weekly bridge game, I realized something was off. "Mama, why aren't you just hosting at your house?"

She didn't turn around to look at me. "Because I'm living here now." She said it lightly, but there was a bit of steel in her voice.

"How long exactly are you planning to live here?"

This time she turned around. "You want me to leave?"

"I didn't say—"

"Of all the ungrateful—I ruined my figure for you, gave up my whole life to help you in your hour of need, and you'd just throw me out in the cold like a day-old newspaper."

"No one is throwing you out. Your figure is perfect. And it's spring, which is hardly the cold. I'm just asking why you're not hosting at your own home, three blocks from here, where I don't have to work myself to the bone making the house the way you want it."

"This is the thanks I get for moving in to help raise your children—"

Which was when I noticed that they were way too quiet and I hadn't seen them in too long. "Speaking of the children, where are they?"

"I dropped them off at Nancy's."

"You—what?"

"Well, they can't be running around during my bridge game."

I stared at her for a moment. "This is *their* house."

"It's mine too right now."

"But Larry is living at Nancy's house."

"He won't be there in the middle of the day. Do you really think I didn't consider that?"

I exhaled forcefully. All I needed was for Robbie to see something of Larry's and put the pieces together. He may have just turned five, but he was a sharp five-year-old. "Okay, well, I'm going to go and get them now."

"Why? Enjoy the break."

"Because I don't want Larry coming home and confusing them."

"Did that man ever come home early in your entire marriage?"

I hesitated. Not since the kids were born, no. But in the early days, yes, he'd sneak home for lunch or come home early when he could, claiming he missed me. Had that ever been true? It felt like a lifetime ago. Different people. Not us, surely. I shook my head at the memory, which my mother misinterpreted.

"See? There's nothing to worry about. I've thought of everything." The doorbell rang, and I startled. "That'll be Jean."

I sighed at the unwelcome intrusion. "I'm going to get the kids."

"That's the problem with your generation. Mine knows that you have to tend your own garden before you can tend anyone else's."

I thought of how many nights Rosa had put me and my brother to bed. But we still always wanted our mother, who prioritized herself over us. "We'll be back."

"Try and keep them out until four, darling. No one will want me to host again if we're interrupted."

I don't want you to host at my *house again,* I thought. But I gritted my teeth. "Fine. I'll take them to the park."

"Maybe stay out until 4:30, then. If anyone stays to talk, I don't want grubby fingers."

"This is their house, Mama. They can have dirty fingers in their own house."

She pursed her lips. "It's mine as well, and I believe the adults make the rules."

She was impossible.

But I took my handbag and left, letting her friend in as I did, and headed for Nancy's.

6

Nancy might have had no problem walking right into my house without knocking, but I wasn't comfortable doing the same.

Well, not comfortable doing the same anymore.

Though, to be perfectly fair, the very reason I didn't feel comfortable just walking in should have led to me knocking on Larry's office door. But I hadn't expected to walk in on a similar scene in my husband's workplace.

I rapped smartly and Nancy appeared a moment later, her eyes widening as she saw me. "Bev, I told her—" Shrieks emanated from behind her, and without even turning around, Nancy yelled, "If that's broken, you're not watching TV tonight!" She lowered her voice. "Your mother said you'd be okay with it if it happened."

"Okay with what?"

Nancy blinked three times in rapid succession. "Larry is here."

"Why isn't he at work?"

In the six years we had been friends, I had never seen Nancy get flustered. Nancy was the woman who walked in and got things done, wherever she was. And it took me a moment to register that the change in her was my first time seeing her actually uncomfortable. Even the final time that I walked into her house unannounced, she just waved at me and continued what she was doing, calling out that she and Arnie would just be another couple minutes.

But Nancy bit her lip and looked away. "Arnie was home for lunch and called him when your mother brought the kids." My shoulders dropped. "Bev, I told him not to. I really don't want to be in the middle of this."

I counted to ten in my head. "I don't want you to be in the middle either. And I wish Larry had found someplace else to stay." *And I really wish he and my mother respected boundaries,* I added silently. "I came to grab the kids. I'll get them out of your hair."

"Do you want to just leave them for a while? Then you don't have to see him."

It was tempting. But I also didn't know what he was telling them and whether he had them each on a knee, spinning a sob story about how mean Mommy wouldn't let him come home. If so, I hoped Nancy's can-do attitude would extend to helping me dig a six-foot hole in the backyard.

"No. I'm going to take them home." Except they couldn't go home. I had been hoping I could have a cup of coffee with Nancy while the kids played before taking them out to kill some time.

Nancy wrung her hands, and I put a hand on her arm. "None of this is your fault. It'll be fine. I promise."

She nodded and pulled me in for a quick squeeze. Then I marched inside, heading toward the sound of voices in the den.

"Well, well, well," I said, surveying the scene. Larry was on the floor opposite Robbie, a half-empty checkerboard between them as Debbie sat on his lap, chewing on a black game piece. It was the first time I had seen him play a game with Robbie in over two years, and I momentarily forgot why we were at Nancy's house instead of ours, taking in the heartwarming scene. *Maybe,* I thought, observing how content the children looked, *he* should *come home.*

"Mommy!" Robbie screamed, launching himself at me and knocking everything off the board in the process.

"Mama!" Debbie cried around the checker in her mouth. "I pay keckers too!"

Robbie looked up, his arms still wrapped around my legs. "She's *not* playing. She's slobbering on all the pieces."

"I pay!"

"No, you don't!"

"Kids," Larry said, rising and dusting off his pants. I glanced over my shoulder to see if Nancy had followed us into the room. She would take that as an insult. There wasn't a speck of dust in her house. But she hadn't come in. "Why don't you go play with Eddie and Patty for a few minutes so your mother and I can talk."

"But—"

"No buts, champ. We don't talk back to adults, do we?"

Robbie's little face fell. "No sir."

If anything had thawed, seeing him on the floor with the kids, it froze back up at the look on Robbie's face. And Larry didn't even notice or care how disappointed he was!

Larry ruffled his hair. "Now take your sister to go find your friends."

Robbie held out his hand to Debbie, who took it, the checker back in her mouth. He looked back once at Larry, who wasn't watching them leave. Instead, he was looking at me smugly. The whole game was a show for me. No. He wasn't coming home.

"What are you *doing* here?" I asked as soon as the kids were out of earshot.

He crossed his arms. "What did you do to your hair?"

"Cut it for myself, not for you for once. Now answer my question."

"Suits you," he said, reaching out to touch the bobbed ends. I backed away, and his face hardened. "I'm living here because my wife threw me out."

"Why *here*?"

"Well, I couldn't exactly go stay with Linda as you suggested. She lives with her mother and sister."

My stomach flipped over. Somehow every time he opened his mouth, the situation got worse. "You are truly disgusting, do you know that?"

31

"Bev, come on. It was just sex." I glanced over my shoulder to make sure the kids weren't peeking around the doorway. "I don't love her. I love you. You *know* that. So let me come home already."

"If you loved me, you'd know that there's no such thing as"—I looked behind me again and lowered my voice—"'just sex' if it's with anyone else."

He shrugged. "Well, that's what it was regardless. I don't expect a woman to understand, but men have needs and—"

I held up a hand. "Yeah, and one of those *needs* is for you to stop talking before your children hear you say something that is going to cause permanent damage."

"And you think their mother kicking their father out won't achieve the same thing?"

I stared at him, wondering how I had ever thought I loved this man. Then I took a deep breath, because it was that or slap him. "No. I think our children will grow up learning to care about others instead of just themselves. Which is not the lesson they'd be learning with you in the house."

His brows closed in, and his face darkened. "Beverly—"

"No. I'm going to find a lawyer this week. I'm not doing this. You can find someone else to handle your 'needs.'"

I turned to walk out, but he grabbed my arm. "The department store called me because of how high the charges were. I was going to let the bill slide if I was coming home," he said as I yanked my arm back and spun to look at him. "But if I'm not, it all goes back to the store."

"That furniture is going nowhere."

"Oh, it's going somewhere all right. That's the next thing—I can't stay here forever, and I can't afford both that house and someplace else to live, especially not the way you spend. So either I come home, or you're going to need to find something smaller. An apartment in Silver Spring would do nicely."

An apartment! I shook my head. I wasn't leaving that house. "Get yourself an apartment. I'll get a job."

He threw his head back and laughed. "A job? Doing what? You've never worked a day in your life."

"I've kept house and cooked and raised our children. That's work."

"But nothing that pays the bills. What are you going to do? Leave the kids with your mother and go be a domestic?"

I set my jaw. "Oh, you just wait." I turned around again, swatting behind me in case he tried to grab me, and marched into the kitchen to get the kids.

7

The following morning, I set out, announcing to my mother that I was taking her car.

"It's customary to ask," she said, then flipped a page in the magazine she was reading at the kitchen table and took a puff of her cigarette. I swiped the cigarette, put it to my lips and took a quick drag, then stubbed it out in the ashtray in front of her. "I thought you didn't smoke anymore."

"I don't want you smoking around the kids. And I need the car for a few hours."

"I need it at two." She pulled another cigarette from her pack.

"Not around the kids, please."

"Do you see them anywhere near the kitchen?" she asked, lighting it. "They never leave that television set."

"Amazingly, you're the one who keeps turning it on for them. Try to get them outside, please."

"I'll have to," Mama said. "How else am I going to smoke?"

"That's the spirit. I'll be back by two." I picked up my handbag and turned to leave.

"Where are you going anyway?"

I stopped and looked back at her. I didn't want to get her more entangled in the details of my marriage falling apart than I had to, and I wasn't looking forward to the fight that was sure to come if I told her about Larry's threat to downsize. She would tell me to move home with the kids, and the idea of moving back into my childhood bedroom with my two children in tow was much worse than the idea of raising them alone. Which she would never understand.

"I have an appointment," I said lightly.

"Is that code for a date or a lawyer?" she asked, flipping another page of the magazine. She glanced up at me to see the effect of her words. "I'm sure you're wonderful at lying to other people, darling, but I see right through you."

"Lawyer," I lied, gritting my teeth.

"Fine, don't tell me, then."

"I'll see you at two, Mama."

"One thirty."

"But you just—oh, forget it. One thirty." I hoped she kept more of those cigarettes in the car. I had gone six years without one. Another week with her and I would be smoking two packs by lunch.

~

Of the two divorced women I knew, one of them, Francine Keller, had also gone to work and was currently employed as a receptionist at Emory Estates Country Club. And while I wasn't willing to go and ask *our* club if they were hiring, I thought checking the other local clubs would be a good place to start. I couldn't type, but I could certainly answer phones and direct people to the changing and dining rooms.

The first two clubs I tried weren't hiring, but the second told me that Emory Estates was. I thanked them, then debated if that was a good idea or a terrible one. Francine and I had never been particularly close, and I wasn't sure if she would forgive me for letting that distance grow when she and her husband separated—even if I was now coming crawling to her on the same terms. But if she was willing to overlook my ignorance, it might be nice to have a friend who understood.

I turned the key and started the car. Emory Estates it was.

The long driveway was tree-lined, and I squared my shoulders as the whitewashed brick of the clubhouse came into view. This was the new beginning I needed. I could feel it. They'd be fools not to hire me. Yes, it was more of a drive than Chevy Chase or Congressional, and being this far off the main road, I would need Mama's car to get to work. But I also didn't know any of the members here, so my employment was less likely to be a cause for gossip.

I gave the keys to the valet and adjusted my hat before walking inside, making sure it had the perfect Jackie Kennedy dent that my mother would purse her lips at. Between my new hairdo and the pink dress, perfectly belted at the waist, I turned heads as my heels clacked on the marble floor.

Francine was seated at the desk. She looked up, and it was a moment before she recognized me. "Beverly?"

"Francine," I said warmly, holding out a hand. "How are you? It's been way too long."

She looked at my hand suspiciously before taking it. "Are you meeting someone here today? I didn't see you on the list."

"Darling, I'm not. But I was hoping I could speak to the manager."

She eyed me warily. "I suppose so. I'll go see if he's available."

"Thank you so much."

"What is it regarding?"

I had been planning to ask her to put in a good word, but the welcome I received was far too cool to hope for that. So I felt it best to keep my cards close to my chest. I could always win her over later, once I had the job. "Just a business opportunity."

"Business? Is Larry trying to host an event here?"

I blinked but shook my head, unperturbed. "I promise I'll tell you after I speak with him."

Francine shrugged, then disappeared through the door behind her desk.

A minute later, she returned and then directed me through the same door. "He's in there," she said, pointing down the hallway to an office, before returning to her own desk.

"Francine," I said to her back. She angled her head in my direction but didn't actually look at me. "It's very nice to see you." Her shoulders softened slightly, and her head dipped infinitesimally in a nod.

Buoyed by the knowledge that she had already begun to thaw, I marched into the manager's office, noting the name, John Harmon, on the door.

"Mr. Harmon," I said from the doorway. He looked me up and down, then rose. "Beverly Diamond."

"What can I do for you today, Miss Diamond?"

"*Mrs.* Diamond," I corrected out of habit. "I heard you're looking for a receptionist, and I believe I'd be perfect for the job."

He held a finger to his lips, then came behind me and shut the door. "Sit, sit," he said, gesturing toward a chair across from his desk. "Where did you hear that?" I named the club that had told me. "We are, but it's a bit of a tricky situation," he said. "Have you worked in reception before?"

"Mr. Harmon, I have not. But my husband works for a politician, and I've been tasked with hosting duties so many times now that I feel like I have."

He smiled at that. "I suppose you're personable enough all right. Do you have children?"

"I do."

"And they're in school?"

"Not yet, but my mother is watching them."

"And your husband is being stingy with the money for clothes and frills, I assume." I inclined my head slightly but didn't exactly nod. "Yes, I believe you'd do well in the job." He leaned back in his chair. "As I said, it's a little sticky right now. We couldn't hire you officially for a week or so."

That was just fine. It gave me time to figure out getting a lawyer and warm my mother up on the job front.

"We need to get rid of that one first," he said quietly, gesturing toward Francine's general direction. "It turns out she's Jewish."

The room tipped upside down. "Excuse me?"

"I know. I couldn't tell by looking at her either. But she is. And that just won't work."

"I see," I said slowly. "Yes, I imagine that *would* be a problem here, wouldn't it?"

Mr. Harmon exhaled. "I'm so glad you understand."

"Mr. Harmon, I understand you perfectly." I rose. "But unfortunately, you would have the same problem with me, so I'll just save you the trouble." I walked out, slamming the door behind me.

Francine had turned around at the noise, her mouth slightly open as I reached her. "Come on, Francine, let's go grab lunch."

"I can't. I'm working."

I shook my head. "They're firing you. They wanted to hire me because you're Jewish. I didn't know."

She stared at me for a moment, then stood. "Where do you want to go?"

"Anywhere but here." Francine nodded, took her purse from a desk drawer, and came around to me. "Wait," I said, pulling a lipstick from my own bag. I uncapped it, then used it to draw a large Star of David on the desk. "Might as well. They're probably going to burn it after we've touched it anyway." Francine let out a choked laugh. "Come on. Lunch is on me. Larry and I are splitting up, but I still have his Diners' Club card for now."

8

Seated across from each other at O'Donnell's, Francine and I fell into an awkward silence. "When did you and Larry split up?" she asked.

"About two weeks ago." I sipped my water. "I caught him with his secretary."

"Such a cliché."

I shook my head. "You'd think they would at least find creative ways to humiliate us."

Francine smiled tightly and changed the subject. "How did they find out I was Jewish?"

"I haven't the faintest of ideas. I went to another club looking for work, and they told me Emory was hiring—I assumed to supplement your hours. It wasn't until I was in that cretin's office that I learned they were trying to get rid of you."

"*Cretin* is right." Francine shook her head. "Probably a blessing in disguise, but now I need to find another job."

"That makes two of us."

"Why are you looking for work? You've got kids. Larry has to keep supporting you."

"He's threatening to make me downsize, and I don't want to move to some tacky apartment with the kids." Then I covered my mouth. Francine's husband had sold their house before leaving her for their widowed neighbor, and, to the best of my knowledge, she was now living in an apartment. "I'm so sorry."

She shrugged. "It's not so bad. Although I could see where it would be with kids. At least Larry didn't burn you as badly as David burned me." The waiter brought our food, and Francine cut a piece of fish, brought it to her mouth, and chewed delicately. "The worst part," she said when she'd finished chewing, "honestly, was all my friends giving me the cold shoulder."

"I'm sorry," I said again. "I didn't know you well, but I—I don't know."

"People think it's contagious," she said, shrugging again. "It wasn't like I had a choice though. He left. What was I supposed to do? Waste away and die in a sanatorium somewhere?" She cut another piece of fish, but stopped short of her mouth with it. "I've made new friends. Turns out, there are a good number of divorcées now."

"Soon to be one more," I said, raising my glass to her. She clinked hers to mine. "Listen, Francine—"

"Fran," she interrupted. "We're in the same boat. We can be friends now."

"Fran. I *am* sorry. I want you to know that."

"Water under the bridge." She hesitated. "But now we both need jobs. Do you have any skills?"

"Skills?"

"Typing, dictation, anything like that?"

I colored slightly at the reference to dictation. "I don't think I want to be a secretary. Not after—"

"No, that wouldn't do, would it? Besides, anyone good would want someone who had gone to secretarial school. Did you finish college?" I shook my head. I had left college my senior year to marry Larry. Papa had thrown a fit at that. Who knew he was going to turn out to be right? "Me neither," Fran said glumly. "I was trying to avoid retail."

"Retail?" I was fabulous at shopping.

"Yeah. I suppose we could go to the makeup counter at Woodies and see if they're hiring." My eyes widened. "You're good at your own makeup. They'd hire you."

"But—then everyone—"

Fran looked at me for a moment. "Oh, honey. They're all going to know eventually anyway." She sipped her drink. "Why don't you just move in with your parents? Then you won't have to work, and your mother's reputation just may save you from suffering my fate."

I shook my head. My desire not to live with my parents outweighed my desire to avoid seeing all my friends—if they were still my friends—while I waited on them at a store. "Woodies it is."

Fran raised her glass this time. "To new beginnings."

I clinked my glass to hers. I knew Nancy would never abandon me, but it *was* nice to have someone to talk to who had been through it all already.

~

My career behind the makeup counter at Woodward & Lothrop lasted exactly two hours and thirty-four minutes.

I left the house the following morning and took the bus to the Woodies in Friendship Heights. I had debated suggesting the Hecht's in Silver Spring to buy myself some time before I ran into everyone I knew, but the reality was that there was no shame in working. And Fran had been right: everyone would know Larry and I had split eventually. Did I actually want to be friends with anyone who would stop talking to me over either situation?

Well, yes. I wanted Larry to be the pariah, while I flourished in my exact same social circle with the largest disruption being the fact that I no longer had to wake up so early.

But even I knew that was unlikely.

It probably didn't help that I arrived late. Mama simply didn't understand why leaving at a set time was important if it wasn't for one of her various social outings. And she peppered me with questions about where I was going and when I would be back.

Miss Llewelyn wasn't exactly forgiving of my tardiness, suggesting I use my first week's earnings to purchase a watch from the jewelry department. "I have one," I told her. She looked pointedly at my empty wrist. "Perhaps you should wear it, then."

She didn't seem like she would sympathize with why said watch was ticking away in the junk drawer, so I just nodded. And I had spent enough time at that exact makeup counter as a customer that I was already quite well versed in where everything was.

The first two hours were uneventful. I sold six lipsticks, three tubes of mascara, and two powder compacts. Fran was opposite me behind the perfume counter, and we chatted when we could until Miss Llewelyn told us that was what our breaks were for. I made a face at her behind her back, and Fran stifled a laugh.

But at eleven thirty, I heard a gasp that I knew all too well, and I smeared the lipstick I was applying on an elderly customer across her cheek to her ear.

"Beverly Ann Gelman Diamond," my mother said. "What on earth—?"

I took a deep breath. "Hi, Mama."

The woman with the lipstick on her cheek turned to my mother. "Millie!" she said. Then she looked back at me. "I knew you looked familiar."

"What are you doing behind"—she gestured to the counter—"that? Come out here right now."

"I can't, Mama. I'm working."

"Working!"

"Yes. I have a job now."

"Absolutely not. My daughter, working behind a makeup counter! You come out here at once."

"Is there a problem, Mrs. Gelman?" Miss Llewelyn asked smoothly. Of course she knew my mother by name.

"I should say so!" Her hands were on her hips, and I suddenly realized there should have been tiny people attached to those hands.

"Mama—where are the children?"

"I'm looking at one of them," she said, pointing a finger at me. "I don't know *what* you were thinking! Does Larry know you're here?"

"It's not Larry's business where I am," I said tartly. "And if he wasn't threatening to sell the house, I wouldn't *be* here. But he is. Now where are *my* children?"

She waved a hand in the air. "I dropped them at Nancy's house. I had errands to run."

"Mama, Nancy isn't free babysitting."

"And I am? While you come and make pennies here?"

"You're making a scene," Miss Llewelyn hissed at me.

"I'm not doing anything! She's making a scene!" I pointed to my mother.

"Well, I can't fire her, but I can fire you. Take your things and go, please. Now."

"Good," my mother said. "Go get in the car. The very idea. I'll never be able to hold my head up in here again."

"What about my lipstick?" the customer asked.

"That color is all wrong for you anyway," my mother said. "I don't know what Beverly was thinking."

"Me?"

She turned to me. "I told you to get in the car."

"Mama, I'm a grown woman. You can't order me around like this."

Her lips almost disappeared. "Car. Now."

I lifted the counter's opening and came out meekly. "Call me this week?" I asked Fran as I passed.

She nodded. "Good luck."

"I'm going to need it," I said as my mother prodded me in the back toward the door.

9

I fumed silently for the first ten minutes of our drive home, while my mother alternated between moaning and lecturing me about the perceived impropriety of my actions.

But somewhere in between her comment that it was bad enough I was about to be divorced, let alone working to support my family, and her insistence that she needed to close her charge account with Woodies because she could never be seen there again and would have to do all her shopping at Hecht's and Garfinckel's now, I'd had enough.

"Mama, stop. This isn't like the time you caught me kissing Nathaniel Gordon in high school."

"No, it's worse than that. I just knew I should have sent you to your great-aunt Ada when that happened, but your father said no. If I'd sent you to her, you wouldn't have married Larry in the first place, and we wouldn't be in this mess."

While I appreciated her use of *we* in describing my situation if it related to the divorce, I wasn't sure if the *mess* part was the end of my marriage or her catching me working at a department store.

"Thank goodness your father isn't still in office. Can you imagine?"

"I can actually," I said. "It probably would have helped him secure some working-class votes—if you didn't spoil that by making a scene about how inappropriate working is. Come on, Mama, it's 1962."

She waved a hand, and the whole car swerved. "There's nothing wrong with *other* people working, darling. But whatever is this about?

You have the children. The courts will make Larry support you. This theater is unnecessary and is going to give me gray hairs."

I suppressed a smirk. It was easier to miss when she wasn't living with me, but her hair color had a distinct change when she returned from the salon two days earlier. That hint of a smile faded when I realized I had to answer her question. "Larry said I have to downgrade. He can't afford to keep the house and someplace else for him to live."

"Can't afford? Nonsense. He's just trying to scare you. Besides, *we* gave him money for the down payment. He can't make you go anywhere."

"You gave it to *him*, Mama. Not to me."

"Whatever would you have done with it? You couldn't have gotten a mortgage."

I sighed. Yes, the courts would likely mandate that I got to keep the house. But my mother had grown up extremely wealthy, and since marrying Larry, who had not, I had learned more about the world outside of my mother's privileged, upper-class New York upbringing.

"Money isn't going to be unlimited—money hasn't been unlimited. But with two households to run, it's going to be tighter. If I have a job, nothing needs to change for the kids."

I held my breath. Here came her suggestion that I move home with them. And I wasn't looking forward to the resulting fight when I said that no, I would rather work than do that.

But no offer came.

Instead, my mother contemplated this, then nodded so infinitesimally that I wasn't sure if I had imagined it or not. "We need to think about a more appropriate source of income. Something that won't bring gossip." She paused. "For your father's sake."

Papa wasn't exactly the one soliciting the makeup counter at Woodward & Lothrop, but I refrained from pointing that out. That avenue was closed now anyway, and to be fair, even just one morning selling cosmetics had bored me. I wanted something where I was challenged and got to use my brain for more than complementary colors on my mother's bridge buddies.

I just didn't know what that was.

~

I dropped my mother off at the house and then took her car to go pick the kids up from Nancy's house. Normally, I wouldn't mind walking, but it was rainy and my feet hurt from being in heels all morning.

I rapped smartly on the door and heard Nancy's voice yelling to come on in.

I walked into a scene of utter bedlam. The cushions were all off the sofa and assembled in a makeshift fort, buoyed by overturned dining room chairs, and the whole concoction was covered in sheets while the older children fought off the younger two with pillows as they tried to dismantle their older siblings' handiwork.

"Nance?"

"In the den," she called. A child screamed. "Fight GENTLY," she yelled. "I already told you that. FIGHT GENTLY!"

The scene in the den lacked children but was far more chaotic as Nancy sat in the middle of the room, surrounded by tools and pieces of electronics. My gaze traveled toward the wall, where the whole television had been disassembled.

"What happened in here?"

She grinned up at me, tightening a bolt as she did so. "TV wasn't working, but I think I got it now. Just need to put it all back together."

"And you did it yourself?"

"Of course. It's not hard. And if I tell Arnie that the repairman charged twenty-five dollars and I paid for it with my pin money, he'll give me twenty-five dollars that I can put toward that new dishwasher he doesn't want to buy."

Had Nancy been born a man, she would be running an empire instead of a household. There was nothing she couldn't take apart and put back together better than it had been assembled in the first place.

"That would be quite a business plan," I said, thinking out loud. "You could charge women half what a repairman would and let them keep the difference. Everyone would call you."

She tilted her head as she began fitting pieces back together. "Not a bad idea. Maybe when the kids are both in school."

I wished I had a fraction of her skills. But I had needed her help just to hang my new curtains.

"How's Larry going to like his bed being used as the Alamo out there?" I asked.

"I couldn't care less. I told Arnie he has to tell him he's out by the end of next week."

"You did?"

She nodded, then walked across the carpet on her knees, holding the TV's insides to begin putting them back in place. "He told Arnie what he told you about the house," she said, still focused on the television repair. "He said that'd scare you into taking him back, and I thought that was rotten."

I exhaled. "Then it's just a ploy?"

"I don't know, but I'm not letting him plot against my best friend from my living room. No sir. Pass me that Phillips-head screwdriver. Not the flat one. The one with the end that looks like a star."

I brought her the screwdriver and leaned down and hugged her fiercely. "Thank you."

She looked up in surprise. "You okay for now? I can loan you twenty-five bucks tomorrow if you need it."

I laughed and told her I just might, before regaling her with my employment adventures of the past two days.

"I would have paid good money to see your mother's face when she saw you there."

"Worth twenty-five dollars?"

Nancy laughed. "Absolutely. I could always break the TV again next week." She thought for a moment. "I can break yours too. Then we can go shopping." She paused. "Maybe not at Woodies."

"Definitely at Woodies," I said, grinning. "Miss Llewelyn won't know what to do with me as a customer."

"Think Millie could handle watching all four kids?"

We both laughed at the idea of eight sticky hands assailing her. "Absolutely not."

10

"I had a dream last night," my mother said over breakfast.

"Oh?" I asked disinterestedly. I was far too busy trying to wipe Debbie's face as she squirmed away from me. "You cannot leave the table with syrup on your face," I told her.

"Lemme go!"

My mother leveled a stern look at her. "Deborah Annette Diamond," she said firmly. "Do you want people to think you're a street urchin?"

Debbie looked up at me, confused. "Do I, Mama?"

"You do not," my mother said firmly. I shook my head slightly to confirm. "Now let your mother clean your face."

Debbie sat stone still while I wiped the remaining syrup from her chin. "All clean."

"I go now?"

"Yes, darling, you can go now." She scampered off happily from the table, and I turned back to my mother. "You know she has no idea what a street urchin is, right?"

She shrugged. "It worked, didn't it?" I had to give credit where credit was due. "Now about that dream—I found the answer."

"The answer?"

She shook her head in exasperation. "To the job problem. You'll host Tupperware parties!"

I blinked heavily. "What?"

"As a job. It's a perfectly appropriate way to pick up some extra money."

I took a deep breath. "That's not a job, Mama."

"You don't *need* a job. Larry will have to let you keep the house and an allowance."

"I'm not a child. I don't want an allowance. I want to stand on my own feet and know that he can't pull the rug out from under me. I don't ever want to be in a position where he can threaten me again. And Tupperware parties aren't going to accomplish that."

"Harriet Lowenstein makes a lot of money off them."

"Harriet Lowenstein's husband is a surgeon, and she lies constantly to one-up everyone. And you know that."

My mother threw up her hands. "And what better idea do you have?"

I didn't have any. And she smirked when I said nothing.

There was a crash from the living room. I started to stand, but she beat me to it. "Think about it," she said, going toward the sound of Robbie wailing. It was his over-the-top crying that he did when Debbie destroyed whatever he had been playing with, not a hurt cry, so I let her go. It was a rare occurrence when I got to actually eat breakfast without putting the television on.

I picked up the newspaper and flipped idly past the front section. Marilyn Monroe's performance at the president's birthday party was still making headlines over a week later with details on her dress and the guests in attendance. There had been an airline crash. And always more nuclear testing because of the Soviet Union.

But when I flipped to the Metro section, I froze.

On the front page, below the fold, was a picture of Sam. Next to it was a younger man. The headline read "Maryland senatorial race heats up, despite incumbent's insurmountable lead."

I studied the other man's photograph, my eyes drifting down toward the caption. "Political newcomer Michael Landau looks to challenge suburban favorite Sam Gibson."

"Michael Landau," I said quietly. I turned to the article.

Thirty-three years old, unmarried, and from Silver Spring. He had attended the University of Maryland for both undergrad and law school. He was too young to fight in Europe but *had* gone to Korea. Sam likely had the edge in that he had been at Normandy, which painted a better picture than being a pilot in Korea, but a vet was a vet. Sam came from old money—based on his hometown and education, this Landau fellow did not. And politics was a wealthy man's game. But the article said he had some strong backers who were passionate about his ability to bring change in Washington.

I looked back at his picture. He needed a better haircut and a tie that didn't look like it came from the previous decade, all of which was fixable. His expression was stern, but there was no denying that he was good-looking, with a straight nose and full lips. He had that edge over Sam—and if the previous presidential election had proven anything, it was that in the television era, looks mattered.

And slowly, an idea began to blossom.

I had grown up in politics. My earliest memories involved visiting my father in the House of Representatives. I had dined at the White House from the age of eight, when my mother finally trusted me to behave as behooved the daughter of the minority leader. And when he ran for reelection, I handed out stickers and pins and posed for countless pictures, telling people to remember to vote for my daddy.

Once I married Larry, while I wasn't the politician's family, I slid comfortably into the behind-the-scenes role, offering advice that I had learned at my father's knee. Larry never credited me, but I saw how many of my ideas he implemented.

I stood up. "Mama!" I called. "I need you to stay with the kids for a few hours."

"Where are you going?"

I deposited the breakfast dishes in the sink to be dealt with later. "To meet with a lawyer."

She appeared in the kitchen. "Where are you actually going?"

I grinned at her. "To meet with a lawyer," I repeated. It wasn't a lie.

11

A quick phone call to the operator got me the Landau campaign office's address—he wasn't anywhere near the Hill, but only a fifteen-minute bus ride down East-West Highway to Silver Spring.

So it wasn't much later when I rapped on the door in an office building, dressed in my sharpest baby-blue suit. It wasn't Chanel, but it was a knockoff of a Jackie Kennedy number, including the hat and gloves. Which might have been overkill, combined with the new hairdo, but, well, if you wanted to be a woman involved in politics, there was no one better to emulate in 1962.

No one answered the door. My last experience entering a campaign office left me hesitant to just walk in, but I could see a figure faintly through the frosted glass and heard a distinctly male voice. So I straightened my hat and turned the knob.

"No!" A man was practically shouting into a phone. "I told you already—we need a smaller venue. If he's speaking in a big room and no one shows up, he looks awful. We need a smaller house that we know we can fill."

"Sounds to me like you need to find more people, not a smaller venue," I said.

The man on the phone looked up, annoyed, and held his hand over the mouthpiece. "Can I help you?"

"I certainly hope so. I'm here to see Michael Landau."

"Regarding?"

I sized him up. He appeared to be in his early thirties, and even without looking at his hands, it was obvious he wasn't married. Not with that rumpled shirt, unbuttoned at the collar, lack of a tie, and—I glanced down—brown shoes with a black belt. I never would have let Larry out of the house like that. I peeked around the rest of the office space. There were three other doors off the main office and four desks crammed into this room, all in a similar state of disarray to the one I was standing in front of.

They needed a secretary.

But that wasn't why I was there. And if he was shouting into the phone about speaking venues, this was likely who I was looking to replace.

"I'm afraid it's a personal matter," I said primly.

"I'm going to have to call you back," he said into the phone. "And by the time I do, you'd better have a smaller room for us." He replaced the receiver with a thunk. Then he looked up, taking his turn to examine me, but I refused to shy away from his gaze. "He's not here," he said brusquely. "You can leave a message with me."

Three chairs sat against the wall near the door, and I sat in the one that didn't have a jacket draped over it. "I can wait."

"Look, Miss—?"

"Beverly," I said, realizing my last name—either my married name or my maiden name—would be enough to set off alarm bells.

"Miss Beverly—"

"Just Beverly. That's my first name."

The man blinked heavily. "I don't care what your name is. I can't sit here babysitting you all day. I have work to do."

I opened my mouth, a sharp retort on my tongue about his appearance indicating he was the one who needed a babysitter, when the door to the office opened and the man whose picture I had seen that morning walked in, carrying a bag from a local delicatessen and a coffee cup.

"They were out of pickles," he said, not noticing me yet. "What kind of delicatessen runs out of pickles?"

"Go to Hofberg's next time," I said. He turned to stare at me. "Better pastrami too."

Michael Landau looked back at the rumpled man behind the desk, who shrugged. "Michael Landau," he said, setting the bag and cup down on the desk, then holding out his hand. "And you are?"

"Beverly." I took the proffered hand and shook it.

"She wouldn't tell me what she wanted," the man behind the desk said.

"It's okay, Stuart," he said. "How can I help you today?"

"Mr. Landau, I am here to help *you*." I glanced at Stuart, whose arms were crossed. "Is there somewhere we can speak privately?"

"Anything you have to say to me, you can say in front of my campaign manager," he said, eyeing me warily. "You look familiar. What was your last name?"

I ignored the question. This was going to be more difficult with Stuart, the incompetent campaign manager, glaring at me. "Look, Mr. Landau, I'm going to be frank with you. You're going to lose this campaign."

His face changed from skeptical to steely. "And why is that?"

"Because Sam Gibson has Larry Diamond running his campaign and you have Stuart over here telling people to find you a smaller room to speak in because he can't fill it with voters."

Stuart started to argue, but Mr. Landau silenced him with a "wait" gesture. "And what do you suggest I do about that?"

"That's why I'm here. If you hire me as your campaign manager, you can win this."

For a moment neither man spoke. Then Stuart threw his head back in laughter, and Landau chuckled. I raised an eyebrow.

"Did you put her up to this? Found her when you went to get lunch and sent her on ahead?" Stuart asked.

Landau shook his head. "I thought you put her up to it?"

I glanced at my wrist for effect, then remembered I still needed to get a new watch. "If you two are quite finished, I don't have all day."

"Look, I admit we could probably use a secretary—"

"We definitely need a secretary," Mr. Landau said, looking at me intently.

"But the campaign manager job is taken. By me. And we're going to win this election on our own."

I shook my head. "I'm terribly sorry to break this to you, but you're not. The *Washington Post* knows it. I know it. Sam Gibson definitely knows it. And I think deep down even you know it. But I'm the one person who can change that."

"Why is that?" Mr. Landau asked, looking at me from the corner of his eye.

"Because my full name is Beverly Gelman Diamond. My father is Bernie Gelman, and I spent six years married to Larry Diamond." I watched as recognition and then alarm spread across their faces.

"Get her out of here," Mr. Landau said to Stuart. "Now."

"Excuse me?"

The two men exchanged a look and then huddled together, whispering. I caught the words *spying* and *husband* and *low even for him*.

"I'm not a spy. I want Larry—and by extension Sam—to lose."

They both turned to look at me. "Why?" Mr. Landau asked.

I took a deep breath. All I had was the truth. "Because he's been cheating on me with his secretary and told me if I didn't take him back, he was selling the house and making me move the kids to an apartment." They took this in. "So, yes, I want a job. But specifically *this* job. I grew up on Capitol Hill. You want to know why Larry is so good at his job? He had me and my father. So if you want to win, I'm how you do that. And I'll tell you right now, you book that bigger room, and I'll help you fill it. You book a smaller space, and you might as well give up now."

"Absolutely not," Stuart said. Mr. Landau turned to look at him, but something had shifted in his face. "You can't trust her. She's *married to Larry Diamond.* She said that much herself."

"Only until we can get divorced," I said. "Trust me, I don't want to be married to him any more than I want to marry you."

Stuart stood up a little straighter at the insult and started to return fire, but Mr. Landau cut him off. "I can't hire you as my campaign manager. But I can hire you as a secretary and see what happens from there."

He held my gaze for a few seconds while I contemplated this. I knew full well that I could win him over. Stuart might be a different situation, which was understandable; I *was* there to take his job. But there was a warmth behind Mr. Landau's eyes that offered a glimmer of hope.

"I don't know shorthand. I don't take dictation. And my typing is atrocious at best."

"How about personal skills?"

I smiled my most dazzling smile, and he softened, smiling back. "I'll take the job—on the condition that you actually do listen to me. And when you see that I know what I'm doing, you promote me and hire a real secretary."

"Promote you to what?" Stuart asked.

I turned back to Mr. Landau. "Why, whatever position you think I deserve, of course."

Something had changed in the room. I couldn't explain it, but there was an electricity crackling that hadn't been there before. Then Mr. Landau held out his hand again. I placed mine in his. "You're hired," he said.

I grinned again. "I'll be here first thing tomorrow. You won't regret this, Mr. Landau."

"I regret not locking that office door," Stuart grumbled.

But Mr. Landau ignored him. "Michael," he said. "We don't stand on formality in this office."

Every junior staffer in Sam's office called him "Senator Gibson." Even Larry did, if it wasn't just the two of them.

"Michael," I repeated. "It'll do. For now. Until we change your title to 'Senator Landau.'"

I didn't wait to see the effect of my words. Instead, I turned and opened the door to the hall.

"What on earth did you just do?" I heard Stuart saying before the door closed.

"I don't know," Michael's muffled voice replied. "But she's right. Book the bigger room. We'll find people."

I smiled again from the hallway. They had no idea what kind of revolution they were in for.

12

Instead of going home, I took the bus one stop further and walked a block to my parents' house.

For a moment, I stood, looking up at the columns of the house I had grown up in. It had never occurred to me in my childhood that I would suddenly find myself ensconced in the political arena. A politician's wife? Yes. Despite my mother's warnings to marry someone out of the public eye, I think Larry's aspirations were part of the appeal.

Unfortunately that was entirely where the similarity to my father ended.

I shook my head. It did no good to wonder what might have been. I'd made my choice, it ended poorly, and I had made the next choice to clean up my own mess.

But despite my assurances to Michael and Stuart, if I was going to win this campaign, I needed help.

So I climbed the front steps and let myself in.

Only to stop short in the foyer. "Papa?" I called out in alarm. Shoes littered the front hall along with discarded suit jackets. A plate with the days-old remains of a sandwich sat on a console table, and there were muddy shoeprints leading down the hall toward the kitchen. I followed them, dread mounting. Clearly someone had broken in. I should call the police, I thought. What if whoever had broken in was still here? But concern for my father propelled me forward. "Papa?" I called again.

"Beverly? Is that you?"

I heaved a sigh of relief. "Yes. Where are you? Are you okay?"

He walked into the kitchen from the living room in an undershirt and a pair of wrinkled pants, barefoot and unshaven. Which, quite honestly, was nearly as jarring as stumbling upon his corpse would have been.

"Papa, what happened?"

He looked at me in confusion, and I wondered if, rather than an intruder, he had suffered a stroke or some other mental lapse. I was going to send Mama home right away. He couldn't be alone in this state.

"Nothing happened," he said mildly, pulling out his seat at the kitchen table, which was covered in dirty dishes. A glance at the sink showed it was overflowing.

I gestured to the house and then to him. "Then why is everything like—this?"

He shrugged. "Your mother took care of the housekeeping."

A euphemism at best. "Did Rosa quit?"

"I haven't the faintest. Your mother always arranged with her, and I don't know how to contact her."

I blinked heavily, then took a deep breath. "I'll talk to Mama when I get home."

My father looked at me sadly. "I don't think that will help."

"Why not?"

He sighed. "Because she said she's not coming back."

"She—what? No, that's not right. You misunderstood."

"There wasn't much to misunderstand. She said she hasn't been happy with me in a long time, and she was tired of pretending."

I closed my eyes and counted to five. "She told *me* that she was moving in for a while to help with the kids."

"And how does Larry feel about that?"

"I don't think that matters much now . . ." I trailed off as I hit the end of my sentence. Papa didn't know I had thrown Larry out. My mind went back to the look on my mother's face when I asked if she would have stayed if she caught Papa in similar circumstances. What on earth was going on? "Did you cheat on Mama?" I blurted out.

"Cheat? Beverly Gelman—"

"Diamond," I added automatically.

He shook his head, angry now. "If you think I ever even so much as *looked* at another woman, I—"

I held up a hand, stopping him. "I had to ask. I—well, I told Larry he had to move out. And that's why Mama told *me* she was living with me."

"I never liked him," Papa said.

I resisted the urge to ask why he hadn't pointed out that little tidbit *before* I married him and had his children. That was a conversation for another day. And this bombshell that my mother's living arrangements in my house were permanent would need to be dealt with immediately. Free childcare or no, it wasn't sustainable in the long term.

"Well, then I'm glad that particular situation worked out to your advantage," I said. "I will figure out how to fix this with Mama. But first I need your help, and then we're going to clean the house because you can't live like this."

"Do you need money?" he asked.

"No. That's why I'm here. I got a job." His brow furrowed, but I held up a hand again. "I don't want to hear any of those prewar complaints. Besides, it's a job you'll approve of." *I think.*

"What is it?" he asked warily.

"I'm going to be Michael Landau's campaign manager." It wasn't technically a lie. I was *eventually* going to have that job. I was determined. And I had never met a challenge I couldn't conquer—if you didn't count the country club position or the makeup counter, neither of which I did. I couldn't help the religion I was born into any more than I could help my mother going shopping and losing her mind in the middle of a department store.

He looked at me, processing this, before a smile spread across his face under the unfamiliar white stubble. "That's my girl." He reached across the table and patted my hand fondly. "Your mother won't like that at all."

"Neither will Larry, which is the bigger victory."

"You've got an uphill battle there though. Sam is going to win in a landslide."

I tilted my head, hearing the unspoken word. "Unless?"

His grin widened. "Grab a notepad from the drawer under the phone," he said. "We have some brainstorming to do. But I have a feeling if anyone can do this, you can."

13

I didn't return home until close to dinnertime. But at least my father was no longer living in filth, even if he was subsisting primarily on peanut butter sandwiches. I had shown him how the washing machine worked, so he would hopefully have clean clothes. And I had six pages of notes filled with my ideas that I had talked out with my father—some of which were going to be a bit shocking. But if Michael would listen to me, well, Papa was confident he could if not win, then at least give Sam a real race. And that was a start.

But it was also a problem for the following morning.

Right now, I had to deal with my mother.

She was in the kitchen when I arrived home, and cooking, a feat I hadn't witnessed in at least a decade.

"You're back late," she said without turning from the stove. "Did the lawyer hire you?"

There were carrots on the children's plates, waiting for the rest of their meal, and I plucked one from Debbie's plate and took a bite. "He did, actually." Again, not a lie.

She looked up. "Really? As what?"

"Secretary. For now."

"But your typing is atrocious. And what does 'for now' mean?"

"It means I didn't go to a divorce lawyer. I went to see Michael Landau."

"Is that Shirley Landau's son?"

"No."

"Rhoda Landau's?"

"No relation to anyone we know."

"Well, that just can't be true. Who is he, then?" She had a point. It seemed that all Jewish families knew someone in common with each other. It was just a matter of finding who it was. Larry's cousin on his mother's side had gone to college with my cousin Marilyn before she inherited some ridiculous fortune from a great-aunt I had only met at my wedding.

"He's running against Sam for the Senate seat." I took another bite of carrot.

She put down the spoon she'd been holding and turned to look at me. "He—what? Start at the beginning, please."

"How about you start at the beginning?"

"Excuse me?"

"I went to see Papa today. Why are you actually living here?"

She picked the spoon back up and resumed stirring the pot with a vengeance. "To help with the children. You wouldn't have been able to get that secretary job without me here."

"That's not what you told Papa."

The only sign that I had gotten to her was a slight droop in her shoulders. Then they returned to their perfect posture as she turned and pointed the spoon at me. "You are the *last* person to be questioning my marital choices."

"Because I didn't stay with a cheater?"

Debbie burst into tears. I didn't realize she had snuck into the room. I gave my mother a warning look and she returned to the meal at the stove, stirring violently, then I picked Debbie up and sat at the table with her, my arms wrapped around her. "What's the matter, darling?"

"You saw a cheetah and I dinn't," she said with a sniff. I turned away so she wouldn't see the smile I was fighting to hide. "I yuv cheetahs."

"You do? Last week it was elephants."

"No. Cheetahs."

I stroked her hair. "I suppose we'll have to get you a stuffed one, then, won't we?"

"We go to zoo?"

"Soon," I said, nodding. "We can go very soon."

"Today?"

"Not today, silly, it's almost dinnertime."

"Tomowow?"

I started to agree and then remembered that I was a working girl now. "No. It'll have to be the weekend, sweetheart." Her little face fell again. "But I promise we'll go soon." I could hear the sound of the television from the living room. "Go tell your brother dinner is almost ready."

I set her on her feet, and she ran out of the room, shouting, "Robbie! We go to zoo tomowow!"

I shook my head as my mother set food on the table. "We're going to talk about this more when the kids go to bed," I said. She gave me a murderous glare but said nothing, and I stood to get drinks. As difficult as she was, it *was* nice not to have to cook after cleaning her whole house.

~

Once the kids were both asleep, I joined her in the living room where she was watching *The Many Loves of Dobie Gillis*. I switched the television off.

"So rude," she murmured. "You get that from your father."

"Well, leave, then. That seems to be your strategy these days."

"I'm still your mother and won't be spoken to that way."

I closed my eyes and rubbed at my forehead. It had been a long day. "I'm sorry. But will you please tell me what's going on? Papa was living in absolute squalor, and I spent the afternoon cleaning *your* house."

"You'd think a grown man would be able to clean up after himself."

"Mama. What happened?"

"Nothing happened." She pulled a cigarette from the pack in front of her on the coffee table and lit it. "I could use a drink." She looked up at me expectantly.

With a sigh, I went to the kitchen and poured two sherries. She took the one I offered with her free hand and took a sip, then another drag of her cigarette. "I do wish you'd smoke outside," I said, opening the window before I sat in the chair across from her.

"You might as well have one too," she said. "The doctors told me to smoke a cigarette and drink a cup of coffee whenever I got hungry when I was pregnant with you. They wouldn't tell you to do that if it wasn't good for you."

"Yeah, they're not saying that anymore. At least the good doctors aren't."

She shrugged. "You turned out fine. Unless you want to blame the failed marriage on me smoking while pregnant. It's always the mother's fault after all."

I rolled my eyes, which I could get away with because she was studying her drink, not me. "If what's happening is Papa's fault, I still want to know."

"No you don't. He's your knight in shining armor."

I wouldn't have put it that way. But I *had* gone to him to talk out my ideas about Michael winning. "Mama."

She took another drink but still didn't look at me. "It was fine when he was in the House. I understood then."

I waited for her to continue, but she didn't. "Understood what?"

Finally she looked over. "That what he was doing came first. He was legislating the *country*. I had no right to complain that he didn't want to travel, or come to a dinner party, or even just hear about my day. But now? Now checkers in the park is more important than me. When do I get a turn to matter?"

I didn't know what to say. No, there hadn't been any infidelity, but I remembered staring at my wedding picture in its silver frame, and I did know what she meant. They say girls grow up and marry their fathers—Larry wasn't Papa. He didn't begin to measure up to him, and to be perfectly honest, I never thought he had. I had hoped he would grow into . . . what exactly, I didn't know. But he didn't. Still, maybe I had married someone more similar to my father in some respects than I had realized.

"You matter," I said softly, more to myself than to her.

"Well, of course I do to *you*. Why do you think I'm here?"

I had never seen my mother make a truly selfless gesture, and moving in with me wasn't the first. I was a means to an end. A way to make herself feel needed and get out of the situation that she felt was making her unhappy. Not that I could say that to her.

Nor could I let her know about the little seed of determination that had just planted itself in my chest. My marriage was dead, but I knew I could save theirs. If all Papa had to do was make her feel seen and appreciated, they would be back together within the week.

What that meant for me and my new job, I didn't know. But I wasn't going to sacrifice my parents for my own independence.

I stood up, my drink untouched. "I'm going to bed. I have work tomorrow."

"This Michael Landau," she said, looking up at me. "Is he married?"

"No. Why?"

She pointed her cigarette at me. "Don't you go falling in love with a politician. There are no happy endings there."

We'll just see about that, I thought, completely intent on restoring the happy ending to her marriage. "I'm not falling in love with anyone. I'm keeping my house for the kids."

"And sticking it to Larry?"

I grinned. "Icing on the cake. Good night, Mama."

"Switch the television back on, please. And leave that sherry. I'll have it when I finish mine. You're awfully stingy with your pours."

I shook my head as I turned on the television. "Don't stay up too late."

She stubbed out her cigarette and reached for the pack, shaking out another one. "May you live long enough for your children to tell you what to do."

"Hah! Have you met my tiny tyrants? They already do."

"That's a parenting choice," she said.

"Good night, Mama," I repeated, shaking my head again. Maybe my father had gotten the better deal and didn't even realize it.

14

I arrived at the office the following morning at 9:15, carrying coffees and a box of Montgomery Donuts.

Stuart looked up from his desk at the sound of the door opening, and his brow furrowed. "We start working at nine."

"Good morning to you as well," I said cheerily. "Coffee?" I placed one of the cups on his desk. "And once you give me a key, I can be here earlier. But I'm not getting here early just to sit outside the door." I cleared a spot on one of the chairs by the door and set the donuts down.

"I'm here by eight," he said, smelling the coffee before taking a sip.

"I swear I didn't lace it with arsenic to steal your job." He looked up in alarm. "The donuts are another story altogether. Eat those at your own peril."

Stuart shook his head but did look over in interest at them. No one could resist Montgomery Donuts.

Still in my jacket and hat, I strode purposefully to the back office that Michael had come out of the day before. "What do you think you're doing?"

I looked at Stuart over my shoulder. "Bringing the boss coffee. Like a good secretary."

"I'm your boss."

"Now, Stuart," I said, turning to face him. "That just isn't true. Because you work for Michael, and *he* hired me. Now don't you worry about what I'm doing and go help yourself to one of those donuts."

"The poisoned ones?"

"I don't need poison," I said. "I'm going to take your job on my own merit. You wait and see."

I should have knocked. Especially after Larry. But it would have ruined the period on my sentence to Stuart, so I did not. "Coffee?" I asked as Michael glanced up in surprise, a phone receiver held to his ear. He nodded, and I placed the coffee in front of him and then retreated, closing the door behind me.

"Which desk is mine?" I asked Stuart as I removed my gloves.

"I don't care," he said, head still bent over his desk.

I looked around the office. "I suppose you'll need to move, then."

"Excuse me?"

"I'll need a phone, assuming you still want me answering calls. And the only desk with a phone is the one you're sitting at."

He glared at me. "We'll get another phone."

"Lovely. Where are you planning to put it?"

"I don't have time for this. Why don't *you* call the phone company and get another phone installed for you to use."

"I'd be happy to," I said. "But you'll still need to move so I can use the phone." If he had brought me coffee, I wouldn't trust it based on the look he was giving me. But the phone rang. "Would you like me to get that?"

Scowling, he answered the phone. "Landau campaign." A brief pause. "NO! I told you that was no good."

~

I spent the morning cleaning and organizing the office. If anyone walked in here, it was going to be obvious what a rinky-dink organization they were running. And I realized quickly that, even without having spoken to Michael other than to say the word *coffee*, I was going to have my work cut out for me here. They had no idea what it took to run a campaign.

"Where are the other campaign workers?" I asked Stuart around lunchtime when no one else had joined us.

"There aren't any yet," Stuart said gruffly.

"Well, who does cold calls and leaflets and press releases?"

"I do."

"You do realize we need an actual staff if we're going to have a shot at this thing, don't you?"

"It's grassroots still."

I shook my head. "With all due respect, the time for grassroots and no help was a year—maybe two—ago. The election is less than six months away. We need a staff."

"Are you planning to pay them?" I didn't respond. "That's why we don't have a staff. I don't even know how he's planning to pay you."

"The *Washington Post* said—"

"Who do you think told the *Post* that we had donors?" Stuart asked impatiently. "It's the only reason they wrote about him at all."

I took this in, the wheels spinning in my head. Cheap labor wouldn't be an issue. But I wasn't going to make the calls I had to make for that in front of Stuart. He would shoot down my plan. So instead I asked if he would like me to pick up lunch.

Orders in hand, I walked down the street toward Hofberg's Deli. But I stopped at the pay phone a block away from the restaurant and fished a dime from my purse. I told the operator whom I wanted and waited.

"Hello?" a woman's voice asked.

"Louise? This is Beverly Diamond—Mildred Gelman's daughter."

"Hi, Beverly. How's Millie doing?"

"Same as she ever was. Just at my house these days."

"Why at your house?"

"Long story—listen, Louise, I have a favor to ask you."

Louise listened and agreed to help. I thanked her, hung up, and then hummed under my breath as I went to get the sandwiches. At this rate, I would have the manager job in under a week.

15

I arrived the next morning at 8:45 and found four college students waiting for me outside the building. I embraced the tallest. "How are you, Paul?"

He returned the hug a little too strongly. He'd always had a crush on me. "I'm well. I'm sorry to hear about Larry."

"Are you?" I asked, the corners of my mouth twitching up.

"Not in the least," he admitted.

I shook my head. "How did I know that would guarantee you'd be here?"

"Actually, I'm thrilled for the opportunity."

I smiled for real. "Introduce me to your friends. Then we'll get to work."

The other two boys were George and Charlie, and the young woman was Claire. "Wonderful," I said. "Now a word of warning—two actually. First, they're a mess in there. But don't let on that you know that. We're here to fix it. And two, don't you mind anything that Stuart says."

"Who's Stuart?" Charlie asked.

"Mr. Landau's campaign manager—for now anyway." I winked at him, and he grinned. Paul hit him in the chest with the back of his hand, and I laughed. "Come on. We have a campaign to win."

I led the way and opened the door to the office. Stuart didn't look up. "At least you managed to come on time today."

"I did," I said. "And I brought reinforcements." At this, he did look up, suspiciously.

"Are these your kids?"

"Yes," I said. "I had them at seven years old. I've always been precocious."

He glared at me. "Who are they, then?"

"They're our campaign staff. This is Paul, Charlie, George, and Claire."

Stuart stood rapidly behind his desk, came around it, and took me by the arm, pulling me into the far corner of the office. "What do you think you're doing?"

"We need help. You agreed with that yesterday as I recall."

"And as I said yesterday, we don't have money for a full staff."

"We won't *pay* them." I rolled my eyes. I could have sworn I saw steam creeping up toward his ears. "They're interns," I said slowly as if I were spelling it out for a child. "They don't expect to be paid."

"Why would they actually do any work, then?"

"They want experience. And when we win, they'll get a letter of recommendation to the employers of their choice from the senator."

He digested this information, and I could see him wavering. "They're not even old enough to vote, are they?"

I shook my head. "They are not. I used to babysit Paul over there."

"I don't have time to babysit kids. What do you plan to have them do?"

I called over to them. "Paul, darling, what's your major?"

"Government and politics," he said.

"Great. You're going to be in charge of going door-to-door and talking about the issues."

"What *are* the issues?"

That was a great question. "We're still working that out," I said, waving a hand in the air. "Charlie, what about you?"

"Journalism."

"Fabulous. You're our press secretary. You'll be in charge of press releases and the media. George?"

"Finance."

"Even better," I said. "We need money. And a lot of it. Quickly. Let's work on a plan to round up donors. Claire?"

"Secretarial school."

I beamed at her. "Excellent."

"What do we need you for, then?" Stuart asked. "If we have a secretary who's willing to work for free."

I ignored him and quickly assigned each intern to a desk. "We'll need additional phone lines installed as soon as possible. Claire, could you—"

"I'll call the phone company right away, Mrs. Diamond," she said.

"Lovely. George—"

"Can you work up a list of Mr. Landau's stances, so I know how I'm pitching him?"

I looked at Stuart. "Do we have that already done?"

"They were over here," Stuart said, gesturing toward a desk I had cleared the previous day.

"Then they're in that file cabinet," I said. "Don't get too attached to them yet though. I'll need to review his platform eventually. Charlie and Paul—"

"We'll get to work with George and that list."

The door opened, and everyone's head swiveled to see Michael walk in. He took in the scene. "Uh—good morning."

"Good morning," I said cheerfully. "Meet your new campaign staff." I gave introductions.

He shook each of their hands, as befitting a politician, before retreating to his office. "Beverly?" he asked before closing the door. "A word?"

I pulled my notepad from my purse and followed him to the small room that housed his desk. "I have some questions," I said, sitting across from his desk.

He looked at me as if I were an alien for a moment. "So do I, actually."

"Oh, after you, of course."

His hands were the only tell that I was flustering him. He didn't quite seem to know where to put them. "Who are those people?"

"Oh dear. If you're planning to be a politician, you'll really need to be able to remember names."

"I remember their names just fine. But who *are* they?"

"My mother is friends with Paul's mother, and I used to babysit him. I asked her to round up some interns for us."

"Interns?"

I nodded.

"So we're not paying them?"

"Not a cent."

He processed this. "Well done, I suppose. As long as they're reliable."

"They'll be reliable. They're hungry for this experience." I hoped that was true. But I was confident Paul would keep them in line, if for no other reason than to impress me.

"And I suppose that answers part of my next question. You told Stuart we needed the bigger venue and to find the bodies to fill it. Can you do that the way you just filled the office?"

"Yes. But this speech tomorrow night—who's it for?"

He looked at me quizzically. "Everyone. Everyone of voting age, that is."

I shook my head. "No, who specifically are you targeting tomorrow?"

"I don't know what you're asking."

"Well, you wouldn't give the same speech at a women's luncheon as you would at a men's club." He dropped his gaze. "Wait. You don't mean to tell me you're giving the same speech all over town? What if someone sees you speak twice?"

"It's not exactly the same," he said meekly.

"Oh dear," I said again, fighting the urge to use a much stronger expression. "We have our work cut out for us, don't we?"

"Stuart says it's best to stick to strong talking points."

"With all due respect, Stuart hasn't participated in a big campaign before. I have."

His eyes met mine. "I'm listening."

I exhaled heavily. "Okay. Where's the event?" He named a recreation center, and I nodded. "I'll need a copy of the speech."

"Why?" he asked, suddenly guarded.

"To figure out who should be there," I said patiently, like I was explaining to Robbie for the nine hundredth time that there were no monsters under his bed. *And to punch it up,* I thought. Better not to tell him I would be making changes though.

He reached into his desk drawer and pulled out a manila envelope. "I'll need this back."

"Of course."

He handed it to me hesitantly, and I replied with a winning smile. The tension in his shoulders loosened. We would have to work on his politician's demeanor too. He was too prickly and quick to jump to conclusions.

But that was all a job for once he trusted me.

16

The speech wasn't *bad*. But it also wasn't anything groundbreaking.

Not that people went for groundbreaking. People liked reliable. Handsome, charming, and reliable.

He had a stronger focus on equal rights than anything Sam was saying, and that was something to build on. Beyond that, the words were different, but the gist was the same. The Soviets were the biggest threat to America, and we had to work to neutralize that without sacrificing quality of life at home, blah blah blah.

I grabbed a pencil and camped out at Claire's desk—the interns were being lectured by Stuart.

No big changes yet. But I added in two jokes at his own expense and one at Sam's. It was always better to let people laugh with you first. Otherwise, making fun of a veteran came across as mean. But if they saw that you could poke fun at yourself, they would enjoy a joke about someone else too.

"Claire?" I called, interrupting Stuart in the middle of some arm waving. With his grumpy face, he looked like a gorilla when he gestured too furiously, and I suppressed a smile. "I need you to type something for me."

"Coming, Mrs. Diamond."

"You work for me," Stuart said.

Claire looked to me, unsure of what to do.

"Are you paying her, Stuart?" He glared at me. "I didn't think so. Claire, darling, I need your help."

She came over, and I stood, allowing her to sit at the typewriter. "Can you retype this for me with the added sections? Exactly as it is. I want it to look like the same document."

"Of course, Mrs. Diamond."

"Thank you," I said. Then I strode over to Stuart's little huddle. "I'm afraid I need to borrow the rest of them as well."

"What did you even bring them on board for if you're not going to let me explain how we do things here?"

I tilted my head. "How you did things wasn't getting anywhere. Don't worry. I'll let you finish your lecture soon. Now, boys, a word outside, please?"

Paul leapt up to open the door for me. "Always a gentleman," I said, reaching up to pat his cheek as I passed him. "But I was your babysitter, and it's never happening."

The other two boys laughed. "Can't blame a fella for trying," Paul said good-naturedly.

Safely on the street, George lit up a cigarette, and the other two quickly asked to bum others. George offered me one as well, but I declined. Just because I was living with my mother didn't mean I needed to get back to my teenage bad habits when I wasn't with her.

"Have you got friends?" I asked.

They looked at me in confusion.

"Listen," I said. "Mr. Landau has a speech tomorrow night, and we need to fill that hall."

"How big is it?"

"About two hundred fifty people," I said. I only knew from listening to Larry talk about Sam's venues. That would have been a small one for him these days. Insurmountably huge to Michael. "And we need it standing room only."

"I can get my fraternity to come out," Charlie said. "But most of us aren't twenty-one yet."

"That doesn't matter," I said, waving a hand grandly. And it didn't. This was a test run. "But try to get them to bring their older brothers too. And parents. Grandparents. Neighbors. I want three hundred people there."

"But the hall holds two fifty?"

I grinned. "Imagine the picture of a packed room and people in the doorway trying to see. No one needs to read the article attached to that to know he's someone to watch."

"I feel like we should be taking notes," George said.

"Maybe you should." I smiled at them. "Finish your cigarettes and go make some calls—from the pay phone down the street. I don't want Stuart knowing what we're up to yet."

"He told us to tell him everything you said and did."

"Well, we obviously won't be doing that." I laughed merrily, and they joined in.

~

When Claire finished typing the revised speech, I read through it once, then slipped it back into the manila envelope. If he read it before the event, I would have some explaining to do. But I had a feeling, if he was giving the same speech all over the state, I didn't have to worry about that.

And at five, when I strode out of the office to catch the bus home, I smiled. It was the first honest day's work I had done outside of the home in my life.

And even better, Larry was going to be furious when he eventually found out.

17

The following day was spent preparing the recreation center for Michael's speech. We hung flag bunting, which I borrowed from our country club's Fourth of July decorations, set out the folding chairs, and placed a mimeographed fact sheet on each chair.

Three hours before the event, I looked around. Everything was ready. I straightened one of the fact sheets, stopping to study the slightly purple photograph. We would need to start getting things professionally printed. But that was a concern for later, when we found the money for it. Michael would need a new set of headshots too, I thought, looking at the smudgy ink. He wasn't smiling and looked too stoic.

Then I went home for an hour to kiss the children, eat a quick meal, and change my clothes before the main event.

"You're never home," my mother said by way of greeting.

"I just started work. We'll get the interns trained up, and it won't be so bad."

"At least when I was married to your father, I had help around the house."

I finished chewing the roll I had shoved into my mouth. "Feel free to hire help—you've got the money to pay for it."

"Honestly, Beverly—"

"Mama, I'm happy to discuss this with you later. But for now, know that I appreciate you." It was true. But I also didn't need her picking up and leaving like she had done with Papa. Not that she had anyone else to go to—my brother lived in New York, and after thirty years in DC, I didn't see her making that move easily.

Besides, she referred to her daughter-in-law as "that woman." She'd happily eat glass before moving in with them.

She muttered something under her breath but allowed me to kiss her on the cheek before I went into the living room to sneak a quick cuddle from the kids, both of whom protested that they were watching television.

"Did you even notice I was gone today?" I asked them. Neither replied. Apparently fighting off snuggles was the only reply I would get while the television was on.

"Don't let them watch TV all night," I called to my mother.

"You have too many rules," Mama said. "Children don't have to follow them at their grandmother's house."

"This isn't your house."

"It is now."

"If that were the case, I wouldn't have to go back to work tonight, would I?" I asked.

"I think you should talk to an actual lawyer—Larry is required to support you."

She had a point. But there was also the matter of the charge card that I was legally entitled to use for "necessities," and I wasn't sure new wallpaper counted. And I also didn't know if he was required to support me in the same house that I had been living in. "I'll find a lawyer," I said.

"How late will you be?"

We had to be out of the recreation center by nine. "Ten at the latest."

"Maybe you should have stayed at the lipstick counter and worked normal hours."

I looked at my mother pointedly. "*Someone* made a scene about that as I recall." I checked the clock on the wall. I really needed a new watch. "I've got to go. Thank you, Mama."

She continued to grumble as I grabbed my handbag. "Take the car," she said finally, speaking clearly enough for me to understand her. "I don't want you riding the bus at night."

"What would I do without you?" I asked.

She gestured to me with her cigarette. "Just you remember that."

I blew her a kiss and left.

18

By the time we opened the doors at seven, there was a line.

"Who are all these people?" Stuart asked me.

"Ask me no questions, and I'll tell you no lies. You can't expect me to give up all my secrets so you can use them against me."

He continued studying the crowd with a sour face. "Half of them aren't old enough to vote yet, and half are likely to drop dead before the election."

He wasn't wrong. It was a mix of elderly folks and college kids, some of the former being held up by the latter. When I told the interns to get their grandparents out, they listened.

"So let's fix that."

"Fix what?"

"The 'not old enough to vote.' Add that into the next round of Michael's speech. Let's get eighteen-year-olds the right to vote."

"Why would we let kids vote?"

"Because they're not kids. They're old enough to drink and go to war. And if Michael shows them that he cares about them as human beings who deserve equality, they're going to work their fingers to the bone to get him elected." I turned to look at Stuart, who was staring at me. "What?" I touched my face, making sure my lipstick hadn't smudged.

"It's not a terrible idea," he admitted begrudgingly.

"Well, of course it isn't. It's mine." Sam had twenty years on Michael, who wasn't yet old enough to be president. And that age gap was the best thing Michael had going for him, according to my father. It had worked in Kennedy's favor, and the nation was enjoying our young, handsome president. But young people didn't just want to *look* *at* a young president. They felt like he was theirs. And they would be excited to vote. Not that it helped us *now*, but that word-of-mouth endorsement from the younger crowd was worth almost as much as a newspaper one.

"Don't get all cocky on me," he said. "One good idea doesn't exactly threaten my job."

"By my count, we're up to four."

"Four?"

"Keeping the larger venue and filling it," I said, ticking off the first item with a raised finger. "Hiring interns. Courting younger people. And—" I stopped myself.

"And?" he asked suspiciously.

Best not to tell him about the edits I had made to the speech yet.

"And borrowing decorations for the hall," I finished, glaring at him defiantly. He wasn't fooled and started to say something, but I took his arm and looked at his watch. "Shouldn't you go introduce him? Unless you'd like me to do it."

"Absolutely not," he said, shaking me off. "Why don't you have your own watch?"

"Long story," I said, shooing him toward the podium at the front. "Now get over there and make our man sound good."

He bristled slightly at the "our" part, but I gave him a little push, and he went to the podium, where he tapped on the microphone.

"Ladies and gentlemen," he said, turning on a charm that I hadn't seen any evidence of before. "I want to thank you for coming out tonight to meet Michael Landau. This is a special venue for us—Michael and I grew up just down the street and helped lobby for them to build this recreation center. Which, in fact, was one of the first issues that made him think he should run for office."

I felt my brows coming together and forced my face into a neutral position. *Michael* should be the one saying this. Not Stuart. He couldn't give a static speech everywhere and have Stuart provide all the local color. So far I'd give Stuart my vote—and I couldn't stand the man.

But we would deal with that later. Baby steps and all. For now, I wanted to see if Michael actually delivered my jokes. And if so, how they landed.

Stuart finished his introduction, calling Michael the next senator from the state of Maryland, and walked back to me as Michael entered to moderate applause. Stuart gave him a good start, but he wasn't there yet. Granted, I wasn't sure many people in the room knew why they were there. If the interns had promised entertainment, this likely wasn't what they had in mind.

Stuart smirked at me, and I resisted the urge to give my criticism now, despite how strongly I wanted to wipe that look off his face. "Very nice," I murmured instead, disarming him as Michael addressed the crowd, his prepared remarks in front of him.

"Good evening. My name is Michael Landau, and I am running for the United States Senate representing the great state of Maryland."

Don't repeat your introduction, I said to myself, making a mental note. *We know who you are now.*

Michael continued: "President Kennedy said last year, in his inaugural address, that we should ask what we can do for our country. My friends, what I can do for our country is make sure that Maryland has an effective seat at the table.

"We may be one of the smallest states in the nation, but we were also one of the first. And our voice—*your* voice—deserves to be heard. Marylanders have a lot to say, which can sometimes be drowned out by the bigger states talking louder.

"We sometimes fall through the cracks simply because people don't know how to characterize us. We're south of the Mason-Dixon Line, so we're Southerners. But we didn't secede. Enslavers and abolitionists lived side by side in our state, sometimes pitting brother against brother.

"We are a land of some of the earliest and greatest cities in our nation, from Baltimore to Annapolis, but also of farmers, of fishermen, of crabbers, of politicians, of federal workers, and of descendants of some of the first Americans."

I looked around the room, watching people's faces. They nodded along as they found descriptions of themselves. He was hitting the right notes with that part.

"But, my friends, my neighbors, my Maryland, many of us have been forgotten by the people in power.

"Make no mistake, the threat of Communism looms large, threatening to take this union we have created and break it anew. But that cannot be the only focal point of our government while folks at home go hungry.

"I firmly believe that if we shift our focus to tending our own garden, the fruit that labor bears will pay off in maintaining our democracy, in defeating the Soviet Union, in keeping this great nation living up to its promise.

"With that said, I also believe that the 'what' of what we need to do is more important than the 'who' of who will be doing it. And if Sam Gibson is going to get the 'what' done, then I want you to go ahead and vote for him."

The crowd murmured, and I watched Michael to see if he would be able to sell the next part.

"Sam Gibson loves to talk. And he's good at it. But the record doesn't lie. And Senator Gibson has used those oratory skills to filibuster no fewer than six bills that would have benefited Maryland residents."

There was more murmuring. Either this was news to the crowd, or they didn't know what it meant. Based on some of the faces, it was a mixture. I waved an arm to get his attention and Michael glanced at me, clearly annoyed. *Explain that*, I mouthed, shaping the syllables carefully. He looked at me, processing what I meant, then at the crowd, evaluating before looking back at me with a nod.

"What do you think you're doing?" Stuart hissed in my ear.

"He's losing them," I whispered back. "Tell me people don't look confused."

"What that means," Michael said, veering off his prepared remarks, "is that he's spending hours talking to prevent a vote. And he did that about a measure to compensate farmers, he did it for one of the civil rights acts that he eventually signed, and he did it about a measure expanding access to healthcare, among others."

More murmurs. But now he had them.

"I may be young," he said, then he stopped, reading the unfamiliar line that came next. He shot a somewhat amused glance at Stuart, then continued. "Although I'm old enough that my mother wishes I'd settle down and get married already." He got the desired chuckles, finally smiling himself. "But I remember what segregation looked like. And I know I don't want to support someone who hesitates when it's time to sign bills that ensure equality."

By the time he told the next joke poking fun at himself, he got real laughter. And when he read the line about Sam acting like Mr. Toad in *The Wind in the Willows*, he had to pause for a good two minutes for the crowd to contain themselves.

Stuart was fuming.

The speech ended, and Michael shook hands, his politician face plastered on. A good two-thirds of the crowd stayed to meet him.

Finally, the hall cleared. We were fifteen minutes past the nine o'clock end time, but the county worker who ran the center was still in conversation with Michael when I instructed the interns to begin packing up the decorations to return to the club.

"I need to be back by ten," I told Paul. "You may need to be in charge of finishing this."

"Turning back into a pumpkin?" Stuart sneered.

"Don't be daft. I'm Cinderella, not the coach."

Michael extricated himself from his conversation and came over. "Are you leaving?" he asked. "I thought we could all go for a drink to celebrate how well that went."

"The fairy princess over here has a curfew," Stuart said curtly.

"First of all, Cinderella has a fairy godmother, she's not a fairy herself. Second, I don't have a *curfew*. I have a mother who is watching my children for me."

"How many kids do you have?"

"Oh for the love of—it doesn't matter how many brats she has. It matters that she changed your speech without telling us."

Michael held his hand up at his waist in his small "wait" gesture as Stuart seethed. "He's not wrong," Michael said, choosing his words carefully, eyes still on me. "In the future, let me know so I don't stumble on any new parts."

"In the future?" Stuart asked. "Are you serious?"

Michael turned to his friend. "How many people did we have here tonight?"

"The hall holds two fifty," he muttered. "But a lot of them were too young to vote."

"And people were standing in the back. So it was more than two hundred and fifty." He glanced back at me before continuing. "And the jokes hit the right mark. They built up. And by the time they got to the Sam one—they won't be able to look at him without seeing Mr. Toad now."

"To be fair, that was my son's joke," I said. "Credit where credit is due."

"Michael. She's got her kid writing your speech. Come on."

"Oh, he can't write more than his name. He's only five." They both stared at me. "A very precocious five."

"Beverly?" Paul called. "Where do you want the bunting?"

"In the car," I said, rummaging through my bag for the keys. "Here. I'll drop it off before work tomorrow."

"We'll see about that," Stuart said.

But Michael turned on him. "We said we'd give her a chance," he said. "So far, she's delivered what she promised." He looked back at me. "Thank you, Beverly. I'll see you tomorrow."

I resisted the ever-so-mature desire to stick my tongue out at Stuart. "See you tomorrow."

I didn't need my mother's car. I could have flown home. But it wasn't time to get cocky. We still had a lot of work to do if Michael was going to steal Sam's Senate seat.

19

Michael and Stuart were both looking at me like I had forgotten to take the rollers out of my hair.

I was in Michael's office the following morning, explaining what we needed to do next, and it wasn't going well.

"Start at the beginning," Michael said. "Again."

"This is nonsense," Stuart protested.

I turned to him. "We gained, if we're lucky, a hundred and fifty votes last night. Against Sam's what? A hundred thousand?"

"Women don't vote," he said again.

"They *will*," I countered. "Especially if we give them a reason to."

Michael sighed. "I'm with Stuart here. Historically women will come to a speech, but they'll stay home in November. Or vote the way their husbands do."

I pointed a finger at him. "That. That right there is the problem. And how I know neither of you is married."

"You want me to get married?"

"No! Actually—" I thought for a moment. "No, better if you're single. Once we get you a haircut and some new clothes, single is better."

"What's wrong with my hair and clothes?" Michael smoothed his hair and adjusted his tie.

"You can't go speak at a women's luncheon looking like that. You have to be dapper."

"I'm dapper," he said, insulted. "Besides, what I look like doesn't matter."

"Then why isn't Richard Nixon president now?" I had a point there, and they both knew it. Nixon still would have had a leg up in the radio era, but once televisions brought him into everyone's living room, he was sunk unless his opposition looked like a drowned rat. And Kennedy was no drowned rat.

"Women's luncheons are a waste of time," Stuart said. He turned back to Michael, the tension evident in every sinew of his body. "I'm telling you, she's here to sabotage." He returned a cool gaze to me. "If it's such a good idea, why didn't you tell your husband to get Sam to talk to women?"

"It wasn't my place. And he wouldn't have listened. Besides, my father agreed with me that this was your best shot at winning."

Neither man responded immediately, but they shared a long look.

"I'm listening," Michael said finally, steepling his fingers.

"Look, Maryland women haven't voted historically because we were one of the last states to ratify the Nineteenth Amendment. It happened in our lifetimes." I gestured to the three of us. I was six when the ratification came down, and I still remembered my father swinging me onto his shoulders and asking whom I was going to vote for when I turned twenty-one. My answer had been "Papa," of course. Back then, I still thought he would be president someday, even though my father repeatedly reminded me that the country wasn't voting to put a Jew in the White House anytime soon. "But women are finally starting to vote. I know so many people who were proud to cast their first vote for Kennedy. But Kennedy isn't running in November. So we need to give them a *reason* to go back to the polls."

"So you just want me to go in and be good-looking, and you think that's going to do it?"

"Not with that attitude, no. If you treat women like they're incapable of thinking for themselves and like they'll vote for anyone with a decent haircut, then no, they're going to go vote for Sam or stay home."

"Why do you keep harping on my haircut?" Michael ran a hand over his head again.

"Because it looks like Stuart did it over the kitchen sink with a pair of garden shears, but that's beside the point. Pay attention." Stuart looked away, and I stifled a laugh. "Oh. I didn't realize Stuart actually cut your hair. No, we need to pay a professional. But that's a problem for tomorrow. Today, I want you to realize that women don't want to just do what their husbands tell them to."

"Then what do women want?"

I thought of my mother, moving out under the pretense of helping me. Would she have left my father if my life hadn't imploded, providing the perfect opportunity? And of Nancy, who had to hide her handiness from her husband, lying to protect his fragile ego and pocket the money a repairman would get. Of Fran, who was now struggling to get by on her own. And of myself. My situation could turn on a dime once we went to court and I knew it.

"Freedom. Self-sufficiency. Respect for who we are, not who other people want us to be. The same life, liberty, and pursuit of happiness that this country promises men."

Michael shook his head. "How am I supposed to deliver that?"

"You can't. But you can show them that you hear them. That you want them to have what they want. And that you'll work to help them get it. That will be enough."

He and Stuart exchanged another long glance.

"I still think it's a waste of time," Stuart said.

"Because I suggested it or because you can't get it through your thick skull that women have their own brains and opinions?"

He stood up, angry, and had I been a man, I think he would have told me to step outside.

"One luncheon," I said, turning back to Michael. "Let me help you write your speech for one lunch. And if you're not convinced after that, I'll drop it. What have you got to lose?"

"Our dignity? Sam is going to be laughing all the way to the polls," Stuart said.

"And if I'm right, he'll be skulking the whole way home. Michael, one lunch."

There was another long pause as we both watched to see which way this would go. If he sided with Stuart, I was done here. He would lose. And if he lost, so did I.

I didn't care about the house. Not really. But I wanted to win against Larry. I wanted to show that I could go up against him, brain against brain, and come away the victor. He, like Stuart, was so convinced that women were the weaker sex and that I was lost without him. And as I sat there for that interminable moment while Michael Landau determined my future, I realized what it was that *I* wanted.

"Set it up," he said finally. "I want to represent the people of Maryland, and that includes women."

20

Of course, once I convinced Michael, I had to actually deliver on a venue and a group of women. A country club was an ideal starting point. These were the women who had time to go to lunch. We would go after the women who didn't later, once we had already established ourselves as the frontrunner among women.

But which club?

Woodmont was firmly out. Larry didn't know what I was up to yet, and that was the fastest way to get that information to him. Someone would slip out and call her husband, who would tell Larry before Michael even reached the podium to speak.

And after my experience at Emory Estates, I wasn't sure a non-Jewish club would host Michael. They likely would—they brought in entertainers frequently of religions and races whom they would never allow to actually set foot on club grounds otherwise. But it was safer to start on something more akin to home turf.

That left Norbeck and Indian Spring. Norbeck was further out in the suburbs and therefore probably a better choice if I didn't want Larry knowing, though Indian Spring was on Michael's home turf. I mulled that over at my desk as the interns buzzed about. My mother would be a good person to ask—she knew everyone at all the clubs. Fran would be a good resource too. She certainly had the inside track on the country club scene.

I picked up the receiver of the newly installed phone at my desk to call my mother. Claire was doing good work because she got the phone company out already. But a familiar raised voice at the front of the office caused the receiver to slip from my hand.

While I had debated the best place to host an event to avoid Larry, the devil himself walked into the office and was currently gesticulating wildly while shouting at Stuart, who stood with his arms crossed, the first look of amusement I had yet seen on his face.

I stood up, and the movement caught Larry's eye. He stopped yelling long enough to scowl at me. "I'm taking *my wife* home," he said and went to move toward me, but Stuart blocked the path. "Move, Friedman."

"She's not going to be your wife much longer from what I hear," Stuart said coolly, not budging an inch. "And I'm not letting you drag anyone out of here like you're some caveman."

I was almost too shocked at the show of support from Stuart to notice that an angry red hue had begun creeping up Larry's neck. I had only seen him mad enough to change color once before and that was when someone had hurled an anti-Semitic slur at me in front of the kids. "She's my wife," he growled. "And she's not working for you another minute. If you have any sense of dignity, you'll fire her."

"With all due respect," a voice said from behind me, "she works for me. And no one is getting fired today." Michael put a hand on my arm. "Would you like to go sit in my office while we handle this?"

I shook my head. "No. I'll talk to him outside."

"I'm going with you."

I looked up at Michael. "He's harmless," I said quietly. "I won't be long." I turned back to Larry. "If you're done with this little temper tantrum, I'll talk to you outside." And I strode past him, to the door, which Paul opened for me, allowing it to shut in Larry's face before he reached it.

I heard the door open and then slam shut behind me, but I kept walking until I reached the street.

"You've made your scene, now what do you actually want?" I asked, spinning around to face Larry.

"Bev, I know you're mad, but this is too far. People are laughing at both of us."

"What people?"

"Everyone!" He gestured widely to the sidewalk, where a woman walked around us, pointedly ignoring our argument.

"Bizarrely, I haven't heard a single laugh—actually, that's not true. Michael had the crowd laughing at his event last night after I tweaked his speech." My hands were on my hips as I stared him down. "So you must mean the people in *your* office are laughing. I can't do much about that."

He opened his mouth to lob a return volley, but instead his shoulders sank. "How much do I need to grovel?" he asked, softer now. "I want to come home. I miss you. I miss us."

"You haven't groveled at all. You blamed me for your affair and only seemed sorry about being caught, not about cheating."

He set his jaw, and I watched the struggle to stay cool play out across his face. "I'm sorry," he said, sounding anything but. "I am."

"That's not enough."

"Dammit, Beverly, I'm trying here. I'm sorry I'm not perfect."

I studied him, trying to remember why I had ever thought this pathetic little man was anything special. "I don't want perfection," I said slowly. "I want honesty. I want respect. I want to feel valued. And you can't give me those things."

"I always valued you."

I shook my head. "You valued having dinner on the table and a pretty wife on your arm. Not *me*."

The look he gave me wasn't that of a man who wanted to fight for the love of his life. A stranger stared at me from behind familiar eyes. "And the kids? You're okay with them growing up in a broken home?"

"You broke our home. Not me."

"I apologized!"

"Are you Robbie's age? You think an apology can fix whatever you did?"

"At least I'm willing to try!" The red splotches were back on his neck, but he lowered his voice. "I love you. I want to make this work." The words were right, but his eyes were still hard as nails.

Don't say it, I told myself as a retort bubbled up into my mind. But it rose in my throat and came tumbling out of my mouth anyway. "Do you actually want me back? Or do you just not want me working for Michael because you know I can win this?"

He laughed heartily. "You? You think you have a shot at winning?"

"I know I do."

He continued to laugh. "Oh, Bev. No. You're going to get crushed. And I don't want to deal with the humiliation of people knowing my wife was the one who screwed up a campaign that badly."

"I think we're done here," I said, moving around him toward the building's door.

"We aren't close to done," Larry said darkly.

I spun to face him again. "Take it up with my attorney. You'll be hearing from him soon."

"You're going to regret this," he said.

"No," I said, smiling humorlessly. "That's you you're thinking of."

I opened the door and walked in, colliding immediately with Paul, who bumped into Charlie, who hit Stuart, who knocked Michael to the ground, the other three men on top of him as they fell like dominos. "Really?" I asked as they tried to extricate themselves from the besuited dogpile.

"We wanted to make sure you were okay," Paul mumbled, shamefacedly.

"Instead you look like something out of the Three Stooges," I said, looking pointedly at Michael, who had the good grace to look embarrassed.

But he dusted off his pants and asked me to see him in his office. My stomach dropped. He had said no one was getting fired, but Larry knew what he was doing making a scene. He couldn't keep me on when that could happen at any moment. My shoulders wanted to sink in defeat, but I wouldn't let them. I could argue my way out of this yet.

Stuart followed us into Michael's office and shut the door behind him.

"Look, I can't promise he won't do that again, but at least you know I'm not spying for him now."

"I shouldn't have said that," Stuart said quietly.

I looked at him, trying to figure out what had just happened. "Yes, you should have. I would have thought the same thing if I didn't know me from Adam."

"Do you have a lawyer yet?" Michael asked gently.

I shook my head, thoroughly confused.

"I'm thinking Greg Patterson," Michael said to Stuart. "What do you think?"

"Him or William Davis."

Michael nodded. "Greg owes me a favor, so let's start with him." He flipped through the Rolodex on his desk, pulled out a card, and copied the number onto a sheet of paper. "I'll give him a call first as a heads-up. But then he's likely your man."

I looked down at the paper that was suddenly clutched in my hand, not knowing what to say.

"He's a shark. You won't have to worry about money or the house—unless you remarry."

"Hah. The last thing I want right now is another husband." *Money though*. I wouldn't have to worry *after* this lawyer did his job. But I would have to pay him a retainer. I'd have to ask my father for help. Which he would give, but how humiliating. "Is this lawyer expensive?"

Michael and Stuart exchanged a glance. "Don't worry about the money."

"But you don't have any," I blurted out, clapping a hand over my mouth as I realized I had said it aloud.

Michael suppressed a smile. "Like I said, he owes me a favor. And I'm a lawyer—my campaign just isn't funded yet."

"Sorry. I . . . Why are you doing this?"

"Purely selfish motivation," Michael said, leaning back in his chair. "How else am I going to keep my junior campaign manager from being harassed at work?"

If I was a crier, the tears would be flowing. But that wasn't me. "Thank you," I said. "I won't let you down."

"Just work on finding that luncheon venue."

I tilted my head. "Oh, that's easy now that Larry knows. We'll hold it at Woodmont. I'll call them right after I call the lawyer."

"Set it up," Michael said, standing as I did.

Stuart even nodded at me as he held the door. "Thank you," I said. "Not for the door—for earlier."

"Also selfish," Stuart said, with a gruffness that I now recognized as bravado. "I've always hated that guy."

I grinned at him, and I thought I saw the hint of a grim smile as he closed the door behind me.

"Junior campaign manager? Are you kidding me?" I heard Stuart say through the closed door.

Clearly it had been a trick of the light, and he was just happy Larry had gotten his behind handed to him by a woman.

But I was a step closer to winning now.

21

The next morning found me dressed in a Chanel suit I borrowed from my mother and seated in a plush chair across from a huge mahogany desk, while an attractive man in an equally expensive suit asked me questions about my marriage to Larry, his secretary taking notes in the corner.

I had thought the Chanel was overkill—wouldn't it be better to look like Larry was keeping me in poverty?

But my mother insisted I needed to walk in there looking like the lifestyle I expected Larry to maintain in divorce, even if he had never quite gotten to this level in marriage. And who was I to turn down Chanel? Though it came with a warning that I had better not even think about denting the matching hat. Better I go in sackcloth and ashes than follow that trend.

I held myself steady when Greg—he insisted I use his first name—asked about Larry's infidelity, not allowing a stray flinch to betray how I felt about discussing this with a perfect (and ridiculously handsome) stranger.

"Do you think this secretary would be willing to testify?"

"Linda? Why?"

Greg was all sympathy as he explained. "The court will need evidence of infidelity."

"I'm the evidence. I caught them."

He shook his head. "It has to come from a source that isn't involved in the divorce."

"Well, Linda's involved in the divorce. If he hadn't been cheating on me with her, we would still be married."

"It can't come from the husband or wife," he said gently. "So we either need her to testify or other evidence that he was illicitly engaged outside of the marriage."

There was no way Linda was going to testify for me. And Larry didn't want to let me out—even if she thought that would set him free, he would be done with her after that. If he wasn't already.

Not shacking up with her certainly didn't bode well for them having a future.

And if I was being completely honest, I wanted nothing to do with her. There had to be another option.

"What else would work as evidence? She's not testifying."

Greg leaned back in his seat and ticked the examples off on his fingers as he gave them. "A private investigator, if you think the affair is still going on. Someone else who saw them in flagrante. Love letters. Things like that."

"And if I can't prove it?"

"A no-fault divorce can be granted after eighteen months of living apart."

"Eighteen months!"

He nodded. "It leaves room for reconciliation."

"There isn't going to be a reconciliation here."

"Not now, no. But a lot can change in a year and a half."

I rubbed at my temple with the base of my palm. "So how does one hire a private investigator?"

Greg grinned. "Michael said you were a fighter." Then his smile faded somewhat. "There is something else I think you should know—your husband called me this morning."

I jumped out of my seat, ready to leave. What kind of setup was this?

But Greg held out his hands, palms facing me, and I didn't move. "Once you called me, I wasn't taking him on. But I was curious so I called a couple of colleagues, and he's retaining people left and right so you can't hire anyone good."

"Can he do that?"

Greg smiled wryly. "Let's just say it's a good thing you got to me first. I don't know who he's going to choose to go with, but there's no one I'm afraid of in this town." I sat back down as he asked me to go over marital assets.

"Legally," he said, "his threat about the house was empty. If he's running around throwing money at multiple lawyers, it won't be hard to prove he can afford for you to stay where you are. And no judge is going to want to uproot the kids."

I finally leaned back in the chair, relieved, albeit furious that Larry could just scare me like that because I didn't know better. "So I don't *need* a job?"

"You absolutely do not need a job. He is legally required to support you in the manner you were accustomed to in your marriage. But you can't abuse that—no big shopping sprees."

This time I flinched.

"How much are we talking?" he asked, not even batting an eye.

"Not *that* much in the grand scheme of things. I didn't buy a car or anything. But I—well—I was mad. So I kind of . . . redecorated the whole house."

"A car would have been easier to spin. You could argue you needed that for the kids. If anyone asks from now on, you weren't mad. You had been planning to overhaul the house for years and now that you're working, you thought you could afford to."

"So I *do* need a job."

"No, you can say you thought that was how you would have to pay for things because you didn't know how a divorce would work."

"Isn't that lying?" I looked at him curiously. Who had Michael sent me to?

"Much less so than committing adultery, so let's call it stretching the truth. Besides, you didn't know that he couldn't sell the house out from under you."

"I can live with that." I thought for a moment. "Assuming we can get evidence, how long will the whole thing take?"

"Usually about six months."

I did the math in my head. December felt awfully far off. And ideally, I didn't still want to be married when the election happened. If we won, I didn't care that much. If we lost . . . Well, we just couldn't lose. "Is there any way to speed that up?"

Greg smiled, a dimple forming in his right cheek. I glanced down almost involuntarily at his left hand. How on earth this man wasn't married, I couldn't have explained—unless dissolving marriages for a living had made him cynical. "I'll talk to Michael. If he's willing to call in one favor for you, he might call in another with a judge. No more spending sprees for now though. Necessities only."

There went that watch I needed. "Unless it's money I earn myself?"

His smile turned into a mild grimace. "For our purposes, it's likely better if you're not working. You're a more sympathetic case if you need Larry supporting you."

My mother would be happier. She could go back to her lunches and bridge games and hair and nail appointments without having to move back home. But something inside me wilted at that idea. It had only been a week, but I was enjoying my work on Michael's campaign. I was useful. And while I had to fight with Stuart, Michael was starting to listen to me.

And more than anything, I wanted to prove Larry wrong: I may not have finished college, but that didn't make me less smart or capable than him.

I knew I shouldn't want revenge, but I did.

The words popped out of my mouth on their own accord. "I want to keep working."

Greg studied me. "I think Michael will be happy with that decision. And we'll make it work." Then the friendly advisor was gone, and he dismissed his secretary, waiting until she was out of the room to speak again. "But no funny business or this is going to go south quickly."

"Funny business?"

"Office affairs."

"Excuse me?"

"I get it. I've been lonely too. And it's easy when someone else is there all the time. But that's going to derail our case, and I can promise that with us hiring a PI, your husband is also going to be looking for any missteps on your part."

"Ha," I said drily, trying to picture a scenario on earth where that was a concern. "I can assure you that not only do I have no interest in any 'funny business' with *anyone* for a very long time, but I am *far* more professional than my husband is in that regard."

"Good," Greg said, holding out his hand. "Had to get that part out of the way. I look forward to working with you, Mrs. Diamond."

"Beverly," I said, taking his hand and shaking it firmly. "Just Beverly."

The smile returned. "Talk to Michael about judges. I'll have my PI call you early next week."

As I left the office, I pressed a palm to the top of my mother's hat in a small act of rebellion. No one was going to tell me what I could or couldn't do anymore.

Of course, I removed the dent by pressing on the underside of the hat before I returned it that afternoon. If I wanted to beat Larry, I *did* still need her watching Robbie and Debbie instead of abandoning me over a dented hat.

22

I set the women's luncheon for two weeks later. Stuart wanted to go in guns blazing and hold it immediately to prove me wrong, but I needed time both to gather women who would be amenable to listening to him (and moreover to voting) and to help him write a speech that would actually send them to the polls in a few months.

For the former, I recruited my mother, who proudly marched to the polls in November of 1942 to cast her first vote for my father and continued to do so every two years until he retired. She had voted for Sam six years earlier, but I doubted she would again at this rate.

She listened more or less attentively, puffing away on her cigarette as I explained my plan.

"What's in it for the women?" she asked eventually. "Your father was an easy choice—I had to live with him, and I'd have never heard the end of it if he lost by one vote. Women who aren't married to a politician need a reason to vote."

That was the issue, wasn't it? Michael wouldn't promise the moon if he knew he couldn't deliver it—though Kennedy *was* promising the literal moon.

I had voted for Sam entirely because Larry believed in him. But that was akin to my mother's reasoning, not a real reason to vote.

"We need to explain to women how politics affect them," I said, thinking aloud. I reached instinctively for my mother's cigarette and took a pull before handing it back to her. "Sam wants the status quo. He doesn't want things to change."

"And your man does?"

I nodded slowly. "I think so. He wouldn't have given me a chance as anything but a secretary if he didn't. And that's most of the work women can do these days. Teacher, secretary, or wife."

"And what about the men who won't want women taking their jobs? You were a kid when the war ended, but—"

"I remember Papa talking about it," I said, mentally transported back to my parents' dining room table as my father explained how women had stepped up, becoming Rosie the Riveter, until the men returned and wanted their jobs back. "Not every woman wants to work outside the home though," I said, reaching for her cigarette again. I thought about Nancy, who could outearn Arnie if given half a chance. And about Larry's derisive laughter over the idea that I could run a winning campaign.

"You're talking about opportunity, not necessity," she said, plucking the cigarette from my fingers. "Either light your own or stop smoking mine since you're so sanctimonious about me smoking around the kids."

"Opportunity," I repeated, ignoring her jab about the cigarette. "But it's about more than just working. I should be able to have my own charge card. My own accounts. You gave us the money for the down payment on this house—why does it belong to Larry and not me?" I was listed on the deed, but as my lawyer had explained to me, I wasn't legally allowed to buy Larry out, as property couldn't be transferred to me. If I wanted my own house, I would have to sell this one with Larry's consent and buy my own, with my father as a cosigner.

"That benefits single and divorced women more than married women. I'm not sure the club is the right audience."

I shook my head and reached for her cigarette, but she held it out of my reach, and I sighed, pulling a fresh one from the pack on the table, holding it to my lips and lighting it. "They should be. No one's marriage is safe. Look at you."

"I don't need my own charge card. I want your father to see exactly how much I'm spending without him. Besides, most of that money came from me."

"Mama, that's petty. You need to talk to him."

"I talked to him for thirty years, and he never heard me. I'm done talking. All those years of making sure he was taken care of, and even after he retired everything was all about him. He wouldn't have won an election without me—how could he? He didn't even wear matching socks when we met."

"I doubt the men who voted for him were looking at his socks."

"No, but the women sure would have. And you may think women will vote how their husbands do, but I'll tell you this much: behind every good man is an even better woman." She pointed her cigarette at me. "That's how you win this thing. You get the women on board, and they'll pester their husbands with everything wrong with Sam."

I blinked at her. It hadn't occurred to me that women would change their husbands' minds in the election. I had viewed it as a battle of the sexes—but it wasn't. There were a million things that I did to make Larry happy, but when something mattered enough, I didn't rest until he came around to what I wanted. I never actually cared what color our bedroom was or that he wanted meatloaf every week, but when he had decided to name Robbie after his father, I launched a six-month campaign against the name Herbert until even Larry agreed it was a terrible name to bestow on such a defenseless child. If we could hit on what women wanted that Sam wasn't willing to provide . . . it was possible Michael could win in a landslide instead of the squeaked-by victory I had hoped for.

"Mama, you're a genius."

"Of course I am. You think your father became Speaker of the House on his own?"

"You'll put the word out at the club?"

"I suppose. What's a mother for? But you may need to watch your own children long enough for me to make some calls."

I stood and wrapped my arms around her from behind her chair. "Thank you, Mama."

She leaned into my hug for a moment. "Although if you dent my hat again, that'll be the last thing of mine you borrow."

My mouth dropped open.

"A mother always knows."

23

"No," Stuart said emphatically for the fourth time.

"I'm starting to think that's the only word you know," I said. "That or you're actually two years old. You and my daughter would get on famously. You could say no to absolutely everything together, throw a little temper tantrum, take a nap, and then do it all again."

"Now see here—" He had a finger in my face.

"Ooh, we added a *w* to the end of your favorite word."

Stuart's face turned red, and he was starting to sputter when Michael interrupted by clapping his hands together once, loudly. We both stopped and looked at him.

"You're acting like children," he said.

"He started it," I said at the same time that Stuart said that I started it. I crossed my arms and leaned back in my seat. "Fair enough."

"You're not writing the speech," Stuart said.

Michael exhaled audibly, cutting off the retort that was about to spill out of my mouth. "She can't write the whole thing, no, but she should have a say in it. She arranged this lunch and, quite frankly, likely knows a bit more than we do about how to sway women voters."

"She can type it," Stuart said.

I still thought a nap and a snack would benefit him immensely. "Why don't you type it? I told you the day you hired me that my typing is terrible."

"Enough!" Michael snapped, raising his voice for the first time in the three weeks I had been working for him. "Do you want to win this campaign?" he asked Stuart.

"You know I do."

"Do you?" he asked me.

"Why else would I be here?"

"Then figure out how to work together, or we're going to lose and spend six more years with Sam Gibson stonewalling every attempt at change for this country."

Neither Stuart nor I responded.

"Now, are we starting from scratch or using the bones of my regular speech?"

"Scratch," I said as Stuart said, "Bones." We glared at each other briefly. And then I conceded a point. "Let's make a list of the main talking points from your usual speech, and we'll figure out how to tailor them to a feminine audience."

Michael looked to Stuart, who finally nodded. Stuart then produced a copy of the speech, and I took notes on a legal pad as he read out the major points.

"What do we need to add that's new?" Michael asked.

Stuart tapped on the edge of the desk with a pen. "Sam talks about wanting to keep Maryland safe for women and children. Let's add that in and say we're going to do a better job."

I turned to Stuart. "This is why you're single."

"Excuse me?"

"Women don't want to be made into china dolls up on some pedestal. We don't break."

"Fine," he said, throwing up his hands. "Let's say we'll ignore women's safety entirely so they can't walk the streets without a man at night."

I sighed. "We don't want you to say you'll slay all the dragons. We want you to treat us with respect."

"Respect doesn't mean a lot when you're getting mugged."

"Except it does, because people who respect women won't snatch a purse."

Stuart blinked heavily at me. "So how do we promise respect?"

"Listening," I said pointedly.

"I'm listening," Michael said. "But I need actual talking points. Not generalities."

"Let's start at the beginning," I said. "Don't introduce yourself again after Stuart does it."

"I assume you're introducing me at this one."

I tilted my head. That was new. "I'd be happy to."

Stuart stood up and strode to the door. "I've got actual work to do. Let me know when you two are done making doe eyes at each other." He slammed the door behind him.

"I—I wasn't—" Michael stammered. His hands seemed to be in the way as he knocked over a pencil holder.

"He's fun," I said wryly. "Let me guess: He's a great guy, just under a lot of pressure?"

"Something like that," Michael said.

"I'm just going to open the door," I said, standing. Michael rose too. "Sit," I said. "I just don't want the office gossiping that there's anything going on. I'm still married, and your lawyer friend warned me that we need to hire a PI to get some evidence of adultery, and that Larry probably already did the same."

Michael colored slightly. "I didn't think of . . . that. Maybe Stuart and I should just write this."

"Not you too. I promise I'm not interested. Are you?"

"Am I—interested? In you?"

I nodded.

"No," Michael said. "Stuart was just—"

"Being Stuart," I said. "Let's just do our jobs, okay?"

Michael nodded. "Okay. So don't introduce myself?"

"No. Dive right in."

"What else?"

I pushed a pen across the desk. "You might want to take notes."

He studied the pen as if he had never seen a writing utensil before, then picked it up and scrawled something on his pad. "What's next?"

I grinned, beating Larry the furthest thing from my mind as I started outlining the points he needed to hit in his speech. For the first time in my life, I was speaking my mind for myself. Not someone else. And it felt like coming home.

24

The day of the women's luncheon came, and I was nervous. Not that I'd let Michael—or worse, Stuart—see that.

But I had taken Michael to the barbershop just over the DC line in Friendship Heights, where my father got his hair cut. I didn't tell him that was where we were going—I told him we were going to test out his speech on a friend. But once he was in the chair, he couldn't say no to a cut.

And when I caught him admiring himself in the mirror, it wasn't a hard sell to go to Hecht's for a new suit. I couldn't quite bring myself to take Michael to the Friendship Heights Woodies after the way I left the makeup counter in shame. I wanted to do a complete wardrobe overhaul, but Michael said we should start slow. I did talk him into ties and a new pair of shoes though. "Women notice shoes," I warned, and the salesgirl agreed with me.

"Size eleven," he said, conceding defeat.

It was a lot easier when Stuart wasn't with us.

And the two of us polished his speech until it shone.

So while my nerves were jangling, I did know we were ready for this.

Stuart drove us up Rockville Pike, past the Colonial Manor motel and the shops at Congressional Plaza. "Such an ugly stretch of road," he muttered.

"It's better when we get to the club," I said, smoothing my dress in the back seat. He wasn't wrong, but I preferred to look on the bright side. "Turn left up there."

Stuart put on his blinker and then made the left turn onto the tree-lined avenue. "Wasn't this in Bethesda?"

"It's been here for ten years," I explained. "The government wanted the old site for NIH." He should have known that though. "Don't you belong to a club?"

Michael and Stuart exchanged a look in the front seat. "No," Michael said cautiously. "Neither of us do."

"Your parents don't?"

"No."

"What did you do all summer as kids?"

They glanced at each other again, and I saw a hint of a smile on both faces. "Ran wild," Michael said.

"We got to be kids. Not tiny adults in top hats."

"I was at the pool all summer," I said. "No top hats. Honestly, though, I was jealous of the families that spent their summer at the beach. Papa had to work." It was a short-lived jealousy, but I thought that would make them feel less self-conscious about missing out on such a crucial part of social life. "I suppose that'll be you soon too. No real point in joining a club when you're working all summer until you have a family."

Michael turned around to look at me as the Woodmont clubhouse came into view. "Our families didn't have that kind of money."

I realized my faux pas. "I'm sorry—I didn't mean to imply—"

"No need to apologize," Michael said. "I'm not ashamed of growing up poor. My parents worked hard to make sure I'd have an education, and Stuart and I both put ourselves through law school after college."

"Is that why you're running for office?"

"Partly. But mostly—"

"Finish this conversation later," Stuart said. "Where do I park?"

"You don't. You pull up at the front, and a valet will take the car."

"I'm not giving my car to a stranger," Stuart said.

I bit the inside of my bottom lip, resisting the urge to dress him down. He clearly hadn't experienced valet parking before. "It's their job," I said, gesturing to a uniformed man in front of the building. "You'll insult him if you don't let him park the car. Is that really how you want to start this lunch?"

Stuart glared at me in the rearview mirror but pulled to a stop and left the car idling in front of the building, while the valet opened first my door and then Michael's.

"Mrs. Diamond," he said, tipping his hat. "Always a pleasure."

"Thank you, Philip," I said, grasping his hand in my gloved one.

The doorman greeted me by name as well, as did Sylvia, the receptionist. "I didn't realize you were the queen of the club," Stuart grumbled.

"Certainly makes it a good testing ground for this plan, doesn't it?" I asked as I led them to the dining room. The interns had beaten us there and were buzzing around the room, arranging chairs and tables according to the map I had drawn them. A podium stood at the front of the room, adorned with the club's Fourth of July bunting. We were lucky the speech was this week—a few days later and the bunting wouldn't have been available. We would eventually have to buy our own, but we needed money for that. Which was the other reason I picked a club as a starting point—every woman here had access to a fully stocked checking account.

Once everything was set up to even Stuart's satisfaction, we retreated into a side room. We would come out after the main course, before the desserts. There was a table set for us in there, and we ate a light lunch that started before everyone else's, to make sure we would be ready when the plates had been cleared.

"It's time," Claire said, poking her head into our room.

"Ready?" I asked Michael.

"As I'll ever be."

I straightened his tie and raked my fingers through his hair. "Now you are."

"If she licks her finger and wipes your face, I swear—"

I turned to Stuart. "Don't be ridiculous. There's nothing on his face. And I'd dip a napkin in a water glass, like a lady." I gave Michael a playful shove toward the door, then looked at Stuart over my shoulder. "No offense intended if your mother used the licking method."

He shook his head but didn't reply. Which I should have known meant trouble. But at the time, I didn't think anything of it.

I walked in first, waving to the assembled crowd. My mother wasn't there—she had stayed home to watch the kids, but she had made good on her promise. The room was full of faces that I either knew or recognized. But it was the blonde hair in the very front that made me smile the widest. Her kids must have been in the pool, because Nancy was there, front and center, to support me and my cause. I reached out and grabbed her hand, squeezing it, before I went to the podium.

"Good afternoon!" I said into the mic, then backed up a little to avoid feedback. "Sorry—I think I've done everything here *except* speak into a microphone."

"You've got this, Bev!" Nancy called out to some light laughter.

"I want to thank you all for coming out here today," I said, which also got a handful of laughs, because where else would they be on a summer afternoon? "That is to say, I appreciate you taking your lunch inside instead of by the pool." More laughs this time.

"But I'm not here to be social. I'm here because I have someone whom I'm dying to introduce you to. Michael Landau is here with us. As you may know, Michael is running for Senate against Sam Gibson." I paused, looking out into the crowd and seeing the confused faces and hearing the whispers. "Yes, *that* Sam Gibson. So why am I here introducing you to his competition? The answer is simple—and it's not because of the rumors I'm sure you've heard by now about my marriage. I'm here because Sam Gibson isn't doing anything for *us*. Men? Sure.

But women? He thinks we're good for raising babies and cooking meals and not much else."

Was I exaggerating? Yes. But it *was* a sentiment I had voiced to Larry previously, only to be dismissed as not knowing what I was talking about.

"Michael Landau is here because he wants your vote—but more importantly, he wants to *earn* your vote. He wants to listen to women, not just make decisions for them. And . . . well, I'm not going to do his whole speech for him, but I want you to know that he has my support. And I think what he has to say is important enough that I'm going to make sure I go out to the polls in November and cast my vote for him. And I hope you'll do the same."

I looked around the room. They were interested. "And without further ado, I present your future senator, Mr. Michael Landau."

The women clapped as Michael came up to the podium. He shook my hand, as he had done with Stuart when he was introduced at the most recent speech, and then I went back to the wall where Stuart was standing.

"Good afternoon," Michael said.

Stuart leaned over. "Well done," he said quietly.

I eyed him suspiciously. "But?"

His mouth twitched up into a smirk. "But nothing," he whispered. "Well—maybe not *nothing*."

I turned to fully face him. "What did you do?"

He shrugged. "Exactly what you did to me with his last speech."

Oh no. He was about to deliver a speech to a roomful of women written by a man who clearly had no clue what women wanted. And worse yet, Michael was going to think that I made the changes. I would defend myself later, obviously, but depending on how this went, going after women voters could be dead in the water.

I wished for the first time that I were a man and could settle this with my fists.

Instead, I hissed that we would talk about it later and turned my attention to Michael, ready to go snatch the microphone out of his hand if things took a turn.

"—I think this might just be my mother's dream. Wait, none of you are single, are you?" He paused for the laughs I knew he would get. "Just as well. I'm not here today to find a wife. I'm here to convince you that you should vote for me to be your next senator."

He paused and looked around the room, making eye contact and smiling. *We* have *to get those new pictures taken,* I thought. With the fresh haircut and a smile, he had suddenly gone from bland to handsome. No one was going to confuse him for Rock Hudson, but the man could turn on the charisma.

"Notice I said *your* senator, not your husband's, father's, brother's, or son's. Because while I'll be theirs too, I think it's important that women have a voice in government. And I want to be that for you. You make up half of the population. We wouldn't have a human race without you. So why is it that Maryland didn't ratify the Nineteenth Amendment until more than twenty years after it became a national law?"

He looked around again. "I'll tell you why—it's because your leaders failed you." He smiled, ruefully this time. "Now, if Maryland was my only goal, I'd be running for the state Senate instead of the national one. But the reality is, there are a lot of women in this great nation of ours who have it worse than you do. And I want to make sure this country is safe—"

Michael stopped and looked over at me quizzically. I shook my head emphatically and pointed a thumb at Stuart. Michael swallowed a chuckle and held my gaze for a moment before looking back out at the room.

"Looks like I picked up the wrong draft of my speech this morning. Will anyone object if I wing it a little?" Several women sat stoically, but most looked amused.

"Not at all," Nancy called out from the front.

"Good. Now listen, everyone wants the world to be safe, not just for women and children. My opponent would have you believe that the way to make the world safe is to keep you in a bubble while we depend on men to protect you. Which may work to a degree. But I'm not interested in *protecting* you; I want to make sure the world is *respecting* you. Because if we genuinely respect women and teach that respect from an early age, you won't *need* some man to protect you."

"Close your mouth, darling. You'll catch flies," a voice whispered beside me.

I whipped around and saw my mother standing at the wall with me. I closed my mouth, which I hadn't realized was hanging open. "Where are the children?" I hissed back.

"With Rosa. I couldn't miss this at my own club."

I shook my head, then turned my attention back to Michael, noting Stuart silently fuming to my right.

"We all know Thomas Jefferson's famous line about all men being created equal, which may have been good enough in 1776. But do you think we would have a country without the women who toiled endlessly while their men fought for our independence?"

He hadn't veered back to the prepared remarks yet, but he didn't need to—in fact, this was better than what we had written. And for the first time since I walked into his office and declared that they were going to have to hire me if they wanted to win, I realized we could win this. All we had to do was give him a push in the right direction and let him talk. Sam was charming as well, but he was a career politician, and there was an oily feeling to speaking with him that you couldn't put your finger on if you hadn't grown up the way I did. My father had grudgingly given his endorsement six years ago entirely for me, a decision that he came to regret in his final term in the House, and I understood why.

"He's quite good," my mother murmured. "Green, of course, but you should have seen your father when he started." I looked over at her. "There isn't much a woman's touch can't fix."

"If you're suggesting I—"

"Will you two stop?" Stuart whispered angrily.

I patted Mama's arm, and we stood in companionable silence through the rest of Michael's speech, which received a standing ovation as he finished.

"That should loosen some checkbooks," Mama said. "Where is he speaking next? People will talk."

"You two did enough of that," Stuart grumbled.

"Who is this angry little man?" my mother asked, more than loudly enough for him to hear.

I tried not to laugh. It wouldn't help the relationship at all. But the way Stuart's chest puffed up like a bantam rooster at being called "little" was too much.

"Oh dear," I said, once I managed to swallow a giggle. People were lined up to speak to Michael, so we had a little time. "Mama, this is Stuart Friedman, Michael's senior campaign manager." He glowered at the inclusion of "senior." "Stuart, this is my mother, Mrs. Mildred Gelman." I put a slight emphasis on her last name to remind him of my pedigree in politics.

The name washed over him, and his entire countenance changed. "Mrs. Gelman," he said, offering his hand. "I'm terribly sorry."

"Had I been Mrs. Smith, would you be as sorry?"

"If you were married to Franklin Smith from New Jersey, absolutely."

My mother let out a peal of laughter, now charmed, as I rolled my eyes.

The two of them continued in conversation as Nancy came over, grabbed my arm, and pulled me a couple of feet away to talk.

"I think I see why you're working for him," she said, waggling her eyebrows.

"Nancy!"

"What? If you really want to make Larry sorry, you've got the perfect opportunity."

"Nance—"

"I know, I know. This went really well. You need to keep the momentum going though. If that other guy . . ." She circled her hand in the air, digging for his name.

"Sam Gibson?"

"That one. If he comes and speaks, this one—"

"Michael Landau."

"That's what I said. He'll need to come back."

She had a point, though she was notoriously terrible with names, often going through her siblings, neighbors, my children, and her dog's names before reaching her own children's correct designations, so I didn't take her inability to remember Michael's name as an indication that she would forget who to vote for at the polls. Besides, the odds of Sam deciding to speak to a roomful of women was on par with him going into space.

"Do you think they'll vote?"

Nancy nodded. "I do. That line about respecting instead of protecting was gold."

I smiled. "It was, wasn't it? That was all him too." Well—mostly. I had said something to that effect in his office, but the rhyme sold it. Maybe we should get that printed on posters.

My eyes drifted toward the front of the room, where Michael was deep in conversation with my mother's friend Mrs. Klein. As if feeling my eyes on him, he looked over at me and smiled quickly before returning his attention to whatever Mrs. Klein was saying.

I didn't even notice Nancy was still talking. "—sent him packing. Do you know he had the gall to go on a date?"

"Wait, start over," I said.

"Larry," she said. "I told him he had to leave. My mother came over, and a pair of his shorts were sticking out from under a sofa cushion. The poor woman nearly had a stroke."

Anyone who birthed Nancy wasn't going to have a stroke over a pair of men's underwear, but I appreciated the sentiment being used to make Larry less comfortable. "Where did he go?"

She shrugged. "I don't care. I just wanted him gone."

I pulled her in for a hug. "Thank you for being here."

"Where else would I be when you need me? But it looks like you have this under control, so I should go make sure the kids are alive and not destroying the whole place."

"Go," I said and turned to watch Michael continue to charm the ladies of the club. *This crazy plan just might work after all,* I thought as a woman walked up and handed Michael a check. If they were willing to donate, they would definitely vote.

25

I wasn't privy to the conversation that led to Stuart storming out of the office for the rest of the afternoon—at least according to Claire the next day—because I stayed to chat with some of the women and then went home with Mama.

Would I have preferred to go celebrate our victory? Yes. But despite having a job, I was still a mother first.

Well, that and Mama informed me that she was playing bridge at someone else's house and that Rosa had to be home by three.

Besides, I owed Debbie a trip to the zoo, so I dropped my mother off for bridge and then took her car home.

"Mommy!" the kids squealed as I came in the door, and I savored the feeling of their chubby arms around me. For a moment, I was willing to throw off the whole campaign. Robbie looked taller. Which was ridiculous. I was home for dinner and breakfast and to bathe them and tuck them in every night.

"I got boo-boo," Debbie said, holding up a slightly grubby finger with an invisible wound. It was a good thing my mother hadn't come with me or that boo-boo would be getting scrubbed with a bar of Dial.

I kissed it and cradled her small hand to my chest. "Do you know what makes boo-boos feel even better than Mommy kisses?" She shook her head, and I pulled her in close and whispered into her ear, "A trip to the zoo."

"ZOO!" she shrieked, nearly piercing my eardrums. "We go to zoo, Robbie!"

"The zoo is for *babies*," Robbie said, arms crossed.

"Lions and tigers aren't. Neither are . . . bears!" I lifted my arms above my head and hooked my hands into claws as both children screamed and ran away from me. "Get your shoes," I called after them.

I thanked Rosa and paid her, then stopped her right before she left. "Rosa," I said. "Have you been going to my parents' house?"

She shook her head. "Your mother told me to come here instead."

That was an interesting development. No, I didn't picture my mother scrubbing toilets, but she hadn't mentioned that her housekeeper was cleaning my house. Not that I minded—I had grown up with Rosa working in the dual role of nanny and housekeeper until shifting fully to housekeeper when we left home. In election years, she put me to bed more often than my mother did. "How many days a week?" She looked a little nervous. "I won't say anything to Mama."

"Three," she said.

"Monday, Wednesday, Friday?" I asked. She nodded. "What would you think about going to help Papa on Tuesdays and Thursdays? He'll pay you."

"I don't think Miss Mildred would like that."

I grinned conspiratorially. "I don't think so either. Which is why we won't tell her."

She smiled back at me. "You're still that same naughty little girl who hid my shoes so I wouldn't leave, aren't you?"

I had forgotten that. And the memory unlocked a series of others. Her kissing my forehead to take my temperature when I was sick. Throwing me a sidelong glance and saying, "We'll be at school tomorrow, won't we?" when that temperature wasn't elevated. The time in high school when I came home and a bottle of gin that had been hidden in my drawer was sitting on the kitchen table. "I found that in the darndest place," she had said. "You wouldn't have any idea how it got there, would you?" But she never once told on me. She didn't have to.

"Some things don't change," I said.

She looked at me fondly. "You tell your father I'll be there on Thursday." And she turned to leave.

"Rosa—thank you. For everything."

Rosa nodded. "That little one could be your twin," she said, gesturing toward the hallway where a shriek sounded.

"I'm glad Mama has you helping her. She didn't need to hide it."

"You know how your mama is with appearances."

Boy, did I ever.

Another shriek came from the direction of the children's bedrooms, followed by a crash. "I'd better go check on that."

"Just like their mama," she said, shaking her head slightly. "Go take those wild animals to the zoo where they belong."

I laughed. "I'll tell Papa to expect you." Then I went to the foot of the stairs. "If you're not down here with your shoes by the time I count to ten, I'm going to the zoo without you! One. Two. Three." Both kids came careening down the stairs, each yelling that they were the leader.

I left a note for Mama and loaded them into the car, all smiles for our adventure.

~

The kids fell asleep in the car on the way home and I woke Robbie just enough for him to get himself upstairs. I couldn't carry him that far anymore. He was usually Larry's job when he fell asleep in the car—not that Larry ever came with us on outings like these. Instead, I'd run in and get him to bring Robbie in. Debbie stayed asleep as I pulled her into my arms, snuggling her head onto my shoulder. I breathed in the scent of her hair. She cuddled me so infrequently these days, wanting to be just like her big brother and as independent as possible.

I set Debbie on her bed, then helped Robbie to the bathroom to wash his face and hands and brush his teeth before pulling his pajamas onto him as he yawned. "Into bed, sleepyhead," I said and kissed his forehead as I tucked him in. "Night night, sleep tight, don't let the bedbugs bite."

Then I grabbed a washcloth and cleaned Debbie's face and hands and even managed to brush her teeth and change her into pajamas without waking her. I brushed her hair back from her face and kissed her chubby little cheek, then turned off the lamp.

I turned to leave, then let out a gasp at the figure in the doorway.

But it was only my mother.

"You scared me!" I whispered.

She smiled sadly. "I remember sneaking in to kiss you good night after you'd fallen asleep."

I couldn't quite picture that. It wasn't something we experienced often awake. She gestured for me to follow her, and we went downstairs to the living room. "Was it hard? Being out so much for Papa's career?"

She took a sip of the half-drunk brandy sitting on the coffee table. "I never knew anything else," she said simply. "Your father was in the state legislature when I married him and was already in the House by the time you were born."

"But your friends—?"

"My friends when you were little were the wives of other congressmen. It helps when people understand."

Fran was my only divorced friend. But she had no children. And even then, we were far from bosom buddies. I supposed Rosa was the only woman I knew who both worked and had a family, though Rosa's children were older than I was.

My mother was studying me. "What's bothering you?"

I sighed and reached for her glass, but she pulled it away. "Get your own. Sharing glasses is rude."

"But sharing cigarettes is fine?"

"No, you need your own of those too."

I shook my head. "Honestly, Mama, were you watching me tuck them in because it was sweet or to make sure I cleaned their hands first?"

"Why can't it be both?"

I chuckled, then turned serious. "Today was amazing, wasn't it?"

"I wouldn't know. You didn't invite me to the zoo."

There was the woman I knew. "Would you have skipped bridge for it?"

"Of course not. But that doesn't mean I don't want to be included. It's rather lonely being home with the children all day."

That was true. Although she had Rosa three days a week. It wasn't quite apples to apples in the comparison of how I had lived before my life imploded.

"I meant at the club," I said, changing the subject back to what I had originally intended. "Michael."

"It was something." She thought for a moment, taking another sip of her drink. "I once told your father that if he was smart, he would try to convince more women to vote."

"And he didn't?"

"God forbid that man take an idea from a woman." She shook her head. "You have no idea how frustrating it is to live like that."

I had a better idea of it than she thought. "Better than Larry, who stole all my ideas and passed them off as his own." But then I realized something. "Mama, when I told Papa I wanted to go after women's votes, he told me that someone wiser than him once said that was the way to ensure a win."

"You're making that up."

"I'm not."

She shook her head again. "Too little, too late." Something in her countenance had changed—maybe it was just the lamplight, but she looked mildly amused. Then she drank the rest of her brandy and stood up. "I'm off to bed."

"Mama," I said, turning on the sofa to look at her as she headed toward the kitchen with her glass. "Thank you for being there today."

She smiled. "It's not every mother who gets to say her daughter is a campaign manager for a future senator. I'm proud of you, Beverly. Even if no man ever will be."

I sat on the sofa pondering that. Except she was wrong. My father was proud of me. And I resolved, as I heard her footsteps in the guest room above me, to find a way to reunite them. That little smile in the lamplight gave me the hope I needed that reconciliation was possible if she could only see how much he did depend on her—for so much more than just keeping the house tidy and keeping him fed.

26

Stuart ignored me when I walked in the following morning, and it wasn't until he went into Michael's office and closed the door that Claire told me in a whisper about him storming out when they returned to the office after the event at the club.

"I thought the speech was great," she said, her voice still low, an eye on Michael's closed office door.

I patted her arm. "I did too. Don't you mind him. He'll come around."

"Did you write that speech?"

I started to nod, and then I remembered. "Part of it. He . . ." As tempted as I was to let Stuart take the fall for his behavior, it wasn't smart. Or professional. "He veered off course though."

Claire nodded. "The 'respect' part."

"He and I had talked about that. I—I wasn't expecting him to use it . . . like that."

She smiled shyly. "Well, he has my vote—or he would, if I was old enough to vote."

I winked at her. "Don't you worry. That's on my list of issues for him. If eighteen-year-olds can go to war and drink, they should be able to vote."

Her smile widened. "When Paul asked me about interning, I thought it was just going to be good experience. I didn't expect to actually care." She looked toward Paul, who was on the phone with someone.

I found myself nodding. Then I noticed the expression on her face as she gazed at Paul and suppressed a smile. *A good experience,* I thought, trying not to giggle. I'd have to give Paul a little nudge there.

"I'll smooth Stuart down," I said. "You don't worry about that at all."

Claire grinned again, and the phone at her desk rang. "I'd better get that. It's been ringing all morning. Women are making donations," she called to me over her shoulder. "And one asked if I thought Michael would go on a date with her daughter!"

I laughed as I made my way to Michael's office door. I wasn't sure if whoever asked that would vote for him when the answer was no. But it was a good sign that she liked him that much. Or her daughter was thirty and she was getting desperate.

Then again, it may have been my own mother.

I shook my head. Mama would wait and put the moves on him for me in person. A phone call to a secretary wasn't her style any more than it was mine.

I fluffed my hair and then turned the knob. "Knock knock," I called as I opened the door. Both men looked up. "Am I interrupting? Or is this something I should be here for?"

"Interrupting," Stuart said at the same time Michael told me to come on in. "Normal people knock instead of saying 'knock knock,'" Stuart added darkly.

"I wasn't knocking, it was the start of a joke. Oh, I'm so sorry, where *are* my manners? You see, a joke is when someone says something funny, and the other party laughs. Do you need me to explain what laughing is too? Or is that something you've done at some point in your life?" So much for smoothing him down. He just reacted so strongly to my very existence that I couldn't help but bait him. He either had a real issue working with a woman or was secretly in love with me.

He glared at me with utter disdain. The former, then. Probably for the best. I couldn't have returned the feeling even if he didn't treat me like I had run his cat over with a car.

"Who's there?" Michael asked.

"It's too late. The joke has died."

"Pity," Michael said. "What did you need?"

"We didn't get to debrief about yesterday."

"Yes, *we* did," Stuart said.

"Well, I didn't," I said, sitting in the seat next to Stuart. "And we have a few kinks to iron out before the next women's speech."

"What next women's speech? We did your little experiment. It's over."

"Stuart," Michael said, a warning tone in his voice.

"Most women don't vote," Stuart said. "We're wasting time, while Sam Gibson gets every actual voter on his side."

For a moment I said nothing. "Have you talked to Claire today?" I asked quietly.

"Why would I talk to Claire?"

"Because she said the phone has been ringing off the hook all morning. People are donating money. One of them even wants Michael to meet her daughter. If they're giving us money, they're going to vote."

"You can't know that."

"And you can't know how marriage works," I said, finally angry. "But take it from someone who has been married, women have a lot more sway in the home than you seem to think. Ever heard the expression 'Happy wife, happy life'? If women want Michael in office badly enough, you'd better believe they're going to wage a domestic war to make it happen."

"I wouldn't call you the marriage expert," Stuart said.

I sprang out of my seat, ready to . . . Well, I didn't know what I was ready to do. But Michael stopped me.

"Enough," he said, also standing, then slapping his hands down on his desk. "We need to work together, or we're going to lose. Stuart,

I get it. We've been friends since we were kids, and you feel like she's taking your job. But we're the underdogs. And we need an edge if we're going to have a fighting chance." He pointed to me. "Like it or not, she's our edge. She knows what Sam's campaign is up to. She's seen her father's campaigns. And she's *not* wrong. We saw what our mothers did when they wanted something." Stuart didn't budge or say a word, but something passed between the two of them, and I felt the tension in the room begin to dissipate. "Can we all be adults now?"

Stuart nodded first, and I followed. Then I sat back down.

"I called Indian Spring Country Club this morning, and we could do next week there. Sometime after the Fourth of July. The manager said they were planning to call us—his wife was at the Woodmont speech and wanted to know why Indian Spring didn't book you first."

Michael looked to Stuart, who inclined his head but didn't speak. "Okay," he said, turning back to me. "Is that a room you can fill as well?"

"Doesn't sound like I'll need to. I think the manager's wife will. But I'll reach out to her and make sure. Word of mouth spreads quickly."

Michael nodded.

"I do think we should do new pictures of you before that. Professional headshots. Ones where you're actually smiling and that don't look like they were taken with a Brownie box camera."

Stuart sat up a little straighter. In addition to being Michael's barber, he was his photographer. "We don't have money to hire someone for something frivolous."

"We do now—all those donations."

"We need that money for the actual campaign."

I started to argue that pictures were a part of the actual campaign—especially with how well Kennedy had done—but then I realized we didn't need to spend a lot. "I can get them for cheap, if not free."

Michael looked at me questioningly. "Are you also a photographer?"

"Me? No. But my cousin's fiancé is."

"Your cousin's fiancé?"

"Yeah, she's an author now, and you should see her headshot on her book—I swear she looks like a movie star."

"Who's your cousin?" Michael asked.

"Marilyn Kleinman. She wrote this book—"

Stuart cut me off. "Your cousin is Marilyn Kleinman?"

I turned to him in surprise. "You've heard of her?"

Michael laughed. "Everyone has heard of her. Her book is a best-seller, and they're making a movie of it. She's been in all the newspapers."

"It knocked the latest Salinger out of the number one spot on all the lists," Stuart said.

"Who knew you two were such readers?"

"I haven't read the book," Michael said. "But we read the news. We have to."

"That's true." I hadn't read it either, truth be told. Taking care of two small children while being the perfect wife was a full-time job. But maybe I'd start it now. "Anyway, I'll give her a call. I'm sure her fiancé will do your pictures."

I rose and turned to leave, then looked back over my shoulder. "Oh, and Michael—that speech?" He looked at me. "Don't change a word."

Neither of them said anything as I shut the door behind me and went to my desk. Marilyn split her time between Philadelphia, Key West, and the New Jersey shore these days, but my mother had all three numbers. We hadn't spoken since Larry and I separated, but I was sure she would help.

I picked up the receiver at my desk and dialed the house, humming to myself as it rang.

27

Marilyn would be driving from New Jersey to Key West the following week and said she and her fiancé would be happy to stop in DC for the day to visit. "Dan won't mind."

"The campaign is short on money still," I warned her.

"Don't you worry about that," Marilyn said. Then she lowered her voice. "My mother said Larry is being a real piece of work too. How are you situated? You know I'll help if you need it."

Of course my own mother had told Marilyn's mother what was going on. The two of them spoke nearly every day. And there were no secrets. When Marilyn went crashing through a stained-glass window while making out with the rabbi's son during Shabbat services a couple of years earlier, I heard all the gory details. So I was sure she knew exactly what I saw when I walked into Larry's office that day.

"I'm okay," I said lightly. I had gotten my first paycheck for my work with Michael, even though I had gone digging for receipts when Stuart stepped out for lunch, and I confirmed I was making significantly less than he was. But that was a problem for another day. Besides, my credit was still good at the grocer, and my paycheck would cover frills for now. And my lawyer had assured me Larry would have to pay for necessities. So no, I didn't want to take my cousin's money—even if she *had* come into a massive family fortune. "But thank you."

"Don't be offended," Marilyn said. "If you need anything, you just call me."

I thanked her and assured her I would see her the following week. I was five years older than Marilyn, and it was strange to suddenly be in the position of supplicant. But family was family. I may not have been able to count on Larry, but I knew I could count on my blood relations.

~

I spent the rest of the week following up with people who had been at the women's luncheon. I had tasked Charlie with getting names as people walked in, and now we had a comprehensive list of people whom we could call, both to remind to vote and to gently ask for money. I started with the former and worked my way around to the latter, amassing nearly two thousand dollars by the close of business on July 3.

"I'm heading home," I called to Michael and Stuart, having let the interns cut out early to begin celebrating the holiday.

"I think we're wrapping up here too," Michael said.

"Not me yet," Stuart said. "I want to get that press release out to the *Montgomery Sentinel* first."

Michael nodded. "I'll see you Thursday," he said to Stuart, before picking up his briefcase and turning to me. "I'll walk you out." He held out an elbow and, in another life, I would have taken it. But when he saw me debating the etiquette of holding my boss's arm, he returned it to his side smoothly, then held the door for me.

We reached the street, and Michael asked where I was parked. "I don't actually have a car," I said.

He looked taken aback by this. "No car?"

"Well, Larry took ours, of course. He didn't exactly think I'd find a job. And I borrow my mother's sometimes. But I don't like her watching the kids without a car in case of emergencies. So I take the bus to work."

"The bus?" he echoed, at a loss. "But we work late sometimes."

"I assure you, the bus is quite safe. No ogres or boogeymen to be seen."

"I'll drive you home."

I looked at him. "What happened to respecting women instead of protecting them?"

The left side of his mouth twisted up in a wry smile. "I respect you too much to make you sit on a dirty bus in that dress. How's that?"

"It *is* a lovely dress."

"It is. And I can assure you that it's the dress I'm protecting."

I laughed. "I'm *only* saying yes because it's hot outside." Which was completely true. July in the DC area was sweltering and usually best spent at the beach, three hours away, or by a pool. In a nonelection year, I would be doing a combination of the two. If Larry hadn't chosen to upend our lives, that is.

"I respect that too," he said. "Come on, it's just around the corner."

Safely ensconced in Michael's car, which I was thrilled to see had an under-dash air-conditioning unit, I directed him to East-West Highway toward Chevy Chase.

"Is that where you grew up?"

"It is."

"Funny," he said.

"Is it?"

"Kind of. We grew up four miles apart. But in different worlds."

I looked over at him. "I don't know what you mean."

"Country clubs and private schools and a congressman father."

"I went to public school," I said. He glanced at me. "Papa was—is—a big believer in public education and civil service."

"That's true," Michael said. "They don't make them like your father anymore."

I shook my head. Papa was still grumbling over his replacement. Mama told him he shouldn't have retired if he still wanted to have a say in what happened in the House, to which he replied that she was trying to kill him. But there was a lot of backseat politicking going on. Or at least there had been. I needed to spend more time with him. I was stopping by once a week after work to stock his refrigerator and cupboards, but he was lonely without Mama. "That they don't."

"I'd love to talk to him sometime."

This time the look I gave him was far sharper. "Is that why you took a chance on me?"

He appeared confused by my tone, which was admittedly harsher than I'd intended. "No. I mean, it was part of it—I knew you'd been around politics. If you had *just* been Larry's wife, I don't think that would have been as convincing. But I'm not looking for an endorsement if that's what you're asking. I just admire him."

I turned to look out the window, unnerved by how perceptive he was. He couldn't have known my suspicion that my father was the entire reason Larry had married me. And yet—

"Besides," Michael continued quietly, "with you raising all that money this week, I think it's *your* endorsement that carries more weight."

"It's a good thing you went into politics," I said, turning back toward the windshield, but not quite looking at him. "You're certainly a smooth enough talker for it."

Michael laughed, a real laugh. "It wasn't a line."

"Mmhmm. Turn left up there."

He put on his blinker and did as he was told, and I directed him to my street and then my house.

"This is it," I said. "Home sweet home."

Michael craned his neck at the windshield to get the full view. "I see why you didn't want to leave," he said. "What did Greg say?"

"That Larry has to pay to support me—as long as I don't go wild with the spending."

"But the house is safe?"

"It is—but I'm not quitting yet."

Michael looked back at me, and for a split second I felt like I was at the end of a date, sitting in the driveway, not wanting to go inside yet. "Good," he said lightly, his eyes locking on mine. He shifted his body slightly toward me and then froze briefly before turning back to look straight ahead. "I—uh—what are you doing for the Fourth of July? Anything special?"

I smoothed my dress. "The club does a barbecue every year. And then fireworks." I glanced over, but he was still looking straight ahead. "What about you?"

"Me?"

"Is anyone else in the car?"

He grinned ruefully. "No. Not unless Stuart is hiding in the trunk."

"A disturbing image."

Michael chuckled. "I don't have anything planned."

I pictured him in a bachelor's apartment with a TV dinner. It was no way to spend a holiday. "Well, that won't do at all. You should come to the club with me and the kids."

It took him a moment to reply. "Is that . . . smart?"

"Couldn't be smarter," I said. "The ladies get to see you're a real person, and you can meet the husbands too."

"I meant—"

I didn't let him finish that sentence. "Bring a bathing suit if you want to swim. They have towels there. And casual—slacks and a short-sleeved shirt. No suits at a barbecue."

He debated internally for a moment before nodding. "What time?"

"Three? Unless you want to just show up for dinner and fireworks."

"What does my junior campaign manager suggest?"

It was my turn to smile. "Pick us up at three."

"I'll be here," he said.

"Good," I said, opening my car door. "I'll see you tomorrow—boss."

Michael laughed again. "Good night, Beverly."

I went up the walkway, fighting the urge to look over my shoulder to see if he was watching me. When I reached the door, I turned back and waved, but he waited until I opened it to begin backing up.

I didn't immediately call to my mother and the children though. Instead, I shut the door quietly behind me and leaned on it. I had clearly been imagining that moment in the car. Besides, I was a soon-to-be divorcée with two kids. Flirting was a thing of the past for me. And even if it wasn't, I was in no position to become an adulterer as well.

No. I needed to focus on Michael's career. And I *had* been telling the truth: going to the club as a person, not a politician, was a wise move.

As I lay in bed that night though, I mentally went through my wardrobe for the perfect dress for the next day to avoid thinking about the way he had looked at me. That line of thought went nowhere good.

28

"So you're working on the Fourth of July?"

"I am not *working*," I said again, flipping the pancakes that I was making for the kids. "He didn't have any place to be, and I thought it was smart for him to come with us from a political standpoint."

"But why on the Fourth of July? No one wants to talk politics on a holiday."

I turned around from the stove. "Actually, Mama, considering that the Fourth of July is quite literally America's first political holiday, I think it makes perfect sense." She opened her mouth to reply, but I cut her off. "And again, it's not about politics. It's about showing up as a person. Remember how much people loved it when Papa would just be a normal dad?"

"Your pancakes are burning," Mama said mildly. I moved the pan to a cool burner and transferred them to the waiting plate, but it was too late. The kids would never trust my cooking again if I served them burnt pancakes. With a sigh, I dumped them in the trash and started again. "Such a waste," she murmured.

"Don't you go starting that Depression-era nonsense," I warned. "Larry can afford an extra box of pancake mix."

"And if Larry comes to the club today?"

That hadn't occurred to me. He wasn't a fan of the club beyond golf. Though if I'd had any doubts about whether the threat to sell the house held any weight or not, that should have been a clue. Cancelling our membership would have been a logical first step before selling the house.

"He won't," I said with a certainty I didn't feel. "I'm sure he'll be working. Besides, he always hated going to the club for the Fourth."

"I'm just not sure that going with another man so soon is in anyone's best interest."

I slapped the spatula down on the kitchen counter and turned around again, arms crossed at my waist. "I'm allowed to have friends."

"Is that what he is now? A friend?"

"No. He's my boss. Is it so wrong to take pity on someone who had no place to be on a holiday? We're supposed to invite people in at Passover."

"This is hardly Passover, and it's a lot more public."

"Which is how you know it's not a date. If we strip naked and go at it on the ninth hole, then I'll agree with your concern."

"Beverly!"

"It's amazing I'm here at all with that reaction."

"Beverly Ann Gelman, if you—"

"Diamond, Mama. Don't forget, I *am* still married. Which is why your concerns are completely unfounded. Even if I were interested— which I'm not—it would be pretty pointless, wouldn't it? It's ironic too: people have no problem voting for an adulterer, but they'd think twice about voting for someone who was *with* an adulterer."

"Beverly," she said, starting again. "I know you better than that. I'm talking about how it will *look*."

I threw my hands up. "I take it back. I'm working on the Fourth of July. Better?"

"Much," she said, sipping her coffee. "But you'd better flip those pancakes."

I swore, then dumped the second batch. "No distracting me this time."

"Who's distracting?"

Rolling my eyes as I spooned a third batch of pancakes into the pan, I dropped the argument.

~

Michael arrived at three sharp with a bouquet of red, white, and blue flowers, complete with two small American flags for the kids.

"I didn't want to come empty-handed," he said sheepishly. "I didn't know the etiquette for—whatever this is."

I glanced over my shoulder to make sure Mama wasn't standing right there. "I appreciate the sentiment, but give them to my mother."

"Your mother?"

"Just trust me."

"I—ah—I didn't realize your mother would be coming with us."

I shrugged. "She moved in to help with the kids when Larry moved out."

"And your father?"

I shook my head. "Don't ask. Long story for another day. And definitely don't ask her about him."

"Mr. Landau," Mama said warmly from behind me, as if she hadn't spent the entire morning telling me what a terrible idea this was. "How lovely to see you again."

"Just Michael, ma'am."

"Until it's Senator Landau," I said.

"So modest," my mother murmured. "Michael," she said, holding out her hand for him to shake.

"I brought—I brought you some flowers," Michael said, glancing at me quickly, which wasn't lost on her.

"How thoughtful. I can't remember the last time anyone brought me flowers."

The last time was her birthday, a month ago. And I knew because I had a longstanding order placed with our florist for them to be delivered from my father. And Mother's Day a few weeks before that.

A crash sounded from upstairs. "I better go check on the kids," I said. "Come on in while I finish getting them ready."

"Hey!" I yelled up the stairs. "What was that?"

"Nothing," they both called back.

I started up the stairs. "*Nothing* always means something expensive got broken," I muttered. When I reached Debbie's bedroom, the rocking chair was overturned, and she was trapped inside it. "What on earth?"

"We're playing jail," Robbie said. "I'm the sheriff."

"I a bad guy!" Debbie volunteered.

"Okay, bad guy and sheriff. It's time to go to the club. Mommy's friend is here, and he brought you a little present, but only children who are dressed and ready to go get presents."

"I ready!" Debbie shouted. "I get present!"

"I don't see shoes on those feet."

"I get shoes!" Debbie went careening out of the room, and I heard her running toward the stairs.

"You're up, Sheriff."

Robbie scowled for a moment at his disrupted game. "Will there be fireworks tonight?"

"There will."

"And I get to stay up for them?" I assured him that he did, and he made his way downstairs.

Michael was in the living room with my mother, and inexplicably, Debbie was on his lap, waving her American flag enthusiastically in his face. Her shoes were nowhere in sight.

"Deborah Annette Diamond, you get down right now."

She looked at me, pouting. "It's okay," Michael said. "She was excited about the flag."

"I 'cited," she confirmed, waving the flag and smacking Michael repeatedly in the head with it.

"You sure about that?" I asked Michael. He laughed.

"I want one," Robbie said. "She doesn't even have her shoes on."

"Robbie, this is Mommy's friend, Mr. Landau."

Robbie looked at him dubiously.

"Hi," Michael said, shifting Debbie off his lap. "You can call me Michael." He knelt to Robbie's level and pulled the other flag off the sofa to hand to him.

"Mr. Landau," I corrected. "We don't call adults by their first names."

Robbie looked from Michael to me and back again as if we were playing tennis. "Listen to your mother," Michael said. "I clearly don't know the rules yet."

"There are a *lot* of rules," Robbie said.

"I bet," Michael said conspiratorially. Then he stood up. "So—I hear there's a barbecue. No one here likes hot dogs, do they?"

"Me! Me!" Debbie shouted.

"Uh-oh. I guess I can't eat them all, then, can I?"

"You can eat the hamburgers," Robbie said, still studying him. "And maybe one hot dog."

"That's very generous of you, sir," Michael said.

Robbie put his shoulders back proudly, and I looked away so he wouldn't see me smile. He always thought I was laughing *at* him instead of *with* him.

"Shall we?" Michael asked, and for a moment it looked like he was going to hold out his arm again. My mother was watching with great interest.

"Yes," I said. "Debbie. Shoes. Now."

29

"Do you think this is smart?" Nancy asked.

I sighed. "It's not a date."

"Well, I know that," Nancy said, taking a sip of her cocktail. "You'd have told me if it was. But it's going to look that way to everyone else."

I shook my head. "We've been here for hours, and I've barely even spoken to him. He's working the crowd." We both looked over to where he stood in a group of men. From the occasional laughter we heard, it certainly sounded like he was charming them as he had their wives.

Paula Rosenblum walked over to us, a drink in her hand. "Hi," she said, using the hand that wasn't holding her glass to shield her eyes from the setting sun behind us. "Is it true that you're dating the senator?"

"How many of those have you had?" Nancy asked. "He's not a senator. He's *running* for the Senate, and he's Bev's boss."

She waved her hand around, sloshing some of her drink. "Tomato, tomahto. And from what I heard, being someone's boss doesn't prevent affairs."

Nancy stood up, hands balled into fists, and I grabbed her arm, yanking her back down onto the chaise longue she had been sitting on. "I'm still married," I said. "And even if I weren't, I'm not dating anyone. But thank you *so* much for your concern. Always lovely to see you, Paula."

Paula stood there, about to say something else, but Nancy beat her to it. "That means scram."

Paula gave her a dirty look, then turned to leave, taking a large gulp of her drink, and narrowly avoiding walking into the pool.

"Tell your buddies over there you have a drinking problem if you need something to gossip about," Nancy called after her, loudly.

"Nance!"

"What?" she asked. "I didn't like her before, and I don't like her better after that."

"We're not going to have any friends left between the people who think I'm an adulterer and the people you offend."

"Who needs other friends? Besides, they're not our friends if they're going to talk behind our backs."

I chuckled and shook my head again. "You've got a point, but I need them to vote for Michael, so we have to be nice. At least until the election."

Nancy nodded sagely, leaning back against her chair and taking another sip of her drink. "Fine. I'll be nice—nicer, I mean—to people to help you win your revenge campaign. But I'm not promising I won't push Paula into the pool."

"She'll fall in soon enough on her own at this rate."

Nancy held out her glass, and I clinked mine to it. "He *is* handsome though," Nancy said. "Did he look this good at that lunch, or am I drunk?"

"Both?"

She winked at me. "Cheers." She finished her drink and signaled to a waiter for another. "You *would* tell me though if something was going on, right?"

I felt a twinge of guilt. But nothing had happened. I had imagined some flirting. That was all. "I would tell you."

"Uh-oh," Nancy said.

"Nancy, there's nothing going on."

"Not that. Your father is here." She pointed across the pool.

"What?" I followed the line of her arm. There he stood, in a seersucker suit that had seen better days. "Oh boy. This isn't going to end well."

"You didn't know he was coming?"

I shook my head. "I just hope Mama doesn't make a scene."

"How many deep is she?"

"Mama? She can drink us both under the table." I watched as he greeted some friends. "He needs a haircut desperately."

Nancy nodded. "He's got that Ebenezer Scrooge look going on."

I started laughing despite myself. "You're terrible."

"Tell me I'm wrong."

Before I could reply, my mother approached him, striding over with furious, long steps. "And now the fireworks." They were too far away to hear, but she had a finger in his face, and people were staring. "I'd better go break this up."

I made my way around the pool, where a crowd had gathered around them. "—just show up out of nowhere, looking like you live on the streets," she was saying. "No word, no calls—"

"You told me not to call you."

"And you listened to that?"

"Mama, Papa, people are staring," I said.

"Let them stare," my mother said. "For thirty years, I stayed behind him and pretended he was the Messiah. But I'm not having another holiday ruined. No sir. Not this time."

"Millie, I miss you—"

"You miss having someone to take care of you, but I'm not your mother. That's not my job."

"Enough," I said. "I'm here working, and you're ruining everything I'm trying to do."

"Working?" my father said, turning around to look for where Michael was. But his arm swung out and knocked me off balance. And suddenly I was swimming.

I surfaced, sputtering in surprise. "Now look what you've done," Mama said. "Go home, Bernie."

My father's shoulders sank. "I'm sorry, Beverly," he said. "I thought—" He shook his head. "No. It was stupid." He looked back at my mother. "I'm sorry, Millie."

She crossed her arms and turned away, saying nothing.

"That's okay. Everyone ignore your daughter in the pool," I said.

Then a hand reached down to help me. I looked up and saw Michael. Behind him it seemed like the whole club was staring at us. If I took his hand, the gossip was going to be brutal. If I didn't, there would be whispers about a tiff. So I did the only logical thing.

I grabbed his hand and yanked him down into the pool as well.

"Really?" he asked me when he came up. Everyone was staring, mouths agape. "Is it too late to fire you?"

I shrugged. "Yes. Besides, I told you to bring a suit." He started to laugh as the first firework went off in the sky above us. With the assembled crowd distracted, I hoisted myself out of the pool. "I'd offer to help you out, but you know what they say about payback. Let's dry off and then head out as soon as the fireworks are done. I need to get the kids to bed before too long."

30

I had hoped we would have new headshots by the luncheon at Indian Spring at the end of the week, but Marilyn said she and her fiancé got delayed and would be in town on Friday. So I invited them to come to the club, and we could figure out pictures from there. Besides, it wouldn't hurt to get some shots of him speaking, which Marilyn assured me wouldn't be a problem.

Stuart was mostly ignoring my existence, but that was better than open hostility. And I chattered away, amiably pretending I didn't notice his silence as we drove to the club.

"So this photographer—" Michael said.

"His name is Dan," I said. "I only met him once two years ago, but if Marilyn says he's good, he's good." I hoped that was true. Although anything was better than the unsmiling pictures he had been using.

Stuart shook his head from the front seat. He was clearly offended even though I hadn't said the last part out loud. But that was the most reaction I had gotten from him all week, so maybe he was thawing.

The interns were already there, setting up the room with the borrowed Fourth of July bunting. "Eventually, we should probably buy our own decorations," I reminded Stuart as we checked their progress.

"We don't have money for a newspaper ad," Stuart snapped, finally speaking. "Let alone stars-and-stripes banners."

"Bunting," I corrected. "Banners are signs. This is bunting."

He glared for a moment, then stormed off.

"He must be so much fun at parties," I said to Michael.

"He'll warm up," Michael assured me. "I promise. He's all bark."

I chuckled at the image of Stuart as a terrier, then straightened Michael's tie.

"I always feel like a kid when you do that."

I dropped my hand. "Sorry."

"Not in a bad way—my mom used to do that too. But she stopped around my bar mitzvah."

Maybe she shouldn't have rose to my lips, but I swallowed the words. I may have been bossing him around, but I still worked for him. Instead, I said nothing but dusted the shoulders of his suit jacket.

As we retreated to a side room to wait for the lunch to begin, I thought about what Stuart had said about a newspaper ad. In theory, new pictures would be good for that. But the reality was that a print ad wasn't worth the amount you paid for it most of the time. Profiles were worth their weight in gold—after all, that was how I found Michael and decided to work for him. And for someone young and good-looking, television was even better. *It's too bad there are no debates to televise,* I thought. That had been the final nail in Nixon's coffin. I looked across the table at Michael. He was still green politically, but he could have given Jack Kennedy a run for his money if the sound was off.

He may get there yet, I thought.

"What?" Michael asked. "Is there something on my face?"

I shook myself out of it. "No. Sorry, my mind was elsewhere."

Claire poked her head in and signaled to us. "Who's introducing him today?" she whispered as all three of us stood up.

"Me," I said as Stuart said, "I am."

We faced each other, but Michael put a hand on Stuart's arm. "Beverly for the women's lunches. You're still my choice whenever we address men."

"I don't know," I said, unable to stop myself. "I bet I could get a roomful of men's attention."

Michael's face contorted as he struggled not to laugh, and Stuart glowered.

"I'm teasing," I said finally. "Lighten up, Stu."

If looks could kill, I would have been floating facedown in the swimming pool that was just visible through the dining room's windows.

Thankfully, his eyes lacked the power to commit murder, so I strolled past him, took my place at the podium, and introduced Michael.

~

I saw Marilyn come in about a third of the way through Michael's speech. He was giving pretty much the same one from the first lunch, but he had written out an approximation of what he had ad-libbed when Stuart tried to sabotage me. And the women here clearly had friends at Woodmont because they were ready for him, hanging on every word and cheering at his line about respecting instead of protecting.

Marilyn's fiancé crept around the side of the room with his camera, blending in so seamlessly that I doubted most of the attendees knew a photographer was present. Marilyn grabbed a seat near the back, spotted me and waved enthusiastically, and then listened as well.

When Michael finished to a round of thunderous applause, she made her way over to where I was standing but was stopped three times by women who were apparently fans of her book. One of them had her sign a napkin.

"Beverly, darling," Marilyn said, throwing her arms around my neck. "How *are* you?"

The emphasis on *are* irritated me. Too much of our mothers talking about my impending divorce.

"Fantastic," I said.

"You look it," she said, completely unfazed if she heard the edge in my tone. "It's been way too long. I haven't seen you since the funeral."

Debbie had been a baby then.

"Honestly, it doesn't feel like that long—but that's because I've been reading about you in all the magazines."

Marilyn pursed her lips modestly and shrugged. "Easy come, easy go. I'm new and I'm cute. We'll see how my second book does." Then she took my hand. "But enough about that. I'm here for you today, darling. How on earth did you get yourself involved in politics? My mother was vague on the details."

I gave her the short account of Larry's affair, though a more graphic version than I gave my own mother, and then the need for a job.

"And you couldn't have found a better way to stick it to him," she finished for me. "Want me to name a character for him and kill him off in my second book? I'm happy to do it."

I laughed. "Sure. But please make it a particularly embarrassing death."

"Drowning in a vat of pig excrement it is."

I laughed again, loudly enough this time that people looked over. "Perfectly fitting," I said.

"So tell me, is he going to win?"

"Larry?"

"No, this Landau fella."

I let my gaze wander over to him. He was talking to a couple of women, who seemed completely enthralled. "I don't know, if I'm being perfectly honest. He should. His heart is in the right place on every issue. He wants equality—not just for women. For everyone. But the guy Larry works for is a powerhouse. And Michael is pretty green. If I had few years to fundraise, we'd be in better shape. It's definitely an uphill battle." I hadn't vocalized my doubts to anyone—not even Nancy. Michael looked over at me, feeling my eyes on him, and smiled, buoying my confidence. "But I'm going to work as hard as I can to make it happen. And if I fail, at least I'll know I did my best."

When I looked back at Marilyn, she was watching me, not Michael. "You really believe in this guy, don't you?" she asked.

It wasn't something I had thought about. When I came to work for him, I didn't care who our senators were, I just wanted to punish Larry. But the speech at Woodmont changed that. I wanted him to win because I trusted him.

But I found myself nodding. "I do. He's exactly what our state and country need."

"Then let's fix one of your big problems. How much money do you need to beat Larry's guy?"

"Marilyn, I'm not taking your money."

"Why not? By all rights, some of it should be yours too. If you'd been bad enough to get sent to our great-aunt Ada, she'd have probably left half of it to you."

"It takes an astronomical amount to fund a campaign."

She crossed her arms. "I mean it: tell me how much."

I had a number in mind, but it was ridiculous. So I threw out a lowball.

"Bev," she said, putting a hand on my arm. "How much do you actually need?"

I sighed and told her.

"Done," she said. "Do I make a check out to you or to him?"

"Marilyn!"

"What? I can't take it with me. And I don't know if I'm having kids or not. If you say he's going to help people, why not make the world a little better for everyone?"

"I can't take that much," I said.

"Then I'll give it to him directly," she said, digging in her purse and bringing out a checkbook. She uncapped a pen and began writing.

I shook my head in disbelief. "Has anyone ever stopped you from doing something?"

She grinned. "Many have tried, none have succeeded." She tore the check out of the book, folded it, and slipped it into my hand. "When the election is over, you should pop on down to Key West. I've got someone there who would absolutely love to meet you."

I couldn't imagine "popping" anywhere with Robbie and Debbie, but maybe if the divorce was finalized by then, I could go on a weekend when Larry had the kids. It would be nice to actually catch up with my cousin, even if I had no intention of being set up with whomever she wanted me to meet.

31

I stopped in to see my father a few days later. The house was cleaner, but his cheeks had stubble, and most of the food I had brought on the previous visit sat untouched in the refrigerator, looking distinctly worse for wear. "Papa, what have you been eating?"

He looked away guiltily, and for the first time, I saw the resemblance between him and Robbie.

"Papa?" When he didn't reply, I opened the freezer, which was full of Swanson TV dinners. I sighed. "What did you do before Mama?"

He looked down at the newspaper in front of him. "I ate at diners a lot," he mumbled.

"At least that's real food. Are you doing that at all?"

He shook his head. "It's too embarrassing."

"Eating at a diner?"

Finally he raised his eyes to mine. "You don't understand," he said sadly.

I came and sat across from him at the kitchen table, reaching over to put a hand on top of his. "What's embarrassing, Papa?"

"I thought—I thought if I went to the club that she would at least talk to me, not make a scene."

I started to say that if he thought that, he didn't know my mother. But he looked so miserable and suddenly so old. And as I studied this man, who had been my childhood knight in shining armor, slaying the dragons of Congress to make a better world for me and my children,

I realized he and I knew two very different sides of the same woman. I knew the one who raised her voice and dragged me out of the Woodies makeup department to avoid tarnishing her image. He knew the woman who did everything she could to make his life comfortable. Who would never make a scene that could cause people to talk about him.

She was the same wife I had been. Until we'd both had enough.

"Oh, Papa." I sighed. "Okay, step one is you have to learn how to take care of yourself. It's good that Rosa is cleaning the house, but Mama doesn't want to come running back to take care of you."

"But she always took care of me."

"She didn't," I said gently. "You got on just fine before you met her."

"I was a young man then."

"Then just give up completely," I said, throwing my hands up. "It doesn't sound like you want a wife. It sounds like you want a mother."

I instantly regretted my harsh words. This was a man who had stood up to Joseph McCarthy when everyone else was too terrified to stop him. A man who dined with presidents, and even with Queen Elizabeth, at the White House. Larger than life in every way imaginable.

And yet he crumpled beneath the weight of my judgment.

I didn't know if he was actually crying. I hoped not. My heart couldn't take it. But his face was in his hands.

"I'm sorry," I said. "But you have to realize, her sole purpose in life isn't to make you more comfortable. And I think you started taking her for granted."

He looked up at me, his eyes shining but his face mercifully free of tears. "I never did."

"Do you know that she wants to travel?"

"We travel every summer."

I shook my head. "A week in the Catskills with her sister isn't what she meant."

"We went to Chicago."

Keeping my cool was becoming a struggle. "That was ten years ago, Papa. And entirely because it was where the National Convention was."

"So if I book a trip to Florida, she'll come home?"

For the first time, I really saw what she meant when she said she was invisible. "No. Booking a trip to Florida will push her further away."

"Then what do you want me to do?"

I counted to ten in my head. And I thought dealing with two children under six was frustrating. "She wants to feel like *she* matters. Like you hear her. Like you care what she wants."

"I give her everything she wants. The house, the car, the handbags—what more could she want?"

I held up a hand to stop him. "She wants you to ask her what she wants and then really listen and work to make it happen. I don't think she gives a fig about the handbags or the car. She wants you to ask her what she'd like to do instead of you just going to the park to play checkers."

He was silent for a little while. "And you think that will make her come home?"

Another deep breath. "No. We're past that now. I think you need to show her you can be self-sufficient. That she'd be coming back because you miss *her*, not the things she did for you. What do you miss beyond her running the house?"

He thought for enough time that I was worried that was all there was in their relationship. And if so, she would be living with me until one of us died—and it was a toss-up whether that would be me from exasperation or her from me losing my mind and pulling a Lizzie Borden.

"Her laugh," he said. "It's the most infectious laugh in the world." A shorter pause. "The way she can make absolutely anyone feel comfortable, from the president to the most unfortunate constituent. The way a whole room would light up when she came in. She knows the right thing to do in every single situation. Nothing fazes her. Ever. She just does what needs to be done. The way her pillow smelled. I used to wake up before my alarm and roll over onto her pillow and doze back off."

A memory hit me, so strong I could feel it, of coming into their room in the middle of the night after a bad dream. I couldn't have been more than five or six years old. But I crawled into the bed, on my mother's side, and she wrapped an arm around me, still mostly asleep, and kissed my hair. I knew that smell. It was the smell of comfort. Of safety. Of unconditional love.

Awake, she smelled of Chanel No. 5. But snuggling into her in bed was the scent of the innocence of childhood.

"That's—that's a good start," I said, uncharacteristically choked up. I didn't know what was wrong with me. If I missed something so bizarre, she was living in my guest room—though I didn't think she would welcome a middle-of-the-night visit to cuddle some twenty-two years later.

But now wasn't the time for sappy emotions. It was a time for action.

"Step one, you're going to shave. And get a haircut. And wear matching clothes. I'm going to make you some food you can reheat, but then . . . Let me think, not this week, but next, I'm going to come over after work one day and teach you how to cook something."

"Cook?"

"Something simple, Papa. We're not going straight to soufflés. But she needs to see that you aren't a giant child and that you can take care of yourself."

He puffed up at the insult, a wounded expression across his face. "Beverly Ann Gel—"

"Do you want my help or not?"

He sank back into his seat. "Go on."

"Then . . . well . . . you're going to need to make some kind of big gesture."

"Like flowers?"

"Flowers? That's your idea of a grand gesture?" I pinched the bridge of my nose. "I don't know what yet. But I'll work on it." I glanced down at my bare wrist and reached for his arm, only to find it watchless as well. "Where's your watch?"

"I don't know," he said mournfully.

As much as it pained me to think such disloyal thoughts about my own father, had I been my mother, I likely would have left too. Instead, I turned and looked at the kitchen clock. "I need to get home. Tomorrow, you shower, shave, and get your hair cut."

He nodded and agreed, and I leaned down to kiss his prickly cheek before I left. "Do you remember what you used to say to me when I was little and would have a problem? There's nothing—"

"—we can't solve if we work together," he finished.

"You do your part," I said, "and we'll figure this one out too. Okay?"

"Okay."

He stood to walk me out, and I noticed his feet were bare. "What happened to your socks?"

It took me a moment to recognize the look on his face as shame. "They're all pink," he said. "I did what you told me with the washing machine, but now all my undershirts and shorts and socks are pink."

"Did you separate out all the whites and colors?"

"I did. Then I put them in the washing machine."

"Together?"

"Well, I only have one washing machine."

I honestly wasn't sure which was the more herculean task: winning a Senate race against an established candidate or reuniting my parents. After this visit, I was leaning toward the latter.

32

The following Saturday afternoon, I heard a key in the front door, then the sound of it opening. "Mama?" I called, coming into the hall from the kitchen, wiping my hands on a dish towel. She had gone out to lunch and shopping, claiming she never got a day off anymore, despite Rosa's evidence to the contrary. "You're back ear—oh!"

Larry was in the hallway. I *knew* I should have gotten the locks changed.

"What are you doing here?" I asked.

"This is my house."

"On paper. What do you want?"

A muscle twitched in his jaw, and I braced myself for the confrontation. "To see my children," he said, a wolfish smile spreading across his face. "Surely you can't deny me that. Especially not when they spent their Fourth of July with another man."

Nancy would have killed Arnie if he was the one who blabbed, so it had to be someone else. He did still golf there; he just didn't enjoy socializing off the course. "They spent the Fourth splashing in the pool and running around with sparklers like every other kid at the club."

"Who arrived and left in another man's car."

My hands went to my hips. "What exactly are you implying, Larry?"

"You had your fun," he said. "I had mine. Let's call it even and get past this."

"My *fun*? Not all of us bring sex into the workplace."

"Come on, Bev, you have to know that's why he hired you."

"He hired me because I know how to win a campaign."

Larry laughed, a deep belly laugh full of malice. "You're married to someone who can win a campaign. So you're right. Maybe he hired you because he thought you'd bring some of my secrets to the table, but what do you know other than how to be a housewife?"

He had moved closer. But I wasn't going to be cowed. "Interesting, then," I said.

"What is?"

"That you married me. Would you have if my father was a plumber and not Bernie Gelman?"

The muscle twitched in his jaw again. Nothing else gave away how angry he was.

"Because once upon a time, you seemed to think my political sense was useful. But some men can be honest and actually recognize that I have value."

"Value? You've got him parading around country clubs and talking to women!"

"Amazingly, women can do more than cook you dinner, bear your children, and service you at the office."

"You're making a spectacle of yourself," Larry said. "I know you want to hurt me, but do you think you'll be able to keep this house if I lose my job because *you* want to dive into pools fully dressed with your new man to make me look like a cuckold? At the club *I* pay the dues for, no less."

"You can't threaten me with that. I hired a lawyer, and I know my rights. And you have to support me in the same manner you did while we were married."

"Not if you're the adulterer, I don't," he said. "And that pool stunt was pretty damning."

I had a meeting with my lawyer set for the following week. I didn't know if the PI had turned anything up yet or not, but I doubted it, because Greg had promised to call me if he found solid evidence. But I had nothing to hide.

"You can waste as much time as you want on that," I said. "But you and I both know that isn't me. And if you find anyone to say otherwise, they're going to be perjuring themselves. Can you say the same?"

"Good luck proving anything," Larry said. "I'm not going anywhere without a fight."

I shook my head. "I'm not afraid of you, Larry Diamond."

"Drop the adultery part," he said. "Agree to that and quit your job, and I won't contest a no-fault divorce after the election."

I stared at the man I had spent six years sleeping next to, waking up an hour before him to be the perfect wife, only to see a stranger in my hallway. "Which part of that is more important?" I asked quietly. "You not having adultery on your record or me quitting?"

"Both."

"And if I'm not willing to agree to either of those conditions?"

His eyes gleamed the way a cat's did before it killed the mouse it had been toying with, and despite what I had said a moment earlier, the expression on his face did scare me.

"Keep the house," he said mildly. "There are worse things to lose."

Then he strode past me to the den, where the kids were watching television. "Daddy!" I heard Robbie shriek.

"Who wants to go on an adventure with Daddy?" he asked. Both kids yelled that they did.

"Not so fast," I said, storming into the room.

"What?" he asked, his voice dripping with insincere sweetness. "No court is going to say I can't see my children." He told Robbie to hop on his back, and he picked Debbie up in his arms. "Who wants ice cream?"

"Me! Me!" Debbie cried.

He kissed the top of her head, his eyes locked on mine. "Good. You're going to be spending a *lot* more time with Daddy in the future," he said. "A *lot* more."

"They need to be back for dinner," I said shrilly.

"What's the matter, Bev?" he asked, grinning viciously. "You sound scared."

And over my protests, he carried them out of the house, without so much as a diaper for Debbie.

I sank down at the kitchen table, my hands suddenly shaking. He didn't *want* the kids. I knew that. He didn't have the faintest idea of how to care for them. No judge would grant him custody over me.

But if he was willing to cheat, he was willing to lie.

And if I didn't give him what he wanted, this wouldn't be a fair fight.

I thought about Fran, who had lost everything.

"No," I said out loud.

"No what?" my mother asked.

I jumped a mile, banging my knee on the underside of the table and swearing colorfully.

"Such language," she said, feigning shock, as if she hadn't uttered a similar phrase when she discovered Debbie had colored on her Hermès purse.

"I didn't hear you come in."

"Should I have knocked?" she asked, removing her hat. "I was under the impression that I lived here now." She cocked her head toward the den. "Where are the children?"

"Larry was here." I rubbed my bruised knee. "He took them." I looked at the clock on the wall—I had been sitting there over an hour, worrying.

"Took them where?"

"I don't know."

She studied me carefully, then took a seat at the table. "I see. Well, they'll be back soon. He has no idea how to change a diaper. They'll get hungry and cranky, and he'll bring them home."

My mouth was dry. "I hope so."

"What did he say?"

I recounted his veiled threat.

"No." She shook her head. "No judge in the world would find you an unfit mother."

"But if he can manufacture some affair—"

"That's where you have a leg up." My whole childhood, she had drilled into me that I was never to interrupt. But when she did it, it was so smooth, I almost didn't notice. "You don't have to manufacture anything. It happened. All you need to do is get the girl to testify."

I shuddered. I had no desire to try to convince Linda to do anything. "She wouldn't."

"Whyever not?"

"Because she's probably in love with him. You know how those young affairs go." She bristled slightly, and I realized she likely didn't. She married my father at twenty after all. I doubted there had been anyone before him. "Besides, he'll fire her. She won't risk that."

"That's easy, then," my mother said. "You offer her a job working for Michael."

"What?"

"Simple. And far less exertion working as *just* a secretary."

"Mama!"

She reached across the table and grabbed my hand, suddenly completely serious. "Beverly, you do what it takes. If I teach you nothing else, you learn that. You do what you need to do to survive."

Then, as suddenly as it had come off, the veneer was back in place, and she stood up. "I'm going to get changed. Then I'll make spaghetti. The kids will be hungry when they get home."

"Spaghetti?" I asked. She never let them have messy food and insisted on leaving the kitchen when I made it for them.

"It's their favorite, isn't it? Let's make sure they remember who knows and loves them best."

I watched her swish out of the room, buoyed by her indomitability.

When she returned, she handed me a slip of paper. "Call while I cook."

"Who is it?"

"A locksmith. We may not play dirty, but that doesn't mean we have to play nice."

I wrapped my arms around my mother. "Thank you."

She patted my back twice and then extricated herself. "Enough of that. Make the call and then be ready with a smile when they get back."

She pulled a pot from the cabinet and filled it with water, then tied an apron around her waist, humming softly as she flitted around the kitchen for pasta, sauce, and a spoon.

~

By the time the food was cooked, the kids were back, hungry and cranky as predicted, Debbie's diaper soaked through. Larry didn't come inside.

Monday morning, I called my lawyer and told him what had happened. "Is there any chance he gets the kids?" I asked.

The pause that followed was enough to worry me. "Under normal circumstances, no," he said slowly.

When he didn't say more, I pressed him. "Why aren't these normal circumstances?"

"They likely are. As long as he can't prove adultery against you."

"Me?" I didn't have to feign outrage.

"Look, Mrs. Diamond—"

"Bev," I reminded him.

"Bev. I believe you. But if he manufactures solid-enough evidence, it turns into a case of 'he said, she said.' And if *we* don't have evidence of his infidelity, things get a lot trickier."

"But isn't that illegal?"

There was a very loaded pause. "Ye-es," he said, drawing the word out to multiple syllables. "How much do you know about Tom Stanton?"

Tom Stanton had been Sam's opponent six years earlier. Sam won in a landslide when a teenage mistress came forward pregnant with an out-of-wedlock child that she said was Tom's. "Mostly what was in the papers," I said.

Another long pause. "My partner represented him in the paternity suit. She dropped it entirely when he lost the election."

I sat for a moment, trying to figure out why he was bringing that up, and then—"You don't think Sam paid her to lie, do you?" I tried to remember what Larry had said about the whole ordeal, but he had been very hush-hush, telling me that I didn't need to worry about things like that. After all, I was a newlywed.

A few months earlier, I would have told Greg that he didn't know Larry if he could even insinuate such a thing.

But it turned out I was the one who didn't know Larry. And the man who had stood in my house threatening to take my children—well, I didn't know what he was capable of.

"I will find the evidence," I said resolutely. "You can count on that."

"Good," Greg said. "He can claim whatever he wants, but if we have solid proof, the court will almost always side with the mother."

I thanked him, and he said he would draft up a visitation agreement to send to Larry's lawyer, as no judge would agree he could walk in and take the children whenever he felt like it.

But that "almost always" echoed frighteningly in my head as I kissed their little heads and tucked them in that night.

33

As July wore on and eventually faded into the swampy heat of August, Michael, Stuart, and I took our show on the road, hitting every country club, Hadassah, and YWCA in Maryland. My father had it much easier as a member of the House, needing only to focus on his constituents in Montgomery County. We had twenty-three counties of varying populations to appeal to.

"Why are we bothering coming way out here?" Stuart complained as we drove to meet with a small group of women way out in Cumberland—a three-hour drive from our office. "You can bet Sam doesn't bother with this nonsense."

"That's exactly why," I said. "Sam focuses on Montgomery, Prince George's, and Baltimore and ignores everyone else."

"Because he knows how to win," Stuart grumbled.

"It's a gamble," I admitted. "But if we can get the outliers, we have a better shot. It's why we started talking to women in the first place." And even Stuart had to admit that was an overwhelming success. Did we know they would vote? No. But if my mother was right and even a fraction of them pressured their husbands into switching their allegiance . . .

"We've got nothing to lose," Michael said, looking up from his notes. "And everything to gain."

"People out here aren't voting for a Jewish candidate," Stuart said. "We're going to get booed out of the hall if we're lucky."

He wasn't wrong. Sam was enough of a WASP (even if he hadn't ever attended church outside of seeking votes as far as I knew) to not be seen as a threat in the more rural populations. And Maryland, once you got out of the DC and Baltimore areas, was the South.

"If we don't mention it, I'm not sure they'll know," I said. "You've got a straight nose, and it's not like you wear a yarmulke."

"So you want him to lie?" Stuart asked.

"Did I say that? No. If anyone asks, you tell the truth. But we don't exactly lead with the Passover story even at a Hadassah speech."

"You two bicker like an old married couple," Michael said mildly. "Should I be worried? Are Mom and Dad getting divorced?"

I leaned back in my seat, stung.

Michael turned around when I didn't reply. "Sorry. I didn't mean—"

"Just focus on your speech, please," I said.

For a couple of minutes no one spoke. "Actually, I kind of have news on that front."

"Your speech?"

"No," he said. "The divorce. I called around, and it's a judge I know. He agreed to hear the case in October."

"October!"

"Is that too soon?"

I didn't know how to answer that question. No. It wasn't soon enough. But the PI hadn't turned up any evidence, and I had yet to figure out how I would prove adultery if we didn't have that. And then we only had two months to find actual evidence, or I would be stuck with him for another year while we waited for a no-fault divorce.

Which was the best-case scenario, I reminded myself, my lawyer's insinuation about Tom Stanton ringing in my ears.

When I finally looked up, Michael was still turned around watching me and even Stuart was paying far more attention to the rearview mirror than he should have been. "October is perfect," I said, feigning confidence. "But while I have your rapt attention, we should probably talk about next week."

"What's next week?"

I grinned wickedly. "On second thought, let's discuss that back in the office. It's a bit controversial, and Stuart may drive off the road." His brows came together in the rearview mirror, and I refused to say more.

~

"Absolutely not," Stuart said.

Michael held up a hand in his direction, but didn't take his eyes off me. "Let her finish," he said.

"We need her," I said simply. "White women alone won't win this election."

"And this woman—?"

"Helen," I said. "Helen Walker."

"Helen."

"I suggest you call her Delegate Walker when we speak to her," I said. "As a sign of respect."

Stuart got up and started pacing. "If we even sit down with this woman, half the men in this state will actively campaign against us."

"Half of the *white* men," I said quietly.

He spun to look at me. "What are you implying?"

I shrugged innocently. "I'm not implying anything. If you took it to mean something, then perhaps you should examine your own conscience."

Suddenly he was in my face, leaning over me in my chair. I didn't flinch, despite how intimidating he was right then, and I stared him down as Michael grabbed his shoulders and pulled him back.

"She's going to ruin us," Stuart said to Michael.

"My father agreed we should meet with her," I said. "He called her office himself to get the appointment."

While I wouldn't admit it to Stuart, my father had initially reacted the same way he did. The parts of the state that wouldn't like Michael being Jewish would be even less happy about courting support from

Helen Walker. But as I explained why the time was right to look at different demographics of voters, he not only came around but became more animated than I had seen him since Mama left.

"She's already in the state House of Delegates," I said. "And she's running for state senator. If she wins that—and she's ahead in the polls—she'll be the first anywhere in the country."

"And she's in Baltimore," Michael said, thinking.

"They don't vote," Stuart said.

"Which *they* are we referring to?" I asked. "Because you told me women don't either."

Michael held his hands up in a "time out" gesture but took a few seconds before he spoke. "There's no harm in a meeting," he said eventually. "Especially if Bernie Gelman thinks it'll work."

I fought the urge to stick my tongue out at Stuart. But he wasn't looking at me. There was some silent conversation that I wasn't a part of happening between the two of them, and eventually Stuart nodded.

"Great," I said, ignoring their little moment. "Because we need Baltimore to win. And if you meant what you said about wanting to represent all of Maryland, we need to actually represent *everyone* in Maryland."

34

Driving into Baltimore to meet with Delegate Walker was a very different experience from driving into the same city to meet with Hadassah groups. Baltimore was one of the first Southern cities to integrate schools after *Brown v. Board of Education*, but housing-wise, it was still very much a segregated city. And as we neared the office she kept near Druid Hill Park when she wasn't in Annapolis, the faces we saw on the street nearly all reflected her constituency.

"I don't think we're in Kansas anymore," Stuart said mildly.

"Don't be rude," I said. "Druid Hill Park is lovely."

"I'm so glad you have so much leisure time for trips to parks," Stuart said. "But this is your harebrained idea, so let's get back to this meeting."

"Are you the tortoise, then? You do drive like one."

Michael started laughing, and Stuart glared at him. We continued on in silence until Stuart parked in a spot on the street.

We got out, bringing a box of Michael's new flyers with the headshot Marilyn's fiancé had taken of him, when a boy, maybe ten years old, ran up to the car. "Watch your car for a quarter, mister?" he asked Stuart as Stuart locked the door.

"Why would I give you a quarter for that?"

I opened my handbag, but Michael reached into his pocket. "Here's a dollar," he said. "When we get back, you go buy yourself some candy and a comic book, okay?"

"Yes sir! Thank you, mister!" The boy grabbed the dollar and shoved it into his pocket, then climbed up onto the hood of the car, his back against the windshield, and crossed his arms.

"What are you giving him a dollar for?" Stuart asked as we walked away. "You don't see any of these other cars being watched. He just assumed we were scared to be here."

"Maybe," Michael said. "But how often can you make someone's day for as little as a dollar?"

Stuart shrugged, and I found myself smiling as I peeked back at the little boy. It was the same scam at Griffith Stadium when Papa used to take me to watch the Senators play. And Papa always paid up, explaining to me that he didn't care about the car; he cared about helping others.

"What if he just spends it on candy?" I asked once.

"What he does with it once it's in his pocket is his business," Papa had said. "But what's not worth much to us may be worth a lot to others."

I should invite Papa to the office sometime, I thought. *He'd love Michael.*

I glanced at Stuart, and my smile faded. Stuart would probably take it as an affront somehow.

~

Her office was small, above a hair salon, but Delegate Walker met us at the door herself. I recognized her because Papa had a stack of clippings I had looked through.

"You must be Mr. Landau," she said, addressing Michael.

"Delegate Walker," I said, making sure he didn't mistake her for a secretary. She was in her fifties, according to the newspaper articles, but looked much younger, with straightened hair and red lipstick. "Thank you so much for meeting with us. I'm Beverly Gelman Diamond—you spoke with my father last week."

She looked me over sternly, nodding her approval as she reached my shoes. She had been a teacher and still commanded that air of not accepting failure in any form. "Won't you come in?" she asked.

A secretary sat at a desk in the corner, a phone receiver held to her ear, typing as she listened, a lit cigarette smoldering in the ashtray in front of her.

Delegate Walker led us to a desk in the opposite corner and moved to pull a third chair to the visitor side, but Michael took it himself, which she noted with a nod.

"You're younger than I expected," she said to Michael. "That picture in the *Washington Post* didn't do you any favors."

"No, ma'am, it did not," I agreed, pulling one of Michael's flyers from the box and setting it on her desk. "That's why we got new ones taken a few weeks ago."

"A much better likeness," she said. "I think I know why you're here, but why don't you tell me anyway?" She spoke with a hint of a Southern accent that revealed her Georgia birth, but the thirty years she had spent in Baltimore were evident in her voice as well.

"Mrs.—Delegate Walker," Michael said, and I wanted to kick him. We'd gone over this at least a dozen times. She raised an eyebrow at the correction but said nothing. "We're here today to ask for your help."

"Not much good typically comes from a white man showing up here to ask for help," she said smoothly. "But let's see what I can do."

Michael paused a moment, flummoxed, and I moved my foot slightly. A kick would be unprofessional though, so I crossed one ankle behind the other. Then he took a deep breath and continued. "Can I be honest?" She nodded. "I'm a little nervous. You've got a much more impressive résumé than I do."

Delegate Walker laughed, a hearty sound that disarmed even Stuart.

"I mean it," he said. "Suing the city over the civic center was a huge gamble."

"And an even bigger victory," she said. "But I know my record. I don't need you to flatter me. Why are you here?"

Michael nodded. "I'm running for the US Senate. And as things sit right now, I'm going to lose to Sam Gibson."

Delegate Walker's nostrils flared slightly, but that was the only hint that she wasn't a fan.

"We're working hard to make that not the case," he continued. "And we're focusing strongly on underrepresented populations."

She nodded. "I heard you've been making the rounds at women's luncheons."

"We have. And we've had a lot of success there. But I don't want it to be close. And to do that, we need your support."

Her posture was ramrod straight in her high-backed chair, hands folded in her lap with a studied lack of motion. Not a stray blink betrayed her reception of this statement.

And for a full minute, she said nothing.

"Let me see if I understand this correctly: you want me to tell my constituents in Baltimore to vote for one white man from Montgomery County over another white man from Montgomery County. Is that right?"

Stuart's shoulders dropped, but Michael's didn't change.

"Yes, ma'am."

She leaned forward slightly. "I'll be very honest with you. Sam Gibson hasn't done anything for us. He may have signed off on the Civil Rights Act two years ago, but I've got a long memory, and I don't forget a filibuster on something that important. But from where I sit, I haven't yet seen how you'll be any different."

Michael leaned in as well, and though I could only see his profile, I could tell he was impressed by her bringing up that filibuster. "He and I may share a race and a gender, but that's where the similarities end," Michael said earnestly. "That filibuster was sickening. The reason I'm here today, instead of just campaigning in white neighborhoods, is because I want to represent all of Maryland. Not just the people whom the Founders thought mattered. You said you didn't see how we'll be different, but has Sam Gibson made an appointment to see you? Do you think he's even read up on what you've accomplished up here?"

"That man wouldn't set foot on this side of town," she agreed.

"No. And he wouldn't ask women to support him either. Much less women of color. He's great at kissing babies and charming those mothers, but his focus is on himself, not bettering the lives of his constituents."

"And yours is?"

I adored her. If it wouldn't take me more than an hour to get to work each day in a car I didn't have, I would have switched campaigns.

"Yes," Michael said simply. "I believe holding office is an act of public service."

"Whereas most people who run for political office like power," she said. Her head turned in my direction. "Your father was one of the few exceptions, which is why I took this meeting."

"He speaks very highly of you," I said.

"I was surprised he remembered me. I only met him once, before I was in the House."

"Yes, but he started in the state House too. And he's been following your career."

She smiled, her eyes turning down at the corners. "They don't make them like him anymore."

I thought about Larry. "No, ma'am, they do not." Then I realized Michael was watching me with an amused smile. "But Michael here is—"

"No Bernie Gelman," he cut me off smoothly, saving me the embarrassment of trying to figure out how to end that sentence. "You're not wrong about politicians wanting power. It's why I picked the Senate over the House." She tilted her head, listening as he continued. "The Senate was designed to make voting more fair, and a lot of the time it does the opposite." Delegate Walker nodded. Michael glanced at me, but I was lost.

"How are you going to fix that?" she asked.

"I can't," he admitted. "Not without tearing down all of Congress, and I don't think I have the power to do that. But I can make a difference from inside. Especially for the people the system hurts."

"It's an uphill battle," Delegate Walker said. "That's for sure."

"It is," Michael said. "But you know better than anyone that you won't get anywhere if you don't try."

She gazed out the window over our heads for what felt like several minutes, though I doubted it was really that long. Then she turned her sharp eyes back on Michael. "And what do I get in return for my support?"

I held my breath. If he gave the wrong answer, we would be politely but firmly shown the door.

"My ear," he said. "I can't promise that I know what your constituents need. But I want to. And I'm not so arrogant to think that I can blindly make decisions that will benefit people with experiences that are different from mine." He looked at me sideways and smiled. "That's why Beverly is here. She came barreling into my office and announced I was going to hire her as my new campaign manager." Stuart sat up a little straighter. "And yes, I liked the idea of having Bernie Gelman's daughter on staff. But Bev hasn't been wrong—about anything really. Women, historically, haven't voted in large numbers. But they should. And your community is the same."

"Congress has made it a lot harder for my people to vote," she said. "Bernie helped, but there's a lot of work to be done still."

"And there's only so much one man can do," Michael said. "I know that. But I want to work toward it. And I promise you, Delegate, that if you help me get elected, I will listen to you as well as I've listened to Bev here."

She looked out the window again, then stood up. The three of us followed suit, but she waved Michael and Stuart back down. "You two sit. I'd like to have a word with Beverly here." She gestured for me to follow her, and I did, out of the office, down a flight of stairs, and onto the street. "Let's walk around the block," she said.

I matched her steps but felt a bead of sweat forming at the back of my dress that had nothing to do with the oppressive heat.

"Is it true what he said?" she asked.

"Which part?"

"The storming into his office demanding to run his campaign part."

I grinned sheepishly. "It is."

"Why?" she looked at me. "The truth now."

"My husband is Sam Gibson's campaign manager," I said. "I caught him with his secretary, and he threatened to sell the house."

"He can't do that."

"I know that now. But I wanted to get back at him."

She took this in, then stopped to greet a young man sitting on the corner by name.

"What about what he said about listening to you?"

I nodded. "All true. Even when he disagreed."

"Then he's genuine?"

"He is," I said slowly, realizing that I meant it. I told her about Stuart changing my speech and Michael pivoting to adjust to what I had said.

"Interesting."

"Delegate Walker—"

"Helen," she said.

I hesitated, the urge to refrain from using my elder's first name as a sign of respect battling with the show of respect involved in doing what she asked. "Helen," I said finally. "Do you remember that scandal that took down Sam Gibson's opponent six years ago?"

She nodded. "I believe I do."

"My lawyer—I'm not supposed to repeat this, but my lawyer thinks they fabricated that. To win."

Helen peered at me carefully. "Haven't you been around politics your whole life? You sound surprised. Of course he made that up."

"That wasn't the kind of campaign my father ran."

"No," she said. "But if you bring that up to him, I'd wager he has the same reaction I did."

"That may be true. Maybe he shielded me from how ugly campaigns were. But Sam *cannot* win again."

"Because of your husband? What happens to you when he's out of a job?"

Larry had said that, but then I was so focused on keeping the kids that I hadn't processed it. Larry would have to get another job. The courts would require he support me and the kids. But we could lose the house—not out of Larry's spite, but because of my own.

I didn't reply for the full length of the block as I thought about what that could mean.

While I pondered this, Helen stopped to scold a boy who was sitting on the hood of a car.

"Julian Barnes, you get down from that car right now, or I will tell your mama that you're scamming people out of quarters again."

This shook me from my ruminations as I realized she was speaking to the boy sitting on Stuart's car.

He hopped down immediately. "Aw, Miss Helen, I didn't mean no harm."

"That man paid you?"

He glanced around furtively to see if Michael was anywhere in sight. "Yes, ma'am."

"How much?"

"Miss Helen—"

"I asked you a question."

"A dollar."

She nodded, biting her lip slightly.

"You ain't gonna make me give it back, are you?"

"Say *ain't* again and I might," she said. "But I think you'd better figure out a way to earn it."

"Earn it?" he squeaked.

"That windshield is looking mighty smudged. Like a boy's been sitting on it."

"I'll clean it, Miss Helen, I promise!"

She patted his head. "That's what I like to hear. Go on and run down to the gas station for a rag. We'll stay here while you're gone."

"Yes, Miss Helen," he said, taking off at full speed.

She chuckled as he disappeared down the block. "I was a schoolteacher for eleven years," she said.

"Oh, I can tell," I said, finally smiling again. "Listen—I'll land on my feet. But this election is more important than what happens to me."

"And you think this Michael Landau will do what he says?"

I nodded. "And if he doesn't, he'll have both of us to deal with."

She let out another hearty laugh. "Yes. I can see where that would be formidable. Let's go tell him I'll work with him after all."

35

I went to visit my father after work to tell him about our meeting with Helen. We'd had our first cooking lesson the week before, and I was pleasantly surprised to see chicken breasts marinating and the oven preheating.

He smiled bashfully as I praised his efforts in the kitchen, and I got to work showing him how to cook the spinach and asparagus I had picked up on my way over. I told him about our meeting—down to the detail of Michael giving the boy a dollar to "watch" the car. He grinned at the same memory I had thought of.

Dinner was on the table when I walked into my own house, and I felt guilty about my mother making my children dinner while I went and did the same for my father. But as much as it would be nice to have the house to myself once in a while, I remembered that I couldn't do the work I was doing if she hadn't moved in.

Helen's words came back to me as the kids prattled on about their afternoon with Nancy's kids. I didn't know what would happen if Michael won. Larry would be out of work—and the reality was that I would be too. Robbie started kindergarten after Labor Day, but only in the mornings, and Debbie had two more years at home. Even if Michael wanted to keep me on staff, I didn't think my mother would agree to that long of a time commitment, and I didn't know that I wanted her to. I wanted to be home with my kids, experiencing their days with them instead of hearing about them after.

Walking away would be better for them.

But what about all the people whom Helen said Sam Gibson hadn't helped?

Who was my responsibility to?

"Beverly," my mother said, reprimanding me. "Robbie asked you a question."

"I'm so sorry, darling," I said to Robbie. "Mommy's head was in the clouds. What was your question?"

~

Exhausted, I excused myself from television with my mother after the kids went to bed, then cleaned the kitchen and changed into my nightgown. I pulled back my lovely pink bedspread and admired the room before turning off the lights. It was strange how getting rid of Larry turned the house into more of a home. Then again, after six years of being Mrs. Diamond, being just Bev meant that I *was* the home.

Maybe it was the cup of coffee I accepted at my father's house, but sleep didn't want to come. And after I mentally created a shopping list for teaching my father how to make meatloaf, Michael's words repeated in my brain. *The Senate was designed to make voting more fair, and a lot of the time it does the opposite.*

I should have asked my father what that meant. A glance at the radium dial on the alarm clock next to the bed told me it was too late to call him. He was in bed by 9:30 most nights. But Michael had said he was a night owl.

I flipped onto my other side. I should just ask him about it in the morning.

But now, tired as I was, I was wide awake. With a sigh, I turned on my bedside lamp, picked up the receiver, and dialed the operator to ask her to connect me to Michael Landau in Silver Spring.

As the phone rang once, twice, and then a third time, I debated hanging up. Then Michael's voice came on the line. "Hello?"

"Hi—it's Beverly."

"Is everything all right?"

"Sorry—yes—I know it's late. I just had a question." *I shouldn't have called him,* I thought. There was a rustling sound and then a click that sounded like a lamp. "You're not in bed, are you?"

He chuckled. "I'm not."

"Good," I said, realizing there was something innately intimate about talking to him from my bed, even if he didn't know that was where I was. Somehow if he had been in bed too, it would have been worse.

"What can I do for you?"

"I wanted to know what you meant earlier—about the Senate."

"About the Senate?"

"You said it was meant to make things more fair but sometimes does the opposite?"

"Ah," he said. "That. You know how the House is divvied up by population?"

I nodded, then remembered he couldn't see me—which was a very good thing. "Yes."

"So Maryland has fewer delegates than New York, California, and all the bigger states. But in the Senate, every state has two representatives."

"Which makes all the states equal."

"Exactly. But they created that system for the Southern states because they had smaller populations of people who were eligible to vote, and the South wanted more independence and didn't want the North making decisions for them."

"Which led to the Civil War."

"Ostensibly," Michael said. I knew what he meant there. "But giving each state—including those with sometimes millions fewer eligible voters—an equal say was designed to make the states equal."

"I understand that—but how is that *not* fair?"

"People in different places have different needs." That was true even just in our small state, as we saw earlier in the day. "And with voting regulations on the books that prevent certain populations from being able to vote easily, the senators in some places wind up representing the people who are keeping other groups down. And even where that isn't the case, it disenfranchises people when it's not 'one man, one vote.'"

I thought back to 1960, when I went to vote and several women at the club asked me why I was bothering. *Because it's the right thing to do,* I had said. Their responses surprised me when they said their votes didn't matter. It was the opposite of what my father had taught me.

But what Michael was saying meant they were right.

"Then—you mean only local elections matter?"

"No, not at all," he said quickly. "Local elections matter, of course, but when the House advances a bill, the Senate can kill it. And when it's mostly just one demographic voting in large numbers, those minority voices get drowned out."

It was a complicated concept, but I could see how the way it was going wasn't benefiting people the way the Founders intended. Or maybe it was—they certainly wouldn't have wanted me voting. And Helen's mere existence had to have them rolling in their graves.

"Thank you for explaining," I said. "I think I'll be able to sleep now."

I could hear the amusement in his voice. "So when you asked if I was in bed, it was because *you* were?"

"You can get your mind right out of that gutter," I said primly.

Michael laughed. "I'm teasing. In my mind you are fully clothed at the kitchen table."

He *had*, after all, seen my kitchen.

"I should go," I said.

"Wait—before you do—thank you."

"For what?"

"For whatever you said to Helen today. I'm not enough of a fool to think she was going to lend her support before that talk you two had."

"I didn't do anything," I said. "She just wanted to know if you were honest or not."

"And what did you tell her?"

I grinned. "That you're as crooked as they come."

"Perfect," he said.

There was a long pause. "Good night, Michael."

"Good night, Beverly. Thank you again."

There was a creaking sound just before he hung up, and I wondered if he had been lying about being in bed.

"You can stop that right now," I said out loud to the empty room.

"Stop what?" my mother asked, opening the door without knocking. "I was just getting changed for bed."

I shook my head. "Nothing. I was talking to myself."

"Sounded like an extended conversation," she said.

"Good night, Mama," I said pointedly.

"You're a grown woman," she said. "If you want to have a boyfriend over, I won't stop you."

"Mama!"

"What? I've been thinking I might dip a toe into the dating world myself."

I put a pillow over my face and mimed suffocating myself.

"Women have needs too, Beverly," she said as she closed the door behind her, and I debated whether using the pillow to put myself out of my misery was better than using it on her.

But inappropriately intimate conversations or not, I realized staying in the campaign *was* the best move for my children. Michael was going to make the world a better place for them if he won. They might not understand it, but that was worth the sacrifice now.

I just wished I could get the way he smiled when he told Helen about me demanding a job out of my head as I lay awake, trying to sleep.

36

We spent the next three mornings in Baltimore, first touring the city with Helen and then preparing for the actual event that they would cohost. She suggested holding it in Druid Hill Park itself on Sunday afternoon.

"Isn't that a gamble with weather?"

"If you're not willing to gamble, you'll never win," she said. "Having it in the park holds special significance. It's one of the few integrated parks. It shows your dedication to the community's needs—that's where they wanted to build that civic center. And it means women can come because their children can play. That won't work in a hall."

Stuart's mouth was hanging open by the time she was done speaking. "Close your mouth," I whispered to him. "You'll catch flies."

He closed his mouth and glared at me, but there was far less malice in it than usual.

"You can admit I was right," I said quietly.

"I'm not going that far. But you weren't necessarily wrong."

I grinned. That was good enough. And thanks to my cousin Marilyn, we had campaign money to rent a microphone, speakers, and a small platform to serve as a stage. Helen said she would deal with permits and making sure people were there.

"I can tell them I'm voting for you," she said. "And for some, that will be enough. But you're going to need to do more than smile and wave."

"Would you be willing to look at my speech?" Michael asked. "I don't want to make any missteps."

She smiled. "You don't think I'm letting you up there without knowing what you're going to say, do you?"

"Believe me, ma'am, I wouldn't even go up to that podium without your say-so."

She leaned over to me. "I see why you like this one." I started sputtering something to the effect of him being my boss, but she winked at me. "You're giving yourself away now."

Thankfully Michael and Stuart were discussing something else and missed that whole exchange.

~

The morning of the speech in Baltimore, I borrowed my mother's Chanel suit again, and had just applied my lipstick, when my mother called to me from the hall.

"I can't be late," I said. "What is it?"

"Where do you keep the thermometer?" she asked.

I looked at my reflection in the mirror. *Not today,* I thought. "In the medicine cabinet," I said lightly. "Why?"

"Debbie is awfully warm," she said.

"It's summer."

My mother shook her head. "See for yourself."

I found Debbie in her bed, and my heart sank. Even getting her to nap now was a struggle. She usually catapulted out of bed the second she woke up in the morning. Her cheeks were flushed, and her eyes were closed, her chest rising and falling rapidly. "Oh, sweetie," I said, sinking down next to her on the bed. "What's the matter?"

She looked at me pitifully. "I sick."

I felt her forehead with the back of my hand, then remembered Rosa's trick. My lips were hovering just above her forehead when I realized I had lipstick on. I reached for a tissue from her nightstand

and scrubbed until it came away clean and then pressed my lips to her forehead. I didn't need the thermometer.

I swore softly. "That a bad word," Debbie said.

"I'm sorry, darling. It is." I stood up. "Mama is just going to get you some medicine to make you feel better."

She grabbed my hand. "Mama, stay."

I hesitated. "You'll feel better with the medicine," I said. "And Grandma will be here while Mama is at work today."

She started to cry weakly. "Want you, Mama."

I closed my eyes and pinched the bridge of my nose as she continued to cry. And then I gave in. "Okay. Mama will stay. Let me just get you the medicine and make a phone call, and I'll be right back. Okay?"

She nodded, still crying, and I turned to find my mother in the doorway. "Can you grab the Tylenol Elixir from the medicine cabinet?" I asked. "I need to call the office and let them know I'm not coming."

"You can go," my mother said. "I'll be fine with her."

I looked back at my daughter in her bed. Debbie *would* be fine. Probably. But what if the Tylenol didn't bring her fever down? I didn't want to be unreachable and an hour away if she had to get to a doctor. And as much as I adored Rosa, when I was sick as a child, there was no substitute for my mother.

Slowly, I shook my head. "No. I'm going to stay." She looked at me for several seconds, then nodded and went toward the bathroom. "I can give it to her," I called after my mother.

"I'm perfectly capable of reading directions on a bottle," she said.

My shoulders drooped as I returned to my bedroom. I sat on the edge of the bed and lifted the receiver, then dialed the number for the office, which would normally be empty on a Sunday. I had planned to drive my mother's car there to meet Michael and Stuart to drive up to Baltimore together.

Stuart answered on the third ring. "Landau campaign."

"It's Beverly."

"You haven't left yet?"

I sighed. "Can you put Michael on, please?"

"He's going over his speech."

"Stuart, please."

He huffed into the phone and then called for Michael, who came onto the line a few seconds later. "Beverly? Everything okay?"

I hadn't cried when I caught Larry with Linda. Not when he threatened to sell the house. Not even when Robbie had colic, and I was so sleep deprived I thought I was going to lose my mind. But I was close to tears right then. This was my speech. I arranged this. If it went well, it would be the biggest victory of his campaign. And I had to miss it because I was a mother before anything else.

"Debbie has a fever," I said thickly.

"Is she okay?"

"Likely yes. Kids get fevers, and it's often nothing. But—"

"You need to stay with her," he finished. It wasn't a question. "Does she need to see a doctor? Stuart can drive you."

I looked up at the ceiling to keep my suddenly moist eyes from spilling over. "No, no. We're giving her Tylenol now and my mother is here with her car. But she wants me."

"Of course," Michael said.

"I'm sorry."

"For what? You didn't get her sick."

"This is my job. Stuart wouldn't miss a speech for something like this."

"Stuart doesn't have kids," Michael said gently. "It's apples and oranges."

Stuart is a man, I thought bitterly. Larry wouldn't have stayed even if Debbie had begged him.

"I'll call you after," Michael said. "You just take care of Debbie. Don't worry about me."

"I'm not worried. I wanted to be there."

There was a pause. "I wanted you there too," he said. "But family comes first. Always and forever."

"We need to go," I heard Stuart saying.

"I'm sorry again," I said. "And do me a favor?"

"Don't worry, I'm going to listen to everything Helen says."

"I know that. I was going to ask you to kick Stuart."

Michael laughed. "I'll see what I can do. I'll call you after," he repeated.

~

Debbie's temperature dropped within an hour with the Tylenol in her.

"I wish we'd had that when you were young," my mother said. "We had to make do with ice baths and cold compresses."

I shuddered. I had blocked those memories out. Tylenol was a relatively new medicine for kids, but when Robbie got chicken pox two years earlier, it had been a lifesaver.

Debbie spent much of the morning on the sofa in front of the television, while my mother took Robbie out to the park. She had suggested the club so he could go swimming, but I didn't want her and her car that far away if Debbie took a turn for the worse.

Larry was going to need to pay for a car, I decided. Especially if my mother moved back home.

And if Sam lost, he had to find a job that paid better.

Debbie napped, and I tried not to worry about what was happening in Baltimore. Her fever stayed down with the medicine, and a telltale rash indicating roseola began creeping across her torso by the time she woke up.

"Phew," I told her. "We can play connect the dots on your tummy, but at least it's nothing serious." She snuggled in tight against me, and I kissed the top of her head. If she wasn't sick, she would have pushed me away, so I would take what I could get.

I made dinner, no longer worried about keeping the kids separate—Robbie had caught roseola just before his second birthday—and bathed them. Robbie went right to sleep, but Debbie asked to sleep in my bed.

"Just because you're sick," I told her.

"I be better tomowow," she promised.

"It might take a few more days than that," I said, smiling as she nestled up against me again.

I waited until her breathing had become regular to leave. She had her thumb in her mouth, which she had stopped doing months earlier, but I wasn't going to worry about it right then.

I was, however, worried that I hadn't heard from Michael.

But as I reached the living room, I stopped short. Michael was sitting in the chair opposite my mother, a drink untouched in front of him.

"How is she?" he asked when he saw me. I was too stunned to speak first.

"Sleeping," I said finally. "What are you doing here?"

"I wanted to tell you how it went in person," he said. "And make sure Debbie was okay."

"A call would have been smarter. What if it was the measles?"

He grinned sheepishly. "I've had the measles. Mumps too."

I shook my head. "I don't know why I bother trying to tell you anything at all."

My mother stood up. "Sit," she said. "I need to go clean up in the kitchen. Michael, always lovely to see you."

That kitchen was spotless, which I knew because I had cleaned it before I bathed the kids.

"So she's okay?" he asked once she left.

"She will be in a few days. Roseola."

"I don't know what that is."

"You had it as a kid most likely," I said. "Everyone gets it once. The pediatrician said it wasn't serious when Robbie had it."

"Good," Michael said. Then he smiled—not his political smile. A big, goofy grin that made him look like a kid. "You should have been there—sorry, I know you couldn't. But, Bev, it was . . ." He shook his head. "Helen thinks there were two thousand people there at least."

"Two thousand?"

"Not counting the kids. She was right about everything. You were right about everything."

I should have been happy. And I was. But I was still upset I had missed the victory.

"Even Stuart said so."

I chuckled finally. "He did not."

"Well, maybe not in those words." He smiled again.

"Tell me what happened," I said, sitting where my mother had been.

He gave the long version, leaving out no details. We saw the way Helen appeared to be a celebrity in Baltimore when she took us around to see her part of town, but Michael had underestimated the drawing power she had. The event was slated to last an hour, and he said he stayed for four, talking to people who waited in a line to meet him.

"Bev," he said, reaching across the gap between us to take my hand. "I think we can win this thing."

I looked down at his hand on mine and remembered Larry's threat. I didn't know if it was the expression on my face or if he realized he had crossed a line, but he drew his hand back quickly.

"It's late," he said. "I should let you go. I just—I'm sorry. I was excited."

"I appreciate it," I said earnestly. "I do." He stood and I followed. "I'll walk you to the door."

"Don't worry if you need to stay with Debbie tomorrow," he said. "I'll handle Stuart."

"I don't give a hoot what Stuart says about it."

"Still," Michael said, lingering at the door. "If he says anything rude, I'll give him that kick."

We stood there smiling at each other until I heard my mother's footsteps in the kitchen. "Right. Well, I'll likely be there tomorrow. Now that we know it's nothing major."

"Whatever you need to do."

"Thank you."

He looked like he wanted to say something else, but the moment passed, and he put his hand on the doorknob. "Good night, Bev."

"Good night."

He looked at me one last time and then left. I leaned against the door once it was closed and exhaled.

"He's gone, then?" my mother asked.

"Why are you saying it like that's a question?"

She grinned at me mischievously. "I could have slept with Debbie."

"MAMA!"

"What? Like I said, you're a grown woman."

I pushed past her. "I'm not having this conversation. Good night, Mama."

"Where did I go wrong with you?" she asked with a sigh. "Good night."

37

The phones were ringing off the hook when I came into the office on Monday. We had gotten a third line installed, and Charlie was manning that one, with Claire and Stuart on the other two. Every time one of them hung up, the phone rang again.

"What's going on?" I asked Paul.

He grinned at me. "You missed a hell of a speech."

"So I heard. But who's calling?"

"The press—the *Baltimore Sun* wants an interview."

"Take it."

"Stuart already did," Paul said. "The *Montgomery Sentinel*, the *Prince George's Sentinel*, the *Frederick Post-Gazette*," he said, ticking them off on his fingers.

"No *Washington Post*?"

"Not yet."

I pursed my lips. That was the one we needed. Then again, I realized, I—or more accurately, my mother—might be able to swing that one if they didn't call on their own. Mama had been friends with Anna Wainwright for decades—a relationship that had certainly been mutually beneficial for my father and Anna's husband, who had taken over management of the *Post* when Anna's father stepped down. I never liked Henry, but Anna was a Washington icon.

"And speaking engagements. All of Baltimore wants him now."

Baltimore was a major victory—especially if the minority groups turned out to vote. Sam certainly hadn't encouraged or inspired them to do so. We would never get the more conservative Annapolis, but if we had a strong-enough foothold in the rest of the state, particularly the most heavily populated areas—namely Montgomery and Prince George's Counties—we wouldn't need it.

Charlie stepped away from the desk in a brief lull, only for the phone to ring again. "I'll take it," I said, shooing him away.

He looked at me gratefully. "Thank you. I'm dying for a cup of coffee."

We need more help, I thought as I sank into the desk chair. And now that we actually had the money to pay for it, I decided to give Fran a call. If she was still working the perfume counter at Woodies, a secretarial job would likely be a welcome reprieve. "Landau campaign," I said into the receiver.

"I'm calling for Beverly Diamond," a woman's voice said.

"Speaking."

"Please hold for Mr. Patterson."

Great timing, I thought as I crossed my fingers, toes, and legs that the private investigator he had hired had turned something up.

"Beverly," he said. "Is this a good time?"

I looked at the chaos of the office and saw the phone ring again within a second of Stuart hanging up. "A little busy, but it's fine. What can I do for you?"

He sighed. "The private investigator has been following Larry for three weeks and hasn't found a thing," he said. "I would guess his lawyer told him to lay low." He paused. "Have you given any more thought to talking to his secretary?"

I hadn't. "Yes," I lied. "I'll do it if you think it's absolutely necessary."

"It's absolutely necessary," he said.

"Right. I'll take care of it."

"In good news, his lawyer agreed to the visitation agreement with only a couple of modifications."

"Which are?"

"In your favor. He's not set up for overnight visits—*yet*, he said. And he only wants a weekend visit every other week during campaign season."

Of course, I thought bitterly. He wanted to take them when I actually had time to be with them. He knew I was working too now.

"And if all goes well," Greg continued, "this will be knit up with a neat little bow by the time the election comes around."

"You're mixing your metaphors there."

"Excuse me?"

"Never mind." It was either *all knit up* or *tied up with a neat little bow*. But what would a man know about knitting or wrapping presents?

I thanked him and ended the call, the phone ringing again immediately. "Landau campaign." At least I was too busy to worry about how I was going to convince Linda of literally anything.

～

By the time I left the office, the sky was ominously dark, thunder rumbling in the distance as a summer storm came in.

I debated going back inside and asking Michael for a ride. He had made it clear he would give me one whenever I needed it. But I had been enough of a burden the day before. And the spark I had felt when he put his hand on mine . . . No—better not.

The rain held off until I got onto the bus, then began to fall in thick drops that pinged off the roof and reduced visibility even with the wipers on full speed.

The bus stop was only a block from my house, but I didn't have an umbrella, and the newspaper I had brought with me that morning did little to protect me from the rain that seemed to be falling sideways. I was soaked through by the time I reached my front porch and wished

I could shake off like a dog. Instead, I opened the door and yelled for my mother to please bring me a towel.

"Your great-aunt Ada would have skinned you alive for shouting in the doorway like that," she said as she looked me over. "Don't you walk in this house dripping wet. I'll get a towel."

"Why *did* your parents send you to spend a summer with her?" I asked as she handed me a towel, and I dried off as best as I could before removing my shoes and stepping inside. "You never would tell me."

"And I still won't," she said primly. "Now go get changed before you catch your death. Why didn't Michael drive you home in this weather?"

I pretended I hadn't heard her as I went to my room and peeled off my wet clothes and changed into dry ones. If the storm didn't let up, I wouldn't be able to wash my hair, so I had to hope wetting and setting it would be good enough.

A huge clap of thunder boomed, and the kids both screamed. "What's all this?" I asked, coming out of my room.

"Scared," Debbie said, running to me.

I felt her forehead with my lips—cool and dry. If she slept through the night and woke up fever-free, we could stop giving her the Tylenol. "There's nothing to be scared of," I said. "You and Robbie make more noise than this when you don't want a bath."

Another boom of thunder punctuated my sentence and Robbie joined Debbie at my legs. I hugged them both to me. "In good news, unless it stops by bedtime, no baths tonight."

Robbie looked up at me. "Really?"

"Really. It's not safe in a storm."

"Gramma will make us anyway."

I laughed. He wasn't wrong. She'd boil water in the kettle and scrub them down that way like people who lived before plumbing. "I'll see what kind of magic I can work with her."

~

When the storm hadn't abated, Mama grudgingly agreed to let them just wash their faces and hands—a true sign that she was softening in her old age. That or the kids had finally broken her.

I got them into bed and then went and joined my mother in the living room, where she was watching television. "I have a favor to ask," I said as I curled up on the sofa, tucking my bare feet under me.

"Ask it at the next commercial," she said.

Thunder cracked again, and the power went out.

"Oh, for Pete's sake," Mama said. "The one break I get. Do you have candles?"

"I'll get them," I said as I rose to feel my way to the kitchen. I found two, then fumbled in the junk drawer for matches.

I lit the candles, brought them back to the living room, and set them on the coffee table.

"What were you going to ask me?"

I sat back down. "Have you spoken to Anna Wainwright lately?"

She pursed her lips at me. "I've been a little busy these last few months. Someone doesn't exactly give me time off—or pay me."

I ignored the last part. "Do you think you could give her a call?"

"Why?"

"I want the *Post* to endorse Michael."

"Darling, Anna has nothing to do with the paper. Her father talked about leaving it to her, but Henry expressed interest and that was the end of that."

"I know she doesn't work there, but I also know being in their social circle is practically a guarantee of an endorsement."

She couldn't argue there. Henry was the one who pushed for Johnson to be Kennedy's vice president. And what the Wainwrights wanted frequently happened.

"I'm not sure Michael is exactly . . ." She trailed off.

"He grew up poor," I said. "But I didn't. And I can give him the *Pygmalion* treatment for a night."

She looked unconvinced. "He's a very nice man. And he'd be a breath of fresh air in the Senate, but the Wainwrights . . ."

"They like people in power. And is there anything Henry likes more than *putting* people in power?"

"They endorsed Sam last time."

I met her eyes over the candlelight. "Who introduced Henry to Sam?" I asked point-blank. We both knew it had been my father.

"I'll call her tomorrow," she said. "But don't embarrass me. I don't want to lose my place at their parties if I ever have time to attend one again."

I stood up and kissed my mother on the forehead. "Thank you, Mama," I said.

After picking up my candle, I told her I was going to bed. But first I wet my hair and set it in rollers as best as I could with the small flame's flickering light. I blew out the candle in the bathroom and made my way to the bed, where I found two squishy, sleeping forms. Thunder cracked again, and Debbie whimpered in her sleep. I kissed her forehead, smoothed her hair, and snuggled in beside her.

38

Two days later, I took Mama's car to work—I told her I would need to drive press releases out to different media outlets, which wasn't a lie. I did that in the morning. What I didn't tell her was that I would also be staked out in her car with a scarf over my hair and sunglasses on outside Larry's office, waiting for Linda to come out on her lunch break. Assuming she wasn't making it a "working" lunch in the loosest of all possible interpretations.

I had no idea what her status was with Larry. I had stopped by to see Nancy the day before. With anyone else, I would have beaten around the bush, but I think that's the true definition of friendship—where you can ask absolutely anything with no qualifying information needed.

"I don't know," Nancy said. "I told Arnie that if he so much as mentioned that jerk's name again, he'd be crashing on Larry's couch instead of the other way around."

"When was that?"

"Right after Larry left."

And even if he *had* still been seeing her, a lot could change in a couple of months.

But without warning, Nancy stood up and crossed to the kitchen phone. "What are you doing?" I asked.

"Getting your answer."

I was by her side in a flash. "You can't call Larry!"

She stopped dialing. "Have you lost your mind? I'm calling Arnie."

"Oh," I said weakly, sinking into the chair closest to the phone.

She told the secretary she needed to speak to her husband and tapped her foot impatiently while she waited. "Get him out of his meeting," she said. "Yes, it's an emergency."

"It's not an emergency," I whispered.

Nancy held her hand over the mouthpiece. "How many times have I seen you in the last two months?"

I had picked the kids up from her house a couple of times after my mother had dropped them off there. And we'd met up at the playground a few times. And the Fourth of July. But when you considered that we were at each other's houses at least four times a week before I started working . . .

"Arnie," she said into the phone. "Is Larry still fooling around with his secretary?" She waited while he said something. "The kids are fine. But I need to know about Larry." Another pause. "Yes, it's an emergency. Never you mind why." I could hear a muffled response and fought the urge to crowd around the receiver with Nancy. "I know I said that, but now I'm asking." More muffled words. "Uh-huh. Thanks. That's all I needed." She hung up without saying goodbye.

"He said yes. Larry made some comment about convenience." She scrunched up her nose. "Listen, if the divorce isn't going well, I've got a backyard and a shovel." Her face lit up as an idea hit her. "If we put a pool in over the body, they'll never find him."

I laughed, despite myself. Getting Linda to testify would have been a lot easier if he had broken things off. But that shovel was a great plan B.

Which led to me sitting outside Larry's office at lunchtime in my admittedly shabby disguise.

I had been there the better part of an hour, ducking behind the steering wheel whenever anyone I recognized walked out, before Linda's blonde bob came into view. I slipped out of the car as she passed it and followed her down the block and around the corner before removing my scarf and calling her name.

She turned around, a smile on her lips, which froze and then died as she recognized me. Then she glanced over her shoulder and turned one foot to flee. "Stop," I said, reaching out and grabbing her wrist.

"Let me go!"

I dropped her wrist. "Don't run. I just need to talk to you."

"I have nothing to say," she said, starting to walk away.

"Linda," I said, "I need your help. You owe me that much."

She stopped walking but didn't look at me. "I don't owe you anything."

"How about my kids, then?"

Her shoulders dropped.

"Look," I said, "I'm not here to argue with you. If you want Larry that bad, you can have him. But I do need your help first—and actually it helps you too. He'll be free sooner."

At that, she finally turned around, her brows together in a wary expression. "What do you want?" she asked.

I took a deep breath. "I want you to testify that he committed adultery."

Her eyes widened. "I can't do that."

"Why not? It's the truth. And if you don't, it'll be another year before he's single."

"I don't care about that," she said, and my heart sank. Of course she didn't care. If she was willing to have an affair while he was married with kids, why would another year matter? But when I met her eyes, there was something pitiful in them. And as much as I wanted to hate her, it was hard to hate someone who looked that pathetic and scared.

"Then what's the problem?" I asked, gentler this time. Not because I felt any real sympathy for her, but my mother always said you caught more flies with honey than with vinegar.

For a few seconds that felt like an eternity, she didn't reply, and I was worried she was going to say she was in love with him. There would be no reasoning with that kind of ridiculousness. Never mind that I once thought I was in love with him too. That was a different person. A different life.

"He'll fire me," she whispered.

"That's all?" I asked with a chuckle. "That's easy. You can come work for Michael, then."

She looked suspicious. "Why would you do that?"

I exhaled. "Because I need the divorce to go through. And Larry is threatening to take the kids."

Her expression turned to unsure. It was helpful that she had no poker face. She was maybe twenty-two or twenty-three, but I doubted I had ever been that naive, even at her age. "That doesn't sound like Larry."

No. It didn't sound like the Larry I had thought I knew a few months earlier. "Larry cares about Larry," I said, trying to keep the bitterness out of my voice. "And he wants to win this campaign. He's threatening me so I'll drop out, and Michael will lose."

"Then just do that," she said. "Isn't that easier?"

I looked at this girl. I remembered when Larry hired her—she had to have been fresh out of high school then. Which should have set off a warning bell, as she couldn't have possibly gone to secretarial school. I remarked on how pretty she was, but I was more worried about Sam or someone else in the office being lecherous. Yes, I had been in the exhausted haze of new motherhood, but Larry was attentive back then. Perhaps *attentive* wasn't the right word as that attentiveness was primarily in the bedroom. But I had been secure in our marital life, and it never occurred to me that he would be the problem.

But age and appearance were far from the biggest difference between us if that was her suggestion.

I shook my head. "I can't do that. I may have taken the job to get back at Larry, but it's not about that now."

She nodded knowingly. "I heard him talking to Sam about that."

I recoiled. "About what?"

"Your affair with him."

An alarm rang in my head, though I didn't connect the dots just then.

"There's no affair," I said. "I'm there because he's a good person. He cares about making the world better more than about himself. He's exactly who we want making decisions for our country."

Her mouth opened, and then she shut it again. She did this twice more as she wrestled with something, and for a few seconds, I held out hope.

"No," she said. "I'm sorry. I can't help you." And she turned to walk away.

I grabbed her arm one more time. "Linda," I said. "Think about it. He'd be free. You could marry him. Start your own family."

She looked back at me, her face naked of any real emotion. "He'd leave me if I helped you. If he asked me to testify, I'd do it. But if I help you, I lose everything."

I released her arm and stood on the sidewalk as she walked away from me.

Sinking onto a nearby bench, I put my head in my hands. And I wished that tears would come. Anything to help wash this feeling of dread from my chest.

But eventually, I picked my head up. I had to get the *Post* endorsement. And if the PI hadn't turned anything up by the time I did, that would have to be enough. I would have to quit.

I just hoped that doing enough for Michael wasn't the same as doing too much for Larry to back off.

Which was a problem for another day. Right now, I needed to talk to my mother and make sure she had called Anna Wainwright.

39

I put my dime in the pay phone and dialed. It rang eight times with no answer before I hung up. My mother was probably at the playground or the club with the kids. Their swimming lessons were on Thursdays, but we had talked about them needing to get more practice. Not that my mother would get in a pool herself. If her hair got wet, we wouldn't have to worry about the Soviets anymore because she would unleash a fury that would make nukes look puny.

But she wasn't averse to slipping a teenager some money to play with them in the pool while she sat under an umbrella with her friends.

At least someone is having fun today, I thought.

Then I remembered I had her car.

Playground, then.

I shrugged and slipped back into the driver's seat of her car, heading back toward the office.

Which was in utter bedlam by the time I returned.

I heard the shrieks from the hall, and I rushed in, half-convinced we were under some sort of attack—from whom I didn't know. But I ran in, ready to do battle, only to stop short at the scene in front of me.

Michael had his tie around his head, covering one eye, the hook of a coat hanger where his left hand should have been, a flagpole in his right as he fought off Robbie, who wore Michael's coat, belted at the middle. Debbie sat on top of a file cabinet, clapping her hands and cheering for her brother, while the interns watched in amusement and Stuart glowered over his typewriter.

"What on earth?" I asked, crossing to Debbie, and pulling her off the cabinet.

Michael turned at the sound of my voice, and Robbie stabbed him with a ruler to the ribs. Michael yelped and grabbed at his injury, and I started toward him but stopped when Paul put a hand on my arm. I watched as Michael took his time about "dying."

"Is this the end of Captain Hook?" he cried, just before closing his eyes.

Robbie took a bow for the applauding interns, then ran to hug me.

"What are you doing here?" I asked him, trying not to sound annoyed about the mess. Besides, whatever the reason they were there, it wasn't *their* fault.

"Gramma brought us," he said with a shrug. "I'm Peter Pan!"

"I see that," I said. I looked down at Debbie. "I suppose that makes you Wendy, then?"

"Nuh-uh," she said, putting her fists at her hips in a far better impression of Peter Pan than her brother. "I Tinkerbell."

"Of course. And that would explain the hook," I said to Michael.

"He can't hear you," Robbie said. "He's dead."

"An assassination wasn't what I expected when I came to work today," I said.

"Why don't you take them home?" Stuart said. "You know, so we can actually get some work done?"

"Lighten up, Stu," Michael said, sitting up. "Your mom brought them by an hour ago," he said to me.

I wondered if Nancy's offer to dig a hole would apply to my mother as well. "Did she say why?" I asked through clenched teeth.

"Lunch with Anna someone," Michael offered with a shrug.

"Hey, you're dead!" Robbie said, pointing his ruler at Michael.

He grinned boyishly, then jumped to his feet. "It'll take more than that to kill Captain Hook," he shouted, brandishing his flagpole at Robbie. Robbie screamed and ran to hide behind Stuart.

"Get him!" Debbie yelled, although I wasn't quite sure who she was talking to as she squealed in delight when Michael growled in her direction. Then she wriggled out of my grip and ran around the room, flapping her arms and proceeding to knock over a huge stack of papers.

Stuart looked ready to commit murder—which could be quite convenient if I could get him to channel that toward my mother instead of him just scowling at me, like this was my fault.

But my rage dissipated rapidly as Michael caught Robbie and threw him over his shoulder. "Let's see how *you* like losing a hand to a crocodile," he snarled.

"Mommy!" Robbie shouted. "Save me!"

"Your mommy is no match for this!" Michael said, holding up the coat hanger.

Robbie made a grab for the hanger and slipped a little. Michael released the hook to keep from dropping him, and Robbie delivered a particularly ill-placed kick. Michael sank to his knees before freeing Robbie, who plucked the hanger off the ground and ran away with it, declaring he was now Captain Hook and telling Charlie to walk the plank and George to swab the deck.

"Are you okay?" I asked, kneeling beside Michael.

"Been better," he said through a grimace. "Children of my own may not be in my future after that."

I laughed. I couldn't help myself.

"Might want a wife before you start thinking about kids. And by the time you find one of those, you'll probably be recovered."

"A wife?" he asked. "No way! I'm never growing up and getting married." He stood back up, taking a first gingerly step to make sure he was okay, before bellowing, "Hook! I'm coming for you!" And then he took off after Robbie again.

"Are all grown men such children?" Claire asked me over the noise and commotion.

I glanced at Stuart. "No." But I smiled as I watched Michael playing with the kids. "The good ones know how to turn it on and off though."

Michael motioned for Paul to help trap the kids in a corner. I turned to Claire to say something else, only to see her watching Paul with keen interest.

I remembered my resolve to do a little matchmaking there, but Paul glanced up at Claire and grinned, and I realized he hadn't been acting on his little crush on me in some weeks. Romance seemed to be brewing without any nudges from me, and I loved to see it.

"Watch out, Wendy!" Michael called, and I realized he was talking to me. "The pirates are coming for you!"

~

They played for another half hour before I made the executive decision to bring them home. Debbie didn't always nap anymore, but she was yawning and clearly needed one after the excitement of the day.

"I'll help you all out," Michael said, pulling his tie off his head.

The car was parked nearby, and I started to say that wasn't necessary, but he knelt down and gestured for Robbie to hop on his back, then picked Debbie up in his arms. "Curbside service," he said as he gestured for me to go first. "Your mother said you had the car today."

That was right: "How did she get here?"

"We took a cab," Robbie said excitedly. "The driver smelled like hot dogs!"

Michael and I exchanged a look, and we both tried not to laugh.

"I'm sorry about this," I said as he helped the kids into the back seat of the car.

"Don't be. We had fun."

"But there's so much to do—"

"And it can wait an hour," he said, standing back up. "Like I said the other day, family comes first."

I contrasted that with Larry, who was using the family as a threat to get his way. And without Linda's cooperation—

"You okay?" Michael asked.

I snapped out of my reverie. "Sorry—I'll explain another time."

"Can we come back tomorrow?" Robbie asked.

"No," I said firmly.

He pouted. "Then can Michael babysit sometime?"

I started to laugh. "If we don't win, you've got a job lined up," I said.

"Perfect. I'll bring the hook."

Get in the car and go home, Beverly, I told myself. But my body didn't cooperate as I still stood there smiling at him. "You'll make a great father someday. Assuming everything is still working after that kick." Then I clapped a hand over my mouth. "I'm sorry—I didn't—I—"

Michael laughed and put a hand on my shoulder. "I think I'll be okay."

"I'm just going to go home," I said quickly, opening the driver's side door and sitting, mortified.

He shut the door for me, then leaned in Robbie's window. "You take good care of your mother, okay?"

Robbie saluted him. "Aye aye, Captain!"

"Are you all pirates now?"

Michael winked. "Have fun, Wendy lady."

I never ate lunch, I told myself as I pulled away. *That's all that fluttering in my stomach is. Nothing more.*

But the thing about Wendy was that she grew up ever so long ago and therefore knew better than that.

40

My mother walked in a little after five, loaded down with shopping bags. I looked at her from the kitchen with raised eyebrows.

"Don't look at me like that, darling," she said, depositing the bags in the hall. "That's how you get forehead wrinkles."

I peeked around the corner and down the hall, making sure the children were still watching television. Which was unnecessary. I would have heard screams and objects breaking if they weren't.

"Did you really just leave them at my office today? No warning, nothing?"

"Well, you told me to call Anna."

"Yes, call her. Not abandon my kids to go shopping with her all afternoon."

"Anna didn't go shopping. But I figured once I was in Georgetown, I might as well make the most of it. I have so little free time these days."

I rubbed at my forehead and its imaginary wrinkles. She was willfully missing the point. "Mama, you can't just leave the kids at my office."

"Whyever not? Your father's secretaries watched you all the time."

I had no memory of that ever happening. "Michael doesn't even *have* a real secretary. We have Paul and his friends."

"Paul who?"

"Louise Lefkowitz's son."

"See? It's not like I left them with strangers. And Michael said it was fine."

"Did you actually ask him?" I asked. "Or just deposit them and say"—I mimicked her voice—"You don't mind, do you, Michael, darling?"

She raised an eyebrow at me. "I sound more like Audrey than Katharine if you're going to do a dreadful Hepburn accent," she said drily. "And either way, it was fine."

"It wasn't *fine*. This is my job!"

"Correction: this is your hobby," she said. "You don't *need* a job. But I have wholeheartedly supported your decision to work, to the detriment of my own marriage and social life. And which I continued to do today, by going to see Anna." I was about to argue that she latched right on to this "hobby" of mine as a way to jump ship on her marriage, not that her marriage fell apart because I took a job, but she cut me off. "Don't you even want to know how that went, by the way?"

I did not want to hear the inanities of gossip with Anna. But I needed to know if Michael was going to be meeting with the Wainwrights, so, silently fuming, I nodded.

"What's that, darling? I didn't hear you."

"How did it go?" I asked through gritted teeth.

"Just lovely," Mama trilled. "Be a dear and get the rest of the bags from the front step, won't you? I didn't want the cabbie to come inside. And then I'll tell you more."

I didn't know how it was possible that more bags could have fit in a cab, but I did as she asked, carrying in several garment bags and two hatboxes. She clearly wasn't worried about outliving her means being an issue in a future divorce.

Then again, as far as I knew, she had yet to even speak to a lawyer. Maybe there was hope there still.

I set the bags in the hall, but she told me to bring them to her room. "Except the Garfinckel's bag; you can leave that here." I draped one over a kitchen chair, but she corrected me—she meant the other one. And I graciously resisted throwing the whole stack at her head.

"Now," Mama said when I returned to the kitchen, "open that one."

"Mama, just tell me—"

"Ah ah ah," she said. "Let me see what you think first."

Inside the zippered bag was an absolutely exquisite dress. Black and beaded, it was strapless with a shrug that gave the appearance of covered shoulders, while drawing attention to the square neckline. It tapered at the waist and flared out in an A-line before it ended just below the knee.

"It's lovely," I admitted, fingering the beadwork. It had been forever since I had needed a fancy dress. Then again, my mother wasn't exactly going out to galas anymore either. "But what do you need it for?"

"I don't," she said. "You do, to wear to Anna's house. I assume Michael has evening wear?"

I looked at her in surprise. "You bought this—for me?"

"You can't exactly turn up to a party at Anna's in your everyday clothes."

"A party?" I asked.

"You wanted an invitation. I delivered."

"I thought she'd invite us for tea or dinner or something."

"How uncomfortable," she murmured. "No, this is far better. You know how connected they are to everyone worth knowing in Washington. Vice President Johnson may even be there—if Michael is going to be in the Senate, he'll need to know him."

She had a point. And that dress—

"When is the party?"

"Tomorrow night." She looked me up and down. "I suggest you get your hair done."

"Mama—"

"No need to thank me, darling," she said, sweeping back out of the kitchen. "You're a mother now. You know how it is to sacrifice for your children."

I looked at the price tag on the dress and winced. A shopping spree on my father's line of credit hardly felt like a sacrifice. Nor did depositing my children with strangers so she could do so. But she wasn't wrong that an invitation to a Wainwright party was a golden ticket to the Washington elite.

"Mama—" I called after her again.

"Don't worry, darling, there are shoes too. I'll put them in your room when I find the bag with them. Did you bring everything in?"

I gave up. She was never going to change or recognize that she could have done anything wrong. And as long as she didn't make a habit of leaving my kids at the office . . .

I peeked in the oven to make sure I still had time on dinner, and then picked up the kitchen phone and called Michael's direct line at the office.

"It's me," I said when he answered. Then I realized how awfully familiar that was and added my name. "Bev. Do you have an evening suit?"

"Is that different from a regular suit?"

I exhaled loudly. "We'll have to go shopping tomorrow, then. I'll—" I looked at the clock and swore. "It's too late to call the salon. I'll call first thing in the morning for an appointment and then work around that."

"The salon?"

"For me, not for you. Although you should get a haircut and a shave. I'll make that appointment for when mine is and then we can just run into Garfinckel's."

"Bev, what are you talking about?"

"We're going to Anna and Henry Wainwright's house for a party tomorrow night."

There was a pause. "The *Washington Post* Wainwrights?"

"Yes. And you need dinner attire for that."

"I—I'm lost. Why are we going to a party there? We don't know them."

"I do. And they are how you win elections in this town."

"But we're in Maryland, not DC."

I threw a hand up in the air even though he couldn't see it. "Listen, how do you think Johnson wound up on Kennedy's ticket? That was Henry. And speaking of Johnson, my mother said he's invited tomorrow night."

Another pause. "Should I go tonight to get a suit?"

I closed my eyes and shook my head, but I was smiling. "No. I don't trust a random shopkeeper to know how to dress you for the Wainwrights. If I send you alone, you'll show up in a top hat and monocle."

"I'll have you know I look quite distinguished with a monocle."

"There's a reason we eat peanuts instead of voting for them."

He laughed. "Point taken. But I can go for my own haircut on my way to work."

I agreed and told him I would see him after that to get a suit. Then, after hanging up, I made a note on the pad next to the phone to call the barbershop and make sure they knew what to do with his hair. Men liked to feel independent even if you couldn't trust them to get the details right.

41

"Stop fidgeting," I said as we walked up to the huge Georgetown mansion that dated to the earliest days of our nation's capital.

"I'm nervous," Michael admitted.

"You do realize as a senator, you'll meet with the president and visiting dignitaries regularly, right?"

"Yes," Michael said. "But you made me feel like the Wainwrights are royalty."

"Hey," I said, grabbing his shoulder so he turned to face me. "The only thing that separates them from us is money."

He tilted his head with a wry smile. "Us?"

I shook my head. "I know you think I'm rich, but compared to this, I grew up in poverty. And besides, I'm just a soon-to-be divorcée to a man who married into a much wealthier family than his own. But believe me, the Wainwrights have their own problems."

"Such as?"

I wasn't going to divulge what Mama had told me Anna confessed about the state of her own marriage. *A shadow of her former self,* Mama had whispered. *She called herself a dowdy housewife. Can you imagine Anna thinking herself dowdy?*

"Listen," I said. "Charm them tonight, and the rest of this election is a piece of cake."

"But no pressure," Michael said.

I grinned. "I wouldn't go *that* far."

"There will be alcohol, right?"

"Flowing like the Potomac."

"Between you and a drink, I can do this."

I slipped my hand into the crook of his elbow as we entered the receiving line that snaked around the side of the house. "You'll have both." He looked down at me like he wanted to say something, but when he didn't speak, I tugged him along. "Into the lion's den we go."

"Better lions than vipers, I suppose."

"Oh, they'll be there too. In fact—" I pulled my hand from his arm and offered a hand to the woman who had turned around in front of us. "Isadora," I said with a fondness that I hoped sounded more genuine than it felt. "It's been far too long. How are you? How's life as a diplomat's wife?"

"Simply dreadful," she said. "We're back home now. I told Harry I couldn't take another posting like that." And she proceeded to tell me how appalling life in Prague had been with only one nanny for the children and none of the amenities of the rich at home.

When Isadora's attention wandered to the much more well-connected wife of an author, Michael leaned in. "I thought this was a dinner party," he said, gesturing toward the assembled crowd that was being directed toward the rear of the house, where at least a hundred people mingled.

"This is nothing," I said. "They hosted a cocktail party for the Kennedys before the inauguration—it stormed, and Anna was in a tizzy because they invited six hundred people, and only two hundred could get here in the snow."

Michael looked at me, blinking rapidly.

"My parents were supposed to attend, but Papa got stuck in a snowdrift."

"Six hundred people," he repeated.

"So you see, this is an intimate gathering." He was staring at me. "What?"

Finally he shook his head. "It's like you're from a different planet," he said finally. "How will we even find the Wainwrights?"

I smiled and adjusted his tie. "You worry too much."

Anna was holding court at the entrance to the garden, where tables were set up beneath twinkling lights that were strung across the porticos. And sure enough, as men and women waited in line for their turn with the socialite, the man monopolizing her was none other than Vice President Lyndon Johnson. Michael's eyes widened. I elbowed him gently. "Pretend you're not fazed," I whispered. "It won't do for you to look starstruck. You have to seem like you belong."

"You act like you're at parties with vice presidents all the time," he whispered back. When I didn't reply, he looked at me. "You *are*, aren't you?"

I shrugged and recounted some of the higher profile guests from my wedding.

"I'm amazed it's Sam who's in office and not Larry."

"Don't be silly," I said. "He wasn't thirty yet when the last Senate race happened."

He started to say something else, but Johnson kissed Anna's hand with more gusto than I'd consider proper, and the line inched forward.

Finally, it was our turn. Anna greeted me with a hug and an air kiss on each cheek. "Beverly, darling, you look divine." I smiled under her praise.

"It's impossible to compare with you," I said. "But I will always take the compliment that I can fit into your sphere."

"Flattery will get you everywhere, my dear." She leaned in conspiratorially. Then she turned to look at Michael. "And this must be your candidate. I was surprised when your mother told me about your new career, but I have to say, it sounds like you're the perfect person for the job." She held out her hand. "Anna Wainwright."

"Mrs. Wainwright," he said, taking her hand. "Michael Landau. It's an honor to meet you."

"Call me Anna." She took in the cut of his suit. "Yes," she said to me, "he'll do quite well, won't he?" She took Michael's arm and, much to the dismay of the people waiting behind us to greet her, led him away. "You simply have to meet my husband. He's the one who knows all about politics. Then Beverly and I can catch up."

I followed a few steps behind them as she took him to another area of the enormous backyard—something unheard of in Georgetown—where Henry Wainwright was in conversation with Johnson and other politicians, a drink in one hand, a cigar in the other.

Anna waited until there was a lull, which was created by Johnson, for her to speak. Her own husband clearly saw her but was ignoring her presence. Which, at a party especially, was quite rude. If Larry had done something like that . . . Well, Larry had done something worse. Although the rumors about Henry had him in the same ballpark of philandering.

"Henry, I want to introduce you to Michael Landau. He's running for Sam Gibson's Senate seat in Maryland."

Henry looked Michael over, then switched his cigar to his left hand and offered his right. "Henry Wainwright," he said. "I think we wrote about you a few months ago."

"You did," Michael said.

Henry quickly did a round of introductions, then asked Michael his opinion on the situation in Cuba, completely ignoring Anna again. Johnson looked me over with interest, but Anna pulled me away. "Come along. Let's go get a drink and you can tell me all about this new man. Your mother told me about Larry. Ghastly business."

"Oh, he's not—no—we're not together," I said quickly.

"More's the pity," Anna said sympathetically. "I didn't see a ring though."

"Strictly professional. But I'll take that drink, and I'd love to tell you about why he should win."

She waved a hand, and a waiter appeared with a tray of champagne flutes. "I don't need to hear about all that," she said.

My heart sank. I had told Michael to just talk to Henry and I would charm Anna into making sure the *Post* ran something.

But Anna was nothing if not an attentive hostess. "How on earth did you decide to go from housewife to political strategist? I couldn't imagine having time to work outside the home, and my children are nearly your age."

"My mother is watching the kids while I work," I admitted.

"She told me she had moved in with you—I wasn't going to pry, but she had a couple drinks and confessed that she had left your father." Anna took a sip of her champagne. "Oh dear, I do hope that wasn't a secret."

"It's not."

"Do you think they'll reconcile? They always seemed so happy together."

"I'm working on that one."

"Good," Anna said, touching my arm. "I'll take your mother to lunch again, and I'll work on her as well. It's such a shame when couples can't make it work." Her eyes drifted to Henry, and my mother's words replayed in my head once more. It wasn't a dig at my parents' marriage or mine. It was a fervent prayer about her own.

"Anna," I said, and she turned her head to look at me. "Did my mother tell you why I wanted to come tonight?"

"She said you wanted Michael to make some connections that could help him."

"That," I agreed. "But I wanted to talk to you while he did that."

"Me?"

"You," I said. "The *Post* endorsed Sam Gibson last time around. We need you to endorse Michael now."

"Darling, I have nothing to do with the business, you know that."

"But it's your father's paper—"

"Was," she corrected. "He gave control to Henry, not me. And that was how we all three wanted it."

I took a long sip of my champagne for courage. "But you know everyone in the editorial department."

"Socially."

"If you just made a call—"

"If I just made a call," Anna said smoothly, but she was looking me directly in the eye, "my husband would be furious. I'm sorry, but you're going to have to hope he charms him on his own."

We both looked over as Michael said something that caused the group of men to laugh. A drink had materialized in his hand, though he hadn't taken a cigar.

But Anna's gaze was on her husband, watching him with thickly veiled concern.

"Mama told me once that behind every good man was an even better woman," I said quietly. Anna turned to look at me. "You know full well he wouldn't be anywhere without you. And Michael wouldn't be here without me. It seems a shame to just let them make all the decisions after we put them in the room."

For a long moment, she said nothing. Then she pulled out a gold cigarette case and opened it, offering one to me before taking one for herself. I refused, though I desperately wanted one to calm my nerves.

She lit the cigarette herself with a gold lighter, which along with the elegant case went back into her reticule.

"I always liked you," she said. "Even when you were just a little thing."

I felt my hopes lift.

"Tell me why I should work on Henry for this man of yours."

I smiled broadly. My mother might have driven me insane, but there wasn't much she didn't know.

42

By the time I had finished with Anna, I apologized for monopolizing her time. "Nonsense," she said. "Now I can't make any promises, but . . ." She winked conspiratorially.

"Anna, I don't know how to thank you."

"Wait until there's something concrete to thank me for," she said. "And then don't be a stranger. Henry loves feeling like he has his finger on the pulse of Washington."

"Invite us and we're here."

"Give my love to your parents," she said. "Maybe I should invite them both to my next party separately. I can lock them in a closet until they reconcile."

Remembering the country club debacle, I wasn't sure my mother wouldn't just burn the whole gorgeous house down, Mrs. Rochester-style, just to get out of there. But I said that if I didn't have them back together by the election, I would take her up on it.

I made my way through the party, knocking back an additional glass of champagne in celebration as I looked for Michael, whom I eventually found in a conversation with Secretary of Defense McNamara.

Catching his eye, I flashed him a discreet thumbs-up. For a moment he just stared at me, then his face split into a wide grin. McNamara turned to follow his gaze, then patted Michael on the arm with a laugh. Michael excused himself and came to me.

"Really?" he asked quietly.

"How did it go with Henry?"

"Well, I think. What happened with Anna?"

I looked around. The *Post* knew better than to report something overheard at one of Anna's parties if the Wainwrights didn't want it reported, but any gathering of such high-profile individuals was bound to have people listening. "When we leave," I said cautiously.

"Is it rude to go now?" Michael asked, his eyes sparkling with reflected string lights.

I took his wrist and checked the time. Even if I had bought a new watch, I wouldn't have worn it with a cocktail dress. "No. Anna knows I have kids."

Michael offered me his arm, and I took it, a warmth spreading through my abdomen that had to have been from the champagne and victory with Anna. Surely that spark hadn't been there when I took his arm on the way in.

Had it?

We made it down the long drive onto R Street and walked past the Oak Hill Cemetery toward Montrose Park, before Michael pulled me to a stop. "Tell me what happened," he said.

"She's going to work on Henry," I said. "They're going to endorse you over Sam."

"Did she *say* that?"

I smiled. "When Anna wants something, it happens."

All of a sudden, I was twirling through the air. Michael had picked me up and spun me around, while I laughed. But as he went to put me down, time slowed to a crawl as my body brushed down the length of his. My head tilted up, and his angled down toward mine, and it was like watching in slow motion as his lips came closer and closer to mine until finally, they touched. That electricity that I had tried to blame on champagne, on proximity, on literally anything except what I felt for this man, was now undeniable as his mouth moved against mine, my lips parting just as hungrily for his.

But abruptly, Michael moved away.

"I'm sorry," he said, and my stomach sank. For him it *had* just been the champagne and the victory of the party and the endorsement. I was a fool.

"Don't be," I said, turning away.

But Michael took my hand and pulled me back to face him. "I have to tell you something."

I didn't look up, afraid to meet his eyes. But he put a finger under my chin and lifted my face. "You asked me once why I was running for office, and I didn't give you the full answer." I looked at him questioningly. What could that possibly matter right now?

"Okay," I said softly, trying to figure out why that made him stop kissing me.

"I—Bev, it was your father."

I pulled back. "My father?" My chest began to hitch with shallow breaths as I connected the dots. Of course. That was why he had hired me. I knew that. It was why I told them who I was. I wouldn't have had a shot if I hadn't been Bernie Gelman's daughter. But I was more and more certain that my father was also why Larry had married me. And here I was, walking right into the arms of another man who wanted me for the provenance of my birth, not for me. "I see," I said, folding my arms across my chest. The night was hot, but I was chilly now.

"No," Michael said. "Let me explain—I didn't want you to think that had anything to do with . . ." He gestured at the space between us. "Your father spoke at my college graduation. I had already been accepted to law school, mostly because it was the career where I could make the most money. I didn't want to be poor anymore. I wanted to buy my parents a house and raise my own kids with everything I never had. But he—he changed my life that day. I was the first person in my family to go to college, and at that graduation, he looked around the room and said he had sat there, graduating from the University of Maryland, and said he remembered the graduation speaker telling them that they would change the world."

Michael took a breath, looking at something in the distance over my head, before he focused on me again. "He said that his charge to us wasn't just to change the world, but to fix it. And he told us to look at ourselves in the mirror every single morning and ask ourselves what we were going to do to make the world better that day." He reached down and took my hands in his. "And I didn't think anything of it. But the next morning, when I woke up, I saw my reflection, and I asked myself that. It became something I did every morning. Something I still do. And when I read about that filibuster on civil rights, I looked in the mirror, and I told myself I needed to do more. Because Sam wasn't just hurting people who grew up like I did; he was hurting people who didn't have a voice. And I—I heard your father's voice when I looked in the mirror."

He looked down at our joined hands. "It felt like fate when you walked into the office that day. But, Bev, I don't want you to think that's why I'm here." He stopped himself. "I'm saying this all wrong. I'm *here* because of that. But I'm here on this sidewalk, with you, because of *you*. And I know—"

But I didn't let him finish. It wasn't a conscious decision by any stretch of the imagination, but I was on my tiptoes, I had pulled my hands from his, and my arms were around his neck. And this time, I was kissing him.

For a second, he was too surprised to respond. I think his lips were still moving in the rest of his sentence at first. But then, he did, as an arm wrapped around my waist, bringing me closer, the other at my neck.

Time stopped altogether. It could have been seconds or years that we stood there. No one had ever kissed me like that. Not the handful of boys in my youth, and certainly never Larry. There had never been a kiss that left me so breathless and dizzy and hungry for more.

When we eventually pulled apart, I bit my lower lip. "Sorry," I said, echoing his earlier apology, feeling anything but.

Michael grinned and wiped at his mouth with the back of his hand. "I have lipstick on me, don't I?"

I nodded and raised a hand to wipe it away, but he caught it, bringing it to his lips and kissing it. Then his smile faded. "This is where you tell me we can't do this, isn't it?"

Reality crashed back onto my shoulders, the weight of it pressing me into the earth, the mugginess of the night suddenly too oppressive to breathe.

"I think this is where we mutually decide that," I said quietly. "You can't be with someone who isn't even divorced yet, and my lawyer said I can't do anything that—"

"Larry would use against you," Michael finished. "He's right of course."

Part of me had hoped, irrationally, that he would say none of that mattered.

But of course, he wouldn't. Even if he cared more about me than the campaign, which he didn't, I wouldn't have felt the same way if he had dropped everything for me after what he had just confessed. And he knew, as I did, that keeping the kids was the most important thing in my life.

"We should head home," I said lightly. "I'll behave."

"I will too."

Don't, I wanted to say. There had been that moment in his car, but I saw now, with the clarity of hindsight, that his behavior the day before, when my mother left the kids at the office, was the tipping point for me.

"Things may be different after the election," I said as we approached Michael's car.

He brought my hand to his lips again, and I had never felt such a strong pull of desire. "That's not so long. It'll be September in a couple of days."

"Not long at all," I said as he opened the car door and I sat. "Especially with how much we still have to do for the campaign."

He walked around to the driver's side and got in. "I can't believe how much you've accomplished for me already."

I smiled wryly. "For us." He looked over at me. "I was at that graduation."

"You were?"

I nodded. "I was sixteen."

"You're that young?"

I smacked him lightly in the chest with the back of my hand. "Are you saying I look old?"

"You look perfect," he said. "Besides, it's a good thing."

"Why's that?"

"You're not old enough to run for the Senate yourself. You'd beat me in a landslide."

I laughed as he pulled away from the curb, taking us through Georgetown and along the Potomac as we headed back toward Maryland and home.

43

The following day was business as usual at the office, except for a single rose on my desk when I walked in, the word *November* written on a slip of paper under it. I looked around, but Michael was in his office on the phone, and Stuart hadn't even looked up at me yet. I smiled, slipping the note into my purse. And for three days, we did what we did best.

Fran had declined my invitation of a job for now. "What happens if he loses?" she asked. "I don't want to be back to square one again. Besides, Miss Llewelyn is leaving next month, and they offered me her job."

I wanted to assure her that he wouldn't lose. But I couldn't promise that. And I, of all people, understood not wanting to depend on what a man did to be secure.

"I understand," I said. "But if he wins and you *do* want to be in an office, we're still happy to hire you in November. Speaking of which, I'm up to my eyeballs until the election, but I'd love to get lunch, or a drink, or dinner, or *something* when it's done."

"I'd like that," Fran said. "We can toast your divorce."

I agreed, thinking what a relief that would be. Assuming everything went my way, that was.

Summer was winding down as we entered the home stretch of the election, and when the weekend rolled around, we spent most of it at the club, the kids enjoying their last weekend of splashing in the pool before it closed after Labor Day. I let them splash me and laughed with them, feeling like I was making up for all the time I had spent away from them during the summer months.

Robbie would be starting kindergarten on Tuesday, and on Saturday afternoon we went shopping for supplies.

"What if none of my friends are in my class?" he asked quietly as we stood in line to check out. The store was noisy, and I wasn't positive I heard a quiver in his voice until I looked down at his face, which suddenly looked so much more grown-up than it had.

"We already know Freddy is in your class," I said. "And that's the fun part. You make new friends."

"I don't want new friends," he said, his bottom lip beginning to shake in a prelude to tears.

I knelt down, ignoring the line behind us. "Here's the secret about kindergarten," I said. "Everyone in your class is going to live super-close to us."

"They are?"

"Uh-huh," I said. A good chunk of his friends were from the club, and they were scattered throughout Montgomery County. "Every last one of them will live within bike-riding distance."

His face fell again, and I could have kicked myself. We had bought Robbie a new bike for Hanukkah, with Larry swearing he would teach him to ride it when the weather got warmer. I had suggested he take it when he took the kids a couple weeks ago per our new legal agreement, but Larry said he couldn't do that with Debbie there too.

My father had taught me to ride in the nebulous past, and all I remembered was begging for him not to let go until one day I didn't even realize he had.

For a split second I debated asking Michael to help teach him. But that would have been inappropriate, and Robbie deserved the security of a parent holding his bike. Which meant it had now fallen on me, like so much of the rest of parenting had.

"Let's go practice on your bike when we get home," I said. "And we'll keep working on it. By spring, when you have a million new best friends, you'll be a pro."

Robbie nodded. He had only asked about Larry a couple of times, usually after being dropped back off. And I wondered if Larry would someday realize how much he had missed and regret it. I didn't care if he regretted me, but I very much hoped he regretted being such an absent father.

"Want to get ice cream before we go home?" I asked him.

He did. There wasn't much an ice cream cone couldn't cure.

~

On Tuesday, I walked Robbie to the elementary school, having already warned Michael and Stuart that I would be late all week. Once he was acclimated, my mother could bring him, but for the first week, I wanted it to be me. October was going to be a mess between the campaign and the divorce, and I wanted to make sure the kids were in a good place before we got to that.

He dragged his feet, pulling on my hand as we approached the brick building. "Hey," I said, stopping and squatting down to his level. "Did you know that on *my* first day of school, I threw up?"

"You did?" he asked halfheartedly.

"I did. All over Grandma."

That wasn't entirely true. It had been all over myself. But it got the giggle I had hoped for. Which was fair—the idea of someone throwing up on my mother was hilarious. Although I was sure she was made of something akin to Teflon, and any bodily fluids would simply bounce off her.

"It's true," I said. "I was so nervous that I threw up. And Grandma was so mad. She had picked out the perfect outfit for me and I ruined it. But do you know what else?"

"What?"

"When Rosa came to pick me up, I didn't want to leave because I was having so much fun."

He looked unsure. "Is that true?"

"It is," I said. "School is scary because you haven't been there. But once you know what to expect, it's a lot of fun. And every other kid in there is just as nervous as you are."

"They are?"

"They are."

"Robbie!" a voice yelled. We both turned to see Freddy Rosenblatt running up the block toward us, pursued by his harried mother.

"Hi, Freddy." Robbie's greeting to his best friend was pretty lackluster, betraying how nervous he was.

"I threw up," Freddy said proudly. "Mommy said I'm nervous, but"—he lowered his voice—"really her breakfast was yucky."

"My mommy threw up too," Robbie said.

Freddy's mother took a step back. "Not today," I said. "On my first day of kindergarten." She looked unconvinced.

We finally reached the building, and I pulled Robbie in for a hug. "Can you pick me up today?"

I hadn't thought about that. We had established that my mother would walk up with Debbie to get him. But the way he looked up at me with those puppy dog eyes that looked just a little too wet broke my resolve.

"I'll try," I said. "But if I can't, it'll be Grandma and Debbie, okay?"

He nodded. "If Michael wins the election, will you be able to pick me up every day?"

I didn't reply at first. But the real answer was that win or lose, I would likely be out of a job come November 7. Yes, Michael would find a way to keep me on staff if I wanted to stay, but that would look bad if we were involved. I didn't know what we were going to be, but I liked the idea of giving us a try. I also didn't know what Michael actually wanted, but that rose was a good indication that it wasn't just a champagne-fueled kiss.

And as I looked at Robbie, my answer was clear. "Win or lose," I said. "I'll be home a lot more after the election."

I didn't know that I would stop working, but I did know that I was going to make sure I had more time for my kids.

I gave Robbie one more hug and kissed the top of his head, something he would have usually squirmed out of. Then I gave him a gentle push. He and Freddy walked in holding hands. Robbie looked back over his shoulder and gave me a wave. Freddy never looked back.

I watched until I couldn't see him through the door anymore, feeling oddly emotional about my baby going off to school. And for a split second, I wanted to call Larry and tell him about the drop-off.

That feeling evaporated by the time I turned to walk to the bus stop, and was completely forgotten by the time I reached the office, where a man sat on a bench outside the building.

When he stood up, I stopped walking.

It was Larry, looking serious and holding a manila envelope.

My mouth went dry.

"Beverly," he said with a nod. "We need to talk."

44

I stared at Larry without responding. He hadn't come to the house to see Robbie off. Did he even remember it was the first day of school for his son?

"I have work to do," I said eventually, starting to walk past him. "Take it up with my lawyer."

He shook the envelope at me. "I thought you might want to handle this one yourself."

I turned to face him. "Why?"

"Let's go sit somewhere."

My hands went to my hips. "I'm not going anywhere with you until you tell me what this is about."

Larry shrugged. "Suit yourself." He opened the envelope and removed a series of photographs, holding them out to me. "Look familiar?" he asked.

I took the stack and then dropped them like they had burned my hand.

They were taken in Georgetown a few nights earlier. The top one was of me and Michael kissing. Another that I could see on the ground was his hand on my cheek, us looking into each other's eyes. I could hear him telling me it wasn't so long until November.

Shaking, I looked up at Larry. "It's not what it looks like," I said.

"I don't care what it is," he said. "But I warned you I wasn't going to play nice if you didn't leave this campaign. And taking him to the

Wainwrights?" He made a *tsk-tsk* noise, shaking his head as he bent to gather the photographs.

The last shreds of what could have been affection for this man, purely because he shared genetic material with my children, turned to stone. "What do you want?" I asked coldly.

"You know what I want," he said. "Drop out of the campaign. Now."

"And if I won't?"

"Then my lawyers present this as evidence that you're the adulterer."

There was a slim chance he could get the kids. But based entirely on a kiss that Michael would testify was nothing—especially when Larry had never changed a diaper, didn't know who their pediatrician was, and would continue to work full-time with no one to raise the children—I didn't see a judge ripping them away from their mother over one kiss.

Okay, two kisses.

And if kissing alone had been adultery, well, I'd probably have a much easier time proving to a court that Larry had cheated.

Moreover, I was done letting Larry threaten me. He had assumed (correctly) that I knew nothing when he said he would have to sell the house. But I wasn't so naive anymore.

"Go ahead and try," I said, turning to leave again.

"I thought you might say that," he said. I stopped walking. "Which is why I gave Sam a copy of these this morning."

I turned back around, the wheels spinning rapidly in my head as I connected the dots between what my lawyer had told me about Sam's first Senate campaign and what was happening now. "That story," I said slowly. "Six years ago. The illegitimate baby. That was you, wasn't it?"

He shook his head but wouldn't meet my eye.

"Even if it wasn't you—you knew. You knew none of that was true."

"As far as I know, it was all true," he said, putting the photographs back into the envelope. "And if it worked then, it'll work now."

"You wouldn't."

"Me?" he chuckled. "Of course, *I* wouldn't. I'm the one who cares about our children's well-being while their whore mother is sleeping with her boss."

I had never hit anyone in my life, but I drew my hand back reflexively. He caught it before it made contact.

"Do you really want to add assault?" he asked as I struggled to free my wrist. "You have until tomorrow morning to resign," he said. "After that, Sam can do what he wants with the pictures." He dropped my wrist, and I rubbed at it. "Here," he said thrusting the pictures at me. "I have extra copies."

Then he started to walk away, pausing only to call over his shoulder. "Do the right thing, Beverly. For everyone."

45

The office was quiet as I made my way in, the envelope of photos clutched tightly in my left hand. I felt like I had aged a hundred years in seconds.

"Where is everyone?" I asked Stuart.

"The interns went back to school," he said, not looking up. "You knew that already."

I did. They'd be coming in odd hours and working around their class schedules, while we scrambled to find volunteers. But I had forgotten.

"Is Bev here yet?" Michael called from his office. Before I could respond, he strolled out, his face lighting up as he saw me, then draining of color when he looked closer. He crossed the office in three seconds and put me in a chair. "What's wrong? What happened?"

"Larry," I said, choking on the name. Then I shook my head and handed Michael the envelope.

He pulled out the contents, then sank into the chair next to mine and swore. "Bev, I'm so, so sorry. This was all my fault."

"Don't," I said.

Stuart hung up the phone and came over to see what was going on. He looked at the top picture over Michael's shoulder and made a sour face.

"You two couldn't have done that inside?" he asked. "You've got a whole back office with a door that locks."

I glared at him.

"Not helping," Michael muttered. He looked at me and took my hand. "Is he going to use it in court?"

I nodded. "If I don't quit."

"That's easy," he said. "I'll testify. It was all me, and nothing else happened."

"You can't do that," I said.

"You absolutely can't do that," Stuart agreed. "It'll be the end of the campaign."

"Her kids matter more than me winning," Michael said. "He can't take the kids."

"He won't get the kids," Stuart said. "You know that as well as I do. But if you testify that you kissed a married woman, everything we worked for is done."

"There's more," I said quietly. They stopped arguing to look at me. "He gave the pictures to Sam." They both stared at me in silence. "If I don't quit, he's going to use them against you publicly."

Stuart let out a string of foul invective explaining exactly what Larry could do to himself, where, and with a goat.

"While I think we could probably sell tickets to that," I said drily, "there's only one answer here. I'll clear out my desk. And I suppose type up a letter to show him as proof."

"No," Michael said.

"It's the only way. It's okay. There's not much more I can do at this point."

"She's right," Stuart said. "Look, I agree, we would have never made it this far without her, but right now"—he picked up a picture and held it out at us—"she's a liability."

"Which is my fault," Michael said. "I want to find a way to fix this."

"You can't," Stuart said. "She can."

"It's not your fault," I said. "There were two of us there that night. If anything, you were the voice of reason."

Michael put his other hand on mine, and for a full minute said nothing. Then finally: "Do you want to quit?"

If he had asked me that morning, when Robbie was all tearful and asking if I would be home more, I might have said yes. But quitting meant Larry won, even if we won the election. And more than that, I wanted to see this through. I didn't want to be like Anna Wainwright, describing myself as a housewife who stayed out of business because a wife should never be her husband's boss.

I wanted to be something, do something, leave a legacy. And if we lost, we would lose knowing we had fought our hardest and not been outsmarted by a man who took me for granted.

"No. I don't."

His hand squeezed mine. "Then we figure this out." He looked up at Stuart. "Together."

Stuart nodded. "The Three Musketeers," he said with a sigh.

∼

"He'll plant a newspaper story," Stuart said as we sat around the table in the back of the office, trying to strategize. "Larry will be the anonymous source of course."

"You think he'll be anonymous?"

Stuart nodded. "He's not going to risk dragging Sam through the mud on this. Then he'll give some on-the-record quote about just wanting what's best for his kids."

I rubbed the bridge of my nose, the beginnings of a headache forming. "That's the biggest joke in this."

"Look, we knew Sam fought dirty," Stuart said. "It's why Michael was the perfect candidate."

"Until I came along," I finished for him.

Stuart didn't argue. "He was squeaky clean. No dirt."

"Let's find the girl," Michael said.

"What girl?"

"The one from six years ago. The one they said Tom Stanton had the affair with."

"Greg said his firm represented him," I said. "She dropped the charges as soon as Tom dropped out."

"They paid her off," Stuart said. "They're probably still paying her. I doubt she'd talk."

"We have to try," Michael said.

"What about the secretary?" Stuart asked. "The one Larry is having the affair with."

I shook my head. "I tried. She seems to think she's in love with him. She won't testify."

Both men thought for a moment. "It's too bad you don't have receipts from the Colonial Manor or something like that," Stuart said. "We could build a case."

The name rang a bell. "That motel on Rockville Pike? Why?"

Michael and Stuart exchanged a look. "It's where a lot of men go to cheat on their wives," Michael said slowly.

My eyes widened.

"That night," I said. "The night there was that big thunderstorm, and the power went out, remember that?" They both nodded, not sure where I was going. "I went looking for matches and I found a book in the junk drawer. I remember putting it away the next morning. It was from the Colonial Manor. I've never been there. But we had a matchbook, which means Larry was there."

"The sign-in book," Michael said.

"Which only works if they'll give it to us and if he was dumb enough to use his real name," Stuart said.

"It's worth a try." Michael stood up. "Come on. We're going over there."

"You are not going anywhere," Stuart said. "The last thing we need is this PI getting pictures of you going into a motel with Bev. I'll go."

"Wait," I said, holding my hands up in a "time out" gesture. "What are we doing?"

"If he stayed there with anyone, the motel will have a record of it," Michael said. "If we can get the pages from the book with him and a woman checking in, we can use that in court."

"And to battle anything Sam's campaign claims in the papers."

"That'll be enough in court?" I asked. They both nodded. "Then I'll go."

"I'm coming with you," Stuart said.

"I can do this."

"No one said you couldn't," Stuart said. "But backup never hurts. And it's all our jobs on the line here."

I picked up my purse. "Let's go."

46

We stopped at my house before going to the motel. Stuart said we would do better if we had a picture of Larry. If he didn't use his real name to sign in, there was a chance the motel clerk would recognize him and agree to help us.

"What are you doing home?" my mother asked as Debbie wrapped herself around my legs. "What's wrong?"

"Too much to explain," I said, trying to pry Debbie off me. "And little pitchers have big ears. But L-A-R-R-Y is trying to blackmail me."

"Blackmail?"

"To quit the campaign."

I could see the gears turning in her head as she put two and two together that something had happened with Michael. Then she nodded. "Rosa can watch Debbie. I'm coming with you."

"Stuart is in the car," I said. "He's coming with me."

"Stuart hates you."

I chuckled humorlessly. "It's been an interesting morning. Besides, I need you to pick Robbie up at lunch."

"I go with Gramma!" Debbie declared proudly.

I knelt down and drew her in for a hug. "You do, you big, big girl." Then I went to the living room and took a framed family picture that I had left out for the kids off the bookshelf. I stopped back in the kitchen and riffled through the junk drawer to make sure I had read the matchbook correctly. Sure enough, it was royal blue, with a white silhouette of the motel, the lettering clear as day. A little more digging produced a notepad and pen from there as well.

I didn't even notice my mother looking over my shoulder, observing the paraphernalia, her mouth pressed into such a tight line that her lips disappeared. We exchanged a look, and she squeezed my arm in support.

"I'm a phone call away if you need me," she said.

I kissed her cheek. "Thank you, Mama." She nodded once and then took Debbie out to play in the backyard.

On the one hand, Stuart was the smarter choice because he was a lawyer and much more physically intimidating than my mother if it came down to that.

On the other, I would love to see anyone try to argue with my mother and walk away the victor. In my twenty-seven years on this earth, it hadn't happened yet.

~

We pulled onto the property, with a central two-story building, adorned with columns to fit the colonial name, and rooms branching out like arms on either side. Daylilies lined the drive leading up to the swimming pool at the front of the property. I had passed it every time we went to the club. The evidence I needed to secure the kids and fight whatever Larry planned to do to sabotage Michael had been hiding in plain sight all along.

"Give me the picture," Stuart said as he pulled into a parking spot. "You don't need to come in."

But I shook my head. "Let me try talking to them first." Stuart looked skeptical. "One of us is slightly more charming than the other."

He smiled sardonically. "Thanks."

"If I can't charm this guy, then we'll do it your way."

Stuart nodded, and I looked at him, seeing him through new eyes.

"Whatever happens in there," I said, "thank you."

He put a hand on mine for a second, then removed it and opened his car door. "Let's do this."

I did the same and, gripping the photograph of my family, followed him into the icy blast of the air-conditioned lobby, where a mustached man in his late forties or early fifties sat reading a newspaper, sweat stains creeping out of his armpits despite the frosty temperature of the room. He looked up at the sound of the bell on the door and set down his newspaper, then flipped a page in the large book in front of him, uncapping a pen.

"Room for the night or the afternoon?" he asked.

I recoiled involuntarily. It hadn't occurred to me, despite Stuart's comment that I couldn't be seen going there with Michael, that the motel clerk would assume Stuart and I were having an affair.

"Neither," Stuart said, nudging me forward slightly.

I gave myself a mental shake and flashed my brightest smile. "I was hoping you could help me," I said, moving forward toward the desk. "You see, I caught my husband with another woman, and he's making divorce proceedings . . . difficult."

The man shifted in his seat uncomfortably. "I'm sorry," he said. "I don't know how I could help though."

"I—we—would like to look through the sign-in book," I said, my fingers brushing against it.

He moved it away from my hand and out of my reach. "I can't do that," he said.

I glanced back at Stuart and saw his jaw tighten. I held up my hand below the counter, indicating for him to wait.

"I understand," I said delicately. "But maybe you can just tell us if you've seen him here? I found a matchbook, a notepad, and a pen, but that's not decisive enough for court." I held out the photo, studying the clerk's face as I did.

He blinked twice. Then said, "I've never seen him before."

"You're sure?" Stuart asked. "He's clearly been here if they had all that in the house."

"I'm sure," he said. "Besides, people leave matchbooks places. Other people pick them up. He could have come to the bar for a drink and never checked in."

My shoulders dropped in defeat. Worst-case scenario, if the clerk had confirmed that Larry had checked in with someone who wasn't me, Stuart could have testified to that, even if the clerk wouldn't go to court. But with him saying he had never seen Larry, we had absolutely nothing.

"Thank you for your time," I said. Stuart looked at me, and we held each other's gaze, his clearly asking if he should intimidate the clerk to get another answer. But it was what Larry would have done. I didn't want to do that, even if it meant my short career had just ended along with my marriage.

I turned to leave, and Stuart begrudgingly did the same.

"I'm sorry I couldn't help you, Mrs. Diamond," he said as we reached the door.

Stuart and I both stopped walking and looked at each other again. Then we slowly turned back to the clerk.

"I never told you my name," I said.

His eyes widened as he realized his gaffe, and he ducked as Stuart lunged at the desk. But Stuart wasn't going for his throat; he was going for the book, which was now left unguarded.

The clerk protested as I flipped it open, but Stuart loomed over him menacingly, and he made no move to stop me.

I turned the pages, seeing an awful lot of George Washingtons, Abraham Lincolns, and the odd Harry Truman before—

There it was. Clear as day. "Mr. and Mrs. Larry Diamond." Again two pages earlier. And again a few pages earlier. I lost count somewhere after eight.

Then I looked up at the clerk. "How many different women?" I asked.

"I don't kn—"

Stuart grabbed him by the collar as the man looked up at him, terrified.

"Two? Maybe three. I don't know."

"Let him go," I said. Stuart did.

"We're taking this," Stuart said, gesturing toward the book that I now had clutched to my chest. "We're going to make copies of a few pages, and then we'll return it."

The clerk started to protest again, but Stuart held up a finger. "I'm good friends with the DA. And running a brothel is illegal in Maryland."

"It's not a brothel!"

"You willing to gamble your whole livelihood on none of those women getting paid?" Stuart asked.

The man blanched and whimpered something that sounded like "No sir."

Stuart gave me a little nudge and said we should leave. Then he looked back to the clerk one more time. "I'm going to be back with the book tonight. And if Mr. Diamond returns, you never saw us. Is that clear?"

He nodded.

"Good," Stuart said. "Because one call to the DA, and you're finished. You hear me?"

Another nod.

"Let's go," Stuart said to me, and he held the door.

I didn't remember crossing the parking lot to the car. But once I was seated inside, I opened the book again, running a finger over the familiar handwriting that said his name and mine.

And then, for the first time in my adult memory, I was crying. Not just tears, but full-out sobbing. I hadn't cried when Larry showed up with those pictures, nor when he threatened to take the kids. Not even when my grandmother died when I was fifteen. My eyes were a well that I thought was dry but that had refilled without my knowledge. And once I started, I couldn't stop, crying out all the pain of the life I had lost, the embarrassment of having been so blind not to see what was happening under my nose for so long, and the fact that, because we had kids, I could never truly be rid of Larry even after our marriage was dissolved.

Stuart, to his credit, didn't panic at the sight of tears, the way so many men did. He simply took the book from my lap and let me cry, eventually passing me a stack of Montgomery Donuts napkins from the glove compartment in lieu of tissues.

I don't know how long we sat there before I was composed enough to apologize.

"You don't have anything to be sorry for," he said.

I looked at him, trying to see how far back that extended. But he smiled tightly at me, patted my shoulder awkwardly, and said he would take me home.

"Thank you," I said as we turned onto my street.

He shook his head. "You've been a pain in my ass since the day we met," he said. "But you've also been right about almost everything. And no one deserves to be treated like that. Especially not someone like you."

It was the closest to a compliment I would get from him. And when he stopped the car in my driveway, I startled him by wrapping my arms around his neck in a tight hug.

He removed my arms. "What if the PI is still on your trail?"

"Then the judge will think Larry and I are both awful people," I said. I released him and opened my car door, leaving the book on the front seat for him to make copies and return. "But don't worry. I won't tell anyone your secret."

"My secret?"

I smiled. "That underneath that tough exterior, you're actually a nice guy."

He raised an eyebrow and shook his head. "Call the office if you need anything."

I said I would and watched as he pulled away.

47

My mother wasn't home with Robbie yet when I walked in, so I washed my face and reapplied my makeup.

I greeted them when they came in, pushing off my mother's questions to ask Robbie all about his first day of school. Apparently there was a boy named Billy who was going to be an issue, but otherwise he had a good time and wasn't particularly unhappy about returning the next day.

To celebrate, we baked a cake together, the kids on either side of me standing on kitchen chairs as we measured, stirred, and poured.

But at four, I removed my apron and asked if my mother would mind frosting the cake with them.

"Why?"

"And I need to borrow your car," I said.

"Beverly, where are you going?"

"I'll explain tonight," I said. "I've got one more loose end to tie up today."

I drove down Connecticut Avenue into the District and made my way down to Larry's office, where I parked in view of the main entrance and waited.

My quarry came out at three minutes past five, walking purposefully in her pumps toward the bus stop at the end of the block.

I slipped out of the car and moved into her path. She stopped when she saw me and froze like a trapped animal.

Then her posture straightened. "I told you, I have nothing to say."

"I know," I said. "But I do have one more question."

Linda didn't reply.

"Did you ever go to the Colonial Manor motel with Larry?"

Her brows came together in confusion. "No. Why?"

I was gambling. She could go running back inside and tell Larry I was asking about that. But as a fellow wronged woman, I was willing to bet on her reaction.

"Because I talked to the desk clerk there today. And Larry has been coming in for a long time with two or three different women. I figured you might have been one of them."

I watched as her expression crumpled. And somehow, I felt bad for her. She was young, and Larry was probably feeding her all kinds of lines about how unhappy he was with me and how he loved her.

"Are you telling the truth?" she asked quietly.

"I am. I can show you the pages tomorrow if you want. One of my colleagues is making copies of the book."

She shook her head. "I'm really stupid, aren't I?" A tear formed in her left eye and spilled out of the center as if poured from a pitcher, leaving a black mascara track as it ran down her cheek. Another followed on the other side, and I reached for a Kleenex, only to realize I had left my purse in the car.

"Come on," I said. "I've got tissues in the car. I'll drive you home." Crying harder now, she let me lead her to my mother's car, where I handed her a ball of tissues from my purse.

I asked where she lived, she told me, and we pulled away from the curb.

"What do I do now?" she asked as we drove north toward the Maryland border.

"My offer stands," I said, especially since Fran had turned us down. "You can come work for us."

"And then what?" she asked. "If your man loses, I'm out of a job. I'm better off finding something completely new."

"Linda," I said. "Look at me." She turned her head. "He's not going to lose. But if he does, we'll help you find something else. Michael will likely go back to law if he loses. Legal secretaries make a lot more than you did working for Larry." I had no idea if that was true. "Would Sam do the same if he loses?"

She ignored the question. "I don't have any formal training," she said. "I can't be a legal secretary."

"We can help with that too," I said gently, though I was mentally cursing Larry. He really hired her because she was attractive. I wondered if the affair started before or after she started working for him. But it didn't matter.

"Why are you being so nice to me?"

My original reason was because I still wanted her to testify. I wanted to win in court without any doubts about my character or his. But even though I had no kind feelings left toward Larry, I could still empathize with this girl and the position she was now in.

"Because Larry lied to both of us," I said after a long pause. "And it wasn't either of our faults."

She looked at me skeptically. "It *is* my fault."

I sighed. "A small part. But you weren't the one who took marriage vows and then broke them. And certainly not with multiple people. And honestly, Linda, you're not the first to fall for a married man and believe he loved you, and you won't be the last. Larry loves Larry. That's it. Period. And we didn't see that because we thought we loved him too."

She nodded and then sniffled, and we sat in silence other than her telling me where to turn until we reached a neighborhood full of small, somewhat run-down houses in Silver Spring. "This is it," she said, pointing to a driveway.

I looked up at the peeling paint of the front porch and wondered if Michael had grown up in a house like this, just a few miles on the map from mine, but a million miles socially.

"Thank you for the ride," she said.

"I meant what I said. If you need a job, you just come to the office."

She looked at me through the open car door for a long time. "I'll think about it," she said.

"And if you do decide to testify—you know where to find me."

She nodded again, then shut the door and walked up the steps to the house. I watched her go inside. I didn't think she would testify or come to us for a job. But even if it didn't help me against Larry, she deserved to know the truth about what he was.

And that motel book would have to be enough.

48

I was manning the phones the following morning somewhat nervously. My deadline for resignation had passed with no word from Larry. But the photocopied pages from the motel—no mimeograph for such an important document—were in an envelope in my handbag to be delivered to my lawyer on my lunch break. Stuart kept several additional copies in a locked file cabinet in the office and said he had brought one home. We were armed, if clumsily, against whatever political weaponry Larry chose to launch at us.

But that morning was quiet—relatively speaking. The phones still rang incessantly, but now it was all people seeking Michael out for quotes and speaking engagements. In fact, when a civic center in Laurel asked for him to come out for an evening, finding a free time slot was difficult. He was booked most nights until the election in one capacity or another.

Which was a great sign. The race was heating up, and people wanted to be informed about their choices.

It didn't hurt that he was young and attractive either, I thought as I watched him shake hands with a reporter from the *Montgomery Sentinel*. They had started a weekly series in which they asked each candidate a few of the same questions and contrasted their answers.

I left for Greg's office at midday, and he was thrilled with the evidence from the motel. "A lot of people use fake names there," Greg said. "You're sure this is his handwriting?" I confirmed that it was. Greg shook his head. "Unbelievable." He grinned at me. "He won't underestimate you again, that's for sure."

"You do your job well and he won't have a chance," I said.

"It would have been great if you could get one of the girls to talk, but this will do." He glanced at a calendar on his desk. "We've got six weeks to go until the hearing. The photographs of you and Michael aren't great obviously, but a public street is a very different situation from checking into a motel with someone." His expression turned more serious. "Do try to keep your hands—and mouths—off each other until the divorce is finalized though, okay?"

I agreed and left to return to the office, hungry but unwilling to waste the time on picking up lunch when there was so much work to be done.

When I reached my desk, however, a wrapped sandwich from Hofberg's Deli was sitting there, my usual order scrawled across the butcher paper in grease pencil.

I looked up at Stuart, who was taking the last bite of his own pastrami sandwich, and held the sandwich up at him questioningly.

"Wasn't sure you'd have time to get lunch," he said. "Besides, you don't want to go in there today. Two kids got into a fight with condiments, and there's mustard everywhere."

⁓

The reporter from the *Washington Post* called a little after 3:00 p.m.

Claire's classes ended at noon on Monday, Wednesday, and Friday, so she came in at one and was back on the phones. Paul had driven her, and I was watching the two of them with great interest to see what might be happening when they weren't in the office.

"Yes," Claire was saying. "Can I tell him what this is regarding?"

She listened, then gestured for me and held her hand over the receiver. "*Washington Post*," she whispered. "They want a quote from Michael on something."

I could feel the color draining from my face. "Did they say what about?"

She shook her head.

It could be something else, I thought. *Or for the endorsement piece.*

But it was only September. They'd endorse a candidate in late October.

"Wait a minute and then transfer them," I said.

I walked toward Michael's office, feeling like I was moving through water. The door was open, so I didn't knock. "Claire is about to transfer a reporter from the *Post* through," I said.

"Great. Do you think it's the endorsement?" He looked up at me, his smile fading as he took in my face. "Oh."

"They didn't say," I said.

Michael nodded, then came around his desk. He guided me to a chair and shut his office door just as his phone rang.

"Michael Landau," he said. He listened for what felt like an eternity. "I see. No, I don't have any comment on that."

I waved my arms wildly to get his attention.

"Hang on just a moment, please," he said and covered the mouthpiece. He mouthed the word *What?* to me.

"Is it about us?" He nodded. "You have to comment."

He held the receiver further away, his hand still over the mouthpiece. "What do you want me to say?"

I tried to come up with the right words, but I was frozen. This was all my fault, and the wrong statement would ruin everything and everyone's trust in Michael.

Finally Michael brought the receiver back to his mouth. "Sorry about that. Yes, the kiss happened. We were celebrating a campaign victory and got carried away. Little too much champagne at your boss's house. We both immediately regretted it and mutually expressed that nothing like that will ever happen again as we have enormous respect for one another professionally, but no romantic feelings toward each other." He listened again. "No, that was the only time anything like that ever happened and the only time it will." Another pause while I heard only the tiny humming sound of the reporter's voice over my heartbeat. "Mrs. Diamond is currently separated from her husband and will be divorced by the end of October. I did not know her prior to June, when she came to work for me after she was already separated from her husband, and our relationship has been strictly professional other than that one indiscretion." More nasal humming. "My record speaks for itself. And I think the fact that I have a female campaign manager is evidence enough of the strong respect I have for women both in and out of the office." The reporter spoke again. "I can get her," Michael said. "It's not like she's sitting in my office." He laughed. "Give me a minute—she may be on another call."

He held the phone out to me, but I shook my head. He held it out again and mouthed, *You can do this.* I took the receiver, but he mouthed, *Wait,* then got up, opened his office door, closed it again loudly, and then said, "Just answer honestly. I already told him what happened."

Uncertainly, but buoyed by his belief in me, I held the phone to my ear. "Beverly Diamond," I said.

"Mrs. Diamond," the reporter said. "James Peyton with the *Washington Post.* I wanted to ask you a few questions regarding your relationship with Mr. Landau."

I couldn't explain what snapped. Maybe it was being referred to by the name Larry had used to sign his women into the motel. Maybe it was the fact that he asked me about Michael instead of asking what happened. Or maybe I was just tired of everything being about a man.

"How about asking about my relationship with my soon-to-be ex-husband instead? He's the reason you have this story in the first place."

I could hear a pencil scratching on paper. "Sure," he said. "Tell me about that."

I began with walking in on him and Linda, though I didn't name her. And I explained how Larry's threats led to me working for Michael.

"And the affair?"

"Larry's?"

"No, yours."

I stood up and started pacing with the phone receiver, the cord pulling me back when I went too far. "Now you listen here," I said. "There's no affair. There was a single, celebratory kiss. Did you track down the woman from that photo in Times Square when the war ended to ask if she was having an affair with the soldier who kissed her? No. The only reason you *think* there's an affair is because Larry told you there was."

"Your husband didn't give us a quote."

I stopped pacing. "What do you mean he didn't give you a quote?"

"The photographs were sent to us from Sam Gibson's office, but Mr. Diamond refused to comment."

I cursed him in my head. What kind of trick was this? Why wouldn't he comment but try to get Michael to?

I didn't know the answer.

What I did know was that I wasn't letting him win.

"Sam got the photographs because Larry hired a private investigator to try to blackmail me. He brought the pictures to me first and said if I didn't quit the campaign, he would use them both to get the kids in the divorce and to make sure Michael lost. And off the record? Why don't you look into that girl who supposedly had Tom Stanton's baby six years ago? I doubt you'll find that child on any school enrollment records."

The reporter let out a low whistle. "That's quite the allegation."

"And I said it was off the record. Try doing your job instead of just printing what Sam Gibson's campaign tells you to." I hung up the phone.

"Beverly!" Michael said.

"What? I'm sick and tired of this, and someone needs to know the truth."

He chuckled in surprise. "I think a whole lot of people are about to know the truth," he said.

"Good."

"You didn't mention the Colonial Manor."

"It slipped my mind," I admitted. "But why play all my cards now when he just has time to find a way around it in court?"

Michael shook his head. "Remind me never to make you mad."

I smirked at him as I went to the door. "Remind yourself," I said. "I'm a campaign manager, not your secretary."

I could hear him laughing behind me as I went back to my desk.

49

A week went by. An agonizingly slow week in which I heard nothing from Larry, nor saw anything in the newspaper, despite combing the *Post* daily.

Stuart came back from lunch the following Thursday spewing profanities and clutching two newspapers. My stomach dropped.

"Michael," he bellowed, barely glancing at me.

Michael came out of his office, saw the newspapers in Stuart's hand, and closed his eyes for a few seconds. "How bad?"

"Front page of both the *Sentinel* and the *Gazette*. I haven't seen the other county weeklies, but I'm sure they're there too."

Michael took the papers from Stuart and put them down on a desk, which the three of us crowded around. The picture of us kissing was on the front of both papers, above the fold. The articles were different, but the gist was the same, with information clearly supplied by Sam and Larry.

Michael put a finger down at a line toward the end. "It says we declined to comment. But they didn't call us."

"They did, actually," Stuart said quietly. We both looked at him. "I said we had no comment."

Michael's shoulders sagged.

"What?" Stuart asked. "We don't comment on gossip."

"This wasn't gossip," I said weakly.

"What's that supposed to mean?"

"We talked to the *Washington Post*," Michael said.

"You—what?"

"Bev thought—"

"If Bev was thinking anything, we wouldn't be in this mess."

"Hey!" I said, but Michael cut me off.

"I kissed her. Blame me," he said. "But she was right. We commented to the *Post*, and they didn't run their story. There's not a lot we can do once this is out there."

No one replied immediately, and I was sure Stuart was going to blow his top. But he didn't. "Next time, maybe fill me in on your strategy meetings," he said. "Sorry I blamed you, Bev."

"It's okay." I looked down at the newspapers again, hating that this was getting delivered across the state as we spoke. "But what do we do now?"

"Press conference," Stuart said. "Michael gets out ahead of it, apologizes, says it hasn't happened since and won't happen again."

I shook my head. "I wasn't going to speak to the reporter, but Michael insisted," I said slowly. "And he was right. But a press conference is too visible. A quote in the *Post* is one thing, but it won't even matter what he says in a press conference. Voters will just remember that there was a scandal."

"Then what?" Stuart asked.

"Give me a minute," I said. "I'm thinking." There was no way I could do a press conference in Michael's place. And no one knew who I was, other than the adulteress the articles painted me as. "I'm going to write a letter to the editor," I said finally, thinking out loud.

"To both papers?"

I inclined my head, still working out the details in my mind. "Only if the *Post* won't run it."

"Why would you write it to the *Post*?"

"Because they didn't run their story yet, which means they're either investigating what I said about Tom Stanton, or they're sympathetic to us and scrapped it. But either way, they can run it sooner because they're daily. They've got a wider readership. And they'll like running a scoop that the locals didn't have." I thought again. "I'll send it to the *Baltimore Sun* too."

Michael and Stuart were both looking at me. "And you think that'll be enough?" Stuart asked.

I nodded, but Michael shook his head. "I don't want you falling on your sword for me."

"Don't take this the wrong way," I said. "But I think you've got the metaphor backward. You're not the knight here. I am." He started to reply, but I cut him off. "You go call Helen and tell her the *Sun* is likely going to run something too, so she'll know how to reply if people ask her. I'm going to call Anna."

The phone started ringing, and Stuart moved to his desk. "Wait," I said as he put his hand on the receiver. He raised his eyes. "Say we're working on a full statement now, but there is not and never was a relationship between us, and this is part of a smear campaign by Sam Gibson and his team."

Our gazes were locked for a full two rings before Stuart picked up the phone. "Landau campaign. He's not available right now. Yes, we've seen the story. We're working on our full statement now, but Mr. Landau and Mrs. Diamond are not now and have never been involved with each other. Mrs. Diamond's husband hired a private eye and caught a moment that they both agreed was a mistake and used that as part of a smear campaign to help his candidate win. Yes. No. That's all I have to say because that's all that happened. Yes. Stuart, S-T-U-A-R-T Friedman. F-R-I-E-D-M-A-N. Mr. Landau's campaign manager. Yes, there are two of us . . ."

I slipped out of the office and went down the street to a pay phone. I didn't want Stuart yelling into a phone in the background when I called Anna. I put my dime in and asked the operator to connect me. Anna's housekeeper answered. I gave her my name and waited while she got Mrs. Wainwright.

"Beverly, darling, how are you?"

There was no emphasis on *are*, so she clearly didn't know. Then again, she lived in the District, so she likely didn't get the Maryland newspapers. And I wasn't sure anything other than the *Post* was allowed to cross her doorstep.

"I've been better," I said, and explained the dilemma we found ourselves in.

"How dreadful," she said. "Although I could tell there was chemistry between the two of you."

I shook my head. No wonder she and my mother were friends. "Listen, Anna, I want to write a response."

"I wouldn't," she said. "No one puts any stock in the local weeklies."

"I know," I said. "That's why I want to write it for the *Post*."

There was a long silence. "I think you're calling the wrong person for that."

I knew that wasn't even a little bit true. She chose to have no say in the business. "You know everyone in that newsroom—"

"Socially," she reminded me. "Not professionally."

"Maybe," I said. "But I'm going to write a letter to the editor anyway. I'd love it if you would maybe just mention to editorial that it's worth running."

Another long pause. "Henry would be furious," she said, and I felt my shoulders drop. "But . . ." I perked back up. "I suppose I could take a couple of wives to lunch."

"You're amazing," I told her. "Truly."

"That'll only get you so far," she warned. "Make sure it's worth running."

"I will. Thank you."

"And just so you know—although I didn't tell you this—they're following the lead you gave them now. So if you have anything solid on that whole situation six years ago . . ."

"I don't," I said. "But I will let you know if I find anything."

"Heavens, not *me*," she said. "Call the newsroom if so."

"Of course."

"Give my love to your mother," Anna said. I promised I would, and she hung up.

50

The phones were ringing constantly when I came back into the office, but Michael told me he would help Stuart and Charlie, who had shown up when his classes ended for the day, and to go sit in the relative quiet of his office to work on my letter.

I sat in Michael's chair, picked up a pen, and got to work writing. Claire could type it when I finished—if I tried, it would be another week before it ran.

But the words weren't coming. I couldn't go in too angry. Angry women were seen as too emotional to be trusted. Nor could I be a doormat. But finding the right balance was difficult, because the truth was that I *was* angry that I was in this position. Angry that I had to write this letter. Angry that Larry couldn't just own what he had done and let me go. Angry that I had so readily put myself in this situation. But also angry that if I didn't do something, Larry and Sam would win everything at our expense.

When Michael poked his head back in an hour later, a dozen balled-up pages sat around the legal pad on the desk. "What do you need?" I asked him.

He took in the crumpled pages. "Um—I'd normally hate to interrupt but . . ."

"Interrupt away," I said, leaning back from the desk.

"There's a woman here to see you, and uh . . . she said you offered her a job?"

I looked at him blankly for a few seconds, then jumped out of my chair. "Linda?"

Michael looked uncertain. "Maybe? Blonde. Said she came from Sam's office, and you said she could be my secretary?"

I hurried past him to find Stuart glaring at Linda at the front of the office as she stood in a cheap knockoff Jackie Kennedy suit and dented hat. Her shoulders sagged in relief when she saw me. "Linda," I said warmly. "Welcome."

"What is this?" Stuart asked, looking from me to her and back to me.

"This is Larry's sec—" I looked at Linda. "Former?" She nodded. "Larry's *former* secretary, Linda Fleming. I told her we could use a new secretary, with the interns back in school."

Stuart took my arm and forcibly tugged me toward the back of the office. "We just need a minute," he said over his shoulder to Linda.

"Let me go," I said, taking my arm back. "You can just say, 'Hi, Bev, can we talk in private?' No need to manhandle me."

"Sorry," he said, sounding anything but. "But what are you doing?"

"Winning my divorce," I said. "If she's here, it means she's willing to testify." He blinked twice rapidly and then a third time, then looked over my shoulder at Linda as he processed who that meant she was.

"Oh," he said, his Adam's apple bobbing as he swallowed.

"I went to see her after we got the motel book. She was scared that if she testified, she would lose her job."

"Does she have any . . . qualifications other than . . . you know . . . ?"

Men, I thought. "No formal secretarial training, but she's been on Larry's staff for"—I called over to her. "Linda, how long did you work for Larry?"

"A little over four years," she said.

"I'd argue there's a lot you can learn in four years on the job that you can't in secretarial school."

Stuart studied her for a few seconds, then turned back to me. "And you trust her?"

Not around Michael, but as a secretary, I thought. But what came out of my mouth was "I do." And I was surprised to find that was the truth. The fact that she quit and came here told me what I needed to know about her character.

"Then I guess she's hired," Stuart said.

I gave Linda a wink, then left Stuart to go to her. "So this means . . . ?"

She nodded. "I'll testify."

I fought the urge to whoop. "Thank you. Really."

"Listen," she said. "That article—they shouldn't have done that. That's why I'm here." I looked at her quizzically. "Larry knew full well you weren't cheating on him. He laughed when Sam suggested hiring a PI. And he wouldn't have the first idea of what to do with the kids. I heard him telling Sam that too." She looked down at her hands. "I—I knew they fought dirty. That whole Tom Stanton thing. I thought that was what all campaigns did. But that's not true, is it?"

"It's not. A lot do, but not all."

"And this one?"

"Clean as a whistle," I said. Then I realized what she had said. "Wait. What do you know about the Tom Stanton thing? You weren't working for Larry then. You had to still be in school."

She didn't reply, but looked guilty.

"Linda," I said. "What do you know?"

"You—you won't let them know I told you?" I mimed crossing my heart. "My sister was the one who said she was pregnant."

I stared at her. "Your . . . sister?"

Linda nodded. "My daddy was sick—he's gone now—but we needed the money for treatment. And Betty met Sam when she was waiting tables at Mrs. K's Toll House." Her eyes were fixed on a spot on the ground. "He took her out and helped a lot. He was married, but . . ." She shrugged.

"Wait, Tom Stanton took her out?"

Linda looked up. "No, Sam did. Came to the house to pick her up and everything."

"Sam had an affair with your sister?"

She nodded again. "But then he talked her into saying she'd been with Tom Stanton. He said he'd pay Daddy's medical bills and then give me a job when I finished school."

I stared at her. "And—and the baby?"

"There never was a baby. They paid her to say that so Sam would win."

"Michael!" I yelled. "Stuart! Get over here!"

Linda backed away, but I reached out and took her wrist as the two men advanced on us. "There's nothing to be afraid of," I said. "But I'm going to need you to tell them EXACTLY what you just told me." I turned to Michael and Stuart. "I think we just won the election."

51

I called my mother to tell her I would be home late, and after we sent Linda home for the day, Michael, Stuart, and I sat around the table in Michael's office strategizing.

Linda told us that she had signed a document stating she would not discuss her family's arrangement with Sam, but both Michael and Stuart explained that was entirely unenforceable from a legal standpoint and in no way binding.

All three of us agreed, however, that it was best to keep her name out of the papers. Both because it would look bad for us hiring her and because we were sure Sam would launch a smear campaign against her, making her testimony at the divorce hearing harder to believe.

"Then it's worthless," Stuart said. "We already knew he was crooked."

"If the *Post* reporter is willing to talk to her anonymously, it could work," I said. "But the sister won't confirm anything. Linda said he got their name and called the house, and she refused to talk."

"How much of that was to protect Linda's job though?"

I didn't know the answer. All I knew was Linda said her sister wasn't saying a word.

"Let's just call the reporter and tell him what we know—in loose terms," I said.

"It's not much more solid than what you told him initially," Michael reminded me.

"We didn't know then that Sam was sleeping with a teenager whom he later bribed to lie about his opponent."

Michael and Stuart exchanged a glance. "Do we know how involved Larry was in all this?" Michael asked.

I leaned back slightly. "What are you implying?"

"Sam isn't stupid," he said. "He's not going to take the fall for anything."

I connected the dots. "If anything actually illegal happened, Larry could go to jail."

"Look, I'll employ you as long as you want," Michael said. "But that makes your life . . . interesting."

On the one hand, if he committed a crime, he belonged in jail. And on a personal level, I had no problem with that.

On the other, I didn't want the kids facing that stigma. Money would work itself out. But Robbie, in particular, would be ostracized at school when the news got out.

I swore viciously. "Honestly, can we just hire a hit man at this point?"

Both men chuckled.

"So we have nothing?" I asked.

"Not nothing," Michael said, putting a hand on mine. "Finish the letter. We'll call the reporter tomorrow. Together."

"Cut that out," Stuart said, plucking Michael's hand off. "You two caused enough trouble today."

"To be fair, it was a couple weeks ago."

Stuart stood up and shook his head. "I'm going home. If you're going to do anything else"—he gestured between the two of us—"keep it between these walls where it can't be photographed, please." He made a sour face. "And *not* on my desk." At the door, he muttered something that sounded like "Teenagers."

Once he was gone, Michael looked at me. "Want to go sit on papers on his desk so it looks like we fooled around there?"

"Absolutely."

He was right. We didn't have nothing.

52

Nancy's car was in my driveway when I got home. Michael had offered to drive me, but that wasn't smart on the day that the story broke.

"Hello?" I called as I walked in the front door.

"If it isn't Hester Prynne herself," Nancy said, coming from the kitchen in my apron. "Look, I don't blame you. He's good-looking. But how could you not tell me?"

"There's nothing to tell," I said, walking into the kitchen and looking at the remains of dinner. She was cleaning up. "He kissed me after we went to a party at Anna Wainwright's house, and we both said we couldn't do anything while I was still married."

"That's something," Nancy said. "We're still fighting though."

I laughed. "If you clean my kitchen when we're fighting, we should fight more often." I looked around. "Where's my mother?"

"Ha," she said slowly, drawing it out to multiple syllables. "She's lying down. I came over when the paper came, and she started waving it around and yelling that she'd have to move to Europe because she couldn't show her face in this country."

I rolled my eyes. "It wasn't even in the *Post*."

"Oh, I know. But it's all about her of course."

"Of course." I sighed. "I guess I should go check on her."

"Bring the sherry," she said. "Not to drink—you can hit her over the head with the bottle and put her out of her misery."

A loud crash came from the living room followed by shrieking. "Hey!" Nancy yelled, charging down the hall. "I told you if you broke anything, I was taking the TV apart!"

I grabbed the sherry bottle and headed upstairs.

My mother's light was off, a faint moaning emanating from the room. "Mama?" I asked, knocking softly at the partially open door.

"I don't know anyone by that name. I'm changing my name," she said.

I flipped on the light, and she squinted at me. "To be fair, Mama isn't your legal name."

She sat up and shook a finger at me. "Now see here, young lady—"

I held my hands up. "Do you want to hear what actually happened? Or just be upset?"

"I don't see why I can't do both."

With a sigh, I sat on the edge of the bed, starting at the beginning about the night of Anna's party. By the time I was finished, she was pacing the room, furious. "I have half a mind to call Larry's mother," she said. "Dreadful woman that she is."

I wouldn't call my mother-in-law dreadful, but her lack of fashion sense damned her irreparably in my mother's eyes.

"You do know we're adults, and this isn't like when Bertie Schwartz put gum in my hair?"

She crossed to me and cupped my chin in her hand. "You're my daughter," she said. "I'm allowed to be angry on your behalf."

Amazing how just ten minutes earlier, she was going to change her name and flee the country because of the shame I had brought on her.

"I called Anna," I said. "I'm working on a letter to the editor telling my side of things."

Mama sank back onto the bed. "So you're going to fix this by airing more dirty laundry? How you could do this to your poor father . . ."

"My father? Really?"

"This is his legacy."

"If his soon-to-be divorced daughter kissing a man and then deciding to do the right thing is his entire legacy, then he wasn't such a great congressman."

She leveled a finger at me. "You know that isn't true."

"Mama, listen, I'm fixing this. I promise. I'm not letting Larry win."

"No," she said. "You're not." She patted my leg. "And I suppose if my mother could survive me, I'll survive this."

"What *did* you do when you were young?"

She smiled. "You're not getting that story this easily."

53

My name is Beverly Gelman Diamond, and if you live in Maryland, you likely saw my picture splashed across your local weekly in a compromising situation with senatorial candidate Michael Landau.

I'm not going to defend the kiss. It shouldn't have happened. But if a movie camera had been rolling, you would have seen us both say exactly that approximately two seconds after the picture was taken.

And that is the entire truth. The article's allegations of infidelity are fabricated. I can't tell you for certain if it was my soon-to-be ex-husband in an attempt to blackmail me into quitting my work for the Landau campaign or if it was planted by Mr. Landau's opponent to discredit him—though my now-estranged husband threatened both. But I do know this was an issue that should have been handled privately between the parties involved and potentially in court next month when the marriage is officially dissolved.

But, because it wasn't, I want to set a few facts straight. The first is that I only joined the Landau campaign after catching my husband in a far more compromising situation. When he told me I couldn't keep the house (and I didn't know better, because who thinks that their marriage will end the way mine did?), I looked for a job. And I quickly realized that the field I knew best—if you know my maiden name, you know why—was politics.

Was I motivated by revenge? Yes. But that changed when I saw that Mr. Landau really is the best candidate for Maryland. I could have quit when my lawyer explained that my husband is legally required to support me. And I wouldn't be writing this letter if I had, because nothing untoward would have happened. But the truth is that this campaign is more important than me being humiliated in the newspaper.

Next, I think it's worth noting that Mr. Landau was willing not only to hire a woman, but to listen *to her. Say what you will about a momentary lapse of judgment, but this is a man who wants to serve all people, not just those who look like him.*

And finally, Mr. Landau is not someone who wants to play dirty to win. And believe me, we could. Maybe that's not the best quality for someone going into politics, but I know that I would rather have someone I trust representing me. Someone who, if I were to bring an issue to his attention, would actually strive to address it, not just pay lip service for a vote. How many of his promises has Mr. Gibson kept?

Mr. Landau isn't perfect. But who is? I prefer to judge a man on how he works to correct his faults rather than the facade of perfection he presents. And I hope, come November, that you will do the same.

Beverly Gelman Diamond
Campaign manager for Michael Landau

~

"Well?" I asked.

"I'm still reading," Stuart said. I continued to pace until he looked up. "It's good."

"Michael?"

He took a few seconds to reply. "I think it's incredibly well done," he said cautiously.

"But?"

He shook his head. "I hate to make you do this."

"Now you can cut that right out. You're not making me do anything."

He smiled wryly. "Fine, I don't like having to be rescued by a knight in shining armor."

"Think of it this way: I'm doing it to help the divorce go through without losing my kids."

"Much better."

Linda poked her head in the door. "Mr. Landau? There's a Mrs. Walker on the phone for you."

"Thank you," he said. Stuart and I stood up to leave as Michael picked up the receiver. "Helen," he said warmly. "Thank you for returning my call."

"She's a better secretary than you were," Stuart said, gesturing to Linda with his shoulder.

"That's because I was never a secretary."

Stuart shook his head. "No. I don't suppose you ever were."

I brought Linda the letter. "Do you mind typing this up for me?"

"Of course, Mrs. Diamond."

"Beverly," I said. "We're coworkers now."

She smiled, and I patted her shoulder before I went back to my desk. Paul was in that morning, and I had asked him to bring the letter down to the *Washington Post*'s office at lunch. Mailing would take extra days that we didn't have to waste, especially if we wanted them to run it on Monday or Tuesday.

54

The weekend was quiet. Well, relatively speaking. Michael had four engagements, but I bowed out—both because I wanted to spend time with the kids and also because I felt it was best we weren't seen together publicly until after my letter ran.

Unfortunately, after running into three women who snubbed me at the grocery store Saturday morning, I realized I couldn't be seen alone publicly until the letter ran either.

Fran and Nancy were the only ones who checked in. And I warned Nancy that between this and my impending divorce, being seen with me was likely to become social suicide.

"I couldn't care less," she said over the phone, the noise of her children practically drowning her out. "If you need to go to another store, you just call me. I'd like to see them try that with me there."

I grinned. Although knowing Nancy, she would be likely to throw a can of green beans at someone's head for not saying hello, and then I *really* couldn't be seen at the grocery store.

So I took the kids to visit my father, who surprisingly didn't think the news story would significantly hurt Michael's odds.

"Really?" I asked as we sat outside, the kids trying to climb the cherry blossom tree in the backyard.

"Really," he said. "Men are pretty willing to overlook an indiscretion. And you're both of age."

"Papa, nothing actually happened."

"Even better. But good luck convincing anyone else of that."

I told him about the letter, which he didn't think would make much of a difference. "In court, maybe," he said. "But this isn't like six years ago. He didn't get a teenager in trouble."

"That didn't happen either though."

He looked at me. "Like I said, good luck convincing anyone otherwise. But as salacious rumors go, this isn't terrible."

"Mama said I was ruining your legacy."

My father laughed. A deep belly laugh, which I hadn't heard since Mama left him. "And here I thought my legacy was civil rights. Apparently it was just a daughter who takes after her mother."

"What's that supposed to mean?"

He chuckled. "She still hasn't told you why her parents sent her away for a summer, has she?"

"You know about that?"

"Beverly, we've been married thirty years. There's not much I don't know."

"Okay, then tell me."

"Absolutely not," he said with a twinkle in his eye. "While that *would* get her to come home, disposing of a body is a lot of work and you know she'd make you do all the digging. There's no way she'd risk getting her hands dirty."

"You two deserve each other," I said, exasperated.

"I know you didn't mean that as a compliment," he said. "But I'm going to choose to take it as one anyway." He looked out at the kids. "Speaking of which, I think I figured out a plan to win her back."

"Which is?"

He shook his head. "I'll surprise the both of you."

"Papa, I really think—"

He put a hand on my knee. "I know you like taking care of me," he said. "But I convinced her to fall in love with me once. This old dog still has a few tricks in him yet."

"Okay," I said, not believing whatever it was would work, but choosing to give him the benefit of the doubt because I just didn't have the room to worry about one more thing right then.

~

Monday morning, Linda answered a call and said it was for me. Moving to my desk, I picked up the receiver. "Beverly Diamond speaking."

"Mrs. Diamond," a woman's voice said in the clipped tones of finishing school. "My name is Mary Dubois. I am the editor of the For and About Women section of the *Washington Post*."

I read the section daily but was a little confused about why she was calling me. "How can I help you, Mrs. Dubois?"

"Miss," she corrected curtly. "I'm calling today in regards to your letter to the editor."

"Wonderful," I said. "Do you know when it will run so we can plan accordingly?"

"It will not be running," she said. "As I understand it, there is an article in the works right now, and the editorial staff does not want your letter running before that."

"Oh," I said, my shoulders sinking. "I see."

"A secretary brought it to me," she continued. "And I disagree with the editorial department. While the format does not work as a letter for our section, I would like to run it as a column."

"You—what?"

"I believe you heard me," she said mildly. "And I do not suffer fools. Are you a fool, Mrs. Diamond?"

I hadn't been spoken to like that since I was in elementary school. "No, Miss Dubois, I am not a fool."

"Good," she said. "Then we'll get along famously. Expect to see it in print tomorrow. Good day, Mrs. Diamond."

She hung up before I could reply.

"Everything okay?" Stuart asked me.

"I—I think so," I said.

Michael walked out, three ties in hand. "Which one?" he asked.

"The blue," Linda and I said in unison.

"Good choice," he said, and he wrapped it around his neck, laying the other two over the back of a chair. Then he looked over at me. "What's going on?"

"They're not running my letter—"

Stuart let out a string of profanity that caused Linda's eyes to widen. "I knew Michael should have addressed it himself—"

"Would you let me finish?" I asked. He stopped talking. "That was the editor of the *Post*'s women's section. She's going to run it tomorrow."

"The women's section," Stuart scoffed. "What good does it do there?"

I thought about what my father had said. "Maybe more than in the news section," I said.

"Explain."

"My father said men aren't going to care about an indiscretion. He—he didn't think it would hurt our chances, but he was talking about with male voters. Women are the ones who aren't going to like this."

"How widely read is that section?" Michael asked.

"Everyone I know reads it," I said.

"We don't get the *Post* at home, but I used to swipe Larry's women's section at work," Linda said.

I looked over at her. "He got a second paper delivered to the office?" She nodded as I thought about how many times I had to read his leftovers stained with coffee rings. "That jerk." I shook my head. "Either way, I *think* this might be a blessing in disguise," I said.

Michael shrugged. "It's what we've got right now. So let's hope for the best."

55

I pushed the news section aside and dug through the section heads until I got to For and About Women. A blurb at the top of the page said a guest column from Michael Landau's campaign manager was on page 2. I turned the page and cringed at the sight of the photograph of us kissing.

Miss Dubois certainly hadn't included that element in our conversation.

But the caption under the photograph wasn't damning: "Photograph obtained by a private investigator hired by Mrs. Diamond's husband. Both Mrs. Diamond and Mr. Landau have confirmed this was a one-time incident that was a mutual mistake."

My eyes darted back toward the text of the column. With the exception of a few grammatical changes and breaking my paragraphs into smaller points, it was what I had written.

"And now we wait," I said.

"Wait for what?" my mother asked.

I handed her the newspaper. She shook her head. "That man deserves a swift punch to the nose."

"Michael?"

"Michael?" my mother asked. "No, Larry!"

I suppressed a smile at the idea of my mother throwing a punch. "I can't disagree."

She shook her head. "To put this in the newspapers. You never should have married him."

I couldn't disagree there either, but I refrained from reminding her that after our second date, she told me I should plan on a June wedding.

"Technically, he didn't put this one in. He tried, but the *Post* didn't run the story."

"Then what's this?"

"Mama, read it!"

She pushed the paper back at me. "Read it to me, darling, will you?"

I looked at her for a few seconds, then something clicked. "You need reading glasses, don't you?"

She sat up straighter. "I most certainly do not."

"Mama. Just get the glasses."

"Those are for old women. I can see just fine."

"Oh, for the love of—you're really going to make me read this to you, so you don't look old to *me*?"

She sipped her coffee. "Are you going to read it? If not, I'm perfectly content to go about my day without knowing what's written there."

"You are the most impossible—"

"Watch it," she said, holding up a finger. "Or you don't have a babysitter today."

"—ly charming woman," I finished.

"Much better," she said, smiling.

I read her the column.

∼

When I got to work, Michael and Stuart looked up at me expectantly. "Is something on my face?" I asked, digging in my bag for a compact.

"Did the column run?" Michael asked.

A copy of today's *Washington Post* sat on the desk next to him.

"Why didn't you—" I reached for the newspaper and then stopped. "Did you not read it because it's in the women's section?"

They both looked down. "It's not for men," Stuart mumbled.

"Really?" Neither would meet my eye. "Do you think someone will rush in here and put a dress on you if you read something in that section?"

"No," Michael said. But he still wouldn't look at me.

"Then what on earth are you so frightened of? Two grown men afraid to look in a newspaper. And you want to be in the Senate?"

"There won't be ads for . . . female products . . . in the Senate."

I blinked rapidly. "You do realize that if either of you ever gets married, you'll wind up sharing a bathroom with a woman who is going to need to use those products and who will very likely keep them in that bathroom, right?"

"That's . . . different," Michael said.

"Oh, for heaven's sake." I picked up the paper, pulled out the women's section, and folded the page so that the column and photograph were all that were visible. "Here. Should I pull the blinds too? Make sure no roving photographers catch you with this in your hands?"

Stuart glared at me and took the newspaper, which they both read, Michael over Stuart's shoulder.

"Is it working?" Stuart asked when he had finished.

"I don't know. Let me use the little transmitter in my uterus to ask all the other women." I placed a palm on my lower abdomen. "Yes," I said. "Mostly. Josephine in Rockville is still on the fence, but the rest of the women are on board now."

"If we lose the election, you have a future in comedy," Michael said, rolling his eyes.

"Better win, then. Because if I have to do comedy, I'm telling everyone about this ridiculousness."

The door opened, and Linda walked in. "What's the matter?" she asked when we all looked at her. She adjusted her hair and skirt. "Did I make a mistake?"

"No," Stuart said, shooting me one more dirty look. "*You* didn't."

The phone rang, and Linda hurried to her desk, answering it before sitting down.

I started toward my desk, but the door opened again, and I turned to see an unfamiliar woman. "Can I help you?" I asked.

"Are you Beverly?" she asked in a coastal Massachusetts accent.

"I am."

She held out her hand. "Evelyn Gold. I read your piece this morning. I want to volunteer."

I looked at her for a moment before shaking her hand. "You do?"

"Of course. That husband of yours sounds like a piece of work." She leaned in conspiratorially. "We were in Massachusetts all summer and my kids are in school now, but you and this Michael Landau are all anyone at the club has been talking about. Then I read that column, and I wanted to see what the hubbub was for myself."

"Great," I said. "How's your typing?"

"Terrible."

I smiled. I liked her already.

We had picked up six more women as volunteers by lunch. By the end of the day, we had booked four more women's club speaking engagements and had a team of fifteen women who wanted to help the campaign.

"What do we do with them all?" Stuart whispered to me and Michael. Michael looked as lost as Stuart did.

"Give them jobs the interns would have done," I said. "And actually—let's print more flyers. We can station them at grocery stores handing them out."

"Will that do anything?"

I smiled. "Don't underestimate what determined women can do."

56

The rest of that week and the next were a whirlwind of activity, and I somehow wound up in charge of the influx of volunteers. At one point, we had over sixty people, which our office obviously couldn't hold. It didn't make sense to rent out additional space for seven weeks, so I had to schedule people in shifts. And the grocery stores were a goldmine for convincing women who were on the fence and reminding women who had already attended one of Michael's events that the election was coming.

Nancy even came in three days a week, depositing her youngest with my mother, who even more unbelievably, was willing to watch someone else's child—providing her hands were immaculate, that is.

But as September wound down, I had to keep reminding Linda and Stuart that no, we couldn't book an event on Rosh Hashanah, which was September 28, or worse, on Yom Kippur ten days later.

"It's really okay," Michael said. "I think the last time I was in a synagogue other than to give a political speech was my bar mitzvah."

I put the heel of my palm on my forehead. "You don't belong to a shul?"

"My parents do."

It was way too late to get high holiday tickets for a nonmember, though I did think a synagogue might be willing to make an exception for a high-profile Senate candidate, which Michael now was, thanks to that kiss photograph. "You'll come with us," I said. "You can use Larry's ticket."

"What if Larry is planning to go?"

I shrugged. "The tickets are at my house. If he wants to go, that's his problem."

"Just a minute," Stuart said. "I don't think that anything . . . polarizing . . . is smart this close to the election."

I looked at him. "We have a Catholic president. People don't care *what* you believe in anymore, they just want to know that you believe in *something*. Besides, Jesus was Jewish."

"Did you just compare—?"

"No," I said firmly. "I stated a fact. And my father always said that it was important that your constituents see that you do normal things. You think he wanted to miss congressional votes for the High Holy Days? No. And if he did have to miss them, he would much rather be home watching the Senators play. But he did it because it showed he put his family and his faith above himself."

"If it's good enough for Bernie Gelman," Michael said.

"Oh no," I said.

"What?"

"I didn't think of that."

"Didn't think of what?"

I scrunched up my nose. "We sit with my parents."

"So?" Stuart asked.

"Are they still not speaking?" Michael asked. I shook my head. "Well . . . at least there isn't a swimming pool at the synagogue."

I closed my eyes for a few seconds. "I will get them to behave," I said. "You're welcome to come to Rosh Hashanah dinner as well, if you're not going to your parents' for that. Stuart, Linda, you too."

Stuart and Michael both said their parents would probably expect them, and Linda wasn't Jewish. "That doesn't matter for dinner," I said.

"I think—I probably shouldn't," she said. And I realized she was referring to her situation with Larry. It had only been a couple of weeks, but I already thought of her as part of our team. It seldom occurred to me anymore that she was the one who set this whole thing in motion.

~

When I went home that evening, I waited until the kids were in bed to sit down with my mother. "We need to discuss Rosh Hashanah," I told her.

She looked up at me. "We'll do dinner here. Just us."

I shook my head. "You're not leaving Papa out of this."

"Beverly—"

"He's my father. He's the kids' grandfather. And he's your husband, like it or not. He's not spending Rosh Hashanah home alone."

Her mouth tightened into a thin line. "And what about *your* husband? *Your* children's father, then?"

"Did Papa publish photographs of you in a newspaper to humiliate and blackmail you? No? Then it's apples and oranges, Mama." Her lips disappeared entirely. "And you're going to behave in front of the kids, both here and at shul."

"I'm not going to shul if he'll be there."

"Yes," I said. "You are. Because Michael is going and using Larry's ticket, and we are presenting a unified front."

"You can't bring Michael to synagogue!"

"Why not? He's Jewish."

"Of courses he's Jewish, but think of the gossip."

She had a point.

"We'll sit you, the kids, me, Papa, then Michael in the row," I said, thinking aloud.

"You and Michael should be at opposite ends."

I looked at her again. "That puts you next to Papa."

Her lips vanished again. "Your father will have to be enough of a buffer." She thought for a moment. "What happens if Larry shows up?"

"I think the odds of him even realizing it's the holidays without me reminding him ninety-seven times are slim. It was a fight to get him there every year anyway."

"Was it?" she asked.

The first year it hadn't been. When Mama invited him to attend with us before we were married, he jumped at the chance. Which had likely been about my father. As soon as I had a ring on my finger, it took every trick in the book to coax him into going.

"Yes," I said. "And if you're not nice to Papa at Rosh Hashanah, you've only got ten days to atone for it. So be civil."

"I'll be perfectly civil," she said, standing up to leave the room. "As long as he doesn't try to talk to me. Good night, Beverly."

It was likely better than nothing. And I would pass the warning along to Papa. Whatever his plan to get Mama back was, Rosh Hashanah services were neither the time nor the place.

57

I left the office at noon on Friday to begin preparing for Rosh Hashanah. I had never hosted the meal at my house before, but it was a low-stakes dinner with only my parents and children attending. It would be nothing like the formal dining of my childhood, with aunts and uncles, cousins, and occasionally politicians galore. At least not this year. Maybe next, I thought as I browned the brisket to prepare to cook it. My mother had taken Debbie with her to pick up Robbie from school, promising them ice cream to give me time to cook, and in the rare silence of the house, it was nice to fantasize about a future in which I would be hosting the way my mother always had.

In the daydream, Michael was there, though I didn't assign him a role. I didn't want to presume what would happen in five weeks' time, win or lose. But it was my fantasy, and if I wanted him consulting my father about the slicing of the brisket, then that's where he would be. He would look awfully cute in an apron.

Larry wasn't allowed in.

Though, I realized as I flipped the meat in the pan, it *would* be nice to get to a place of civility with him for the sake of the children. Eventually. When the wounds were less fresh.

By the time the kids were back, I was ready to greet them with open arms. I led them to the living room and read to them, telling my mother to go relax. A child nestled on either side of me, I could turn off the election for now and just enjoy motherhood. As rewarding as my work on the campaign had been, this was the job I had chosen when I accepted Larry's proposal. And Robbie and Debbie were still the most important and best part of my day.

~

On Saturday morning, I scrubbed the children until they practically glowed before putting them into their new holiday clothes, purchased a month earlier by my mother.

"I don't yike dis dress," Debbie said petulantly as I pulled a brush through her hair.

"Why not?"

"I told Gramma, I yike *yellow*!" She stomped her foot.

I had anticipated that when my mother brought the pink dress home and showed it off to me. "Oh dear," I said gravely. "But if you wore yellow, you wouldn't match this." I reached under my bed and pulled out a bag.

"What is it?" Debbie asked, her voice full of distrust.

"Open it," I said.

She did and squealed as she pulled out a new Barbie doll in a dress the same shade as her own. She hugged the doll to her chest, and I smiled down at her, hoping she would always be this happy.

Robbie complained about his tie but otherwise behaved. And my mother swept into the room eventually in a new suit as well.

"Aren't you going to get dressed?" she asked me, as if I hadn't just spent the last hour on the children while she completed her look.

It hadn't occurred to me to get anything new. And people would most definitely look with Michael there. I was going to ask if I could borrow a dress of hers, but she left the room.

Sighing, I went to my closet to look through my options for something that wouldn't be memorable as having been worn before, when I heard my mother walking back into the room. I poked my head out of the closet to find her holding a garment bag.

"What—?" She unzipped the bag and pulled out the most gorgeous turquoise dress, with a high neck, a belted bow waist, and slightly flared skirt. "Oh, Mama," I exhaled.

She took it off the hanger and held it out to me. "I know you think I had it much easier when you were little—and maybe I did. But I also remember what it's like to put yourself last and put everyone else first."

I blinked rapidly to keep my eyes from filling. I didn't know what was wrong with me. It was like crying in that motel parking lot had flipped switches inside my tear ducts, and now I couldn't shut them back off.

"Thank you," I said thickly.

She held out a gloved hand to each child. "Come along, darlings. Let's let Mama get dressed in peace for once."

~

Dressed and made up, I looked in the full-length mirror. It took me a moment to recognize myself. This wasn't Beverly, who ran a campaign, or Mrs. Diamond, the perfect wife. It was me. The woman in the mirror winked, and I smiled back at her.

"Let's go, slowpokes," I called down the hall.

"What do we say today?" my mother asked the children.

"*L'shana tova,*" they said in unison.

"Good," she said, crouching down to straighten Robbie's tie. "Now remember, best behavior."

Debbie clutched her doll tightly. "Barbie behaves too."

It wasn't until we were in the car that I realized how much additional stress Larry had created around the holidays. We had never made it to shul without a tantrum on someone's part before. And as I glanced over at my mother, I took a hand off the steering wheel and placed it on top of hers. "Thank you," I said. "For everything."

She smiled at me. "What are mothers for?"

58

We parked, waving to the police officer who was directing traffic on the holiest of days to make sure people who chose to walk to shul were safe on the busy street, and we each took a child's hand as we made our way to the front doors of the synagogue.

Services had already started—we never went for the very beginning, especially not with the kids, but planned to arrive in time for the Torah service. And we weren't the only ones, as there was a crowd of people in front of the building, talking and admiring each other's finery before going inside.

As a teenager, I often felt that our two-holidays-a-year trips to synagogue (three, if you counted Kol Nidre, the night before Yom Kippur, as a separate holiday) were hypocritical at best. Yes, my father said the Hebrew prayers, but as we seldom even hosted a real Shabbat dinner unless someone Jewish and important was coming to the house on a Friday, it felt like lip service to the congregation to secure votes. And for my mother, it was purely a chance to preen and show off.

But Papa had explained to me, when I announced at sixteen that I was not going, that it was about community more than religion. And that it was a mitzvah to go, not because we believed we would be punished if we didn't, but because our religion required a minyan—ten Jews—to say certain prayers. "If we stop going," he said, "who will be left?"

And I understood that he didn't mean "we" as a family. He meant "we" as the Jewish people overall.

My heart swelled as I saw Michael standing in the congregated group. He was next to my father and speaking to several men as my father nodded approvingly. I didn't know if Michael had shared his rationale for entering politics with my father, but it felt like the sun was shining entirely for this moment, a sign from the heavens that I was doing the right thing.

Michael turned his head as if he sensed my presence and smiled broadly when he caught my eye. My father saw where he was looking and excused himself, then both men came toward us.

I smiled back, perfectly content.

And then a voice called my name from across the parking lot.

A voice I knew all too well.

As I turned to look, Larry walked in our direction, dressed in a suit and carrying a blue velvet *tallis* bag.

"Daddy!" both kids yelled, throwing off my mother's and my hands and running into the parking lot toward him.

I swore softly, then felt a hand on my arm. Nancy was there. She nodded at me, and I felt my spine stiffen, bolstered by her presence. We exchanged a look, no words needed.

Larry embraced the children, and my irritation rose. He needed to get them out of the parking lot, where a car swerved around them. But he eventually stood, swept Debbie up into his arms, wrinkling her dress in the process, and then took Robbie's hand to join us on the sidewalk.

"Beverly," he said with a nod. "I was hoping we could talk."

"You have some nerve—" I started, but Nancy interrupted me smoothly.

"Come on," Nancy said to the kids, taking Debbie from Larry and smoothing her skirt, then holding out a hand to Robbie. "Eddie and Patty are inside already and kept asking when you'd be here." She nodded to me again and led them inside.

Michael moved to her place at my side, and Larry looked from me to him and back to me. "I see," he said, setting his jaw firmly. "I should have known he would be here today. Sitting in my seat, I assume."

"What are you even doing here?" I asked. "You hate coming to services. And if you think after that stunt with the newspaper—"

"Well, it was right, wasn't it? Is he sleeping on my side of the bed too?"

"Now see here," Michael said, stepping in front of me. "You can't talk to her like that."

"Can't I?" Larry asked. "She's still my wife after all, no matter what the two of you are doing in my house."

"Larry," I said warningly, "this is not the time or place."

"I couldn't agree more," he said. "You don't see me bringing the people I'm sleeping with to synagogue, do you?"

And then the floodgates opened.

It happened so fast that at first, I wasn't sure that it wasn't me. Michael pulled an arm back, presumably to defend my honor in a way that would have ended his campaign—which might have been what Larry wanted in the first place—but my father grabbed his arm, stopping him. And then, from nowhere, a fist advanced, and suddenly Larry was clutching his bleeding nose.

I looked down at my own knuckles, expecting to see blood on them, but they were clean. And then I turned my head and saw my mother shaking out her right hand, a smear of red on her glove.

My mouth dropped open, as did those of the people around us. And for what felt like minutes, no one moved or spoke.

Then the yelling began, people shoving each other out of the way to get a better view of what had happened, a million voices going at once. Someone offered Larry a handkerchief; someone else patted my mother on the back. I stood rooted to the spot until a whistle shook me from my stupor.

The police officer who had been directing traffic ran over, parting the crowd like the Red Sea, until he reached the five of us. He took in the scene. Larry's nose. My father still holding Michael's arms. Then his eyes settled on my mother's glove.

"Did you assault this man?" he asked her.

She looked him right in the eye. "Why, yes. I did."

"Did he harm you first?"

"Only my daughter's reputation."

And then, unbelievably, he pulled the handcuffs off his belt and ordered my mother to place her hands behind her back.

"Excuse me?"

"You're under arrest," he said. "We'll sort the rest out down at the station."

"I most certainly am not," my mother said adamantly. "And you will *not* be putting those . . . things on me. Heaven knows the last time they were cleaned."

"Ma'am," he said, "I don't want to have to use force. But you *are* under arrest and are coming to the station with me."

The two of them stared at each other, saying nothing for what felt like a week. Then finally, my mother said, "I'll go to the station with you, but you will not put those on me."

Somewhat flummoxed, the officer agreed and began escorting her to his car.

"Wait," my father called. "Officer, I'm Representative Bernie Gelman, and this is my wife. I think you'll find there's been some kind of mistake."

"No mistake, Congressman," he said. "And I know who you are."

"Officer—"

"Take it up with the chief at the station," he said, opening the door for my mother.

She looked at the seat, making sure it appeared clean enough to sit on. "Bernie, give me your coat. I don't want to ruin my dress."

My father did as she asked, laying it across the seat, and then she sat on it. "Thank you," she said quite civilly. "I suppose I'll need a lawyer. But they're all in there." She gestured toward the synagogue.

"I'll take care of it," Michael said, his eyes wide.

"Thank you, darling," she said to Michael, then she turned to the police officer. "You may go now."

I hadn't yet moved, as I watched the police car drive away with my mother—MY MOTHER—on charges of assault.

59

Nancy's husband said they would take the kids home, and Michael insisted on driving me to the station, my father following in his car.

"What were you thinking?" I asked after a few minutes.

"Me?"

"Were you going to hit him?"

Michael smiled ruefully. "I don't know, honestly. It was instinct."

"You can't go around hitting people if you want to get into the Senate."

"No," he said. "Although there was a time when duels were appropriate."

"And how did that work out for Aaron Burr in the end?" I asked.

"Hamilton may have gotten the better part of that deal, if I remember my history."

"As I tell Robbie, fight with your words, not your fists."

Michael glanced over at me. "Yes, Mother."

"Don't you start."

We drove the rest of the way in silence.

∼

At the station, there was a kerfuffle in progress as my mother was fine with a mugshot, provided she could freshen her lipstick first, but she drew the line at fingerprints. The entire station seemed to have turned out to watch as the chief argued with her. Finally, he put her in a cell, giving up on the prints for the moment.

Michael and my father went to talk to the chief, and I followed while they began explaining the situation.

A few minutes later, a secretary came in and gestured for the chief. He excused himself, and when he returned, he told my father and Michael to follow him to speak to my mother and said there was someone there who wanted a word with me.

The secretary led me to an interrogation room with a small table and two chairs. Larry was sitting in one of them.

"No," I said, turning to leave.

"Bev, wait," he said. "I told them I'm not pressing charges. I deserved it." I looked at him warily, and he gestured to the other chair. "Please? We really need to talk."

I moved the chair so it was as far from him as it could possibly be in the tiny room and then sat.

"What do you want?"

"I—" He stopped and thought. "I'm sorry."

My expression didn't change. "For which part?"

"All of it. Today. The pictures. Cheating." He looked down at his hands, then back up at me. "Marrying you."

I stood up. "Goodbye, Larry."

"No, I don't mean it like that. Please. Sit. Let me explain."

Curiosity got the better of me, and I sat down, though I was close to joining my mother in her cell after that last part.

"Sam—Sam encouraged me to propose."

"You *married* me because Sam wanted you to?"

"It wasn't just—I liked you. I liked you a lot. But I wasn't head over heels in love with you, and I should have been."

"This isn't getting better," I said.

"I wanted to be. And he said—he said the best marriages are built on friendship and respect and grow into real love."

"What does Sam Gibson know about a good marriage?" Sure, he and his wife put on a good show. But knowing what I knew about Linda's sister . . .

"I didn't know—then—about all that." He looked down again. "I saw him as my mentor."

"We have kids," I said. "Did Sam tell you to do that too?"

He still couldn't look at me. "No. I wanted us to be happy," he said. "But being your husband wasn't always easy."

"Yeah. I know. You blamed me for Linda."

"No, I—I wanted to feel needed," he said. "You never needed anything. And it seemed like there was never anything I could do. It was—it was emasculating sometimes."

I didn't reply. I had spent so much of my life making sure he never wanted for anything. That he was comfortable. Happy. Fed. Cared for. And he was sitting here telling me he didn't want that?

It was what a wife was supposed to do. Wasn't it?

"Maybe *emasculating* isn't the right word," he said. "I—" He sighed. "I knew I was doing the wrong thing, and it just made me feel worse when you did everything right."

I wanted to go put my head down. My whole marriage was just something Sam Gibson told him to do.

Larry reached across the table for my hand, but I moved it away. "The first couple of years, I really was happy," he said. "I couldn't believe someone like you would want to be with me. And I shouldn't have said it was your fault with Linda. It wasn't. It was mine."

"Yes. I know that."

He pulled his hand back when he realized I wasn't going to take it and nodded. "And I came to synagogue today because I wanted to tell you that I didn't plant the stories in the *Sentinel* and the *Gazette*. Then I saw you with Michael, and . . ." He trailed off, shaking his head.

"You literally told me you were going to do that if I didn't resign, and I didn't resign."

"I wasn't really going to," he said. "Sam—Sam apparently sent the pictures to the papers before I even talked to you."

He seemed to think that was enough of a mea culpa. "You still gave the pictures to Sam."

Larry threw his hands up in exasperation, then made an effort to remain calm. "My job is to win. When our personal lives blended with professional, it got hard to know the right thing to do. I'm not perfect, Beverly."

The implication was that I thought I was. "No one asked you to be perfect," I said. "I wanted you to be a good person." He reached up and touched his nose, then winced. "You're going to need to see a doctor for that."

Larry nodded. "Sam isn't a good person," he said finally. "I do see that now. I still think he's a good politician, but I don't have blinders on. But listen—I was telling the truth. I didn't know the whole story about the Tom Stanton thing until much later."

Neither of us spoke for a little while. "So what happens now?" I asked.

"I won't fight for custody," he said. "I know Linda is working with you now. I won't bring the pictures into court."

"In exchange for?"

He shook his head. "No exchange."

"You don't expect me to quit the campaign."

"I mean, I'd like it," he said. "But I'm leaving after the election regardless."

"You are?" This was news. "What will you do?"

"I committed to seeing it through. But I don't really know after that. I always thought maybe I'd go into politics myself. Maybe start local."

I didn't think he had the charisma for that. But I had just seen the ugliest parts of him. And once upon a time, I had thought he was charming. I wouldn't vote for him. But that didn't mean other people wouldn't.

"Bev—I don't want us to hate each other. It's bad for the kids. It's bad for me."

I waited for him to say it was bad for me as well, but he didn't. And I realized that was the contrition I needed. I wasn't ready to forgive him, but he wasn't telling me what to do. He finally saw that I was my own person who could decide what I needed.

"I don't want that either," I said. "I'm not inviting you to Rosh Hashanah dinner yet, but I'd like us to be civil for the kids."

"That's fair," he said. "Do—do you think I could have them for some weekends? Maybe even overnight?"

We looked each other in the eye for the first time in the conversation. And I saw how much effort it took to ask that. He hadn't been a very engaged father, and taking them for a weekend—well, he had no idea what he was in for. But it meant the kids weren't just a byproduct of following Sam's orders after all.

"Debbie isn't fully potty trained yet," I warned. "You'd have to change diapers."

He smiled tightly. "I think I can figure that out."

Was that part of the problem? Would he have helped more if I had asked for it?

There were a lot of questions that didn't have answers. And I wasn't sure they all needed to be answered. For now, this was enough.

"Then I think we can arrange that."

"Thank you," he said. I nodded.

~

When we left the room, Michael was sitting on a hard chair in the station lobby. He rose when he saw me, then he and Larry regarded each other solemnly. "Be good to her," Larry said eventually. Michael nodded, and Larry left the station without looking back.

"You okay?" he asked me.

"Yeah," I said. "I think I am." Then I remembered where we were and why. "We should go check on my mother. Larry isn't pressing charges."

"I know," Michael said. "The chief told us."

"Then why—"

"Go look," he said. "I don't think we should interrupt."

I went down the hallway and peeked into the corridor where the holding cells were. My parents were both sitting on the floor, which in and of itself was shocking to see—my mother settled on my father's jacket, which was spread beneath her. They were holding hands, their foreheads touching between the bars.

My mouth dropped open.

"I think," Michael said quietly in my ear, "that she may be moving home soon."

I started to laugh, tears rolling down my cheeks, and I turned around, wrapping my arms around Michael's waist.

"*Shana tova*, I guess," I said, my tears wetting his shirt.

He kissed my hair gently. "*Shana tova*," he repeated.

60

My father brought my mother home to my house. Michael wound up calling his parents and staying for dinner, which was not the formal affair I had pictured, but instead the six of us pretending not to notice that the brisket hadn't been properly reheated.

After dinner, I went up with the kids to put them to bed—they'd had baths that morning and honestly, after the excitement of the day, I was too exhausted to make them do more than wash their hands and faces.

I assumed Michael would leave, but he was sitting in the living room with my parents when I came back down, a drink in front of each of them. My parents looked awfully cozy on the sofa, so I sank into the chair next to Michael's. "Got one of those for me?" I asked.

Michael got up, poured a fourth drink, and brought it back to me. My parents hadn't budged, and I noticed they were holding hands. I took a long drink, welcoming the burn because I knew it would provide some release from the day's stress.

"What are we talking about?" I asked.

"Your mother's right hook," Michael said with a smile.

"No," she said. "We were talking about Michael's college graduation."

I smiled at him. My father had to have loved hearing that. "Back to that right hook though." I turned to my mother. "What were you thinking?"

"I wasn't," she admitted. "But I did tell you he deserved a swift punch in the nose."

"Yes, but I didn't think you'd actually *do* it. What if you'd broken a nail?"

My father laughed. "Millie the Magnificent never breaks a nail. She's got excellent form." And my mother leaned her head on his shoulder and *giggled.*

"You've clearly had enough," I said, reaching for her nearly empty glass and moving it away from her on the coffee table. "And Millie the Magnificent? Huh?"

"She's already seen you in a jail cell," Papa said. "You might as well tell her."

"Tell me *what?*"

My mother snuggled in closer to my father. "That's how we met."

"You punched Papa?"

"No."

"I'm extremely lost here."

"I was dating an older man," she said, then held up a hand. "No names. But you've heard of him."

"You can tell her," my father said. "He died a couple of years ago now." She gave him a look, and he shut his mouth.

"Anyway, he was quite famous—not as famous as he *would* be, but a well-known person. My family didn't approve, obviously. Show people and all. And he wasn't Jewish. And was divorced. Well, he left town for a bit for work, and when he came back, he had married someone else. And he thought that didn't matter and that we'd continue on as we had been—she was out in Hollywood, and he was fine having me on the side in New York. He grabbed my arm and tried to kiss me when I said I wasn't that kind of girl, so I hit him."

I looked at her, wondering what was in that drink I'd just had. And also wondering who it was. "And you met Papa—?"

"Well, I got arrested, and my parents shipped me off to my aunt Ada for the summer. She was none too pleased with the idea of having to go back and forth to New York to meet with a lawyer, so she found one whose family was also in New Jersey for the summer."

I looked at Papa. "You—you were her lawyer?"

"I was," he said. "She was a firecracker." He kissed the top of her head. "Still is apparently."

"Pow!" she said, holding up a fist.

"I—this is a joke, right?"

"No joke," she said. "You wanted to know."

"What year was this?"

She thought for a second. "It was 1931."

Four years before I was born, and I was born in their third year of marriage. But who were the actors back then?

"Well, you have to tell me who it was."

She giggled again. "Frankly, my dear, I do not."

My eyes widened. "No. You dated Clark Gable?"

"More like dodged a bullet," she said. "Five marriages? No thank you."

I looked at Michael, whose eyebrows were practically at his hairline. "I got into a car accident, and I'm in a coma, right? None of this actually happened."

"Call your aunt Rose if you don't believe me," my mother said mildly. Then she stood up, still holding my father's hand. "Come on, Bernie. Let's go home."

And the two of them walked out together.

I looked at Michael. "I think I need another drink."

"It's been . . . quite a day. But I shouldn't. I need to drive home."

I began to tell him to stay. It wouldn't matter for the divorce, and Larry had called off his PI. "You should—"

"Mama," a small voice said from the doorway. "I had a bad deam. I seep in your bed?"

I groaned quietly, and Michael stood up. "I should go," he said.

"Yeah." I sighed.

"I'll call you tomorrow."

I smiled at him, then gestured for Debbie to come sit on my lap as he left. "Come here, honey." She crawled onto my lap, her thumb in her mouth. "You know you can't keep sleeping in my bed, right?"

"Pease, Mama? Just tonight?"

I kissed the top of her head. "Just tonight," I said, picking her up to bring her to my room.

Clark Gable could have been my father, I thought as I got in bed beside her. And somehow that wasn't the craziest part of the day.

61

I felt like I barely sat down in October. My mother gradually moved her things back home, where she was now sleeping, but still came to watch the kids—an arrangement that I promised would end after the election. I did worry vaguely about what money would look like if Larry quit Sam's campaign to run for office and I wasn't working, but, legally, that was his problem, not mine.

My parents attended Yom Kippur services without us.

Nancy came with me to the divorce hearing in the middle of the month. Michael offered to as well, but I didn't think that would look great after the kissing photos, even if the judge was supposed to remain impartial to anything not presented in the hearing. Besides, Michael had multiple events a day leading up to the election.

And the reality was that I didn't need him there. Greg had thoroughly prepared me on how it would all work, and now that Larry and I were no longer in contention about the facts of the divorce or the specifics of child custody, it was easy. And I was spared details of Linda's testimony. A simple statement that Larry was unfaithful with her was considered enough, especially combined with the hotel logs, and Larry offered no objections.

Larry nodded to me as we left the courthouse, and I offered a half smile. It was a strange, ridiculously quick dissolution to something that we had vowed would last forever. But even Rome had fallen eventually, and it was narcissistic to believe that I could, by sheer force of will, be the one to stop a clearly sinking ship. And if I was being perfectly honest, I felt a sense of relief that it was finished.

"So are you and Michael going to make it official now?" Nancy asked me in the car. She was dropping me back at the office before heading home. Stuart had driven Linda to the hearing. I had said she could come with us, but he thought that would look bad and said that he would bring her instead. He waited at the back of the courtroom while she testified and then left with her once she was dismissed.

I shook my head. "I don't know where he is on that, but we need to focus on the election. And if we're together right after we both said there was nothing between us, we look like liars."

"So November 7, I should plan to take the kids overnight?"

I couldn't help but laugh.

~

My mother was smoking at the kitchen table when I got home from work. "How did it go?" she asked me.

I opened the window over the sink and fanned smoke toward it. "As well as it could," I said. I heard laughter through the screen and looked outside to see my father playing catch with Robbie, while Debbie perched on the patio table, clapping loudly every time either of them caught the ball. I smiled at the scene.

"Excellent," my mother said, stubbing out her cigarette and standing. She pulled an apron from the drawer and tied it around her waist. "I suppose someone needs to start dinner."

The clock over the stove told me she should have started it an hour earlier. The kids were going to be cranky messes. "Mama," I said, reaching out to put a hand on her arm as she put a pan on the stove. "Thank you."

She didn't reply immediately. "You're welcome," she said finally. "And I suppose thank you as well."

"For what?"

She gazed out the window at my father and the kids, the edges of her lips curling up in an unconscious smile. "I don't think I would have left if you hadn't needed me."

"And that's a good thing?"

"Yes," she said. "I think it was."

"I don't follow."

She crossed to the refrigerator and pulled out the chicken breasts that had been marinating since the morning. "Do you remember when you were little and you would get croup?"

I shuddered. I had spent two nights in an oxygen tent in the hospital. I mostly remembered the sterile room and the sense of terror, but I still had nightmares about that. "I do."

"I dragged you to every specialist there was until we found a doctor who told us to take you outside. It was the opposite of what everyone else was saying, but we were desperate. And it worked. I wrapped you in a blanket and sent your father out in the cold with you while I packed a bag for the hospital. But when I came outside to get in the car, you had stopped coughing. The doctor explained that the cold air shocks your system and stops the coughing."

"But what—?"

She turned toward me. "We needed a shock to our system. I resented your father so much. I had thought, when he retired, that it would be our time. And it wasn't. And he couldn't hear me." She looked out the window and smiled again. "He hears me now."

I let my eyes drift out the window as well, only to watch Robbie's throw hit my father in the groin. I moved toward the back door as he doubled over, but my mother stopped me with a hand on my arm. "He's fine," she said.

"Are you sure?"

She shrugged. "It's not like we're trying to have more kids."

"Mama!"

"What? Besides, I hear him better now too. Do you know he cooked dinner the other night? I mean, it was awful, but he wants to do more. If we go running out there now, it looks like we don't think he can handle the kids."

I returned to the window. He was standing, a child wrapped around each leg as he tried to walk toward the house. "It looks like you're right," I said.

She winked at me. "I always am." She speared a chicken breast with a fork and laid it in the pan. "And absence really does seem to make the heart grow fonder. He's like a teenager in the bedroom now."

"Ew," I said. "I'm going to go change out of my work clothes. Don't worry about food for me. I may never eat again now."

The sound of her laughter followed me down the hall and up the stairs.

62

Michael, Stuart, and I crisscrossed the state those final weeks until it started to feel like there wasn't a person of voting age whom we hadn't spoken to personally. And we got a little help in reaching those we didn't meet as well.

On a rare morning when I was actually in the office, Evelyn handed me the phone. "Who is it?" I asked, assuming it was a press contact who had a question that Evelyn couldn't answer.

She shrugged. "She asked for you."

Mildly annoyed, I put the receiver to my ear. I didn't have time for minor concerns. "Beverly Diamond," I said. My name had been an interesting subject in the divorce—but I didn't have to decide immediately. And I liked having the same last name as my kids.

"I have a present for you," a voice said over a staticky line. "Call it a happy divorce gift."

"Marilyn?" I asked, pressing the receiver closer to my ear. "Where are you? The line is bad."

"Down in Key West. Make sure you watch Walter Cronkite tonight."

"What did you do?"

"Just watch the show," she said mysteriously. "Also, I know you're swamped right now, but Key West is lovely at Christmas, and you have an open invitation."

I told her I would think about it, then let Michael and Stuart know that *something* was happening on the news that evening.

"Something for the campaign?" Michael asked.

I should have asked Marilyn that. "I *think* so. Although it's Marilyn, so it could be anything at all."

~

My parents were both over again when I got home, which was happening more and more frequently. The kids loved having Grandpa there too. I told them about my call with Marilyn, and my mother didn't react at all.

"You know what she did, don't you?"

"Me? Why would I know what Marilyn is up to?"

"Because you talk to Aunt Rose long distance every day. I saw the phone bill when you were living here."

"Darling, I don't know *what* you could be talking about."

My father didn't make eye contact but hummed something that took me a few minutes to recognize as the "I like Ike" campaign song.

As instructed, I sat down to watch Walter Cronkite deliver the news. But when the broadcast ended with the anchor's signature, "And that's the way it is," an animated screen came on, with the words "A paid advertisement," and underneath that, "Paid for by the People of Maryland for Michael Landau."

My eyes widened. "What on earth . . . ?"

A rich voice began narrating over images of Michael from the photoshoot Marilyn's fiancé had done. "President Kennedy told us to ask not what our country can do for us, but what we can do for our country. A good start would be voting for Michael Landau . . ."

The ad continued for another twenty seconds, outlining our main talking points. The phone rang, and I picked it up, mostly to stop the ringing so I could hear the rest of the ad. I didn't even say hello.

"Is that—?" Michael asked.

I suddenly placed the narrator's voice. "It can't be."

We both stopped talking and listened again. "Gregory Peck," we said in unison.

My mother laughed.

I looked at her, the phone still held to my ear as the screen faded to black and was then replaced by an ad for cereal. "Mama, just how much money *did* Marilyn inherit from that aunt of yours?"

"All of it, it would appear."

"That—" I heard a phone ringing in the background on the other end of the line. "Are you still at the office?"

"I am," Michael said.

"Go home."

He laughed. "I'm just finishing up a couple of things."

A second phone rang. "This is crazy," I said.

"Is there anything you can't do?"

"I didn't do this."

"You kind of did," Michael said. "I'm going to answer these calls, then I'll go home. I'll see you tomorrow, Bev."

I turned to my parents. "I think we're going to win this thing."

"It's hard to say," my father said. "Ike was the first to use a television ad, and it certainly worked for him. But the presidency is different. You have a real shot though. Which is something he couldn't have said a few months ago. Win or lose, you should be very proud of yourself."

I was, I realized. But I still wanted to win. Even if that did make things more complicated for me and Michael personally.

63

I received another interesting call in mid-October, this time from Miss Dubois at the *Washington Post*.

"Mrs. Diamond," she said by way of greeting. "Have you given any thought to your career after this campaign is over?"

"I—uh . . ." My hand hovered over the press release I had been editing in pencil, the phone cradled between my ear and my shoulder. "I'm sorry, is this for an article?"

"No, Mrs. Diamond. I am an editor, not a reporter."

"I see. I haven't—I don't have a real plan. I'm going back to being a full-time mom, I think. Win or lose."

"Are you open to another option?"

Was I? "Maybe—but likely not until my daughter is in school. My mother has made it clear she doesn't intend to be my babysitter past the election."

"I'll speak plainly, Mrs. Diamond. Your column was popular. Wildly so. And I would like to offer you the opportunity to write for us on a weekly basis. I would assume that is something you could do even with a daughter at home."

I didn't speak for long enough that Miss Dubois asked if I was still on the line.

"Yes, I'm sorry, I'm here."

"I will need an answer, Mrs. Diamond. I am quite busy."

"What would I write about?"

"It would be a political column, Mrs. Diamond. About what you feel women voters should know."

I started to say I would need to think about it. But what came out was "Yes. I would love that."

"Your first column will be due on November 19. Five hundred words. And I don't tolerate tardiness. Good day, Mrs. Diamond."

She was gone before I could reply.

I wasn't my cousin Marilyn by any stretch. I would never write a novel or be a famous author. But I had learned in the last few months that I had a voice and a lot to say with it. And especially without a husband to cater to, I could write while Debbie napped or after the kids went to bed. Apparently, it *was* possible to have it all in the modern world.

~

The morning of October 22 started like every other. I woke up to the sound of my alarm at six. It had taken two months before my body adjusted to sleeping past five, and now, if I didn't set an alarm, I slept until the children woke me. Which, with Debbie's new fondness for my bed, wasn't typically past six, but we would get there. I quickly showered and dressed and made the kids their breakfast, then slipped outside to grab the newspaper from our front step while they ate. My mother had taken to arriving at eight, usually driven by my father, and just in time for me to leave. With them living together again, she had graciously granted me the use of her car.

I returned to the kitchen and set the newspaper at my place at the table, ruffling Robbie's hair as I went to grab my coffee from the counter. Then I flipped past the front section to Metro, as had become habit. It was where news of the campaign would be, along with issues that were most pressing to local people as opposed to national events.

My toast was halfway to my mouth when I dropped it.

The top headline on the front page of the section read "Maryland's Senator Gibson paid young woman to lie about opponent's affair."

For a split second, I thought it meant me and Michael. Then I read the first paragraph.

Linda's sister must have agreed to talk to them, I thought. But as I read further, the source was named as a member of Sam's campaign staff.

I leaned back from the table, looking at the kids, but not seeing them. *Could it have been Larry?*

Everything I knew about him said he wouldn't sabotage his own campaign. Even after his acknowledgment that he was leaving, and that Sam wasn't a good person. But who else could it plausibly be?

Either way, I raced to the office as soon as my mother arrived, waving the newspaper triumphantly like a flag as I entered.

Michael picked me up and spun me around, and Paul, whose classes began at noon that day, popped the cork on a bottle of champagne that someone had gifted Michael and poured it into paper cups that Claire passed around. She returned to his side when she was finished, and he pulled her in for a long kiss that didn't look like a first. I smiled even wider and raised my paper cup in a toast.

But once we finished celebrating, our conversation turned to the same thing I had wondered, with Michael asking if it was possible that Larry was the source.

"Anything is possible," I said. "Just look at us."

"It wasn't Larry," Stuart said, taking a sip of his champagne.

Michael and I looked at him. "How do you know?" I asked.

Linda ducked her head, and Stuart's face spread into the most genuine smile I had seen from him yet.

"No," I said. Linda nodded. "Why?"

But she wasn't smiling. "Because he's controlled my family for too long," she said. "I don't want to be scared of him anymore." She looked up at Stuart. "But Stuart said I didn't have to be." He wrapped a protective arm around her, and I found myself swallowing a lump.

"I don't know what to say."

"I appreciate that you trusted me," Linda said. "I wouldn't have been as kind as you have been if it were me."

I held out a hand to her, and she took it, and I looked around at the people gathered, who had become my second family. "No matter what happens two weeks from tomorrow," I said, "we're all going to be okay because we did this together."

Then Stuart yelled at me in typical Stuart fashion for being maudlin when this article was a clear indicator that we were going to win in a landslide.

"I love you too, you big lout," I said. "And just so you know, if we *do* win, I'm pouring a whole bottle of champagne on your head."

He grinned.

~

And then that evening, everyone forgot Sam Gibson existed.

President Kennedy addressed the nation, telling us that the Soviets had built nuclear missile launchers ninety miles from Key West, in Cuba.

My aunt Rose called the house in hysterics, telling me I had to talk some sense into my cousin and get her to fly home to New York immediately. I said I would try, which wasn't good enough for her, but the reality was that if Khrushchev launched missiles from Cuba, it didn't matter if Marilyn was ninety miles away or nine thousand. And to be honest, she might be better off being closer if it came to that.

Larry called, asking if we were okay. I said we were, but it was a lie. No one was okay.

And for the next week, all we could do was watch the news in absolute terror.

"Jack has a good head on his shoulders," my father said of the president the following morning. "He'll de-escalate this quickly."

"*Jack*," my mother snapped, mocking his familiar use of the president's nickname, "is practically Beverly's age. What does he know about avoiding nuclear war?"

"Would you rather have Nixon right now?"

"This doesn't help anything," I said. "And you're just scaring the children when you bicker."

"I don't see how you can send Robbie to school and then go off to work in times like these."

Part of me agreed. I wanted to hold him and Debbie and never let go. If the end was going to come, I wanted them in my arms when it did. And the idea of Robbie cowering under a school desk broke my heart. But I repeated the president's words to my mother. "The greatest danger of all would be to do nothing," I said. "That's what the president told us. We can't stop our lives and hide."

"If Khrushchev attacks, there won't be an election."

I looked at her from the doorway. "If Khrushchev attacks, there won't be a world. If he doesn't, I want to make sure that world looks safer for my kids." She started sputtering arguments, but I just couldn't. "You decide what to do with Robbie," I said. "I trust your judgment. But I'm going to the office. I love you both."

Stuart had brought in a small television, and we kept it on in the corner all day, watching to see if the programming would be interrupted with an update. Campaigning slowed to a crawl. The phones stopped ringing, except for the odd call asking what Michael would do to stop the situation with the Soviets if he won.

Sam, on the other hand, launched a television ad toward the end of the week. It was him, speaking to the camera, talking about the situation in Cuba and the importance of not changing horses in midstream.

"He does know a single senator can't do a damn thing to stop a nuclear war, doesn't he?" Stuart asked.

"He does. But he's hoping voters don't," Michael said.

"If this is still going on, no one is coming to the polls."

"If it's not still going on, we might all be dead," I said. "And by the time this is over, no one is going to remember the *Post* story."

That was the salt in the wound. We had him. And then we didn't.

"Let's worry about what we can control," Michael said. "This is scary for everyone. Marilyn's ad is better produced, and Sam has to be running his budget into the ground with his."

"What can we control right now?" I asked.

Michael smiled tightly. "Let's use Sam's playbook. We talk about de-escalation tactics and our desire to make sure the world is a safer place for our children."

"You already talk about making the world safer."

"Can we tweak our flyers to the situation though?"

I grabbed one off the top of the stack at the front of the office and picked up a pencil. "Better than sitting around waiting to be blown to kingdom come."

Linda typed up the changes once Michael and Stuart approved them, and I used rubber cement to affix a photograph of Michael to it before going to get them photocopied. Our volunteer squad had dwindled down to ten of the hardiest, who felt that sitting around worrying wasn't helping, and we dispatched them around town to hand out the new flyers.

And like the rest of the country and world, we waited, hoped, and prayed.

~

Then, as quickly as it began, the threat lifted—well, mostly. On October 28, Khrushchev announced he would dismantle the missiles, and we went back to work. But the story about Sam and Linda's sister was dead in the water. And the latest polling numbers had us trailing him by seven points.

"Polls are notoriously unreliable, especially for local elections," my father warned. "A lot of people who answer don't vote, and a lot of people who vote aren't polled."

The *Post* issued their endorsement, in an editorial listing their selections for all the candidates in the DC metro area, and Michael was the clear choice. They cited Sam's filibustering of one of the civil rights acts and the situation six years ago.

But as I got into bed on November 5, exhausted from our last round of efforts, I couldn't sleep, wondering if I had achieved anything these past months. This wasn't a case where there was glory in coming in second. It was a firm win-or-lose. And if we lost, I wondered how much more I would lose. Would Michael still want to pursue a relationship if I failed him? Would the *Washington Post* still trust me to provide insight for women voters? Debbie would be too young to remember my months of working, but would Robbie view it as nothing more than his mother's pitiful attempt at revenge? And as I looked down at Debbie's sleeping form next to me, I realized my absence during the day was likely behind her refusal to sleep anywhere but at my side.

Had I upended all our lives to chase something that would remain just out of reach?

In a perfect world, of course Michael would win. He was the better man. The better candidate. We had all the passion of nobility on our side.

But if the past few weeks had shown me anything at all, it was that our world was far from perfect. And greed, corruption, and scheming were often rewarded over virtue.

I sighed as Debbie snuggled in tight to me, her little body fitting itself perfectly into the nooks of my own. No. I did this for her as much as for me. Because I wanted this little girl to grow up to know she could do so much more than just marry well and make the perfect brisket. I wanted her to see that she could do anything, be anything, from a wife and mother to an astronaut. Okay, maybe not an astronaut. I'd worry too much. But the doors that had been locked for my mother's generation were merely shut firmly for me. And by the time Debbie grew up, I wanted them open, so she could walk right through, to whatever future she wanted. Because she deserved to be the person she wanted to be, not just who the world expected her to be.

And come what may tomorrow, I would make sure she learned that lesson, just as I had these last few months.

64

I woke up in the gray predawn of five and rolled over, willing myself to fall back asleep. But it was no use. Not with the polls opening in a couple of short hours.

I brought Debbie and Robbie to the polling station with me, my parents meeting us there. They would take them home, and then I would join Michael and Stuart to drive around to different polling places throughout the day.

As we went to walk in, someone called my name. I turned around and was blinded by a flashbulb, then another. Then a third. There was a news camera there as well, the reporter holding a microphone out toward me.

I hadn't expected that.

"Who are you voting for today, Beverly?" the one with the microphone asked.

I smoothed Debbie's hair down and then looked up at the reporter. "Why, for Michael Landau of course," I said with a big smile.

"Why?" another asked.

"Because he is the best choice to represent Maryland in the Senate," I said. "To represent *all* the people of Maryland." I saw a pop of color from the corner of my eye and turned slightly to see my parents walking toward us, my mother wearing an expression that said she was ready to revert to Millie the Magnificent if the reporters were harassing me.

"Here's my father, former congressman Bernie Gelman," I said. "Why don't you ask him who he is voting for today?"

"Representative Gelman," a reporter called, and I took each child by the hand and led them to the polling center doors.

I knelt down to their level before we went inside. "Now this is a big day," I told them. "Who knows why?"

"It's Election Day," Robbie said.

"Yeah, 'lex sin day," Debbie echoed.

"Very good. And what does that mean?"

They both thought for a minute. "We get ice cream?" Robbie asked hopefully.

I smiled. "Yes. If you're good. But it means today the adults choose who we want to represent us in the government. And who do we want?"

"Michael," they said in unison.

"And why is that?"

"Because he gave us flags?"

I laughed and ruffled Robbie's hair. "I suppose that's the way to win a five-year-old's vote. Come on. Let's go see if Mama made history or not."

~

Proudly brandishing their flags, the kids waved as they drove off with my parents. I would see them that evening, after the polls closed. We originally had planned to watch the news to find out the results at the office, but it turned out that all the volunteers wanted to be there as well, many with their families. So I arranged for the club to host us, and they agreed to provide televisions and refreshments. My parents refused to miss it as well, so the kids would be up late, despite it being a school night for Robbie. But I had fond memories of sitting on my father's lap, waiting to hear if he had won or not, though I never made it to the end of the evening when I was little. I doubted Robbie and Debbie would either. Especially if it was close.

We went to four spots in Montgomery County, shaking hands and handing out flyers to people as they walked in, before making the drive up to Baltimore, where Michael was photographed with Helen, their hands clasped together triumphantly in the air in front of a sea of primarily Black and brown faces.

I leaned in to Stuart. "If they win, that's the front page shot right there."

"Maybe in ten years," he said. "We're not there yet."

I felt my smile fading. He was right, of course. "Maybe sooner," I mused. "If they win, they'll make progress."

He nodded. "No matter what, we gave it our best, didn't we?"

"That we did."

Stuart squinted at his watch. "Don't get all sentimental now. We have to be in Bowie by four." He started gesturing subtly at Michael.

"What time is it now?"

"Time for you to get a watch. Why don't you have one anyway?"

"That's a long story for another day."

"We'll have nothing but time after today."

I looked over at him. "What are you going to do when this is over?"

His eyes were still on Michael. "Assuming we win, stay on as his chief of staff." He glanced down at me. "Unless you're planning to steal that job as well."

I shook my head. "My only job title is mom, come tomorrow. Well, mostly. The *Post*'s women's section offered me a job."

Stuart's whole body turned toward me. "Really?"

"Writing a column about politics for women."

He leaned away slightly, his arms crossed, then let out a whistle. "I couldn't have dreamed up a better job for you if I tried."

I grinned. "Why, Stuart Friedman, was that a *compliment*?"

He shrugged. "Maybe. Unless they expect you to turn it in typed. They'll fire you in an hour if that's the case."

A huge, unladylike laugh bubbled out of me. "Never change," I told him.

"I don't intend to."

I wrapped an arm around him in a side hug. He stiffened at first, then returned it.

"Well, you two look cozy," Michael said, surprising us. "Don't we have to be in Bowie by four?"

We just laughed.

65

I was exhausted, and my feet hurt. But I wasn't going anywhere. "Would anyone notice if I slipped off my shoes?" I whispered to Nancy.

She looked down at my feet. "Those are way too high. Have you even sat down today? Take mine."

I glanced at her shoes, which were brown. "They don't match my dress," I said. "My mother would have a heart attack."

"Your mother is three sheets to the wind and wouldn't notice."

"Trust me," I said. "She could be dead and still notice my shoes. Besides, there's press here." I gestured with my chin toward the photographer roving the crowd. And it was quite a crowd. I had told the club to plan for two hundred people, and it would appear I underestimated.

"It's a good sign," she said, looking around the room.

She wasn't wrong. And everyone looked so festive, almost like New Year's Eve. The only underlying tension came off in waves from our core team, and it was an effort not to bite my nails, something I hadn't done in at least fifteen years.

We had televisions stationed in three separate corners of the room, each tuned to a different channel, but no one expected returns to begin in earnest before eight. And we had sent Charlie to Annapolis with instructions to call the phone that Paul was manning as each district came in. Counties reported their results individually as their polls closed and they tallied votes. It would still be an estimate until we got official word from the state capital, but keeping track of the county winners would give us a solid idea of where we stood. And none of us wanted to wait a second longer than we had to.

Robbie and Debbie were yawning but running around with friends. I grabbed Nancy's wrist and saw it was a quarter to eight.

"Fifteen more minutes or so," I said.

Nancy shrugged. "Want me to take an inch off your shoes while we wait? I keep a hacksaw in the trunk."

I would have laughed except I knew she was serious. But then someone touched my arm. "Mind if I steal Bev for a few minutes?" Michael asked Nancy.

"I hope you take more than a few minutes," she said, grinning wickedly.

"Nancy!"

Michael chuckled, then led me out into the hall.

"What's going on?" I asked him. He suddenly looked like Robbie when he had done something wrong. "What is it?"

"I got you a present," he said. "I was going to give it to you after but—if we don't win—"

I held up a hand. "You stop that kind of talk right now."

"Okay. But, Beverly, I—I just want you to know, win or lose—" He stopped. "I'm mucking this all up, aren't I?"

I looked at him, suddenly suspicious. "You're not proposing, are you?"

"What? No! Oh no, is that what you thought?"

"Just making sure," I said. The official decree of divorce had come to Greg's office, but it was still a little too soon to be thinking about any of that.

"No. I just—you've been so amazing these last few months. And I wanted to say thank you." He pulled a long, rectangular jewelry box from a pocket. "So I got you this."

"What is it?"

"Open it and see."

I took the box and opened it. Inside sat a lovely gold watch. I looked up at him questioningly. "Is this a retirement gift?"

"I hope not," he said. "I just noticed you didn't have one and were always looking at everyone else's."

"It's not because I'm late so often?"

He looked confused. "Who would give a gift with a reason like that?"

I smiled, taking it out of the box and fastening it on my wrist. "It's perfect," I said, meaning it. "Thank you."

Stuart came out into the hall. "Charlie called from Annapolis— Sam got Garrett County."

Michael's shoulders sank, and I touched his arm. "We knew we wouldn't get Garrett. Or Allegany for that matter. But like Stuart said when we went out there, there aren't many people. Montgomery, Prince George's, Anne Arundel, and Baltimore are the big ones. They're the ones we need, and they're where we're strongest."

"We should get in there," he said.

I checked my new watch. "More results are about to come in. Let's go."

Paul was stationed at a table in the corner with a phone, Claire at his side, a notepad in front of her as she tallied up the number of votes we got from each county. Every once in a while, he signaled for quiet, which Stuart yelled for. "Allegany is Sam," he said. "We got Carroll!"

"One is a start," I said. "It's not over until it's over."

"And sometimes not even then," Stuart said. "Dewey defeats Truman and all that."

I smiled as I saw Fran enter the room. She looked around uncertainly, no longer a member of the club. But Sheila Meyers, who had been her friend prior to her divorce, greeted her warmly. Maybe my status had started a shift away from that stigma.

Between calls from Annapolis, Michael brought me to a table where an elderly couple sat, looking out of place. "Bev, I want you to meet my parents," he said. "Mom, Dad, this is Beverly." They both smiled warmly, and I sat to talk until Stuart called for me.

"I hope we see more of you," Mrs. Landau said, putting her hand on top of mine and squeezing it when I got up to leave.

"I would like that."

The crowd thinned out around nine as the parents of young children took them home, wiping out a good chunk of our volunteers.

Debbie was asleep on my mother's lap. "They should go home," she said.

"Are you volunteering to take them?"

"Absolutely not. I worked just as hard as you did for this campaign. You think it's easy chasing kids all over creation at my age?"

She had a point.

I took Debbie and laid her on a pallet I made out of coats in an out-of-the-way spot on the floor, then found Robbie and coaxed him with the promise of ice cream the following afternoon to lie down with her for "just a couple minutes." He was asleep as soon as his head hit the floor.

By eleven, we were neck and neck, with Montgomery, Prince George's, and Baltimore Counties still tallying votes.

"It shouldn't be this close," I said quietly to Stuart.

"The Soviets," he said back. "If they could have waited another month to build those missiles, we'd have had him."

"Helen won!" Paul called out.

Stuart threw a fist in the air. "That means we took Baltimore!"

"Not necessarily," Michael said. "But good for her."

"Good for everyone," I said. "I hope she runs for president next." The men chuckled, but I meant it. If she was born a hundred years later, she would be running the world.

"We got Baltimore!" Paul yelled.

Michael, Stuart, and I looked at each other and then suddenly we were hugging, laughing, and jumping up and down all at once.

"We're gonna win this," Stuart said. "We're gonna win!"

The room took up the chant. "We're gonna win! We're gonna win!"

"Prince George's went to Sam," Paul said.

The room fell silent. It came down to our county. The most populated and wealthiest in Maryland. And a Sam stronghold in the last election. The polls had given Sam a lead here, but a slim one at 50.4 to 49.6.

The only sound was the televisions in the corners, where newscasters worked late into the night providing updates from around the country.

Five minutes ticked by. Then ten. And then—

"You're sure?" Paul asked into the phone. "It's official?"

I grabbed Michael's arm. I had never fainted in my life, but the edges of my vision began to darken.

Paul looked up from the phone, his face breaking into a wide smile. "We did it," he said.

The room erupted.

I was spinning through the air, and everywhere I looked, people were hugging. Claire had jumped into Paul's arms. My parents were making out like a couple of teenagers. And Stuart—where was Stuart?

I scanned the room only to find him locked in a kiss with Linda. *I knew it,* I thought triumphantly.

And then Michael was in front of me.

"You did this," he said. "Bev—I—"

But I cut him off. "Fire me."

"What?"

"Fire me. Right now."

He looked confused. "I'm not firing you. You're the best thing that ever happened to me."

I sighed and rolled my eyes, but I was smiling. "Do I have to do *everything* myself? Fine. I quit." And then I threw my arms around his neck and brought my mouth to his.

"What just happened?" he asked when we surfaced for air.

"A United States senator can't date someone on his staff."

324

He laughed, his eyes shining with tears, and I found my own cheeks were damp. "No. Then I suppose it's a good thing you're not employed anymore."

"No," I said as he leaned in to kiss me again. "My work here is done."

66

As much as I wanted to stay and celebrate, the kids needed to go to bed. And while Nancy repeated her offer to keep them overnight so Michael and I could "celebrate properly," as she put it, Robbie had school in the morning.

Besides, Michael was on the phone giving an interview to the *Washington Post.* So I flagged Stuart over, and he carried Robbie out to the car while my father lifted Debbie.

Once they were in, I hugged Stuart tightly around his waist. "Don't get all mushy on me now," he said. But he wasn't grumbling for once.

I smiled and released him, holding out a hand, which he shook. "We made a good team, you and I," I said.

"We did. Although somehow I don't think I've seen the last of you."

I laughed. "I think that's a safe bet. Tell Michael to call me tomorrow?"

Stuart raised his eyebrows. "I don't think I need to tell him that."

"No. I suppose not."

"You did well," he said. "Really, really well."

It wasn't an apology for being a jerk when I started. But it was better than one. This was no grudging praise.

"You take care of our guy," I said. "And Linda."

He looked uncomfortable. "You saw that?"

"I did."

"I like her," he said. "But she's so young still . . ."

"I already had Robbie when I was her age. Besides, she's got life experience." I touched his arm. "Be happy. Life's too short not to."

Stuart ducked his head slightly, but I saw the smile he was hiding. "Drive safe," he said before turning to go back into the club. But he looked over his shoulder. "Give me a call when it's time for your campaign."

"My campaign?"

He grinned broadly. "I know a good candidate when I see one."

Laughing, I turned to the car to see my mother tucking a jacket around Robbie. Debbie was already similarly covered, a lipstick kiss on her forehead.

My father watched in amusement as his coat became a blanket for his grandson, then looked up at me and smiled. He put a hand on my arm and squeezed gently. "I'm so proud of you," he said, his voice thick.

"Are you okay to drive?" I asked.

"What? Of course I am. I just . . ." He wiped at an eye.

"Oh, Papa," I said, wrapping my arms around him, my own eyes watering. "Don't cry."

He squeezed me back. "My little miracle worker."

"I couldn't have done it without your help."

"Yes," he said. "You could. And don't let anyone ever tell you otherwise."

I wiped at my eyes with the back of my hand.

The valet brought their car around, and my father hugged me one last time before releasing me. My mother took my hand and squeezed it as she passed.

"What will you do with all your free time now?" I asked her.

She smiled. "Oh, I don't think I'll have trouble keeping busy. Besides, you'll still need someone to watch the kids while you write that column."

I looked at her, realizing that she hadn't reconciled with my father entirely because he bailed her out of jail. My needing her had given my mother a sense of purpose that had been lacking in the last few years. The same way working on Michael's campaign had for me.

"I'll always need you, Mama."

She squeezed my hand again. "Need me a little later tomorrow. After all this excitement, I'm going to sleep in."

"You should," I said. "And thank you. For everything."

"That's the secret, you know. You never stop being a mother. Even when your kids are grown." She climbed through the door my father was holding open for her. "And keep the car," she said. "Call it a congratulations gift."

I thanked her again, then watched, smiling as their car pulled away.

The air was chilly, and my coat was tucked around Debbie, so I got into the driver's seat and put the car—my car—in drive.

We headed up the tree-lined drive to Rockville Pike, which was quite deserted so late on a Tuesday. *Fitting that it ended here,* I thought, remembering how Stuart had changed my speech their first time at the club.

Except all that had ended was the campaign. The real work was just beginning. And I would be lying if I said a part of me didn't want to be in on the rest. But a glimpse in the rearview mirror as we passed under a streetlight reminded me that I already had the most important job.

Debbie let out a sigh in her sleep, and I smiled again. That was at least one little girl who would grow up knowing mommies could slay dragons too. I didn't know that Stuart was right about me, but Debbie would be thirty-five in 1995. Maybe by 1996, the world would be ready for a female president. My eyes darted to Robbie. He'd hate that. Not because she was a girl, but imagine having to tell everyone that yes, your baby sister was the president.

Maybe she'd let me work on her campaign though. I did have the chops now.

I woke Robbie to get him inside and carried Debbie in, humming "Hail to the Chief" softly as she stirred. I laid her on her bed, then got Robbie changed and tucked him in.

"Did we win?" he asked through a yawn.

"We did," I whispered, leaning in to kiss his forehead.

"Yay," he said, then rolled over and was asleep.

I got Debbie into her pajamas, but her eyes opened when I tried to brush her teeth. "I seep in your bed. Pease, Mama?"

I shook my head. "No, honey. Big girls sleep in their own beds." She started to protest, but I smoothed her hair and kissed her forehead. "But Mommy will be home with you tomorrow. Should we make a cake to celebrate?"

She yawned. "Chocolate?"

"Whatever kind you want."

"Okay," she said. "I seep here. Love you, Mama."

I kissed her one more time. "I love you too. Good night, Madam President."

For a long moment, I stood in her doorway, watching her sleep. Then I made my way downstairs, where I poured myself a drink. The house was strangely quiet with the kids asleep and my parents gone. *Maybe we should get a dog,* I thought. The kids would certainly love it. My mother wouldn't, but, well . . . it wasn't her house. It was mine.

Mine. I sipped my drink, then almost dropped the glass when there was a knock at the door. Glancing down at my new watch, I saw it was after midnight.

Larry, I thought. Even if it was congratulatory, he was the last person I wanted to see when I was riding such a high. I debated pretending I was already asleep, but with the lights on, he'd know that wasn't true.

With a sigh, I went to the front door and opened it. "Listen, it's late—oh!"

Michael was standing on the doorstep, flowers in hand. "You left without saying goodbye," he said.

I inclined my head to invite him in, and he held out the flowers. "Where did you get these this late?"

He grinned sheepishly. "Swiped them from a centerpiece at the club."

I laughed, then looked up at him. "The kids are sleeping." I bit my bottom lip suggestively.

"Now you listen," Michael said primly. "I'm not that kind of girl."

I laughed again. "Think you can find a sitter for tomorrow night?"

"I think I can arrange that."

"Good," he said. "I want to take you out on a proper date. Now that you're not my campaign manager anymore."

"I'd like that."

He put the flowers down on the console table and took me in his arms, kissing me deeply.

"Good night," he said after breaking the kiss. "And thank you. For absolutely everything."

"Are you sure you don't want to stay?" I asked.

"More than anything," he said quietly. "But I'm doing this right. Because you deserve it." He kissed me one more time and then left, closing the door behind him. I leaned up against it, wiping at a leaky eye. Who on earth was I with all these tears?

Me, I thought. *And that's enough.*

I shut off the lights and climbed the stairs, only to find a Debbie-shaped lump in my bed. *Rome wasn't built in a day,* I thought. But I wasn't worried. If I could win a campaign, I could move mountains. And I could certainly train a future president to sleep in her own bed.

Maybe.

Author's Note

While Bev and her family are entirely my own creation, a few real-life people inspired some of the supporting cast.

I'll start with the most obvious: Kay and Phil Graham, who owned the *Washington Post*. While Kay did stay out of running the newspaper entirely until after her husband's death, Anna Wainwright shows the beginnings of the gumption that the real-life Kay Graham demonstrated in her decision to publish the Pentagon Papers. If you haven't watched the movie *The Post*, Meryl Streep gives a fabulous performance as Kay Graham. The *Washington Post* also has a fantastic tribute to her, which can be found at https://www.washingtonpost.com/brand-studio/fox/katharine-graham/.

Next up is Verda Freeman Welcome, who is the inspiration behind Helen Walker. I stumbled upon Verda Welcome as I was researching Black voters in the early 1960s, and it's unfathomable that I grew up in Maryland but had never heard of her. Verda Welcome was the first Black woman elected to a state House of Delegates and the second Black female state senator in the country. And similar to what Bev says about Helen, I firmly believe that if she had been born fifty years later, we'd be watching her on the national stage. To learn more about Verda Welcome, visit https://wanderwomenproject.com/women/verda-freeman-welcome/ and be sure to watch the video of her speaking at the end.

Mary Dubois from the *Washington Post* is based on (the absolutely formidable by all accounts!) Marie Sauer, who ran the For and About

Women section. Her obituary is fantastic, and I especially love Judith Martin's anecdote that she'd rather ask a president an awkward question than face Miss Sauer's wrath. You can find that here: https://www. washingtonpost.com/archive/local/2001/10/09/pioneering-post-journalist-marie-sauer/6f513f06-a4c4-418d-af48-48a619c66367/.

The anti-Semitic incident at the (fictional) country club actually happened to my grandmother, Charlotte Chansky, at a Maryland country club in the late 1960s. I will refrain from naming the actual club, but I do want to point out that this was a real problem, as Jewish people were barred from most country clubs until relatively recently.

And one bonus: the two kids who got into a fight with mustard bottles at Hofberg's are my father, Jordan Goodman, and his cousin, Mark Kamins. Mark's father apparently never took them out to eat again after that!

Acknowledgments

Someone asked me at a book event last year why my acknowledgments were so long—did all those people actually help, or was I thanking people out of obligation?

The real answer lies in the question I get asked most frequently, which is: How do you find time to write while teaching and being a mom to two little boys?

I find time to write because being an author has been my dream since I was eight years old, and I'm able to do it because I have a huge support network that helps me make the time. So they're alllllllllll getting thanked.

First and foremost, thank you to my editor extraordinaire, Alicia Clancy, and the whole team at Lake Union Publishing. It's still amazing to me that I can basically email you an idea, and you're like, "YES! Write that!" AND THEN YOU PAY ME. Like . . . how is that real life? Thank you for being the best advocates I could ever hope for.

Thank you to Rachel Beck, the best literary agent in the world. From wanting updates while you were on leave, ALWAYS having my back, and everything in between, here's to another fifty books together!

Thank you to Liza Dawson for negotiating this deal so smoothly with Rachel out. I was nervous I couldn't live up to *Don't Forget to Write*, and your email about my "delightful" pages gave me the boost I needed to get this story on paper.

Thank you to my husband, Nick, for taking over at night so that I can write, and do book clubs, and sometimes just sit and stare at a wall and recharge. Your constant support means more than I can say.

Thank you to my children, Jacob and Max, who steal finished copies of my books as soon as they arrive because they are so excited for "Mommy's next book." I'll keep them coming for you. (Just don't let Gracie and Sandy eat them!)

Thank you to my mother, Carole Goodman, for being my alpha reader, book event date, babysitter, one-woman street team, and personal shopper. I couldn't do any of this without you.

Thank you to my father, Jordan Goodman, for answering a million questions and being too excited to wait on a finished draft to read this. Love you!

Thank you to my grandmother, Charlotte Chansky, for sharing your experience of getting a job in the 1960s and letting me borrow liberally from your history.

Thank you to my aunt Dolly and uncle Marvin Band. I don't know anyone else who has their own personal research team, but you've made writing about an era from before I was born a breeze. See? It pays that Dolly is older than the dinosaurs. (Sorry. Had to do it.)

Thank you to my brother, Adam, sister-in-law, Nicole, and nephews Cam and Luke for always being so excited and encouraging. I love you all.

Thank you to my uncle Michael Chansky, aunt Stephanie Abbuhl, and my cousins Andrew, Peter, and Ben for your eternal support.

Thank you to my cousins Allison Band and Andy Levine, Ian and Kim Band, Mindy and Alan Nagler for always believing in me—no matter what Ian says to the contrary.

Thank you to Jennifer Doehner Lucina—the best of friends, neighbors, moms, teachers, beta readers, and everything else there is. You complete me.

Thank you to Sarah McKinley for our peapod. I like how Jen threw us in a group chat one day and we just rolled with it and were like yes, we are also besties now. I'm grateful every single day that we did. Thank you for dropping everything to read and for offering to get the shovel without even needing an explanation.

Thank you to Sarah Elbeshbishi for literally everything. It would take a whole separate book to list how much you help me. And the offer to live in a tiny house in my backyard stands!

Thank you to Jessica Markham, for taking the time to research divorce codes from 1962 and keeping me dressed in style while you do it. You're my personal Wonder Woman and the only person I know who works harder than I do!

Thank you to Kevin Keegan—for making me the writer, teacher, and human that I am today. Although all those bestselling humor flags mean I probably don't need to ding a bell to get laughs.

Thank you to Ann-Marie Nieves, for being the best publicist in the world. You've opened doors to me that I never even knew existed.

Thank you to my cousin Mark Kamins, for always being there to make me laugh and for understanding money so I don't have to (and for reading my work the second tax season ends).

Thank you to Haben Asghedom, for being the best neighbor and stalker with me. We definitely wouldn't have been allowed to sit next to each other in school, so it's hilarious that we get to live next to each other!

Thank you to Jan Guttman, Katie Stutzman, Reka Shammugavel Montfort, Jeremy Horton, Rachel Friedman, Laura Davis Vaughan, Kerrin Torres, Joye Saxon, Christine Wilson, Sonya Shpilyuk, Mike Asghedom, Christen Dimmick, Kim Thibault, Sophia Becker, Katilin Johnstone, Max Giammetta, Scott Tarzwell, Amy Shellabarger, Sherry Antonetti, Julie Dean, Jamaly Allen, Caroline Dulaney, Denyse Tannenbaum, Anita Rajeev, Sam Lee, Heather Bergman, Shelley Miller, Mary Dempsey, Alexandra Robbins, Katie Samsock, Jenna Levine Liu, Brigid Howe, Jen Kramer, Diana Pajewski, and Allison Kimball, for being my people (and putting up with all the book talk!).

Thank you to Paulette Kennedy, Jean Meltzer, Annie Cathryn, Erin Branscom, Rochelle Weinstein, Maddie Dawson, Heidi Shertok, Meredith Schorr, Felicia Grossman, Stacey Agdern, Dara Levan, Alison Hammer, Liza Wiemer, Lisa Barr, Ellen Won Steil, Swati Hedge, Georgina Cross, Rea Frey, Ann Garvin, Aimie Runyan, Jenifer Goldin, and Jessica Guerrieri. I'm beyond honored to call you my peers and friends.

Thank you to Renee Weiss Weingarten, Andrea Peskind Katz, Melissa Amster, Leslie Zemeckis, Fay Silverman, Leslie Shogren, Leighellen Landskov, Kristy Barrett, Lauren Blank Margolin, Barbara Libbin, Nicole Lau, Susan Peterson, Jaime Gazes, Susan Zabolotzky, Stacy Smith, Brittany Rassoolkhani, Kelly Kervin, and Ticey Geyer, Ginny Velazquez, Kate Vocke, and Cheryl Koch, for being the best reading champions an author could ever hope for.

Thank you to my youngest fans, Charlotte, Genevieve, and Nathaniel Lucina; and Aurora, Elena, and Zara (bestie!) Asghedom.

Thank you to the Peloton Moms Book Club for your love, support, and constant enthusiasm.

Thank you to the Confino family.

Thank you to my students, current and former.

And finally, thank you to all my readers, who have made the dreams of a little girl scribbling stories in a notebook and wanting to one day be a real author come true.

Book Club Guide

1. The initial reaction from Mildred and Nancy to hearing about Larry's infidelity is that this will solidify their marriage. In what ways does that represent how marriage was viewed in the era?

2. Was Beverly happy with Larry? Or is part of her quickness to throw him out due to her realizing that she wasn't?

3. What barriers to working did Beverly face that aren't there today? Did she have any advantages over today's working mothers?

4. Why is Mildred so against Beverly working at a department store? What job options did Beverly have available to her?

5. Why isn't Nancy honest with her husband about her handiness?

6. Why do you think Michael gives Beverly a chance?

7. Bernie (grudgingly) endorsed Sam in the last election and seems more politically aligned with Michael. Would this kind of bipartisanship happen today? Are there any politicians today whom you would compare Bernie to?

8. Why didn't Mildred tell Beverly that she left Bernie?

9. Why does Stuart change Beverly's speech? Is it revenge or not trusting her?

10. What barriers were there to women and minorities voting

in 1962? Are we still seeing fallout from that now?

11. Mildred tells Beverly that if women decide they want Michael over Sam, they'll pester their husbands until they vote for Michael. Is this an accurate reflection of marriage? Does it go both ways?

12. Beverly struggles with reconciling her desire to work with her desire to be home for her kids. Has this struggle gotten easier? Or is it still the same for working mothers?

13. What specifically do you think wins Helen Walker over?

14. Do you agree or disagree with Michael's assertion that the Senate actually makes things less fair? Are there any political structures that the Founders put in place that work against true democracy today?

15. How is Michael's confession about Bernie influencing his decision to go into politics different from Larry's admission about Sam wanting them to get married?

16. Why do you think Linda changes teams?

17. We don't hear Mildred and Bernie's reconciliation in the jail. What do you think made her move home?

18. Do you think Bev and Larry will ever reach a point where they can be friends?

19. When did your opinion of Stuart change? Why?

20. Do you think Beverly will run for office someday? Or would she prefer staying behind the scenes?

About the Author

Photo © 2022 Tim Coburn Photography

Sara Goodman Confino is the bestselling author of *Don't Forget to Write*, *She's Up to No Good*, and *For the Love of Friends*. She teaches high school journalism and creative writing in Montgomery County, Maryland, where she lives with her husband, two sons, and two miniature schnauzers, Sandy and Gracie. When she's not writing or working out, she can be found on the beach or at a Bruce Springsteen show, sometimes even dancing onstage. For more information, visit saraconfino.com.